For Uncle Kenny, Uncle Charles, and Nanoo—
the world is now gray without you.

"Beauty is a dying flower."

—Orléansian proverb

*The God of the Sky fell in love with the Goddess of Beauty after the world began. Sky showered Beauty with gifts of his loveliest objects—the sun, the moon, the clouds, the stars. She accepted his offer to be his wife, and together they had the children of Orléans. But Beauty loved her new children so much, she spent all her time with them. After she refused to return home, Sky sent rain and lightning and wind to drown the first humans. When Beauty protected the people from harm, Sky cursed them with skin the color of a sunless sky, eyes the shade of blood, hair the texture of rotten straw, and a deep sadness that quickly turned to madness. In return, Beauty sent the Belles to be roses growing out of the dark and ravaged soil, destined to bring beauty back to the damned world, as the sun brings light.*

*from* The History of Orléans

We all turned sixteen today, and for any normal girl that would mean raspberry and lemon macarons and tiny pastel blimps and pink champagne and card games. Maybe even a teacup elephant.

But not for us. Today is our debut. There are only six of us this year.

My fingertips leave fog teardrops on the paper-thin glass walls. The carriage is beautiful and clear and fashioned into a ball. I am a delicate doll poised inside a snow globe. An adoring audience surrounds my carriage, eager to see what I look like, and what I can do.

A net made of my signature pink flowers stretches along the glass curves in order to tell everyone my name—Camellia—and to hide me until I'm revealed to the royal court.

I am the last in line.

My heart races with excited nervousness as we snake through the crowds in the Royal Square for the Beauté Carnaval. The festival happens once every three years. I peer through the tiny spaces between the petals with a pair of eyescopes, and try to soak in my first glances of the world, wanting to fold up each bit and tuck it into the cerise layers of my dress.

It's a wonderland of palace buildings with golden turrets and glittering arches, fountains full of crimson and ivory fish, topiary mazes of clipped trees, shrubs, and bushes in every possible geometric shape. Imperial canals circle the square, holding jeweled boats bright as gemstones and shaped like smiling moons on midnight-blue water. They spill over with passengers eager to watch us. The royal hourglass that measures the length of day and night churns with sand the color of white diamonds.

The sky and its clouds are made of melting cherries and flaming oranges and burnt grapefruit as the sun sinks into the sea. The dying sunlight flashes my own reflection on the glass. My powdered skin makes me look like an overly frosted piece of caramel cake.

I've never seen anything like it before. This is the first time I've visited the imperial island, the first time I've ever left home.

The Orléans archipelago is a string of islands stretching like a rose with a crooked stem out into the warm sea. Most of them are connected by golden bridges or can be reached by lavish river coaches. We came from the very top—the bloom—and we've made a long journey to the heart of the stem to display our talents.

A breeze pushes its way through tiny breathing holes in the glass carriage, carrying with it the scent of the sky. Salty rain, spiced clouds, and a hint of sweetness from the stars. It all feels like a dream that's held on and lingered past the dawn. I never want it to end. I never want to return home. One minute here is richer than a thousand moments there.

*The end of the warm months brings change,* Maman always said. And my life is bound to transform tonight.

The horses tug us forward, their hooves clip-clopping against the cobblestoned square. Vendors are selling sweets in our honor: small mountains of shaved ice topped with strawberries the color of our lips; intricate little teacakes shaped like our signature flowers; sweet puffs molded like our Belle-buns; colorful strings of sugar pinwheeled around sticks to mirror our traditional waist-sashes and dresses.

A hand thumps my carriage and I catch a sliver of a face. The square is overflowing with bodies. There are so many of them. Hundreds, thousands, maybe millions. Imperial guards push the crowd back to give our procession space to pass. All the people seem beautiful, with skin in various colors, from fresh cream to a drizzle of honey to a square of chocolate; their hair is in blond waves or brunette curls or raven coils; body shapes are petite, round, or somewhere in between. They've all paid to look this way.

The men wear jackets and top hats and cravats in a prism of colors. Some have hair growing on their faces in neat patterns. They stand beside women adorned with jewels and draped in luxurious, pastel-colored dresses made full with crinoline and tulle. Intricate hats cover the ladies' hair; some clutch dainty parasols and oilpaper umbrellas, or cool themselves with patterned fans. From the blimps above, I bet they resemble candies in a box.

I recognize the more popular looks from the stacks of gossip tattlers left in the mail chest a day too long, or from the weekly beauty-scopes Du Barry's daughter, Elisabeth, sometimes dropped between the velvet cushions of the parlor-room couch. The *Orléans*

*Press* says strawberry blond hair and jade eyes are the new windy-season trend. All the newspaper headlines read:

AWAKEN LOVE...LOOK IRRESISTIBLE WITH
STRAWBERRY AND JADE

FILL YOUR TOILETTE BOX WITH BELLE-APPROVED
RHUBARB HAIR POWDER

A COMPLEXION OF LILIES AND BELLE-ROSE LIPS—
THIS SEASON'S COLORS OF BEAUTY

The newsies say that's what everyone will want in the coming months.

Coins jingle. Hands wave velvet pouches in the air. The spintria inside creates a tinkling melody. How much does each pouch hold? How many treatments can they afford to purchase? How much are they willing to pay?

I adjust the eyescope lens, zooming in on excited onlookers, noticing how some of their skin tones have faded, like paintings that have faced the sun too long; how their hair is graying at the roots, and age-lines are creasing several brows.

It's a reminder of why I'm here.

I am a Belle.

I control beauty.

# 2

The carriages stop before the royal pavilion. Embroidered chry-santhemums coil around its peaks. Trumpets sound. Bells chime. I adjust the eyescope lens, and squint to see the king, the queen, and their daughter. They remind me of the porcelain dolls my sisters and I used to play with as children. The chipped face of the little king in his purple robe, and the queen with a bent crown pinned into her dark hair, both sitting inside a miniature palace made of cypress wood scraps in the playroom.

They look the same here, though not as worn, of course. The queen glows like a faraway star, her ink-black skin catching the last rays of sunlight; the king's copper beard hits the waist-belt of his robe; their daughter has her golden hair pinned up like a beehive. I used to paint the arms and legs of the princess doll each time the *real* princess altered her skin color, keeping up-to-date with the scandal sheets Maman used to smuggle past Du Barry.

The blimp screens sparkle with her picture. Tonight she's snowy white like her father, but with peach-pink freckles expertly dusted across her nose. I want to be the one who makes them all beautiful. I want to be the one the queen chooses. I want the power that comes with being Her Majesty's favorite. And if I can be better than Amber, I will be chosen. The rest of my sisters are good, but deep in my heart, I know it will come down to her and me.

Madam Du Barry speaks into a voice-trumpet. "Your Majesties, Your Highness, ministers, comtes and comtesses, barons and baronesses, ladies and gentlemen of the court, people of Orléans, welcome to our kingdom's most notable tradition, the Beauté Carnaval." Her voice is thick with authority. The noise rattles my carriage. Even though I can't see her, I know she's wearing a hat full of peacock feathers, and she's squeezed her curvy frame into one of her black dresses. Maman told me that Madam Du Barry likes to maintain a large and intimidating figure.

"I am Madam Ana Maria Lange Du Barry, Royal Gardien de la Belle-Rose." She says her official title proudly. The people of Orléans would most likely gasp if they knew we called her "Du Barry" at home.

Applause rumbles. High-pitched whistles echo. The noise vibrates inside my chest. My entire life I've wanted nothing more than to be here, before the kingdom.

"This tradition goes back to the very beginning of our islands, and to the onset of our civilization. For generations my ancestors have had the grand privilege to be guardians of our most treasured jewels." She turns to her left and motions to the previous generation of Belles. All eight of them sit in high-backed chairs, and hold Belle-rosebuds in their hands. Black lace veils mask their faces. The favorite—Ivy—wears a glistening crown on her head. This is the end of their time at court. They will return home once they train us.

When I was a little girl, they all played with us between their lessons with Du Barry. But then one day, the servants packed the older girls' things.

I wanted to hole up inside those steamer trunks and carriage cases, hide within their silk dresses and soft furs and fluffy tulles, to stow away and catch glimpses of the world through a trunk's keyhole. I remember reading about the older Belles in the papers after they left. I have their official Belle-cards tacked to my bedroom wall.

I want to be Ivy. I have always wanted to be her.

*You have to be the favorite—just like me,* Maman told me before she died. *The people of Orléans hate themselves. You must change that.* The memory of her words warms me from the inside out as the sting of missing her swells inside my chest. *The favorite shows the world what is beautiful. She reminds them of what is essential.* I wish she had lived long enough to be here, watching from the stage.

I picture myself living at the palace as the personal Belle of the royal family, being the left hand of the Beauty Minister and helping her draft beauty laws, experiencing the wonders of the Imperial City of Trianon and all its quartiers, swimming in La Mer du Roi, sailing in royal ships, visiting every island, and roaming every town to taste all the world has to offer.

My sisters will be placed at one of five imperial teahouses, or will stay at home to tend to Orléans's newborn citizens.

I will be a vessel for the Goddess of Beauty.

I hold the dream inside my chest like a breath I never want to let out.

"And now, it is my pleasure to present the newest generation of Belles," Du Barry announces.

A shiver of anticipation makes my heart threaten to burst. My hands shake, and I drop the eyescopes.

The crowd cheers. The driver pulls the netted covering of flowers from my carriage.

I'm revealed to the crowd. I grab the fans from my lap. Their latches fall open, exposing the fans' primrose-pink pattern. I cover my face, then flap and twirl them together so they flutter like a butterfly's wings. I toss them above my head and catch them effortlessly. The hours of lessons pay off in this moment. Whistles and shouts rise up from the throng.

I look to the left at my sisters' carriages. We're all lined up like a row of eggs in a carton, moving in time with one another. We exchange smiles. The same blood runs through us: the blood of the stars, the blood of the Goddess of Beauty.

Crimson lanterns float into the air. Against a darkening sky, the thin paper burns big and bright with our names: Edelweiss, Ambrosia, Padma, Valeria, Hana, and Camellia. Fish jump from nearby fountains, changing from ruby to teal mid-flight, teasing onlookers. Their leaps hold the promise of our powers. The square explodes with cheers. Little girls wave Belle-dolls in the air.

Many men and women are sporting monocles to have a closer look at us. I smile and wave, wanting to impress them, wanting to be good enough to be remembered.

Du Barry presents Valerie first. Her carriage rolls forward.

I close my eyes.

*Don't watch them,* Maman had said. *Don't ever covet their use of the arcana. Envy can grow like a weed inside you. Be the best without trying to be better than the others.*

We weren't allowed to discuss our instructions in the weeks leading up to the carnaval, but Amber and I had swapped our dossiers. Her subject needed to be given skin the color of toasted walnuts, hair full of large barrel curls, and a pretty, plump face;

mine had to have skin the shade of alabaster stone from the Fire Isles, hair so dark it blended into the night, and a mouth so perfect and so red it would be indistinguishable from a rose. We practiced our looks on house servants, perfecting them in solitary chambers under the scrutiny of Du Barry. *Practice begets perfection,* she'd yelled for hours.

I shift around in the carriage as the demonstrations continue, with Hana following Valerie. My legs fall asleep from having them crossed for so long, and my eyes flutter, fighting my desire to keep them closed. Pained moans cut through the noisy square like silver knives as the little girls endure their transformations. I wince as the cries peak and fall, and the onlookers cheer at their crescendos.

Some of my sisters receive louder reactions than others. Some get *ooh*s and *ahh*s. The roar deafens me at times.

I love my sisters, especially Amber. She's always been the one I loved the most. We all deserve to be the favorite. We've worked so hard to learn the art of beauty. But I want it so much there's no room inside me for anything else.

My eyes feel like they've been closed for an eternity before my carriage trudges forward again. Imperial attendants approach, and their gold uniform buttons catch the lantern light. They arrange themselves at four corners around me, unlatch the hitches, grip the levers jutting from the sides of my glass ball, and lift me off the wheeled bottom like I'm only a soap bubble. Thin and weightless.

I lock my legs in place and focus on my balance. The men march me to the center platform. I try not to be nervous. Du Barry re-created this entire set inside our home, complete with the gold cylinder where my platform will eventually come to rest. I've been preparing for this day since my thirteenth birthday; all of the lessons, the lectures, the practice. I know exactly what I'm supposed to do. It's been rehearsed, yet I can't stop my fingers from trembling and my body from quivering like there's a tiny landquake inside my glass ball.

I whisper to myself: "I will have the best showcase. I will receive the loudest applause. I'll be named the favorite, just like Maman. I will get to live at court. I will get to see the world. I won't make any mistakes. I'll make people beautiful." I say it over and over again like a prayer until the rhythm of the words erases my fear.

The men turn a lever. Gears clink and clang and wheeze. The platform under me rises just above the crowd. Plush royal boxes sit on stilts high above. People lean out of them with eyescopes and spyglasses pressed to their faces, and ear-trumpets jutting out like elephants' trunks. Faces look up in wonder and anticipation like I'm a star caught in a vase, ready to explode.

The platform stops. I turn a tiny lever on the carriage floor. The glass ceiling above me cracks open like an egg. The night's warm air skates over my skin like soft fingers, and it tastes even sweeter up here. If I could bottle the tiny winds, they'd turn to sugar dust.

The stars twinkle. I feel close enough to grab one and stow it away in my beauty caisse.

The square grows so quiet, and the sounds of the ocean swell. The people of Orléans gaze up at me, the last Belle to demonstrate her talents. Du Barry didn't prepare me for what it's like to be stared at. There are so many pairs of eyes, all different shapes and colors. My heart leaps.

Du Barry winks at me, then taps her full lips—a reminder to smile. The crowd believes I was born knowing how to make them beautiful. They don't know how hard I've worked to perfect the traditions and master the arcana. They don't know how hard I've struggled to learn all the rules.

"Now, it is my pleasure to present our final Belle, Camellia Beauregard!"

She fills the syllables of my name with pride, triumph, and magic. I try to hold on to that, and use it to combat my worries.

Light shines everywhere: the lanterns and blimp screens and sky candles and a bright rising moon. I can almost taste it, soft and bubbly and sweet, like pink champagne on the tip of my tongue.

I face a semicircle of smaller platforms. Three to the left and two to the right. Seven-year-old girls stand on them like jewels on velvet cushions. They're as different from one another as pearls and rubies and emeralds, showing how uniquely we can use our arcana to beautify.

I know my sisters' work: Padma's subject has limbs the rich color of honey bread; Edel shaved her girl's head close to the scalp; the eyes of Valerie's subject twinkle like amethyst stars; Hana's girl has the body of a dancer, long legs and arms and a slender neck; Amber's subject has a cheery round face just like her own.

The other Belles have created tiny masterpieces.

It's my turn to transform a girl.

The king and queen nod at Du Barry. She waves her hand in the air, signaling for me to get ready.

I glance up to the heavens for strength and courage. Belles are the descendants of the Goddess of Beauty, blessed with the arcana to enhance the world and rescue the people of Orléans. Blimps crisscross above me and block the stars with their plump forms and silhouette banners.

The last platform lifts directly across from mine. It completes the set of six and creates a perfect half-moon curve. The girl wears a long shirt, which is an excuse for a dress; its frayed hem kisses the tops of her feet. Her hair and skin are as gray as a stormy sky, and wizened like a raisin. Red eyes stare back at me like embers burning in the dark.

I should be used to the way they look in their natural state. But the light exaggerates her features. She reminds me of a monster from the storybooks our nurses used to read to us.

She is a Gris. All the people in Orléans are born this way—skin pallid, gray, and shriveled, eyes cherry red, hair like straw—as if all the color was leeched out of them, leaving behind the shade of freshly picked bones and ash. But if they earn enough spintria, we can lift away the darkness, find the beauty underneath the gray, and maintain their transformation. We can save them from a life of unbearable sameness.

They ask us to reset their milk-white bones. They ask us to use our gilded tools to recast every curve of their faces. They ask us to smooth and shape and carve each slope of their bodies like warm, freshly dipped candles. They ask us to erase signs of living. They ask us to give them talents. Even if the pain crescendos in waves so high it pulls screams of anguish from their throats, or if the cost threatens to plummet them into ruin, the men and women of Orléans always want more. And I'm happy to provide. I'm happy to be needed.

The girl fidgets with the camellia flower in her hands. The pink petals shiver in her grip. I smile at her. She doesn't return it. She shuffles to the platform edge and looks down, as if she's going to jump. The other girls wave her back and the crowd shouts. I hold my breath. If she were to fall, she'd plummet at least forty paces to the ground. She scoots back to the center.

I exhale, and sweat dots my forehead. I hope she earns a few leas for the stress of participating in this exhibition. Enough for her to purchase a square of bread and a wedge of cheese for the month. I hope to make her beautiful enough to receive smiles from people instead of fearful whispers and frenzied glares. I don't remember being that small, that vulnerable, that terrified.

I flip open the beauty caisse beside me. Du Barry gave each of us a different chest, engraved with our initials and the flowers that we're named after. I run my fingers across the golden carvings before lifting the lid to reveal a medley of instruments tucked inside endless drawers and compartments. These items mask my gifts. Du Barry's morning instructions repeat in my head: *Display only the second arcana, and what has been instructed. Keep them wanting more. Show them what you truly are—divine artists.*

Three scarlet post-balloons, carrying three trays, float up to the little girl's stand. One sprinkles little white flakes—bei powder—all over her, and she ducks as it coats her like snow. The other dangles a porcelain teacup full of Belle-rose tea, an anesthetic drink steeped from the roses that grow on our island. It sloshes and dances near her mouth. She refuses to have a sip. She swats at the cup like it's a nagging fly.

The crowd cries out as she nears the platform edge again. The last post-balloon chases her with a brush smudged with a paste the color of a cream cookie. To her left and right, the other girls shout at her, telling her not to be scared. The crowd roars. Onlookers try to convince her to drink the tea and wipe the brush across her cheek.

My stomach knots. Her constant squirming could spoil my exhibition. A surge of panic hits me. Every time I imagined this night, I never thought my subject would resist.

"Please stop moving," I call out.

Du Barry's gasp echoes through her voice-trumpet.

The crowd goes silent. The girl freezes. I take a deep breath.

"Don't you want to be beautiful?"

Her gaze burns into mine.

"I don't care," she yells, and her voice gets carried off by the wind.

The crowd erupts with horror.

"Oh, but of course you do. Everyone does," I say, steadying my voice. Maybe she's starting to go mad from being gray for so long.

"Perhaps they shouldn't." Her fists ball up. Her words send a shiver through me.

I paint on a smile. "What if I promise it'll all turn out well?"

She blinks.

"Better than you expect? Something that will make all of this"—I wave at our surroundings—"worth it."

She nibbles her bottom lip. A post-balloon putters back up to her with tea. She still refuses it.

"Don't be afraid." Her gaze finds mine. "Drink the tea."

The post-balloon returns.

"Go on. I promise you will love what I do. You'll feel better."

She reaches toward the post-balloon, then pulls back like it will burn her. She looks at me. I smile and motion for her to tug it forward. She grabs its golden tail ribbons, then lifts the teacup from its tray and sips.

I examine her, noting the details of her small, undernourished frame. Fear flashes in her red irises. Her body shakes even more.

"Now, take the brush," I gently goad her.

She wipes it along her cheek, and it leaves behind a milky streak as a color guide for me.

A blimp shines a sky candle over the carriages, and I catch

my reflection in the glass again. A smile creeps into the corner of my mouth as I see myself. I abandon Du Barry's instructions: the snowy skin, the black hair, the rosebud lips. An idea leaves behind the warmth of excitement.

The risk might cost me, infuriate Du Barry further, but if it allows me to stand out from my sisters, the gamble will be worth it.

It will be unforgettable. It has to be.

I close my eyes and picture the girl inside my mind like a small statue. When we were little, we practiced our second arcana by manipulating paint on a canvas, shaping clay on a pottery wheel, and molding fresh-dipped candlesticks, until we were able to transform them into treasures. After our thirteenth birthday, we moved on from using our teacup dogs and the stray teacup cats that lurk on the grounds to enlisting our servants as subjects of our beauty work. I'd give my room servant, Madeleine, bright sea-glass-green eyes when the red seeped in. At fourteen, we changed the babies in our nursery chambers, giving color to tiny fat legs and little wisps of hair, and just before our sixteenth birthday, the queen gave out voucher tokens to the poor to help us train and perfect our skills.

I am ready for this.

I summon the arcana. My blood pressure rises. My skin warms. I heat up like a newborn fire in a hearth. The veins in my arms and hands rise beneath my skin like tiny green serpents.

I manipulate the camellia flower in the little girl's hands. I change it, just as I will the little girl, shaping the flower's fibers and veins and petals.

The crowd gasps. The stem lengthens until the tip hits the platform, like a kite's tail. She throws the bloom and inches away. The flower quadruples in size, and the petals lengthen to catch her.

They wrap around her small, squirming body, until she's swaddled inside a pink chrysalis like a writhing worm.

The crowd explodes with claps, whistles, and stamping. The noise turns into a rolling boil as they wait for me to reveal her.

I will be the best.

It will be perfect.

I love being a Belle.

I hear the whoosh of the little girl's blood racing through her body, and the thrum of her pulse floods my ears. I say the mantra of the Belles:

*Beauty is in the blood.*

# 3

My childhood is a blur of quick images, like the twirling of a télétrope. I can never quite remember it fully. Not my first word or image or smell. Only the first thing I ever changed. The memory appears like a sharp ray of light. Du Barry took us into the solarium in the north wing of the house for a lesson. My sisters and I were folded into the scent of flower nectar, and arranged ourselves around a table.

Garden servants buzzed about, pruning, watering, and extracting perfume to be used in the Belle-products. The sun beamed down through the curved glass above me, warming my day dress, turning me into a hotcake. Du Barry gave each one of us a flower potted inside a wire birdcage, and instructed us to change its color and shape. I was so excited that my flower exploded, the petals bursting through the wires like thick tentacles, knocking my sisters' cages to the floor, and stretching between us like an octopus creature.

I have more control now and make fewer mistakes, but I still feel that tickle creep over my skin. When that happens, I know the arcana have done exactly what I wanted.

I open my eyes. The camellia flowers peel away from the Gris girl's body like wax, exposing her to the crowd. Voices gasp and cry out with excitement.

"Bravo!"

"Magnificent!"

"Impossible!"

"Brilliant!"

The chants make the glass vibrate. My blood pressure decreases. My heart slows to a normal pace. Sweat disappears from my brow, and the flush in my cheeks drains away.

The girl wears a small replica of my pink dress, made from the camellia's petals. Her skin matches the exact shade of mine—a sugared beignet fresh from the oil, golden brown and glistening under the lantern light. I've put a tiny dimple in her left cheek to mirror my own. Dark curls are swept high into a Belle-bun, the hairstyle only we wear.

She is my twin. The only difference: her eyes glow crystal blue, like the color of the water in the Royal Harbor, while mine are an amber brown like my sisters'.

The other girls gape and point at her in awe. I name my little subject Holly, after the flower that can survive even the coldest Orléans snows and still remain lovely. The crowd thunders with applause. The excited rumble fills up every part of me.

She gazes at the reflections of herself, and her mouth falls open. She twirls around like a spinning toy, gazing at her arms, legs, and feet. She touches her face and hair. The blimps drop new screens that capture her image. Her look will only last a month before she fades back to gray. But in this moment, no one thinks about that.

After Holly's picture appears in the paper and on the news-reels, I hope a childless lady adopts her. I want her life to change so much she won't recognize it anymore. The people of Orléans love beautiful things. She's now one of them, ready to be collected.

Her eyes find mine again. They spill over with happy shock, and she curtsies.

I gaze down at my sisters. The moon winks light across the carriages. They stare up at me with heavy eyelids and tired expressions, but clap and wave. Each one of us looks different from the next: Edel is as white as the flowers surrounding her, Padma's black Belle-bun catches the light, Hana's eyes are bright and slope in a beautiful curve, Amber's copper hair looks like curling flames, Valerie's figure is like the beautiful brass hourglasses Du Barry turns over to time us when we practice the arcana. We're the only ones in Orléans born unique and full of color.

The crowd shouts a Belle-blessing: *"La beauté est la vie."*

The queen lifts a golden spyglass and stares at me and Holly like we're bugs trapped in bell jars.

The world goes silent.

My breath catches in my throat. I clasp my hands.

The queen sets the spyglass in her lap, and she claps. Her jeweled rings sparkle like tiny stars caught between her elegant fingers.

My heart thuds to the beat of her applause. It might burst with excitement.

She leans to her right, whispering into the ear of the Royal Minister of Beauty. Courtiers lift ear-trumpets, eager to catch any words they can. I wish I could do the same.

The Beauty Minister rises to stand beside Du Barry, and the two of them converse. I'm too far away to read their lips. The princess's fan freezes in front of her. She glares at me so hard, it burns deep in my chest.

Du Barry motions for me to bow. I press myself all the way to the carriage floor to thank the queen and the Beauty Minister and the crowd for watching my exhibition. My chest heaves as I wait the customary minute to show the utmost level of respect. The queen must've whispered good things about me. That's what I tell myself.

"One more round of applause for Camellia Beauregard!" Du Barry announces. "And for all the new Belles. Before the appearance of the evening star tomorrow, as tradition demands, all will know the name of the favorite. Until then, happy guessing and wagering. May you always find beauty."

Women and men wave their gambling tokens in the air. The kingdom's lotteries try to profit from being the first to know the favorite, readying women to cash in any royal tokens earned from the queen for a chance to dine, socialize, or even have a beauty service completed at the palace by the favorite Belle.

Blimps release little Belle-cards that feature our portraits. They shower from the heavens like rain. A smile fills my entire body. I look for my own, but I can't make out a single detail among the flurry.

My platform lowers. The little girls watch me descend. They hop and jump and wave. The imperial attendants place me, glass carriage and all, back on the wheeled base. The crowd whistles even louder. Fireworks streak across the night sky, creating the emblem of the Belles—a golden fleur-de-lis, with a red rose twisting around its center like a ribbon of blood.

New silhouette banners sail overhead, reminding future customers of our names and faces. For a brief moment, I spot myself high above, my face massive and full of light. My eyes look clever, my smile sly. *Well done, little fox,* Maman would say if she could see me now. I feel like one of the famed courtiers depicted in the beauty-scopes or painted on Trianon's promenades and avenue boards.

The previous generation of Belles stands up onstage. They throw their Belle-roses at our carriages. The roses burst open in full bloom, their petals as big as porcelain plates. I wave at the crowd.

I want to stay forever.

# 4

I used to believe my sisters and I were princesses living in a palace at Maison Rouge de la Beauté. I loved the house's pointed roof, the four wings, the endless balconies and their gilded railings and silvery spindles, the soaring ceilings full of house-lanterns, the coral-pink salons and wine-red chambers and champagne-blush parlors, the legions of servants and nurses.

But none of it compares to Orléans's royal palace.

The carriages sit before the southern gate like a series of pomegranates dipped in honey and lined up on a tray. Red velvet covers cloak the glass. Brass handles and glistening wheels sparkle under the night-lanterns. I press my face against the gate. The outline of the palace shines in the distance, stretching out in so many directions it has no beginning or end.

I don't join my sisters just yet. Du Barry fusses with Edel. I linger near my carriage at the very tail of the procession, wanting a moment to myself. The excitement of the carnaval wraps around me like a pair of arms. Maman's arms.

An imperial guard patrols just a few feet away. He walks back and forth in circular motions, like one of the wind-up soldiers in our childhood playroom. My legs tremble and my arms shake. I might be exhausted, or still exhilarated. Perhaps both.

The roars of the crowd in the Royal Square taper off, like the winds of a storm drifting out to sea. The blimps and festival-lanterns leave light streaking through the night. It holds the promise of something new.

We will sleep here. The queen will announce the favorite tomorrow afternoon. Everything will change.

"You were better than expected," a voice says.

A boy leans against the outside of the gates. His jacket and pants blend into the night, but his bright persimmon cravat burns like a flame in the dark. He doesn't wear a house emblem to identify himself. He scratches the top of his head, loosening his hair from the short knot he wears it in. His smile shines like moonlight, and the soft glow of the night-lanterns smoothes out the hard edges of his pale white face.

I look for the guard. He's gone.

"Don't worry, he'll be back in just a minute. I'm not here to hurt you."

"*You* should be afraid. Not me," I say. He could be arrested and spend years in the palace dungeons for being alone with me. Two months ago, the queen put a man in a starvation box in the Royal Square for trying to kiss Daisy, the Belle at the Fire Teahouse. His portrait filled the newspapers and télétrope newsreels. After he died, the guards left his body, and then the sea buzzards carried it off in pieces.

"I'm never afraid," he says.

It's strange to hear an unfamiliar voice. A boy's voice. A buzzy feeling settles under my skin. The only other boy I've spoken to outside of a treatment salon was the son of Madam Alain, House Glaston, who I caught in the Belle storeroom powdering his face and smothering his lips with rouge-sticks while waiting for his mother to finish her treatments. He wanted to be a Belle. We were eleven and had laughed more than we'd talked.

This boy is more of a young man. Du Barry taught us to fear men and boys outside the confines of a treatment salon. But I'm not scared. "Who are you? You're not wearing an emblem," I say.

"I'm no one." His mouth lifts in the corner. He moves forward, closing the gap between us. He carries the scent of the ocean, and watches me with such interest, it's as if he's touching me. "But if you want to know so badly, feel free to have a look at my name. I'll even unbutton my shirt so you can see the ink better."

My cheeks burn with embarrassment. At birth, Orléans citizens are marked with permanent imperial identification ink that not even Belles can cover up or erase. Even if you cut out the skin, the ink will rise again from the blood. Most wear their emblems on their clothing, near the spot where they're marked.

I watch him with newfound curiosity: the way he tucks the fallen strand of hair behind his ear, the few freckles he has on his nose, how he adjusts his jacket. "Where did you come from?"

"The *Lynx*."

"I've never heard of such a place."

"They must not teach you much."

I scoff. "I've had an excellent education. Is it in the south?"

"It's in the harbor." He grins. "My boat."

So he was trying to make me feel stupid.

"You're rude." I start to walk away. The argument between Edel and Du Barry is dying down in the distance.

"Wait! I just wanted to see if the newsies were right." His eyes are a cedar brown, the color of the trees that grow out of the Rose Bayou waters at home. Navy emblems twinkle on his jacket like newly minted leas coins from the Imperial Bank.

"Right about what?"

"They say that you can create a person from clay with your arcana, like magic."

I laugh. "Like a court magician paid to entertain royal children with fireworks and tricks?" The newsies always call what we do magic, but Maman said the word is too simple an explanation for the arcana.

"So, can you?" He fusses with his cravat until it loosens, and the silk tumbles down his chest like a spill of orange champagne.

"It doesn't work like that."

"How does it?" His eyes burn with questions as he takes another step forward.

My heart hitches. "Don't come any closer."

He raises an eyebrow. "Are you going to murder me?"

"There are laws," I remind him. "And maybe I should."

"You follow those?"

"Sometimes." I fuss with the ruffles of my dress. "It's forbidden for men to be alone with Belles outside the confines of beauty appointments, or to speak to them unless the conversation relates to beauty work."

"And what of women? They can be just as dangerous, if not more."

"The same applies. We're not to fraternize with non-Belles."

"Why all the fuss? It seems silly, if you ask me." He smiles like he already knows the answer.

"Bad things have happened in the past."

"But they don't always have to." He rubs his chin as he studies me. "You don't seem like a rule-follower."

A blush rises to my cheeks. "You have a keen eye."

"I'm a sailor. I have to—"

"Camellia!" Du Barry calls out. "What are you doing back there?"

I flinch at the sound of my name and pivot around. "Coming!" I shout.

The guard returns.

I turn back. "Who are you?"

But the boy is gone. The guard gives me a pointed look, but I rush to the palace gates anyway and look left and right.

Nothing.

"Camellia!" Du Barry shouts again.

I go to the opposite side of my carriage.

Nothing.

Already the memory of the boy feels like a dream you try to remember the very first moment you wake up. Fuzzy, wispy, and out of reach.

# 5

The Beauty Minister opens the southern gate, prancing forward in a body-length mink coat. She pets the fur with her red-tipped nails; peacock feathers are woven into her dark hair. She points up. A gold-and-white post-balloon dances over her head. The House of Orléans's emblem blazes on its side. The queen's personal post correspondence.

"Welcome, my lovelies; I am Rose Bertain, House Orléans, and Royal Beauty Minister to our great kingdom. I have a message from Her Majesty." She slices the back of the balloon with a hooked letter opener. Glowing sparks spray from its rear. She pulls out a tiny scroll boasting the queen's wax seal.

She breaks and unravels it, then reads:

*"My Dearest Belles,*

*Welcome to my home and the capital of your beloved kingdom. Each one of you was so beautiful tonight. I think the Goddess of Beauty watched proudly from the heavens above. I look forward to determining the best*

*placement for you. Thank you for your divine service to this land. May
you always find beauty.*

*— HRM Queen Celeste Elisabeth the Third, by the Grace of the
Gods of the Kingdom of Orléans and Her Other Realms and Territories,
Defender of Beauty and Borders."*

I hold my breath until the Beauty Minister finishes reading
the queen's title.

"Shall we go inside?" she says.

"Yes," Valerie blurts out a little too loudly. We all laugh. Her
light brown skin turns pink.

Du Barry and the Beauty Minister lead us forward onto the
imperial grounds. Guards flank our sides. We walk down a sloping
promenade and along curving pathways, headed for the palace.

Night-lanterns wander overhead, leaving footprints of light in
front of us. I pass by bright green lawns and ornate trees trimmed
into shapes favored by the gods, flowerbeds that burst with scarlet
Belle-roses and snowy lilies shimmering like blankets of red and
white stardust. Royal beasts parade along the grass—cerulean peacocks, rosy teacup flamingos, and fire-red phoenixes.

Amber looks back at me. I stick my tongue out and race up to
her. "You did so well," she whispers.

I try to pluck a flying bug from the waist-sash around her
sunset-orange gown. She sweeps it up and sets it free.

"So did you."

Her pale nose scrunches. The angles of her face curve into a
perfect heart shape. Her complexion is as smooth and delicate as
a piece of the fine porcelain from the formal dining salon at home.
The Belle-makeup she wears makes her skin look even whiter. A
slight wind pulls her ginger hair out of place. Her high bun looks

like a split peach on account of the color. "I messed up with the skin. It turned out too bright." Her eyes shimmer with tears.

"It was fine." I trip over my dress skirts, but she catches me. I feel so light and so tired from using the arcana.

"My nerves were a mess. I did everything Maman…" Her voice breaks in half.

I lace my fingers through hers, and they look like twists of butterscotch and vanilla. Amber's sadness is painted all over her. I bury my own. We both did what our mothers told us to do.

"You did great. Your girl's hair had perfect ringlets. Maman Iris would've been so proud." At home, Amber lived next door to me on the seventh floor. Her maman would set up tea parties with sugar cakes and marzipan rose creams just for us. Despite the fact that we were thirteen, and a little too old for it, I loved them. I'll always remember when Maman Iris taught us how to use the bei-powder bundles, and how the chalk-white sprinkles made her skin look like dried-out dirt.

In our Belle-trunks, little stone mortuary tablets are packed alongside our dresses, in memory of our mothers.

"Amber, you did wonderfully."

"Liar," Amber says. "You didn't even watch. I could see you. You had your eyes closed." She elbows me.

She's always seen right through me.

"I saw her after you were done." I'll sneak a newsreel and watch the whole thing later.

My few childhood memories have Amber in them: tiptoeing into Du Barry's chambers to see what size brassiere she wore, hiding out in the nursery where people brought infants for their first transformations, placing bei powder in our playroom mistress's tea just to see her spit it out, pushing all the lift buttons to get to the restricted floors, breaking into the Belle-product storeroom to test all the latest concoctions. We've shared our friendship for so long, I can't pinpoint when it first started.

"Look at the sky." I wave above our heads. "It's different here than at home." No cypress trees blocking the stars. No hum of bayou crickets or the bleating of frogs. No tiny curling bars on the house windows. No thick northern clouds; just a clear stretch out to the ends of the world.

"The queen was supposed to stand up after my exhibition, Camille. So I would know. So everyone would know. Maman told me I had to be the favorite. There's no point in being anything else."

My chest tightens. We were told the same thing. I feel selfish for wanting to be better than her, and all my sisters.

"She didn't stand up for me either," I remind her. And myself. "I know you did well, even if I didn't see it."

"Yes, but you were spectacular!" She throws up her hands. "I've never seen you perform like that."

"And you were just as good, so stop it."

"We all did what we were told to do. What was in our dossiers. Except you. Turning the little girl into your mirror image— so clever. And, I didn't even think to use my ambrosia flower as a little cocoon. It really heightened everything. Made it such a reveal. None of that crossed my mind. Which is my problem. I don't do the unexpected. You take the rules as suggestions, and go beyond." She balls up her fists. *"Just change their hair and skin color."* She parrots Du Barry's nasal-toned voice. *"Nothing more. Anything else is a waste. . . ."* She covers her face with her hands. "It was a show, and you understood that."

"I made the cocoon so she'd stop squirming," I say, not wanting her to know that I'd spent a lot of time thinking about how to be better than her, better than everyone. I reach to squeeze her hand, but she moves it to fuss with a flower that's threatening to drop from her bun. I remind her how she never struggles with the arcana. She earns high marks on each challenge Du Barry assigns. Based on lesson grades, Amber's the top of our generation, always getting perfect scores from Du Barry. If the decision were based on that, she'd be chosen easily.

"If we could've shown the first arcana, I know they would've all seen more of your skills," I say. Amber is exceptional at Manner. She's able to soften even the voice of a teacup monkey, make the most oafish person charming, and give someone any talent they desire—cooking, dancing, playing the lute or a stringed misen—as easily as donning a different dress.

"I was supposed to be the best. I was supposed to be named the favorite."

"We all want to be the favorite," I say.

Her eyes narrow. "Don't you think I know that?"

Her tone feels like a slap. She's never spoken to me like this before.

"Ambrosia! Camellia! You know the rules." Du Barry hitches up an eyebrow. "You're too old for reminders."

Amber moves two paces away, and that tiny space feels like the width of an ocean. We're not supposed to show favoritism with one another. We're all sisters. We're all supposed to be equally close. But I've always loved Amber a little more than the others. And she, me.

Amber flashes irritated eyes at me. I don't understand her anger. We are, each of us, in the exact same place right now. Shouldn't we support one another?

Once Du Barry turns her back, I move close to her again and touch her hand, wanting to fix whatever just broke between us. She brushes away and cuts to the front of the group to stand near Du Barry. I deflate like a post-balloon that's lost its air, but I don't follow her.

We cross a series of small golden bridges that crest over the Golden Palace River. Newsies lean out of charcoal-black newsboats with their light-boxes, trying to capture portraits of us. Their animated quills scratch against parchment pads at lightning speed. They shout our names and ask us who we think will be chosen as the favorite.

"You're a little late to place your bets, gentlemen. You'll get no hints here," the Beauty Minister calls out.

We cross the final bridge and stand before the royal palace. The pink marble building stretches up with turrets so high that if you climbed one, you might be able to whisper to the God of the Sky. Sugary white and gold trim each layer. My sisters and I glance up, and it feels like we're all holding our collective breath.

I lift my skirts and trail the group up a massive staircase, losing count after one hundred steps. The click-clack of our feet pushes my heart to beat faster. At the top, the front door opens like a great mouth, and the grand entry hall swallows us. Jeweled chandelier-lanterns drop from the high ceiling, like spiders with bellies full of candlelight. The walls hold beautiful marble carvings of the stars. I want to run my fingers over them, to feel the grooves, but I can't reach them through the row of guards at our sides.

We enter a new hallway. The ceiling paintings change as we pass. Animated frescoes arrange and rearrange into different celestial scenes: the gods and goddesses, an everlasting rose, the kings and queens of old, the islands of Orléans, the heavens. I almost fall while trying to crane my neck to look up at them.

"The Belle apartments are in the north wing," Du Barry informs us.

"Facing the Goddess of Beauty's direction," the Beauty Minister adds.

We venture into the palace wing on gilded walkways that feel like massive bridges. I gaze over the railings and down onto the floors below. Royal chrysanthemum trees grow up toward the ceiling, but even their branches can't reach us. A series of chariots drifts along a shiny lattice of cables, lifting well-dressed people from one balcony to the next.

We move past an imperial guard checkpoint. They salute us. We stop before a grand set of doors carved with Belle-roses.

I bite my bottom lip.

Imperial servants line both sides of the entrance, heads bowed, hands resting in front of them; their faces are angular with peach lips, rosy cheeks, brown eyes, and milk-white skin. They are mandated by the Beauty Minister to look this way. She's dressed them in colorful work-dresses pinched at the waist, and they sport servant emblems proudly around their necks.

The Beauty Minister pushes the doors open.

# 6

My room at home used to be shared with Maman. Her four-poster bed and my smaller cot were tucked into a corner of our apartments on the seventh floor of Maison Rouge de la Beauté. Tattlers pilfered from the mail chest created secret mountains beneath my bed, and Belle-cards slipped from Du Barry's office decorated the ivory screen separating my side of the room from Maman's. Trinkets lined our shelves: dried petals, tiny bayou pebbles, and rainbow pearls sat like shrines to our adventures together, along with tomes of folklore and fairy tales about the God of Luck's phoenix or the Goddess of Deception's little silver fox. A vanity table held a washbasin, and a fireplace always roared with light. My heart flutters with the memory of it.

But I don't know how Maman ever left these Belle apartments to go back to it.

I turn around in a thousand directions. Walls soar up in gold-lacquered stripes to a ceiling adorned with curling Belle-roses.

Their petals wink and stretch as I move under them. The room
holds claw-footed sofas clutching jeweled pillows; a gold-stitched
tapestry of the great kingdom of Orléans swallows one whole wall;
a large white desk is nestled into the far corner, boasting an abacus
with pearly white beads and cast-iron spintria safes.

Royal servants light night-lanterns and set them afloat. Their
pale glow illuminates more of the room's wonders. Glass cabinets
contain beauty-scopes—tiny brass kaleidoscopes clustered by season and year—featuring images of the kingdom's best and brightest courtiers, taken by the Orléans press corps. Padma holds the
slender tip of a scope up toward the floating night-lanterns. The
cylinder catches the light, projecting a group of elegant men and
women on the wall like glittering, colorful beads. No amount of
money can buy you entry into these collections. Not even the princess has a spot. Every man, woman, and child wants to be featured.

Du Barry never allowed us to look at the beauty-scopes, or to
read pamphlets, tattlers, or newspapers. We weren't supposed to
be tainted by the outside world.

"Take it all in, girls," the Beauty Minister coos.

"Yes, enjoy the spoils," Du Barry adds.

Stacks of beauty pamphlets, including *Dulce*, *Mignon*, *Beauté*,
*Sucré*, and the *Dame's Journal de la Mode* cover ornate side tables. Edel
and Valerie flip through their pages, flashing them out at us. The
pamphlets profile Belle-created looks, feature polls guesstimating
which Belles could land someone in the beauty-scopes, and showcase each Belle in our generation and the depths of our rumored
arcana, comparing us to the older generation now leaving court.

Newspapers are fanned out on a series of coffee tables. The
*Trianon Tribune*, the *Chrysanthemum Chronicles*, the *Orléansian Times*,

and more from every corner of the kingdom. I run my fingers across them. Headlines cluster and flash across the parchment, announcing Princess Sophia's upcoming engagement, and the latest imperial beauty laws to be passed by the queen and the Beauty Minister.

ANY BONE RESTRUCTURING OR MANIPULATION
MEANT TO DEEPLY ALTER THE SHAPE OF
ONE'S BODY OR FACE IS PROHIBITED

THE WAIST MUST NEVER FALL BELOW FIFTEEN
INCHES IN CIRCUMFERENCE IN ORDER TO
MAINTAIN THE HUMAN SHAPE OF THE BODY

SKIN TONE GRADIENTS MUST STAY WITHIN
THE NATURAL COLOR PIGMENTATION AS
SPECIFIED IN ARTICLE IIA, SECTION IV

NOSES SHALL NOT BE SO SLENDER AS TO IMPEDE
THE NATURAL ACT OF BREATHING

CITIZENS OLDER THAN SEVENTY YEARS OF AGE SHALL
NOT HAVE TREATMENTS THAT ENABLE THEM TO
LOOK BELOW SAID AGE, IN ORDER TO PRESERVE THE
NATURAL PATH OF THE BODY'S DEVELOPMENT

Amber looks over my shoulder, the heat of our earlier argument gone. "When I'm named the favorite, I'll add more."

"Why? There are so many already. Or did you forget the endless lists of laws we memorized?" We repeat this same debate all the time. "I don't want to get rid of *all* of them. Just a few."

"Like always." She winks at me before sauntering off.

I lift the *Imperial Inquirer* and grin at images of royal women stuck in carriage traffic the day before the Beauté Carnaval. I spot the headline the boy from the gate mentioned:

CAMELLIA BEAUREGARD RUMORED TO BE
ABLE TO CREATE A PERSON FROM CLAY

I trace my finger over the curving letters.

On a footstool, tattlers sit in piles like stacks of warm sugar crepes. The pages hold potential suitors for the princess. The *Parlor of Titillating Tidbits* accuses the princess of having multiple torrid affairs, even with her ladies-of-honor. Another, *Speculations of the Foulest Kind*, broadcasts royal and courtier relationship breakups, blaming them on appearance shifts or lack of beauty maintenance, and a third, *Scurrilous Scandals and Secrets*, speaks about a series of black-market beauty products rumored to perform the same feats as the Belles themselves. I laugh at the ridiculous headline. No tonic can act as a substitute for what we do.

Tiny perfume blimps drift about, leaving their scented trails.

"The space will be re-accented to the liking of the favorite," the Beauty Minister says. "This is where one of you will meet your clients before their treatments begin." She does a lap around us, touching the most luxurious pieces of furniture, then waves a hand at the servants. They pull back a series of curtains, revealing a glass wall and a magnificent garden alive with roses of every color, flowers of every shape, and plants of every kind. "This is the solarium courtyard to inspire your arcana. I encourage all favorites to walk in it daily. Very therapeutic."

If Maman were here, she would tell me to pluck flower petals to help me create perfect natural shades, and ignore Du Barry's extensive color guides. Hana rushes to my side. "Can you believe it?"

"No," I say.

We race around squealing, scattering like beautiful marbles cast in all directions. I follow one of the perfume blimps down a hall. Gold-framed portraits of past favorites line the walls. I stop in front of my mother's. Her bright eyes stare back at me. I imagine her drifting from room to room. I imagine her creating one beautiful person after another. I imagine my face beside hers.

I step into a chamber. By the look of the space, it must be a treatment salon: a series of cabinets stretch to the ceiling with drawer labels like ROSE CREAM, SWANSDOWN PUFFS, OILS, and POMADES; portraits and canvases sit on easels; ladders click left and right as servants stock supplies; cases hold pigment-paste pots in every skin color imaginable; baskets contain bundles of candles and wax blocks and pastille cakes and metal instruments; a pot-bellied stove lurks in the distant corner, boasting trays of hot irons and steam curlers; a large table is covered with fluffy pillows and towels.

Hana peeks her head in. "Camille, c'mon," she says. She drags me out.

The Beauty Minister leads the group through another set of doors. "This way, my girls. Here's the sleeping chamber." Six canopied four-poster beds are lined up and draped with rich tapestries the color of our signature flowers. The floor is covered in plush rugs. A fireplace roars with light and warmth. "The extra beds will be removed, of course, after the naming of the favorite." She walks ahead again and two doors open, leading us outside onto a terraced balcony. The royal beach sits below; the waters of La Mer du Roi are crashing along the shore, and imperial ships drift down the coastline. Some ships are docked at the palace pier—alive with light and late-night merchants and markets. Du Barry hovers behind us.

It's better than I ever imagined, better than I dreamed. Behind us, the golden tops of three palace pavilions catch the moonlight.

"I daresay this is one of the best views in the whole palace," the Beauty Minister declares before leading us back inside. She points down a hallway. "The bathing onsens are toward the end of that corridor, and the treatment salons and recovery rooms."

"How many in total?" Padma asks.

"Eight grand apartments, all interconnected. Many years ago, the queen would invite the teahouse Belles to come here for treatment parties. She would provide beauty services for her favorite courtiers, and they'd try out new trends and experiments. They were quite the affair."

We follow her back to the main salon.

"Each and every favorite has stayed here. This is truly hallowed ground," she says.

I shiver, thinking about Maman walking through these rooms.

I envision how I will make the apartments my own: by replacing the white candles with beeswax ones for a honeyed scent; swapping out heavy drapes with thinner curtains to welcome the sun; having the bed moved closer to the balcony doors so the ocean sounds can help me drift off to sleep; bringing the desk inside the bedroom so I can look out over the terrace while I write letters and send post-balloons.

I circle the furniture, letting my fingers drift over its plush cushions. I stop at a bassinet hanging from a set of delicate ceiling chains. "Will the favorite have to change infants?"

"Very rarely, a royal will use her beauty tokens for her child, bypassing the nursery chamber at La Maison. It's quite unusual, but it happens." The Beauty Minister snaps her fingers at a servant, and the woman springs into action. "While on the subject of beauty tokens, there's very beautiful craftsmanship this season. I chose the artisan myself from the House of Smiths." She claps her hands together. "The keys to beauty."

Two servants present dainty skeleton keys nestled onto a velvet board. They glitter like fallen stars tucked in place.

"Very clever, Madam Minister," Du Barry says.

"The newsies just loved it. You may receive a token like this from men or women at court. They are worth more than spintria. Only given out by the king, queen, or princess, or even the favorite herself at times. My office tracks them." The Beauty Minister waves away the servants.

"I loved the hand tokens, too," Valerie says, "from two seasons ago."

"Those used to be my first loves," the Beauty Minister says. "Until the keys." She knocks on the wall behind her. "One last important thing. In addition to Ivy, our past favorite who will be here for a month to help the favorite transition..." A hidden door cracks open to reveal a small office drowning with circuit-phones that look like endless rows of candlesticks. Their tinny sounds ring out. A sliding ladder clicks along the wall. Receivers dangle from their bases like temple bells.

Out pops Elisabeth Du Barry, Madam's daughter. Du Barry beams at her. Her face is long and narrow like a grain of rice, and she wears her hair cut into a mushroom-shaped bob. No amount of beauty work will erase the sour expression she always has on her face.

The Beauty Minister scrunches her nose while inspecting Elisabeth's features. "Miss Elisabeth Du Barry will also be stationed at court," she says without enthusiasm.

"I'll be in the circuit center," Elisabeth says with a sniff. "I answer the phones and book the beauty appointments for the Belles at the teahouses, and also for the favorite. I take orders for Belle-products and arrange the court delivery balloons." She pauses and clucks her tongue. "People are phoning nonstop."

At home, whenever Elisabeth speaks, we pay no more attention than we do to the stray teacup cats. She's always liked to tell lies about the other islands to scare us, and will do anything else she can to make us feel inferior.

Edel groans. "I thought we were rid of her."

Padma pinches her. I try not to laugh.

"Elisabeth is to be obeyed in my stead. I'll be back and forth between home and court," Du Barry says. "Do you understand me?"

"Yes, Madam Du Barry," we say in unison, like we're little girls in her lesson room again.

"Well, girls." The Beauty Minister moves underneath a tapestry depicting an ancient map of Orléans. "Look how far you've come." She points to the very top corner, where golden embroidery outlines our island and its old name—Hana. "I'm delighted you're finally here. Relish this night, for the world—yours, mine, the kingdom's—shall change tomorrow."

Du Barry gives her a round of applause, and we all join in.

"See you first thing." The minister saunters out, her mink trailing behind her.

"Young ladies, wonderful display of talent tonight." Du Barry rests her eyes on each of us in turn. "Even your big sisters were mightily impressed. They look forward to helping you with your transitions once you learn your placements tomorrow. Several remarked how a few of you may not even need a full month with them to acclimate to court and teahouse life."

I flush with anticipation, excitement, and a little fear.

"Tonight was one of the strongest debuts I think we've had since my maman was still alive." She kisses two fingers and places them over her heart. We mimic her to show respect for the dead. She removes prayer beads from her dress pocket and wraps the string around her hands. "Your arcana levels will be checked and balanced. Then you will be dressed for bed." Du Barry places a warm hand on each of our cheeks. "You must be sure to get plenty of rest. Tonight is your first time experiencing this much stimulation. You must rid yourselves of it, and reestablish your balance. Always remember that emotions are tethered to the blood, and the blood is where your gifts are. Any excess passion can cause contamination and too much pressure. It can damage the arcana. I cannot stress this enough."

During the weeks leading up to our birthday and the Beauté Carnaval, I had heard this over and over again, as if a needle were stuck on a phonograph record. From our mothers, our nurses, and especially from Du Barry, as if I'd forgotten what I had been taught about the arcana my whole life.

*Beauty is in the blood.*

My sisters and I chanted the mantra even as we learned our letters and numbers.

She tugs a cord on the wall, then turns to me. "Camellia and Edelweiss, you both will be woken early." Her tone is ominous. "We need to speak."

# 7

My cheeks flame as my sisters gawk in my direction. A nervous sweat slicks my makeup. Elisabeth grins at me.

"Why?" I ask.

Du Barry bristles.

"Yes, I want to know as well." Edel steps beside me.

"Camellia and Edelweiss, when I ask you for something, no explanation need be given. Whether at home or here. All of you should remember that." She sweeps her skirts behind her and storms out of the room.

"Good night, girls." Elisabeth blows us a kiss, then follows her mother.

"It'll be fine," Amber whispers, and takes my hand.

Edel starts to laugh.

"It isn't funny, Edel," Amber snaps.

Servants pour in. They herd us to the bathing onsen, where they feed us honey-soaked peaches to help reset our arcana levels, undo our Belle-buns, remove our expensive gowns, wash out our hair, and bathe us until we're soft as tea cakes.

Nurses wait for us outside the baths. Their white uniform dresses make stiff noises. Their shiny Palace Infirmary emblems sparkle around their necks. There are a few pushcarts spilling over with towers of chocolate squares, pots of spiced tea, orange slices, sugar-coated blueberries, and skewers of smoked salmon and beef sprinkled with garlic and ginger. Other nurses hold arcana meters.

I sink into the chaise lounge, wondering what Du Barry wants to talk to me about. My mind races with all the things she might say. I hope she tells me how much she loved my exhibition. I hope she tells me that the crowd clapped the loudest for me. I hope she tells me my use of the second arcana was unique.

But a voice inside me whispers: *She didn't like it.*

My sisters file into the room one by one and find seats.

The servants leave.

"Look at these." Padma drops the *Orléansian Times* in my lap. The headlines scatter, then settle again. "I can't read enough of them."

LADY FRANCESCA CARNIGAN, OF HOUSE HELIE,
RUMORED TO HAVE A BEAUTY ADDICTION

QUEEN MIGHT LIFT SAILING RESTRICTIONS,
OPENING KINGDOM TO TRADE

SOME HAIR TEXTURES DON'T CATCH
THE BEAUTY-LANTERN LIGHT

SERVANT OF HOUSE CANNEN JAILED FOR ILLEGAL BEAUTY
WORK AND IMPERSONATION OF DUCHESS CANNEN

COUNTESS MICHELLE GIRARD OF HOUSE EUGENE TO WED

ROYAL MINISTER OF FINANCE LÉA BOYER IN GLASS ISLES

Edel takes the paper from my hands as she crashes into the chaise lounge beside mine. "We're in trouble, little fox." She looks like a spirit; her snowy nightdress is the same shade as her skin and hair.

"Edel, you're always in trouble," Valerie says, as she sticks her nose into a cart of sweets and her wet hair gets frosting in it.

"Well, Camille, you too—maybe just a little bit. You don't always follow instructions," Padma adds, then smiles.

"I wanted them to remember me," I say. "And my girl kept squirming."

"Oh, so that explains why you made her your twin?" Valerie teases.

I laugh. "Not quite."

"Your girl turned out so lovely, Camille," Hana says through a yawn. Her straight black hair spreads around her body like tentacles. Her eyes fight to stay open, and when closed, fold so smoothly and neatly in the corners, like creases in paper.

"I didn't plan on breaking the rules," I say.

"Of course you did, Camille." Edel's mouth curves in the corner. "Du Barry looked absolutely pinched. Cheeks red as cherries. I was so proud. I should've refused to do beauty work at all. Let them put me on that platform, raise it all the way to the top, then do nothing. Can you imagine? Then Du Barry's face would've been the ugliest in the entire kingdom. I really considered it, but I figured she would bleed me if I did it. She gives me the meanest sangsues. I swear she does."

"The design you shaved in that little girl's hair was rude," Padma says, then giggles.

"So rude it made you laugh." Edel's grin is so wide you can almost see all of her teeth.

"I didn't see it," Hana says. "What did you do?"

"I put the letters D-U-N-G there. That's why she wants to talk to me," Edel says.

We all burst with laughter, imagining the late-night newspapers circulating all over the kingdom with pictures of Edel's little girl, the word shaved into her hair beside a picture of cow feces. When we were little and we wanted to sneak out of our rooms late at night, we'd leave each other notes with that word etched into them, and Du Barry's exact location.

Amber enters the room. "I don't think either of you should've done what you did. I even heard the servants whispering about it. So disrespectful."

Edel sighs. "Of course you don't. You always do exactly what you're told. And, just so you're aware, I had a guard slip my girl one of Du Barry's beauty tokens, so she can come see me—wherever I end up—and I'll fix it. It was just a bit of fun."

Amber turns to me. "And you? What's your excuse?"

"I just got inspired," I say. "That's what I'm telling Du Barry."

Amber purses her lips together the same way Du Barry does, and flashes me an *I-told-you-to-follow-the-rules* look.

"Who cares, Amber. Both of us gave the crowd a show, and gave the newsies something to fill their papers with. That was the point," Edel snaps.

Amber balls her fists like she's readying herself for a challenge. The sting of our earlier conversation returns. Her eyes flicker with tears.

"Or maybe Camille or I will be named the favorite." Edel's gaze burns as she stares at Amber.

"It hasn't been decided," Amber says. "We shouldn't—"

A servant enters with a carafe of warm oil and we fall quiet. As silently as a floating feather, the servant combs the oil through Padma's hair, making it shimmer in the subtle light like onyx. The servant then moves on to me, twisting the frizz out of each curl with the sweet liquid and pinning it up. Another servant drapes a blanket over a snoring Valerie; then they leave again.

"Du Barry said we shouldn't speculate," Amber says.

Hana and Edel flash me a look of annoyance. It's the same one Valerie gave me earlier while the hairdressers created our Belle-buns, and Amber bragged about being the best at creating the perfect curl. The girls have always called her Du Barry's "bird" behind her back.

"Scared to lose, Amber?" Edel's words stir up Amber's growing fury.

"It's not a game," I say, and now I'm the one sounding like Du Barry. "Calm down, everyone." I try to smile at Amber, and get her to let it go. Her hands are shaking, and she's flushed from head to toe like she's been scalded.

"Why do you even care, Edel? You hate being a Belle," Amber says. Tension spreads out like a thick blanket ready to suffocate us all. As we've grown older, spats like this have begun to ignite over the silliest of things: the chair one sits in on the breakfast veranda, whose lesson marks are the highest, who knows the most about Belle history, who Du Barry praises. The heat of the arguments lasts for weeks, like too much sun in the warm season.

Hana waves her hands in the air. "Stop! We're too old for this."

"And it's our birthday," Padma reminds us.

"Oh, I don't care." Edel rises from her chair. "I just don't think it should be *you*, Amber, just because you always do everything you're told."

Amber's glare stings. "Being a Belle is an honor—"

"There was a boy near our carriages," I blurt out.

Edel, Hana, Padma, and Amber turn to stare at me. I'm sure my cheeks are glowing pink.

"He was standing next to the gate."

"A boy?" Padma claps her hands.

"What happened? What could he possibly have wanted?" Amber zips through a flurry of questions. "And how did he get past the guards?"

"What did he say?" Hana says.

"He asked if I could make someone out of clay, like the news-paper headline—"

"Those newsies have no idea—" Amber starts to say.

"Yes, Amber, we know. Let her finish." Edel scowls.

"It was just the two of us," I say. "I don't know where the guard went."

"Were you afraid?" Padma asks. "I would've been shaking."

"No." I remember how the boy made me laugh. The memory rushes through me.

"Well, you should've been. It's forbidden," Amber says.

Hana scrunches her nose like she's tasted a lemon.

"Be quiet, Amber. What did he look like?" Edel leans over the edge of her chaise toward me. "And someone wake up Valerie. She needs to hear this."

Padma walks to Valerie's chair and jostles her shoulder. She rolls over and releases another snore. "She's going to whine about missing everything."

Amber crosses her arms against her chest. Her flush matches the deep ginger of her hair. "Why does it matter what he looked like? She shouldn't have spoken with him. She should've called for the guard or joined us. It's unsafe."

"He was handsome," I say. "Very much so." Padma, Edel, and Hana burst into laughter.

Edel's eyes stretch wide. "He wanted to kiss you."

Amber scoffs.

"No, he didn't," I say.

"I've heard about it. Some people think it's lucky to kiss a Belle. That it'll bring good fortune to their houses. A daughter of the Goddess of Beauty is the luckiest person in the kingdom of Orléans. That's probably what he was after," Hana says.

"Don't be ridiculous," Amber says.

"A kiss wouldn't be terrible, would it?" Hana jumps up, pretending to kiss someone and dance with them across the room. Edel joins her. They morph into a tangle of pale arms and legs. Everyone laughs except Amber.

"It would be catastrophic." Amber throws her hands in the air, and her eyes fill with angry tears. "We're Belles, not courtesans. They already have plenty of those girls at court—ready to be kissed—tripping over themselves and their high pianelles to get to titled courtiers from high houses."

I reach over to touch Amber's arm to get her to relax, but she brushes me away.

"Maybe he's fallen in love with you." Edel presses back into her chair, staring dreamily at the ceiling. "I'd give anything to feel something else, to see something else."

The curiosity of love and being kissed fills me with a blush so deep, sweat beads form along my brow. It's intriguing, but I don't know if I want to experience it.

"Don't be fools. You can't have both. Who wants love when one can be powerful?" Amber says.

"I just spoke to him. That's all," I say. "It was a great night. Let's talk about that instead."

"Remember what happened to Rose Marie? The Belle from the past generation who tried to marry?" Amber speaks as if she's a Belle historian, when we all know the same information. Du Barry had warned us that Rose Marie caught a sickness that plagues the Gris. When Rose Marie returned home from court, we'd just had our fourteenth birthday. She rarely left her room. We used to dare each other to get a look at her, and see what was under her veil. First one to get closest would earn glory, and be entitled to each girl's dessert at dinner. No one ever won.

"It was the son of Madam Bontemps, House Reims, one of the queen's ladies-of-honor. They were caught together—"

"We know, Amber," Edel says.

"They put him in one of those starvation boxes," she adds.

Padma jams her fingers in her ears. "I don't want to hear about this. You know I can't handle it."

"Amber, I didn't say I *wanted* to fall in love—"

Amber yells out an exasperated scream and leaves the room.

"What's happening with her?" Hana asks.

"She cares too much," Edel says.

"It's all the stress of the night. Has to be." I gaze behind me, looking for her outline in the corridor. I stand to go after her, but nurses flood through the door before I can leave.

"Sit, please," one says to me. Dread sinks through my gut. No matter how many times I've been pricked, I never get used to it. I wish Madeleine was here to do it, because at least she'd tell me all the house gossip—how the courtier guests argued over color choices or traded insults after beauty appointments—and by the time she'd finish, the whole level check would be done.

Each nurse bears the same unenthusiastic expression. The women divide themselves between us with trays. My nurse takes my left arm, bunching the wide sleeves of my night robe, and ties a red string around my bicep. I invent a story about her life and pretend I'm telling Madeleine. Her name is Jacalyn, and she has two little girls in the Silk Isles, and they drink rose lemonade and lie in hammocks on their private beach overlooking the Bay of Silk. Jacalyn's husband is a scoundrel who left them to run off to the Fire Isles.

The nurse pops two fingers in the crook of my arm and inspects the veins there. The green channels rise beneath the brown. She removes a needle from the silver tray and shows it to me before piercing my arm. I still hate how it breaks through my skin so easily, like the spot is no tougher than a tract of silk.

I grimace and clench my fingers. She taps my hand to tell me to release them. Blood snakes through a long tube. She takes three vials. One for each arcana. She unties the red string. The needle retracts. The piece of cotton she presses on the prick feels like a tiny cloud. When she lifts it, the wound heals as if she never stuck me.

"The arcana meter," she says.

I take the small machine from her tray and hold it as she fits each vial into one of three separate compartments. My blood swirls inside the meter's different chambers, churning, separating the proteins related to each arcana, determining which ones need rebalancing. I run my fingers over the brass body of the machine, feeling the vibrating hum of the gears working, and the indentations of the numbers that will soon fill with light to reveal my levels.

Above the first compartment, the word MANNER is illuminated, as if a flickering candle is nestled inside. Perfectly balanced, as it should be for an unused gift. She repeats it for the second vial. The word AURA shines. I touch the letters. It's my favorite gift. The number three shows.

The nurse's eyes bulge a little with surprise. I look up at her. She presses it again. The same number fills with light. She makes a strange, shocked sound, and notes it in a ledger book. In our lessons, Du Barry said our bodies all adjusted differently to using the arcana. She warned that if the levels dipped close to zero, a Belle could faint, sicken, or even die. We must be careful not to abuse our gifts. *What the Goddess of Beauty gives, the Goddess of Beauty can take away.*

Edel peeks at my meter. "That's low. Du Barry said it would only dip to four and a half after the carnaval."

"What was your lev—"

"Shh." My nurse taps my arm. "You aren't supposed to comment on each other's levels."

"Don't tell us what to do." Edel rises up.

"Calm down," Padma says.

"The reading will be over in another minute," Hana says.

I reach for Edel.

She pushes my hand away. "Aren't you tired of it? Always being ordered around."

The word *yes* booms inside of me.

"You are not a nurse," the woman tells her. They argue back

and forth until she calls for the servants to take Edel from the room.

"Just listen," I tell her.

"I'm done listening." She swats at the encroaching servants, but she's restrained and dragged out, kicking and screaming. When we were younger, Edel would explode like a firework if she didn't want to read the pamphlets and books Du Barry assigned, or go to bed before the first night star appeared, or eat the blood-strengthening foods made by our chef.

My nurse doesn't react. Her face bears no trace of what just happened. She presses the final button on the arcana meter. The word AGE glows and the number five appears. Amber marches back into the room holding an arcana meter. I wonder if her levels were similar. I wonder if she's calmer now.

Servants wheel in carts of porcelain jars with perforated lids. They lift them and reach silver tongs inside to retrieve black leeches out of freshwater. The sangsues. They wiggle and writhe, their suckers opening and closing, exposing tiny sharp teeth, as they're placed on trays and presented to each of our nurses. Empty diamond-shaped vessels dot their backs. My insides twist with disgust. I should be used to them by now. We tended to the sangsues as children, mating them, learning how helpful their species is to Belles, discovering how they help keep our blood clean.

"These look different. Bigger. Why the diamonds?"

The nurse lifts one above my wrist. "They're the same. Just bred to be larger and take more blood." She pushes the leech near me. "The vessels help the sangsues filter and share more of their purifying secretions with you." She dangles the leech over me.

"No, I'll do it," I say. She hands me the silver instrument. "Only two."

She shakes her head and shows me four fingers. "Madam Du Barry's orders. You broke protocol and your arcana level is low."

I squirm, just like the leech stuck in the grip of the tongs. I bite my bottom lip. The quicker I do it, the sooner I get to go to bed. Then it will be morning, and one step closer to when the favorite will be named.

"Do I need to get the arm straps?" she asks.

"No." I hold my breath and place the creature on my left wrist. It stretches out, hooking around my wrist like a bracelet made of black pearls. Its bite feels like a pinprick. The tiny suckers pull at my skin and the vein beneath. A bloom of red glows under its thin black body. The diamonds fill with my blood. I set a second one on my neck, and it leaves behind a slimy trail like a streak of paint as it finds the thick vein right under my jawbone.

"No more," I tell her, and drop the tongs on the nearest side table. Padma whines about the biting. Hana starts to pant as three leeches affix themselves to the crook of her arm. Valerie sleeps through it all as they climb the flesh of her thigh.

The nurse shakes her head at me, removing another pair of leeches from the porcelain jar. She puts one on my right wrist and the other on my forehead. I close my eyes, take deep breaths through my nose, and try to relax as the tiny creatures fill themselves with my blood and inject me with proteins to help increase my blood flow, reset my arcana level, and drain away the excitement of the day.

# 8

All night I drift in and out of dreams where I'm a child again and Maman is telling me stories about the Goddess of Beauty. I hear Maman's voice and am swept into our old room. The red sill-lanterns flutter in the windows and bathe the walls with ruby light. Younger versions of Maman and I are curled up like sweet-rope bread in the bed.

"Tell me about her?" asks a tiny me.

Maman's long hair falls in waves across the pillow. She pulls me closer, almost burying me in it. We don't look like mother and daughter. The mothers and daughters in fairy tales match like a pair of socks, but we are opposites. Her skin alabaster, and mine golden brown. Her hair cherry red and straight; mine chocolate brown and curly. Her thin lips, my full ones. Whenever I ask why we look so different, she says, "We fit like puzzle pieces," and reminds me that our eyes are the same amber hue. The only part that matters.

"Why did Beauty create the Belles?"

"At the beginning of the world, the God of the Sky fell in love with the Goddess of Beauty, which was easy to do. To call her beautiful would be too small a word."

"What did she look like?"

"She would change herself. One day she might look like you, and another day, me. This entranced Sky. He liked all her incarnations. It made him feel like he was with a new woman every night. He wanted her all to himself, so he gave her compliments and promises and kisses, all that her heart desired."

"What did she want?"

Maman rubs my cheek. "Beautiful things," she says. "Clouds, a sun, a moon. And he told the God of the Ground to make delicious fruit in her honor."

"The pomegranates," I say.

"Yes." She wraps one of my frizzy curls around her finger. "With his love, Beauty birthed all the children of Orléans and spent her days making them look perfect and unique from one another. But she started spending more time with them, leaving her beloved in the sky alone for long spells of time. He called her home, but she was busy tending to their children. She'd always tell him, 'Soon, I'll come.' She lost track of time. So finally, he sent storms and rain and lightning down in anger. The land flooded. Many died."

"She should've just stayed up in the sky with him."

"Love isn't a cage, petit," she says. "It's more like a post-balloon—sent off in a specific direction, but allowed to make its own path."

"A red post-balloon," I say.

"Of course, little fox." She kisses my nose. "Shall I continue?"

"Yes, please."

"Beauty returned to her husband full of grief, and noticed he wasn't sad. She discovered he'd troubled the skies over Orléans to lure her back, so she left him." Maman pauses, lengthening her words like sweet dough, as my eyes grow wide with wonder. "She told him her only and true love was beauty. In furious anger, he cursed all of their children. He gave them skin the color of a sunless day, eyes the shade of blood, hair the texture of rotten straw, and a deep sadness that turned to madness. She would have had to work hard to restore them."

"Did she try?"

Maman shushes me. "Do you want me to finish the story?"

"Yes," I whisper into her shoulder. "Please tell me."

"The hours she spent trying to fix her beloveds stretched into eternity after eternity, until..."

The fire hisses in the hearth. I jump up.

"She's listening," I whisper.

"She is," Maman replies, "always listening to us."

"What happened?"

"She made us." Maman circles her fingernail along my wrist, tracing the path of the vein there. "Her blood is inside you. Her arcana are inside us. She is inside us. We are blessed. We are destined to do the work she could not. We are her vessels." She kisses my forehead.

"Camille."

I wipe the sleep from my eyes, and it erases my dreams and the memories of Maman. Amber's pale face looks back at me. She squeezes my hand under the blanket.

"You awake?"

"Yes, what's wrong?" I whisper.

"I wanted to apologize for earlier." She smells like the orange-blossom treatment they always put in her hair to bring out the rich coppery color. "I just...I don't understand what happened, and I get so..."

"Worked up?"

She thumps my shoulder playfully, then traces soft fingers over my forehead. "Yes."

"I don't know what happened either," I say.

"You're my best friend." She scoots closer and reaches her arm over me. Right now she's not the girl that fusses with me about the rules, the arcana, and court. She's not the girl who is always competing with me. She is my sister.

"And you're mine."

"I just get worried." She plucks the feeling right out of me, as if she's listening to my heart. "I don't want this to change us."

"Our whole lives will be different tomorrow."

"We have to still be *me* and *you*." Our legs tangle together beneath the covers. "Promise me we'll be all right." Her lips tremble and her body shakes. The sobs come hard and fast.

"We're sisters. You're my best friend. Nothing will ever change that." I squeeze her hand tight. "Just breathe."

I take a handkerchief from the nightstand and try to clean her up. We take deep breaths together. The red flush leaves her cheeks.

"How do you know we'll ever see each other again?" she asks.

"I can't go the rest of my life without talking to you. I need you."

She smiles. "I need you, too. But—but—I just feel like this is—"

"We will all be fine."

"But we all want to be the favorite—well, except Edel."

We both chuckle.

"Your maman was the favorite of our mamans' generation—" she says.

"And if I don't get picked as the favorite, I hope you do," I blurt out.

"Really?"

"Of course. Our mothers were best friends. That's why we're best friends. We must always be. That's what they wanted." I push away the tears that come with thoughts of Maman. She wouldn't want me to waste them. She would want me to be happy that my exhibition went well. She would want me to focus on the things to come.

She sighs. "I just don't know if I can handle it."

"What?"

"Losing."

"But what if it's to me?"

She clenches the covers. "I have to be the favorite."

"I want to be the favorite, too."

Silence coils between us.

The redness returns to Amber's cheeks. "You don't understand." She tries to roll out of the bed, but I catch her arm.

"I do." I pull her back toward me. "Stay. Don't leave."

She sinks back under the covers with me. Her skin is still warm with anger. I roll over and bury my face in the pillow. She hugs me from behind, and twists a few of my curls around her finger like they're ribbons on a pole. She whispers, "I'm sorry," and then we're little girls again, slipping in and out of each other's beds, full of worries and wishes, falling into dreams of the future.

I wake to sounds of steaming water splattering into a porcelain bowl. The scent of lavender mixed with rose drifts through my bedcurtains. My eyes flutter. The curtains are drawn slightly.

"Good morning, Lady Camellia," a servant whispers. She looks just like the others—pale white skin, brown eyes, rosy cheeks—except she has freckles.

She helps me out of bed, careful not to wake Amber, who is sprawled out across the covers. I look around the room at the five other beds. The curtains around them remain closed.

"Wash up, and I will take you to Madam. She's waiting in the main salon."

I wipe the sleep from my face, and slip into the turquoise day dress set out for me. She returns and pulls my hair up into a simple, unadorned Belle-bun, and ties a cream-colored waist-sash around my middle.

If this were a morning at home, the sound-box would've woken us. Breakfast would be served on the veranda. Hana would be the last one out of her room and the first to complain about cold hotcakes and picked-over fruit. We would bathe, dress, then rush off for lessons, where Du Barry would have a list of assignments for us.

But this is the first day of my new life.

The Belle-apartment corridor buzzes with activity. Flower garlands droop from the ceiling like beautiful spiderwebs. Morning-lanterns drift overhead. Teapots cry out with steam. People move in and out, carrying parcels and linens and trays.

"What's your name?" I ask the servant.

"It doesn't matter." She looks down and continues to move forward.

"Yes, it does. Please tell me."

"Bree, my lady," she whispers.

"Nice to meet you."

"And you, too, my lady."

We pause before the main salon doors. I shiver.

"She's waiting," Bree whispers.

I shift my weight from left to right, right to left, as she leads me forward. "How angry is she?"

"She's eaten a whole tray of citron tarts."

She opens the door. Du Barry sits in a high-backed chair, facing the fireplace. She clenches a jade cigarette holder between her fingernails. The end burns as bright as the flames in the hearth. She grunts, inspecting a tray of Belle-pots and rouge-sticks, and gives notes to Elisabeth.

Bree leads me forward and into the adjacent seat. She pats my shoulder before slipping out of the room.

"The testers are complete. The windy season's colors are in: bright cobalt, misty mauve, cognac, purple-red wine, radiant orchid, cypress green, and storm gray. Madam Pompadour sent her daughters with new pomander beads to consider for the cold season. The scents will be lovely. Juniper berry, lavender, and snow-melons. They've used sky pearls from the Glass Isles to hold the perfume. Every woman in Orléans will want these for her toilette box," Du Barry says. "Aren't they gorgeous, Elisabeth?"

"Yes, Maman. Will fetch many leas," Elisabeth says.

I ease into conversation with them. "When will the queen release her official announcement regarding toilette-box allotments?"

"Soon, and we shall be ready when she does." She waves at the servants to take the tray from the side table. Then she faces me, her eyes full of disappointment. "You did not follow protocol last night, Camellia."

Elisabeth gulps down her tea and starts to cough, then apologizes. I swallow and tell myself not to break eye contact with

Du Barry. Her steely blue eyes burn into mine. I try not to be the little girl who always jumps as soon as she walks into a room. I try to be the girl who isn't afraid of anything. Or anyone. But a twinge of fear grows inside me despite myself.

"Though your exhibition was quite enchanting and clever, I'm concerned. And I've spoken with the Beauty Minister." The servants display a platter of sweets before her. She pops a raspberry cream puff in her mouth, chewing quickly, then takes three madeleine cookies. "You were told to use the second arcana to provide the look laid out in your carnaval dossier. Small changes that demonstrate you're ready to serve the great land of Orléans. Nothing more. Nothing less.

"Your blatant disregard for the rules, Camellia, in front of the entire population of Orléans, has put us in a compromised situation—do we disqualify you from being the favorite, or allow you to be considered despite this? In order to be a successful Belle, you must be able to follow instructions. It was reckless, and reminded me of all the low marks you received during your training because you simply ignored the rules. You just can't—"

"The crowd loved it." The words bubble up and brim over my lips. Elisabeth puts a hand over her mouth. Servants re-enter the room with tea carts. Bree serves me tea and almost drops the teacup in my lap. I gently take it from her. I worked so hard to get that response from the crowd. I won't let her erase it like a picture wiped from a chalkboard.

Du Barry's shoulders crumple like I've hit her. Her sharp eyes narrow, waiting for me to look away, but I don't. Anger rises inside me. I thought she would be happy with the crowd's response.

"Disrespect will not be tolerated," she says. "Rule-breaking will be punished."

The teacup in my hand wobbles. I drop my gaze. "I wasn't trying to—"

"This isn't a game to be won," Du Barry says. "These traditions have been in place for hundreds of years. Time-honored and tested—they keep us all safe. You think you showed the world what you can do? You think they were amused? Really, what you did was let the queen know that you can't follow directions. That you're more interested in what *you* want than what your client might want."

The possibility of being the favorite shrivels like a dying flower. Du Barry's words dry out each and every petal, and snap the stem.

"You showed Her Majesty that you may not be trusted to carry on the work of the Belles in the way it should be carried out— that although you're talented enough to be the favorite, maybe you're not disciplined enough for such a grand title. Too risky to be picked. Too wild to take over such a hallowed responsibility. And all that pomp and circumstance lowered your Aura arcana level significantly."

Her words link together into a chain that digs its way under my skin, all the way to my heart. I think of the little girl, Holly, standing on the platform. I think of the flower chrysalis and the banners flashing her new face. I think of the grinning crowd and remember the chants. The cleverness of that moment drains away. The stupidity of my feat replaces it all.

"Using your powers to manipulate fabric and plants pushes the arcana outside of its intended use. It weakens it." She releases her deepest and longest sigh yet. "You've always had an excessive appetite—an ambitious soul." She spits each word out at me. "But, Camellia, ambition leads to insanity. The God of Madness feeds on it."

"I thought I was supposed to show them all what I could do. Isn't that the point of the carnaval?" I say with caution.

Du Barry snaps back in her chair. "Have you been paying attention during your studies? Has all this been lost on you?"

"Of course not." I ball up my fists. "I just don't under—"

"That's right. You don't understand. Because if you did, you wouldn't have done something so foolish. The point is to show them that you're strong enough to complete your role. That you're capable, confident, and proficient in the arcana. That you can serve this great world." Du Barry sets her teacup down. "Your little exhibition could've set us back. There was a time when everyone wanted to be the same. Remember your history lessons? The reign of Queen Ann-Marie II of the Verdun Dynasty. People were indistinguishable from one another. Imagine if everyone went around wanting to look like *you*. What if they'd only pay if they could have your features? There'd be millions of your lookalikes walking around. We'd be better off being gray again. Beauty is variety. Beauty is change."

I wouldn't want the world to look like me. I wouldn't want everyone to look the same. Shame and embarrassment ripple through my core, and my stomach threatens to empty. I avoid my reflection in the mirror over the fireplace mantel.

"We will not have any more displays like these again. You are to follow the rules and stay on the path. Understood?"

I nod.

"And if you can't, we will be forced to take more drastic measures. Simply because you're born a Belle doesn't mean you're entitled to be one," Du Barry says.

Her words slam into me. I drop the teacup. Bree rushes to help me. We wipe at the streaks of brown on my day dress. My wrist is puffy and red from the burn of hot liquid. But nothing shocks me

more than Du Barry's words. What does she mean, I'm not entitled
to be a Belle? I'm one of only six. What else could I be? Where would
I live? What would I do? Would the Goddess of Beauty take away
her blessing, my arcana? Would I become a Gris? The questions
knock around in my head.

"I bet, in all your vigorous plotting, you didn't learn about
Heather Beauregard."

"I tried to tell her about that Belle once, but Camellia never
likes to listen, Mother." Elisabeth smiles at me.

I remain expressionless, even though I'd love to slap the smug
grin off her face. I don't want Du Barry to know the worries and
questions humming inside me. I don't want Elisabeth to see that
she's gotten to me.

"She was three generations before your mother. A very talented
Belle, named the favorite. But she didn't follow my instructions, or
respect the honor that the Goddess of Beauty bestowed upon me.
So I took her from court and kept her at La Maison Rouge. I never
let her return to court. I will do that again if you can't fall in line.
There's far too much passion in your blood, Camellia."

She waves to Bree, and I'm dismissed. I stand and walk to the
door with the servant at my side. Each beat of my heart echoes in
my ears.

"Whether you're chosen to be here or are assigned to one of
the teahouses, I can bring you home at any time," Du Barry says.
"Elisabeth will be watching. I will be watching. Now, fetch Edel."

The doors close behind me.

# 9

Through breakfast and then bathing in the onsen, Du Barry's words drum through me like a vibration whose ripple won't stop. I'm floating outside of everything around me, unable to stay anchored. After lunch, I stand on a seamstress block in a slip and hooped petticoat in the Royal Dress Salon. Servants drape tape-ribbons along our waists and arms and legs, and scribble numbers on parchment pages.

Elisabeth watches us. The memory of the morning conversation creeps over me again.

"What happened with Du Barry?" Padma asks me. "Are you all right?"

"Fine." I try to smile. *Everything will be fine.*

"You don't look it." Hana reaches over to rub my shoulder.

"She threatened me," Edel says proudly.

Elisabeth clears her throat, and Edel speaks even louder. "She got so mad, I thought a vein would pop right out of her neck."

"Do you take anything seriously?" Amber asks.

"You do enough of that for all of us," Edel replies. "Du Barry told me she'd have the Beauty Minister speak with me. Like I'm supposed to be afraid or something." She laughs, but I can't stop being scared. I don't want this to slip away.

"I can't tell if the Beauty Minister is mean or nice," Hana says. "I haven't decided what I think of her yet."

"Who cares if she's nice?" Edel fusses with the servant attempting to measure her arms. "I don't plan on talking with her about my *behavior*."

"She's been elected twice," Valerie says, then touches her stomach. "Why can't one of you give me a smaller waist? My numbers are bigger than yours."

"It would make us sick, Valerie," Amber snaps.

"I know . . . I was just—" Valerie's tawny brown skin pinkens, and she frowns.

"Still upset, Amber?" Edel's pale eyebrow lifts. "Because there's no excuse for your annoying temperament after we've had such a delicious lunch."

Padma *tsks* her tongue like Du Barry.

Hana shakes her head.

"Just stating the truth," Amber says.

"Well, *your* body is a pole," Edel says. "Nobody would want you, even if you were interested in experiencing it."

"You don't have to be rude. I swear, you're the most unmannered of us all," Amber says. "I didn't mean to hurt your feelings, Valerie. The Goddess of Beauty made you just the way she wanted you. At least you have breasts."

"Yes, and you're flat as a crepe, Amber." Edel leaps off her block, shoving away another servant. "Hourglass figures and beautiful round bodies will always be coveted if I'm the favorite." She grabs Valerie and pulls her down as well. She hooks her arms around her waist, nuzzling her face into Valerie's neck. "I'd give anything to be shaped like you."

Valerie giggles. Edel reaches for me, yanking me down with them. She spins us around and around. We laugh and screech and skip away from the servants.

"Don't be so sad, or let Du Barry get to you, little fox," Edel whispers. "Who cares what she says?"

Elisabeth tugs at us. "Get back to your places."

"No." Edel blows her a kiss.

I wish I could be more like Edel—want this life a little less.

"Back to your dress blocks," the servants say.

We keep spinning.

"Girls!" Elisabeth shouts.

We turn again and again. We don't stop. Hana joins us. Amber sighs. Padma laughs hysterically.

"There will be order," Elisabeth hollers.

*"There will be order,"* Edel parrots, and we all giggle.

"Ladies, please. We must proceed," one of the seamstresses says.

The doors snap open.

Edel, Valerie, Hana, and I freeze. Amber and Padma scream and try to cover themselves.

"Royal Fashion Minister Gustave du Polignac," an attendant announces.

"Why, hello!" A purple-suited man saunters in, followed by a train of powdered and prim-looking men carrying notebooks, and a set of tailors and seamstresses who wheel in massive spinning looms. "I see we have quite the festivities going on in here. And not to worry, girls, there's nothing I haven't seen." The man has beautiful features, with a deep-brown face freckled like a chocolate chip cookie. He presses a hand to his chest, drumming jeweled fingernails.

The Beauty Minister trails behind him. Her dark hair is fashioned into a bird's nest, complete with a pair of live blue jays in it. They chirp out at us. She smiles at me, and her teeth look stark white like the keys of a piano.

"They're a spirited bunch," he says to the Beauty Minister. He kisses both of her cheeks, careful not to leave behind the bright purple rouge-stick he wears.

Du Barry enters last, starting a round of applause. The rest of us join in.

The Fashion Minister bows, then smiles up at us. I've seen him in newspapers, demonstrating the proper way to wear a corset according to imperial beauty laws—tight enough to fit within the desirable measurements for a proper citizen of Orléans, but fashionable enough to create the perfect silhouette, like an hourglass. He's the fashion tastemaker of the kingdom, and is in charge of all garment production. "At your service."

"He's here to work his magic," the Beauty Minister says, "with his team."

The other well-dressed men smile at her, and a few blush.

"Yes, my dandies and I are here to the rescue. A Belle needs an elegant wardrobe, just like an artist needs a variety of ink and paint." He waves a gold-tipped cane in the air. His heels click and clack as he circles us, his gaze like a strong beam of light. He leans in and whispers, "Welcome to court."

We jump, and then laugh.

"Stop frightening them, Gustave. You know they're not used to men lurking about," the Beauty Minister says.

"No need to be afraid of me, little dolls. I'm so uninterested in female comfort. I'm here to make sure you always have the proper dress to wear. I would dare say—upon penalty of death—that fashion is the most important element of beauty."

The Beauty Minister gives him a light push. They kiss each other's cheeks again.

"You are looking well," he purrs.

One of the Fashion Minister's attendants slides his ermine-lined robe from his shoulders, exposing a gold medallion with his royal minister emblem. Another attendant fluffs his hair with a wide-tooth comb. He waves a flash hand made of diamonds around, thanking his team.

He inspects Elisabeth. "Is this the little Du Barry, here at court to learn the ropes?"

She curtsies. "I'm Elisabeth Amie Lange Du Barry, daughter of the Gardien de la Belle-Rose, and I know plenty about court."

"But do you know the slightest thing about beauty?" he asks. "By the look of you, I'd say not."

Edel chuckles, but a look from Du Barry silences her.

"Of course she does, Gustave; she is my daughter," Du Barry says with pride.

He does a lap around Elisabeth, then returns to Du Barry's side. "There's much work to be done, Ana, for her to fill your shoes." He kisses the reluctant cheek offered up by Du Barry. "But for now, it's time to dress the Belles, and for the whole world to find out who has been chosen."

Servants put up privacy screens and unpack trunks. Silks, woolens, crinolines, cottons, satins, taffetas, tulles, and velvets are stretched over long tables by teams of people. Tiered trays hold buttons, lace, ribbons, gems, jewels, and hundreds of other baubles. A servant rushes me behind a screen and helps me up on a dress block. She unties the sash around my slip, undoes the petticoat ribbons, and removes my crinoline. A seamstress joins us, towing a kit.

"What kind of dress will you make?" I ask.

"The kind the Fashion Minister told me to. He picked out colors for you based on your complexion." She sits at a massive machine that boasts three spindle wheels and two looms. Her thick hands lace the string through a series of loops and pegs. She presses her foot on a paddle. The machine roars to life, creaking like a rickety carriage on a cobblestone street. Red, black, and white threads zip in and around a set of dowels.

Even though I've been dressed and measured and primped so many times, I still hate the feeling in these moments that my body doesn't belong to me. I become a doll—an object to be embellished. I wonder if this is how women feel on our treatment tables. I wish I could pick out my own dress. I'd choose something simple—a shade of red to match Maman's hair, a high waist with a cream waist-sash, and a sweeping skirt that flows out like a silk river behind me.

Another servant helps me into a robe and leads me to the bathing chamber for our second bath of the day. Beauty-lanterns cast a warm light on pink-tiled walls and gilded mirrors. A series of claw-footed tubs lines one side.

Amber sits in front of a mirror with her beauty caisse. Valerie and Hana are rushed into the tubs. Edel's wet hair is fanned dry by three people.

I tangle my feet up in plush floor rugs. My bath is drawn, and I'm in and out of it before the water can soak fully into my skin. An onsen servant leads me to a vanity. With fluid movements she wipes my arms, legs, and face with a damp rose-scented cloth and cuts and buffs my nails, then paints and dries them. She puts my feet into little red shoes. Another woman touches my eyelids, making me close them. I hear them unhook the compartments of my beauty caisse. Now I'm the one to be made beautiful. She powders my face and rubs a rouge-stick over my lips.

The clicks of Belle-pencils echo. She lines my eyes with two different kohl tips. Layer after layer of Belle-powder and rouge are applied to my cheeks and eyes. She rubs a waxy perfume-stick behind my ears and along my wrists. The soft powders and pencils and warm creams relax me. It would be easier if I could use my arcana on myself, even though Du Barry says it's impossible. The arcana are for the service of others.

I imagine my new life-to-be: being chosen, living at the palace, enjoying all the court has to offer, creating beautiful people. I take deep breaths. But Du Barry's words hover around me like the beauty-lanterns.

"Hair is next." The servant sections my hair, combing it through. The steam from the rollers creates a cloud around me, and their warmth seeps into my scalp as she sets my curls with them. Big waves hit my shoulders and are quickly pinned up into a signature Belle-bun, with Belle-rose petals to prevent frizzing.

The women rush me from this room to our dressing stalls. Bree waits for me. She fits me in a patterned long-sleeved gown in black and white. I've never worn any other color besides the deep pink Du Barry claims brings out the honey undertones in my brown skin. Bree's deft fingers close a series of hooks and clasps along my back. A bloodred waist-sash is tied at the middle to gather the skirts into the perfect bell shape. "You look beautiful, my lady," she says.

"Thank you," I reply.

"Are you excited to see the royal family and court?" Bree asks.

"Yes, I am." Our eyes meet in the mirror. I welcome the conversation. "What is the queen like?"

"Gracious, my lady," she whispers.

"And the princess?"

"Gracious, my lady," she says again, but her voice quivers. "Long live the queen and the princess."

I repeat the blessing as well.

"It's time, little dolls," the Fashion Minister calls out.

We step out from behind the dressing screens. The Beauty Minister gasps and claps. She fawns over us, and the dresses, and our new looks. The Fashion Minister beams, and takes us one by one to parade around the room.

Padma wears a bright purple dress with an empire waist that falls in a clean line to the floor. The silk ripples out behind her in waves, and jewels crawl in a pattern up her arms like snakes. Edel's dress spills over with layers of rubies and her edelweiss flowers. Her movements echo through the near-silent room. The cream strapless gown Valerie wears hugs tightly around her curves before blooming out in a fish's tail. Hana's silk gown boasts hand-painted images of our island and its cypress trees, and her sleeves swing low to the ground. Soft golden silk wraps around Amber's lean frame, and her Belle-bun is bursting with yellow ribbons like sunbeams. She's never looked more beautiful.

A mirror is brought out. My heart punches inside my chest. The reflection in the mirror looks like a stranger. My makeup is done up like a courtier in a beauty-scope—thickly lined eyes with gold accents, red jewels dotted along my eyebrows, a powdered face, bright lips. My Belle-bun spills over with Belle-roses, and the dress hugs me so closely I have a shape I've never seen on me before. The shape of my mother.

Du Barry goes down the line, kissing each of us on the cheek. When she gets to me, she whispers, "You look nice. Your mother would approve." She touches the textured pattern of my gown. I picture my mother's face, and I feel her proud and admiring smile deep inside.

"What do you think?" the Fashion Minister asks us.

"I love it," I whisper as my sisters squeal.

"I figured I shouldn't dress you traditionally. It's time to modernize Belles, in my humble opinion. Du Barry has been so ancient in her preparations," he says under his breath.

"What was that, Gustave?" Du Barry asks.

"Oh, nothing." He winks at us.

The Beauty Minister taps his shoulder with a fan, then looks at me and my sisters. "It's time to go learn your fates."

# 10

A plush red carpet cuts through the middle of the Receiving Hall like a thick river of blood. On either side of the aisle sit high-backed chairs filled with undeniably elegant women dressed in colorful silks, taffetas, satins, and crepes. Men ring the perimeter, and a sea of top hats peeks above the women's headdresses, fans, and tall hairstyles. People place eyescopes and spyglasses to their faces, squinting to see us. Over my head, a glass ceiling etched with the Orléansian royal emblem lets in light from the early evening stars.

"Eyes forward," the Beauty Minister whispers before we take our first steps inside.

Imperial guards wear deep purple vestments. The queen's divine color. I drown under the weight of the many stares. These people are the most important in the entire kingdom.

The Beauty Minister is silhouetted ahead, her pace slow and steady as we approach the pure gold chrysanthemum throne. My knees shake a little as I move closer. I try to steady them. I follow behind Padma. The lotus flowers in her hair open and close, winking at the onlookers.

A rustling of sound follows me. Women lean in to one another and mumble behind lace fans. They look at me like I'm a slice of spiced cake waiting to be eaten. Newsies sketch pictures of us, and black gossip post-balloons shift in and out of the crowd, their tails whipping in all directions, trying to catch a scandalous word here or there.

At the front of the room, a set of golden gazebos cluster to the left and right of the throne platform, each one covered with a canopy of flowers and garlands. A royal attendant helps me step into one marked with my name and camellia flowers. My sisters stand beside me in theirs.

A pyramid of stairs leads up to four thrones. They glimmer in the light of the dusk-lanterns, and hold the three most important people in the entire world: King Francis, Queen Celeste, and Princess Sophia. The second-to-last chair is left empty to represent the invalid Princess Charlotte. She hasn't been seen for years. Newsies speculate she's being kept alive so the monarchy doesn't pass the crown to Princess Sophia. The papers say Princess Sophia will make a terrible queen. That she's a spendthrift and loves to gamble and entertain with extravagant parties. But if the stories are true, I'm more than intrigued. She sounds impulsive, thrill-seeking, explosive, and above all, fascinating.

The queen descends from her throne. Guards fan out behind her like a cluster of shelled insects. Streaks of golden paint shimmer and twist into beautiful shapes on her skin. Sapphires decorate the slopes of her bright eyes. Her dark hair has a shock of gray in the front, like a vanilla swirl in a crème-cone. The tattlers say she leaves it there to pay homage to the roots of Orléans, the Gris.

The princess joins her. She matches her mother today. Same beautiful brown skin and soft oval face. Most families desire to be a matched set. Mothers determine the family features and manage their children's outward appearance, especially the families from high houses. But Princess Sophia has always changed what she looks like, as if she were merely donning a different dress. A teacup monkey perches on her shoulder.

I suck in my breath and hold it in my chest until the queen speaks. Every whisper, murmur, hum disappears.

"Welcome, my trusted advisors, my beloved ladies, and my ever-loyal court"—she waves a hand in the air—"to the most important day in our kingdom. The naming of our most glorious treasure." She faces us. "Beautiful Belles, welcome to my court and the beginnings of your divine service to our world. Without you and the gods, we would be nothing."

The room rumbles with applause. Its echo beats in my chest.

"Feast your eyes on our new generation of Belles!"

I knit my fingers in my lap as the entire crowd turns its attention from her to us. Servants open one of the floor-to-ceiling windows along the east wall, and scarlet post-balloons fly in. They sail over us, zipping and dipping and spinning, their little compasses guiding them to the throne platform. The tiny blimps dangle Belle-cards from golden ropes. Rich, animated, glossy. They tease the hands grabbing for them, coming close enough to be touched but not caught.

I spot my face on one, but the ink waxes and wanes, changing too quickly for me to read it and know my fate.

"These royal Belle-cards will be sent to every single citizen of the kingdom: the five major islands, and the smaller outlying clusters. If anyone has forgotten your names after the Beauté Carnaval, they'll remember them all in a matter of moments," the queen says.

The spectators clap.

"Now, my dearest court, cast your coins before I reveal the favorite. Let us see if we've picked the same Belle. May you always find beauty."

The women and men, and a few children, rush from their seats like a swarm of bees. They buzz around the gazebos, dropping coins into baskets held by servants who kneel beside them. They push eyescopes and spyglasses to their eyes and squint at our faces. They flap their fans at us. They listen through ear-trumpets for responses to their questions.

"What are your thoughts on coral-colored eyes?"

"Pale white skin turns gray faster, can you remedy that?"

"Could you give me a new face?"

"Do you think the laws should adjust, and allow for smaller waistlines?"

"My skin is getting old and doesn't take color well anymore, can you fix that?"

"Any opinion on smaller breasts this season versus larger ones?"

"I liked the trend of darker skin and light eyes; will that be back in fashion?"

"Any ideas on extending how long beauty treatments last?"

I can't answer one question before another one comes. The faces and voices blur into a spinning mass.

One face sticks out of the herd crowding around me.

The boy from the gate.

I feel his presence like a teacup dragon. Loud, commanding, full of fire. Courtier girls are watching him; some giggle behind their gloved hands and painted fans, and others ask him questions he leaves unacknowledged. He struts to the front of the line, and people clear a path for him. My eyes travel from the sapphire-blue cravat at his neck to the royal emblem pinned to it. Two ships sailing along the curve of a chrysanthemum stem. He's one of the sons of the Minister of Seas.

A drum beats inside me. I try not to stare. I try to pretend he's not gazing at me. I try to act like I don't remember him.

He starts to drop his coin in my basket, then pulls his hand back. His gaze burns my skin. A deep flush climbs from my stomach to my cheeks.

"Did you have a question?" I ask.

"Oh, she speaks." The pitch of his voice is richer than the darkest chocolate. He hides a smile behind his hand.

"I'm not a doll."

"I didn't think you were." He reaches for my hand. I feel the heat of it through my lace glove.

I pull away.

A guard steps forward. "No touching."

He flashes his palms. "I meant no offense. I'm Auguste Fabry, son of the Minister of the Seas, a harmless sailor. Just wanted to offer Lady"—he cranes to look up at the sign twinkling with my name—"Camellia my sincerest apologies. She's upset with me."

I bite back a smile, fighting with the corners of my mouth. "What is it? I'm very busy and have a long line," I tease.

"Very well. Do you think men should be as beautiful as

women?" His question curls around me like smoke, sliding over and under my skin, and through my dress. His words hold a challenge. One I want to win.

The women around my gazebo grow quiet. A nervous tremor flutters in my stomach.

"I think it's unfair that women must parade around like peacocks and men do not. There should be an equal effort."

The left side of his mouth lifts in a smile. "But aren't women supposed to be more beautiful than men in order to be enjoyed?"

"Are women quills or télétropes or new carriages?" Heat rises to my cheeks. He doesn't break eye contact.

Women fan themselves and trade whispers and gasps. Their eyes dart from me to him, and back again.

"No, they are not." He hides a smile beneath his hand. "It seems I know just what to say to make you angry with me."

"It seems you say stupid things."

"But it was a question, not a statement."

I sigh, even though I enjoy sparring with him. It's different than arguing with my sisters.

"Final question," he says, lifting his coin in the air.

"I think you've asked enough questions, and slowed down my line."

"Just one more. Is that all right?" He pokes his bottom lip out, like he's a child on the edge of a tantrum. The women fuss, goading me into allowing it.

"Go on," I demand, feigning annoyance.

"If you could change anything about me, what would it be?" he asks.

"You will have to make a private appointment for us to discuss your options."

"I'll take that answer to mean you'd change nothing."

The women snicker, coo, and shower him with compliments. He grins at me as he basks in it. I want to laugh, but hold the outburst in my chest. I will not smile. I will not let him know that he amuses me.

"But if you want my coin . . ." He rubs his hand under his chin, and his dark brows slant up. "You'll have to tell me. Because maybe I should give you my vote." He dangles the coin over the basket again. "Or maybe I shouldn't."

"Save your coins, I have plenty," I say. "My sisters are just as talented."

"But are they as beautiful?"

Nearby women burst with chatter.

I blush.

"I think you might make for an interesting favorite. Plus, I like to place a good bet." He drops the coin in just as the baskets are collected, then he disappears into the crowd. Traces of his smug attitude linger like perfume, distracting me from an onslaught of new questions. I search for him in the masses, wanting to tell him I'm not here for him to find me beautiful. I'm here to help the world. I'm not an ornament.

The queen returns to her throne, and she nods at the Beauty Minister.

"It's time," the Beauty Minister says into a voice-trumpet.

New scarlet post-balloons zip through the room, glowing bright with our Belle-emblem. They circle over the Beauty Minister like tanager birds looking for their nest. She reaches for one of the blimps and removes the card. "First up, Valeria Beauregard."

Valerie steps out of her gazebo.

"You will return home to Maison Rouge de la Beauté."

Valerie bows. When she returns to her platform, she looks at the ground and tries to catch the tears falling down her face.

We all clap for her.

The Beauty Minister reaches for another card. I resist bunching my dress.

"Edelweiss Beauregard," she says.

"Yes," Edel accidentally calls out, before clapping a hand over her mouth. The Beauty Minister smiles at her.

"My lovely, you will be at the Fire Teahouse in the Fire Isles," she says.

Edel curtsies.

"Hana Beauregard."

Hana snaps upright. Her hands dig into the folds of her dress as she walks out of her gazebo. She doesn't look at the Beauty Minister; her eyes are fixed on the ground. A few cherry-blossom petals fall from her Belle-bun. She takes in a large breath.

The Beauty Minister scans the Belle-card. "You will be at the Glass Teahouse in the Glass Isles."

Hana exhales, claps her hands together, then bows.

"Padma Beauregard, you will be at the Silk Teahouse in the Bay of Silk," the Beauty Minister says.

Padma's chin drops to her chest. Tears stream down her cheeks, and she does her best to wipe them away. A sob escapes her. She covers her mouth. A nearby servant rubs her back, and whispers something to her.

Two blimps linger over the Beauty Minister's head, chasing each other in a perfect circle.

This is it.

I look at Amber to my left. She winks at me. I blow her a silent kiss and cross my fingers for both of us. I tell myself: *If it isn't me, then I'll be happy it's her.* I hope she feels the same. I ignore the tiny voice inside me that whispers, *You're lying.*

The Beauty Minister reaches for the cards displaying our faces. I stand up straight and ball my fists in anticipation of what she's going to say. The girls watch and wait.

"Camellia Beauregard," she says.

I walk forward. Fear and excitement climb over me like vines. My palms itch. My face feels flushed. I don't know whether I want to vomit, shriek, or both. My heartbeat hammers in my ears.

"You'll be at the Chrysanthemum Teahouse in the Rose Quartier of our Imperial City of Trianon."

My cheeks flame and I know they're red as strawberries. My heart plummets into my stomach with a crash. Sweat streams down my back. "But..." I start to say, before Du Barry glares at me.

I bow and return to my gazebo. My chest heaves. I might never be able to catch my breath again.

The queen stands. The Beauty Minister turns to her.

"Ambrosia Beauregard." The queen stretches out the syllables of her name.

Amber steps forward—eyes gazing ahead, shoulders back, slight smile on her face—looking exactly how Du Barry trained us to. Gracious. Alert. Always ready.

"You have been named the *favorite*," the Beauty Minister announces. The word explodes through the room like a cannon.

I put a hand over my mouth.

The queen claps. "Ambrosia is the favorite."

A servant dumps out Amber's basket. Coins splatter on the floor and make a golden mountain. The court cast many bets for her.

I can't take my eyes off Amber.

The queen smiles at my sister. My heart shatters like a glass mirror, the tiny shards shooting out into every part of me, cutting at my insides, spreading pain. They will never be put back together.

Du Barry keeps her arms crossed over her ample chest. She gives me a satisfied look.

I am *not* the favorite.

The words smash into one another inside my head.

I am *not* the favorite.

Hands reach for me. Lips kiss my cheeks, leaving smudges of rouge-stick behind. People swarm in a thousand directions. Women squeeze my hands. They tell me how excited they are to book appointments with me at the Chrysanthemum Teahouse. People applaud, lights flash, arms pull me into hugs and twirls. Some whisper that they thought it should've been me. Newsies flock around, shoving voice-trumpets in my face and pestering me with questions about Amber and my opinion about the queen's selection of the favorite.

I bite back tears. I push them down with too-sweet champagne.

Amber is surrounded, her ginger Belle-bun a tiny crest above the crowd. Du Barry gives an interview about what she was like as a child: studious, deferential, loving. The Beauty Minister tells royal listeners what criteria the ministers and the queen used to choose the favorite this season: disciplined, dutiful, responsible. My sisters bounce around in their beautiful dresses and speak to other courtiers and newsies.

The room swirls around me. The queen's words ring out— *Ambrosia is the favorite*—alongside the racing thrum of my heart.

# 11

The evening whizzes by like the spinning of a newsreel. My sisters dance and laugh and give interviews and kiss cheeks and eat sweets. We have our portraits painted and talk to our big sisters—the previous generation of Belles. I hide in an adjacent tea salon to avoid the newsies until we return to the Belle apartments. Amber doesn't come with us. She lingers in the Grand Imperial Ballroom surrounded by well-wishers and courtiers, who clamor for her attention.

I watch the doors. I wait for her to walk in.

Belle-trunks are lined up in the middle of the main salon like coffins. Servants fill them with beauty caisses, new dresses and shoes from the Fashion Minister, the latest Belle-products, and sangsue jars.

Hana peers into her trunk. "We're not going to be together anymore."

"Is it time already?" Padma whines. "I don't want to go yet."

I don't either. The pinch of it comes sweeping back, and I'm near tears. I face the wall and pretend to admire the tapestry map of Orléans.

"The carriages will be here soon." Valerie collapses into a nearby chaise. Her dress rips, but she's too tired to look down at the fishtail train that's threatening to fall off.

"And I saw our big sisters leave another apartment in traveling cloaks," Hana says.

A pause settles over us. Tears well up in Padma's and Hana's eyes. Edel's cheeks flush. Valerie sniffles. I look away. The uneasy silence feels suffocating.

"I'm ready to get this over with." Edel throws her shoes into her Belle-trunk.

Servants present trays of fizzy water overflowing with raspberries, snowmelon slices, strawberries, and limes. Carts hold late-night treats: petit-waffles, sugary syrups, fried sweetbread and chicken, and luna pastries. Three télétropes project pictures on the walls. The magic of the night flashes all around us, but I feel only disappointment. A sad tremor lives inside my chest, and my arms and legs buzz with the memory of not being chosen.

"Where's Amber?" Valerie asks.

The sound of her name feels like a sparkler explosion.

"Gloating somewhere, no doubt," Edel says.

"I haven't seen her since the dinner." Hana opens the doors of the Belle apartments to peek out.

"She probably has a dozen things to do now," I mumble.

"I didn't want her to win," Edel states.

"That's terrible to say." Padma gives her a playful shove.

"Why do you think the queen picked her?" Valerie asks.

"Because she's always perfect." The words slip out heavy and hard.

My sisters turn to me. I bite my bottom lip to keep it from quivering. A tiny hiccup works its way up my throat. I'm relieved when the servants take us to the dress salon.

Servants remove our gowns. We're given soft traveling dresses made of cotton and chambray and voile and gauze. The sadness of leaving hits me in a wave. I've never *not* seen my sisters every day. Hana's morning grumpiness, Edel always getting in trouble, Valerie's tinkling laugh, walking the grounds with Padma, and sharing secrets with Amber. I didn't think about how far away they'd be after we received our assignments. I didn't think about how different things would be between us.

We pile back into the main salon and eat food from the carts.

"I think it's time for a toast." Padma grabs a glass from a tray. Bubbly green liquid spills on the front of her travel dress, and she curses.

"Should we wait for Amber?" Valerie asks.

"No," the rest of us say.

Hana lays her head on my shoulder. "I thought it would be you."

"Thanks," I whisper. *Me too.*

"Quiet down and come on." Padma tries to get everyone's attention. "Get a drink. I don't know how much longer we have together tonight."

Edel gulps down a flute of red liquid and takes another. Valerie fusses at her for drinking the last one.

Padma clears her throat. "Cheers to each other. Cheers to this night. And cheers to what's to come."

We lift our glasses and sip.

"Me next!" Valerie leaps up from her chaise. "Even though I was upset about my placement earlier today, and I love all of this..." She waves her hand around. "In my heart I've always known I was supposed to go back home. My maman was the Belle of Maison Rouge de la Beauté, so deep down I knew that I had to fill her shoes. But please don't forget about me. Send me post-balloons about the things you get to see and do. And better yet, don't get too busy to come visit." Her voice cracks. "I will miss you all."

We take another sip. Her words hit me. She's doing what her mother did. I was supposed to be the favorite, like my maman. I've let her down.

"Ugh, you girls are getting emotional," Edel complains. Hana jostles her shoulder, which makes Edel break out in a smile. "I guess I'll miss you all, too."

Servants present us with thick traveling cloaks lined in white fur and covered in tiny gold stitches in the shape of Belle-roses and our royal emblem.

We're slipping our arms into the cozy sleeves when Amber strides into the room. Her heavy footsteps pound the floor as if it should crumble under the weight of their importance. The petit-crown on her head glitters like it is made of stardust.

"Hello, my sisters!"

She prances about, swishing her gown left and right, beaming brighter than a morning-lantern as she waits for us to gush over her.

"Congratulations." Valerie steps forward to hug Amber.

"We're so happy for you." Hana swirls her around and around until both of them collapse in laughter and dizziness. A selfish emotion bubbles up in my chest. It grows larger by the second, stealing my breath. It won't pop. I want to wrap my arms around her, sink my face into her neck, and whisper how proud I am of her, but my feet won't move, and my mouth is full of syrup, the words stuck.

"You're going to make a beautiful favorite." Padma blows her a kiss.

"Well." Edel looks her up and down. "I suppose someone had to win." And then she sweeps out of the room.

A travel attendant steps aside to let Edel go, then taps an hourglass hanging from her jacket lapel. "Carriages will soon depart."

Everyone gives Amber one last hug. I linger in the room after my sisters leave.

Amber and I stare at each other.

"I can't believe Edel," she says. "Are you happy for me?"

"I am," I say. "Just trying to let it all sink in."

"You're at the most important teahouse. The Chrysanthemum. It's where the royal ladies-of-honor go. At least you'll be here in the city—"

"Don't try to make it sound better, Amber. I'm not the favorite." The sound of it out loud sends another surge of disappointment through me. I hear Maman's disappointed voice and see her furrowed brow.

"But you're still important. We're all important."

"It's not enough." I finally let out the little sob in my chest.

She rushes forward, grabs my arms, and pulls me close. I sink my face into the nook between her shoulder and neck. "It's going to be fine." Her words land on my cheek. She smells like a mishmash of courtier perfume. She's been hugged a hundred times tonight. "You'll be able to visit me, and I'll invite you to everything I can. Also, I'll come see you."

I pull away from her embrace. My failure crashes back in, hitting me in a hot wave. *I am not the favorite.* I can't take her pity, and when she reaches for me again, I push her away.

"Stop," I say.

She looks hurt, but there's nothing I can do. "You can't be happy for me."

A tornado of heat swirls around me. My stomach flip-flops, and my face runs with sweat. "I am." I fight back tears. Can't she see how hard this is?

"You thought you'd beat me easily. You got to go last at the Beauté Carnaval. Anyone who goes last gets to leave the best impression. Placement drowned out those of us in the middle. Du Barry set you up to be the favorite, but the queen chose me."

"Is that what you really think? Du Barry doesn't like me. Never has. She's never understood what I have to offer," I say, searching Amber's face for traces of my friend. "Do you know how hard I worked? Researching for months about past carnavals, thinking through different looks, stealing Du Barry's pamphlets and beauty magazines from the mail chest to study trends. I worked just as hard as you did."

"Well, you didn't follow the rules at the carnaval, or ever, really," she says. "You didn't deserve to be the *favorite.*"

I glare at her. A wrinkle of concentration mars her forehead.

"You're my best friend," she says. "You should've been the first one to kiss me after the announcement and the first one to tell me how proud you were. Instead, you're sulking and being jealous. I followed the rules, Camellia. I deserve this. You don't. You always get so upset when I beat you at anything. What would Maman Linnea think of your behavior?"

"Don't bring up my mother." My eyes fill with tears. My fists clench. I shake with anger.

Amber leans in close. "She would be ashamed of you." She grabs my wrist and I yank away, pulling her off-balance. Amber lets out a half-surprised, half-anguished shout as she falls to the ground.

I gasp. "Amber! I didn't mean—"

Her eyes drill into me. Her cheeks burn with redness, and her once-elaborate eye makeup runs down her cheeks in orange-and-gold streaks.

"I'm so sorry." I reach for her.

She scoots away and crawls to her knees, then stands. "Don't touch me."

A travel attendant peers into the salon. "Lady Camellia, your carriage awaits."

Amber won't even look at me. I turn and run from the room. An angry knot hardens inside my gut, and a headache punches its way up my neck and into my temples. I race down the stairs to catch up with the rest of my sisters as her words repeat over and over again to the beat of my footsteps.

*She would be ashamed.... She would be ashamed.*

# 12

The carriage wheels thump against the cobblestones in the Royal Square. I peel back the curtains, and diamond-paned city-lanterns illuminate rich limestone mansions and townhouses in the aristocratic Rose Quartier. Their pillars cut the skyline like expensive blades. The moon paints the sky in deep violets and indigos. The horses whinny and neigh as the driver navigates the sharp turns and narrow lanes of the Imperial City of Trianon.

"Lady Camellia," a familiar voice says.

I glance away from the window. A pale face peeks out from behind a curtain. It's the servant from the palace's Belle apartments. Her brown dress is a smudge of chocolate against the wine red of the carriage's interior.

"I'm—"

"I remember you, Bree."

She flushes pink. "I've been assigned to you as your imperial servant."

"Wonderful." I try to be gracious, just as Du Barry has taught me.

"Would you care for something to eat?"

"No." I return to the sights beyond the carriage.

"How about tea?" She takes a pot from a tiny hearth that holds a warm, crackling fire.

"I'm not thirsty."

She removes the lid and flashes the steeping Belle-roses inside. "It's to help you relax before your arrival." She pours me a cup. When served to clients, it's supposed to keep their arms and legs from trembling, quiet their fears or anticipation, and help dull the pain of beauty transformations.

On second thought . . . I swallow the liquid down in one gulp. It burns all the way to my stomach, and I wish it had the power to erase the memory of my fight with Amber. I want to forget the whole night.

I peer outside again as the world becomes a blur of light and color. Spires of smoke twist up and disappear into the sky. We move through the Market Quartier, still busy with merchants selling wares better suited to the dark. Cobalt-blue lanterns hang from every stall and swing above every saloon, beckoning late-night patrons. Vendors holler that they have the best spyglasses for sale; a trio of women hold up bracelets on raised arms; a man offers carved pipes and powders that promise wishes and dreams, while another curves ear-trumpets in the air like a series of elephant trunks. There are scowls, the flashing of teeth, and sluggish smiles. The fuss of haggling tongues deafens me.

The lantern colors change from deep blues to emerald greens as we enter the Garden Quartier.

*The world should be like a garden with people bright as roses and lilies and tulips, otherwise it's all a waste,* Maman used to say. Towers curve above painted avenue boards. The promenades boast animated cameos and portraits of famed courtiers that wink and wave as we pass. Rose-shape pavilions sell snowmelon cider, peach champagne, fluffy beignets, and luna pastries. The scents slip in through the window.

Bree takes my cup. "We'll be arriving soon."

A scarlet glow pushes into the carriage, washing my arms and legs in red stripes. Beauty-lanterns drift along streets paved with glistening stones, past mismatched shops painted in pastel shades and lined up like the frosted pastries in a bakery window. The stores branch into a maze of twisting alleys. Belle-products twinkle behind glass windowpanes. I try to get excited. I try to take in how pretty it all is. But my mind reminds me that I'm not the favorite and I am not at the palace. This is the consolation prize.

The Chrysanthemum Teahouse glows in lavenders and magentas and reds. Ten stories high, its elegant turrets hold balconies trimmed with shiny night-ivy. It climbs the walls, scaling so high it could grow off the teahouse and make a path to the God of the Sky. A golden walkway licks out like a tongue. Crimson sill-lanterns sit in each window and cast their bloody light over the courtyard. People crowd along the teahouse grounds. Newsies hold up light-boxes. Men and women affix spyglasses to their eyes. Children, up too late, wave their little hands.

The carriage stops. The door opens.

"Lady Camellia!" An attendant presents me with his arm. "Right this way."

I step out. A full staff awaits.

"Camellia!"

"Camellia!"

I wave to the shouting crowd, and try to smile with the perfect amount of teeth, just as Du Barry taught us. I pretend to be happy.

I'm led across the walkway.

I bow, then wave the onlookers good-bye as the teahouse doors shut behind me. The inside blazes with light. Soft golden rays dance over the floor. The space carries the scent of charcoal and flowers. A bubbling fountain sprays water. The foyer looks up into the belly of the house. Nine balconies rim its perimeter, with gilded rails and oil-black spindles that curl along each floor and twist into the shape of Belle-roses. Chandelier-lanterns hang from the high ceiling, floating up and down like jeweled clouds, bathing each floor with a tiny glow. A grand staircase splits into two like a pair of pearl-white snakes.

Bree takes my traveling cloak, then sweeps my gown with a handheld broom, batting at it for dust, bugs, or any other unwanted occupant I may have picked up on my journey. She removes my shoes and replaces them with silk house socks that button along my ankles.

"Thank you." My connection to the palace isn't completely lost if she's here with me.

"Of course, Lady Camellia." She bows.

A woman saunters in wearing a dress the color of sunlit honey, which dips low in the front to display three diamond necklaces. Her long and elegant hair is pinned up in a golden swirl, and she reminds me of the chrysanthemum flower on the Orléansian emblem. Her fingernails shimmer like the bright color of its leaves.

"Camellia," she says. "I'm Madam Claire Olivier, wife of Sir Robert Olivier, House Kent, baby sister of Madam Ana Du Barry,

and the mistress of this glorious teahouse. My, my, that's a lot."
She chuckles to herself.

I curtsy. I have faint childhood memories of her visiting the
house.

She smiles, and the rouge-stick on her teeth makes her look
like she's eaten a box of colored pastels. Sweat dots her top lip, and
she obsessively blots her face with a handkerchief.

"We're so happy the queen placed you here. Though my sister says you're a handful, with a naughty temperament. But you
have the sweetest face. I don't believe her. She can be so fussy." She
touches my cheek. "Now, now. Let me take you on a tour of the
great Chrysanthemum Teahouse."

I follow her up the grand staircase. She jingles from a strange
set of keys around her waist.

"There are ten floors, with thirty-five rooms on each one. They
used to be brimming over with Belles, their ledgers chock-full of
courtiers. The queen had the hardest job, sifting through so many
talented Belles to select the favorite. The Beauté Carnaval lasted a
month when I was a child."

I run my fingers over ornate banisters. Some doors remain
closed, and others flash their themed interiors. Snowy white
chaises with chartreuse pillows, jade bedcurtains and saffron
drapes, fuchsia walls and garnet tapestries. I imagine each room
as the beauty workshop of a Belle. House-lanterns follow behind
us. Their tiny whooshing noises echo.

Du Barry never told us why there are so few of us now.

"I wonder if my sister knows how to nurture Belles anymore."
Madam Claire winks at me.

I keep my face blank. Du Barry's threats still ring in my ears.

Madam Claire shows me the beautiful breakfast veranda and

the game salon and tea parlors. "Historically, this teahouse was where the queen and her ladies came, before Queen Anaïs built the palace Belle apartments in the Charvois Dynasty. My family lives on the tenth floor, and your quarters will be on the third."

We return to the grand staircase.

"Where's my big sister, Aza? Will we share a room as she trains me?"

Madam Claire stops and pivots around. Her mouth crumples into a frown. "You won't be needing her help transitioning."

"But Madam Du Barry said we had a month together. She's supposed to show me how to do everything perfectly and take over her clients."

"I sent her home to La Maison Rouge early. She had an unpleasant disposition, if you will. But not to worry, you have me. I've been mistress of this teahouse for fifteen years. There's no one better to show you what's expected."

More disappointment piles on top of the growing mountain inside me. I thought I would have an elder sister to rely on—at least for a time. That was what we'd been told.

We walk along the third floor. Servants open a set of doors. Bree and I follow Madam Claire inside.

"These are your chambers"—Madam Claire motions—"and your imperial servant will be in nearby quarters."

The most enormous bed I've ever seen sits in the middle of the room. Velvet drapes hang from gilded posts tied with gossamer bows. The bed is covered in silk pillows made of swansdown, and thick blankets embroidered with the Chrysanthemum House emblem. Flames curl and hiss in a stone fireplace, even though it's the end of the warm months. Bowls hold floating tea lights and flower petals. Gold-framed portraits swallow the walls. Marble statues of the Goddess of Beauty and famous Belles peek out of every corner. I spot my mother in the long row. I wonder what she'd say if she were here. Would she admit her disappointment? Would she tell me to be grateful?

Bree works with the others to unpack my Belle-trunk. The beauty caisse is lifted to a vanity complete with three mirrors and a series of beauty-lantern hooks. A Belle-book sits on the table, embossed with my portrait and name, and an instruction card from Du Barry demanding that I record everything. Dresses are hung in a closet so big my new bed could fit inside it.

"The Fashion Minister sent a hundred dresses. I advised him that I'd like for you to match the house, so he used the teahouse colors as inspiration." Madam Claire's words fade into a distant murmur.

I think of the beauty of the room in which Amber now sleeps. The whole scene with her replays over and over again: the hurt in her eyes and the noise she made as she fell. A heaviness settles into me, like a post-balloon with too much to carry. And even though this is a beautiful room in an even more beautiful house, and I am the second most important Belle in the kingdom, all I see are images of the palace Belle apartments, and all I hear are Amber's words, and all I feel is that this room isn't good enough.

"I think you will be perfect here. You already seem to fit with the space." Madam Claire giggles. "Your skin is the right shade of brown to match it. The designers worked hard to ensure it'd be the right fit." She runs her hands over the furniture, then leans on the vanity, staring in the mirror. "Oh, dear, I've put on too much rouge-stick again." She rubs at her teeth.

The servants stifle laughter. She clears her throat, and they stop. She looks at me in the mirror's reflection. "I thought the queen was going to choose you."

I meet her gaze, and tears well in my eyes.

"Your exhibition was so clever. I rooted for you because it was markedly different from the others. And because you made my sister so mad."

I bow so she won't see the smile that her statement inspires. "Thank you, Madam."

"But Ambrosia is the right favorite for the current royal family," she says, and the momentary happiness disappears like a popped bubble. "They've had enough strife. They need someone who will do exactly as told."

"I could've done that," I say, even though it feels like a lie.

She walks over and places a hand against my cheek. "Who are you trying to fool, me or you?" She smiles, the rouge-stick now coating more of her teeth, and leans forward to sniff me. "You smell like lavender. How lovely. I'm happy to have you here. Tomorrow we'll get to work." She excuses herself, sending in nurses to check my arcana levels.

I climb into the too-large bed and let the nurses poke and prod me. After they leave, I take out the cameo of my mother and set it on the pillow beside me. I trace my fingers over the silhouette of her face, carved from blush-pink stone, glass, and white quartz.

"What should I do, Maman?"

I close my eyes and imagine her beside me. The scent of her hair, the feel of her skin, the sound of her breathing. I listen hard for her voice like it's only a faraway whisper.

*Do what you've been asked to do,* she'd say.

"What if I don't want to?"

*You must. The queen has made her decision. You weren't raised to covet the path of others. It allows the God of Envy's snake to enter your veins.*

"I yelled at my best friend."

*You should never let your anger bubble over. It blinds you. It shatters hearts.*

"I'm sorry, Maman. I'm sorry I failed. I didn't work hard enough."

I wait for her voice. I wait for her to tell me it's all right. I wait to feel her arms curl around my waist, to feel the soft beat of her heart pushing through my back.

Nothing comes.

I sink down in the new mattress, wishing for an indentation like the one left behind by Maman in our bed at home, and drift into disappointed dreams.

# 13

Unfamiliar noises and new scents wake me early, and I'm swept into the day. Breakfast on the veranda, and a list of morning appointments.

*Mistress Daniela Jocquard, House Maille 7:00*
*Lady Renée Laurent, House of Silk 8:00*
*Countess Madeleine Rembrandt, House Glaston 9:00*
*Lady Ruth Barlon, House Eugene 10:00*
*Duchesse Adelaide Bruen, House of Pomanders 11:00*

The small treatment salon has pale blue walls and a circular shape, like the inside of a robin's egg. Servants work to fluff pillows and drape blankets across a long table. Bree opens up my beauty caisse and sets out instruments on a silver tray.

A skylight window reveals angry clouds ready to thunder and rain down. It's as if the sky reflects my insides.

"Lady Camellia," Bree whispers.

"Yes?"

"Your first clients have arrived in the parlor. Tea has been served."

"Thank you."

I take a deep breath and smooth the front of my canary-yellow work dress. Bree squeezes my shoulder, and I flash her a thankful smile.

Madam Claire strides in. "Camellia, darling, how are you feeling this morning?" Rouge-stick bleeds around her smile. She mops sweat from her brow.

I curtsy. "Fine."

"I trust you slept well." She rubs my shoulder. "It's your first day here, so I wanted to check on you."

"I'm fine."

"You keep saying that." Her nose scrunches.

"Because I am."

She eyes me suspiciously but says nothing more, and we walk together to the adjacent waiting parlor. A little girl marches around in circles. She chases a tawny teacup lion.

"Come here, Chat. Little Chat, come back." The teacup lion yelps out a tiny roar as the girl yanks its tail. The girl's jeweled pinafore balloons around her small waist, and the little hat on her head threatens to fall off. She can't be more than five years old. Her elegant mother grabs at her, demanding she sit down.

"Lady Jocquard and Mistress Daniela, may I present the new Belle of the Chrysanthemum Teahouse at your service."

I bow. "I'm Camellia Beauregard."

"I know exactly who you are," Lady Jacquard replies, waving my Belle-card at me. "And I'm quite excited to see what you can actually do. It will be such a relief to work with an official Belle again."

"Official?" I say.

"You are the *official* Belle of the Chrysanthemum Teahouse, Camellia," Madam Claire says. "I shall leave you two to discuss Daniela's treatments."

Daniela climbs into a small wing-backed chair. Her legs dangle, and she clicks her little heels together. "You're the new Belle?" Her voice is as small as she is.

"Yes." I sit in the chair beside her. She stares at me with big hazel eyes, and blinks rapidly as if I might disappear.

"Camellia," she says.

"Lady Camellia," her mother corrects.

I reach for her hand. "It doesn't seem like you need any work done. May I take a closer look?"

Daniela jumps up, and I twirl her about like a tiny top.

"Are you sure?" Daniela cups her hand around my ear. "Mother says I'm a complete disaster," she whispers.

The little girl only needs a few small refreshments—a new coat of skin paste, an eye brightening, reinforcement of her hair texture.

"We could give you a tail, and maybe some whiskers—then you two can match." I point to the teacup lion licking her leg.

She picks him up and nuzzles her face in his fur. "Really?"

"Nonsense," Lady Jocquard says. "Her looks have been a mess lately. Can't you see her eyes and nose? They've always been a problem. Her natural template is flawed."

Daniela's eyes are a little sunken, like two finch's eggs in a nest, and her nose hooks left. I want to tell her that Daniela's little hooked nose gives her character—natural individuality, uncreated by Belles. I want to remind her that Daniela's bones will always drift back to their original shape, and that some are more stubborn than others. I want to tell her Daniela's distinctive features make her appear sweet and curious.

"I'd like for you to give her a new, darker hair shade, and work on her face," Lady Jocquard says. "We might have to discuss giving her a completely new one at some point."

"She's a very pretty little girl—"

She scoffs, then lifts a bag from her pocket and jingles it.

A long silence drifts between us. I stare into her eyes.

"I like it when my daughter looks a certain way. She must learn how to maintain herself well. Even at this age." Lady Jocquard snaps her fingers at her attendant. "Here's a beauty board I had created. I'd like her skin to be the color of the night sky, but with a tinge of blue. I'm going to dust her with the new glitter sparkle opera singer Geneviève Gareau is wearing. Did you see her in the *Trianon Tribune*? Just shining. The next trend, for sure. My whole family will be first to do it."

Her attendant hands it to me. Color smudges streak around an old cameo of Daniela. Hair-texture swatches line the perimeter, boasting an array of types—coiled, straight, coarse, wavy, fine, curly, frizzy, and smooth. The portraits of other courtier children circle hers.

I glance from the board to Daniela, and then to her mother. I wish Lady Jocquard could see her the same way I do.

"I really love how Lady Élise Saint-Germain—from House Garlande—styles her twins. You know, they made the newsies' new child beauty-scopes. Twice. She updates them in the perfect way."

"Have you thought about leaving—"

She puts a hand up. "I didn't come here to argue about what's best for my daughter. I came here to spend money. I can just as easily go to the Silk Teahouse, and make sure all my courtier friends know exactly what type of experience they'll get here with you."

My cheeks flame and my heart skips. I stutter out an apology.

"I'd rather you get started. Save the formalities."

Her words are a slap.

"Yes, of course; off to the bathing chamber first," I say.

Daniela wants me with her at every step of the process. I lead her to the bathing onsen. Beauty-lanterns glide through the room. Candles float in three small pools: the first is full of rose petals, the second is thick with an infusion of aloe, and the last one simmers with salt, sulfur, and steam. Four poultice rooms line the wall, holding the promise of healing from red clay, oakwood charcoal, amethyst gem, and blue onyx.

Daniela takes a dip in each pool and visits each poultice room just to take a peek. She interlocks her hand with mine as we enter the treatment salon. Her mother follows closely behind.

A long table cuts through the middle of the room like a knife. Servants fluff pillows and turn down blankets.

"She will need more tea," Lady Jocquard says. "Her pain tolerance is low, unfortunately."

"Bree, would you mind bringing more?" I ask.

She returns with a tray of teapots, and she pours Daniela a cup. Bree adds three ice cubes to cool it. Daniela gags and tries to spit it out.

"Nope, down it goes." Her mother pushes the cup to Daniela's lips and tips it upright. Most of the liquid dribbles down her chin. She wiggles, but her mother's grip tightens. Daniela's tea-soaked pinafore is removed. She swings her naked arms and legs all around.

I tuck Daniela into the treatment bed. "Snug as a little bug."

She giggles. "Are you going to make me beautiful? What will you do?"

"It's a secret." I cup my hand near her ear. I feel the hugeness of her smile. "You're already very pretty. I'm going to make you the most beautiful little girl in the whole wide world."

She gasps, and turns to whisper in my ear. "I'd like that. Maman would like that, too. She would stop being so worried all the time."

"I hope so." I fluff her pillow. "Time to get started. You ready?"

She nods. I examine Daniela's features. I run my fingers through her stiff hair; the strands remind me of hay in the carriage-house stables at home. The brown color is dull and ashen at the roots. A million looks flash through my head, like a deck of cards being shuffled.

"Are you going to do it?" Daniela asks.

"Yes," I say, trying to keep my hands from trembling. "I'm thinking. Close your eyes."

"But I want to see," she protests.

Lady Jocquard paces around the bed. "Do what the Belle says, now." Her voice makes me jump.

I close my eyes. I block out the noise of Lady Jocquard's heels. My body warms like I've swallowed a blazing star. Maman said that we are made of stardust, of the Goddess of Beauty herself, and to envision the arcana like a comet zipping through us.

Her voice guides me. *Be gentle, go slowly. Children require a light touch. You were born knowing how to do this.*

The veins in my body swell. They rise in my hands.

Daniela appears in my head like a painting: doughy skin, dull hair, sinking eyes, crooked nose, long face. Bree and I coat her limbs with bei powder and darken her skin. I place a mesh marked with quadrants over her face. I paint a new color on a single strand of her hair. I imagine a raven sitting on Daniela's shoulder, and I blacken her hair to match its wings. I tug lightly on the strands, forcing her hair to grow, and soon it tumbles over her shoulders in coiled ribbons.

"Ow." She winces. Sweat beads dot her forehead. She bites her bottom lip and bursts into tears. I rub Daniela's shoulder. Tears stream down her cheeks, wetting the mesh.

"Maybe we should stop for a bit?" I say to her mother.

"No, she's fine. She always does this," her mother says. "She's going to be the most beautiful little girl now." She holds Daniela's arms down, but the little girl starts to kick and scream. The shrill sounds hit me in my chest. Servants rush forward to help Lady Jocquard pin her in place.

I try to work faster. I fine-tune her hair, placing a nice wave in the strands, adding a shiny gloss like Padma's black hair, and thickening it in the crown. She hollers even louder. She shakes her head left and right. The mesh falls to the floor.

"I need her head to remain still."

"You stop it this instant. I will send Chat away immediately to be stuffed like a doll," Lady Jocquard scolds. Daniela freezes and whimpers. Lady Jocquard cups Daniela's head, firmly holding it in place.

I pull her eyes a little out of their sockets, like spoons lifting eggs out of a cup-server. Her screams turn cold and sharp as ice. I flinch at each crescendo. I straighten out her nose into the perfect slope. The bone pops and cracks. Bree holds a handkerchief to the base, and a small stream of blood trickles out. I smooth out the break.

"Hush all that noise, Daniela," Lady Jocquard hollers. "Quit carrying on like that. You're becoming an embarrassment."

"I'm done," I say.

Daniela's cries turn to hiccups. "It...I...it..."

"Wipe your face," Lady Jocquard says to her. "And someone bring a mirror." She snaps her fingers at Bree.

Bree scurries off and returns with a mirror. I help Daniela sit up. Her skin is warm to the touch. Daniela gazes into the mirror. She pants, but flashes me a pained smile.

"See?" Lady Jocquard hovers over Daniela. "Simply gorgeous. I love it." She gazes up at me. "You're such a talent. Much better than the others at this teahouse."

"Others?" I ask.

A servant clears her throat. The two of them make eye contact.

"What did you mean, Lady Jocquard?"

"The last Belle here," she explains.

"Lady Camellia," the servant starts. "Your next client is here." She leads me forward as Lady Jocquard continues to talk.

"Job well done. You can be sure I'll tell Madam Claire," she says as the doors close behind me.

# 14

The rest of the day zips by like a lightning flash. Women come with their beauty boards, attendants, and friends. I alter bodies, change hair colors and skin tones, give a man a songbird voice, erase age-lines, and try to reassure frantic courtiers about how beautiful they are. Finally, I crawl into bed, every part of me exhausted.

But my arms and legs buzz with the fervor of the day, and I can't sleep. I thumb through hand-drawn Belle-cards, searching for mine. Portraits of my smiling sisters—and past generations of Belles—are set in circular frames.

I am in the middle of the stack. My face stares back at me: smiling eyes, a Belle-bun full of camellia petals, a rosy blush set in brown cheeks, and the Belle-emblem stamped on my chest. Beneath the picture, calligraphy script announces my full name—CAMELLIA BEAUREGARD—and my best arcana: AURA. The assignment space says CHRYSANTHEMUM TEAHOUSE.

I cover it with my thumb. I want to scratch it out and write *favorite*. When I turn the card left and right, my tiny portrait winks. I comb through them again, staring at my sisters' faces, missing the sound of their laughter and the noise of their company. I linger on Amber's, and her eyes hold a glimmer like she has a secret. Her Belle-bun looks like flames wrapped up in a bow. When you rotate her card, she smiles. I trace my finger along her mouth, wondering if she'll ever smile at me again.

I tuck the stack under my pillow. Servants blow out all the night-lanterns in my room except for one. They close the bedcurtains. I stare up at the canopy and wait for my dreams to sweep me away. Maman always said, *Dreams remind us of who we are and how we feel about the things around us.* But my mind is a frantic mess of worries that pull me awake each time I drift off. Will Amber forgive me? Will I be able to help the people of Orléans discover their beauty and make my mother proud? Will I be able to accept that I'm meant to be here, instead of at the palace?

The shuffle of heeled feet and the hum of tiny cries drift through the house. I listen for a few moments, thinking it might be a servant. The cries continue.

I pull a robe from the closet, then walk to my bedroom door.

It's locked. I wiggle the doorknob. It opens, but not from my side. A sleepy-eyed servant stares back at me. "Lady Camellia, how can I help you?"

"There's crying. What is it?"

"I didn't hear anything, miss."

I brush past her into the hall. I listen again. The whoosh of night-lanterns and the sounds of one of Madam Claire's parties drift through the foyer. The clink of glasses, the giggling of excited women, the laughter of men. "I heard it."

"Maybe it was a night-lantern. They screech a little when the candles are about to go out," she says. "That must be it." She tries to guide me back into my room.

I plant my feet. She avoids my gaze. A sheen of sweat appears across her forehead.

"Why is my door locked? And where is Bree?"

"Just a precaution, miss," she says. "Your safety is important to Lady Claire. Bree is having her nightly meal. Would you like me to get her?"

"No, it's all right." I walk back inside the room.

"Good night, miss," she says before closing the door. The tiny click of the lock echoes.

"Good night," I whisper back. I bite my bottom lip and go right past the bed to the wall. I rub my fingers along the beautiful cream of the damask-printed paper. Tiny air streams push through the panels.

"Bree?" I whisper.

No answer.

I nudge at the hidden door Bree uses to enter my room. The panel swivels forward and reveals Bree's quarters.

Two oil lamps cast their yellow glow through the space like a pair of great eyes watching for movement in the dark. The walls hold cupboards lined with cutlery and plates, piles of silk, linen, candles, and bottles of every kind. Sets of wing-backed chairs spill over with laundry. A lap-size washbasin sits at their feet. On a footstool sits a half-eaten meal of soup and a hunk of bread and cheese. Steam still rises from the bowl.

I listen harder for the crying. The sharp sobs ring out beneath the party noises. I exit through the room's back door and land in a

salon room made rich with russet sofas and ivory tea tables. I slip
out, and up the back staircase that the servants use. Night-lanterns
nip at me as if they know I shouldn't be out of bed or using these
stairs. I follow the whimpering noises and the laughter.

Dark sets of doors lead to sprawling chambers and bold apartments. The cries grow louder and louder alongside a crescendo
of laughter. I enter an adjacent tea parlor to peek into the party
room. The floor is a stretch of marble with gilded piping; cushioned chaise lounges in shades of indigo and crimson sit in a circle;
tiered trays spill over with tarts and petit-cakes and sugar-dusted
fruit; beauty-lanterns whiz above well-dressed guests, providing
them with the perfect amount of light to look their best.

"You'll be fine, Sylvie," one woman says.

"It really isn't that bad," another adds.

"But it's terrible," the woman cries out. "You're all lying." She
paces the center of the room, and her dress blooms around her, the
color of fresh blood. A deep gash cuts across her face in the shape
of a sickle. She dabs it with a handkerchief.

"Men will still find you attractive," says a third person.

"Don't speak for all men," a male voice says, sending raucous
laughter through the room.

"Well, they'll still be attracted to your purse, if nothing else,"
someone says.

"I don't care if men want me. To be found beautiful by other
women is worth more leas than affection from any man," the
injured woman snaps back.

"Anything can be fixed," the man calls out, "with the right
amount of spintria. And we all know you have a bounty of it."

"I can't believe your teacup bear did this. Did you get her at
Fardoux's? I hope you return the little beast," a woman says.

"Where is she, by the way? Lurking about this room, ready to maul someone else?" another man says.

The women scream, and glance over and under their chairs and chaise lounges.

"She's off hiding," the injured woman says. "And where is Claire with the Belle? I'm terrified my skin might fall right off." She snaps at a nearby servant, "Go and fetch Madam Claire. Tell her that her hospitality is lacking, and I don't like to be kept waiting."

The servant scoots out. *The Belle?* I panic, wondering if Madam Claire is in my room right now, looking for me. I turn to leave, but hear Madam Claire's high-pitched voice.

"We're here. We're here to the rescue," she screeches.

I return to my hiding spot at the door. Madam Claire parades a girl with a Belle-bun and veil around the room. My heart thuds. *Is that Aza? Did she lie to me about my big sister being here?*

I crane to see.

The woman in the red dress circles the Belle. "Why can't I have your new Belle? Camellia, is it?"

The sound of my name knocks into my chest.

"Lady Sylvie, Camellia has just arrived. Her ledgers are chock-full of daytime appointments. She does not work after dusk. I reserve specific Belles for the night."

*Belles for the night?*

"This one will suffice and is talented," Madam Claire says.

"I want to see her before she works on me," Sylvie demands.

The Belle whimpers and cries. The same sound I heard before. The pain of it sends a shiver across my skin.

"What's wrong with her?" Sylvie asks.

The rest of the room bursts into laughter.

"She's just nervous," Madam Claire assures her. She tightens her grip on the Belle's arm.

"Lift her veil. Let me see her," Sylvie says. "Hurry up."

"Perhaps we should go into one of the treatment salons. We have dozens. Anything that suits your fancy. It would be more appropriate to inspect her in one of those."

"I don't care what is proper. I want this over quickly so I can go back to enjoying myself. We're headed into the Rose Quartier just before the midnight star. We've got a card game. I need to be fixed now."

Madam Claire forces a smile. "Yes, yes, of course."

I hold my breath.

"Lift your veil, Delphine," Madam Claire orders.

*Who is Delphine?* I crane my neck farther. The Belle slowly uncovers her face, but her back is to me, and I can see nothing.

Sylvie leans in and frowns. "Why does she look that way?"

"They don't all come out the same. Or as beautiful. It's an imprecise art, is what my sister says."

Sylvie turns the Belle around so everyone can inspect her. I press my face so close to the door it's slick with my sweat. The left side of the Belle's face is fused into hard wrinkles, like melted wax. I cover my mouth with one hand and step back.

*What is this? What is going on?*

"I don't want her," Sylvie says. "I demand you wake Camellia." She removes a coin purse from the folds of her dress and jingles it. "I'm prepared to spend thousands of spintria for the trouble. And you don't want to run me off to the Silk Teahouse, because I will go and take all my rich friends with me."

Madam Claire trembles and clutches her hands together,

almost like she's begging. She points at a nearby servant. "Wake her. Get Camellia up and dressed."

I race out of the room and back through the servant entrance to the staircase. I bolt through Bree's quarters. She jumps from her seat.

"Lady Camellia, what are you doing—"

"I'll tell you later." I shove through the panel door into my bedroom, just as I hear the click of the lock. I open the bedcurtains and dive under the covers.

The door creaks open.

I hear the soft patter of approaching feet, the whisper of echoing voices. The bedcurtains flutter. My heart knocks against my chest, wanting out. Sweat soaks my gown.

"Lady Camellia," a voice calls in.

I press my eyes closed.

She jostles my shoulder. I don't move.

"She's not waking up," she whispers to someone else. The woman tiptoes back to the door. "Tell Madam Claire she's fast asleep."

I wait for them to go, trying to calm my breath. When all is silent I slide out of bed again and go back to the wall panel.

"Bree," I whisper.

The door panel creaks open.

"Yes, Lady Camellia. What's wrong?"

"Are there other Belles in this teahouse?"

"I don't think so."

"I saw one."

"One of your sisters?"

"No, someone else."

"A big sister?"

"I know every big sister. I've memorized everything about them. This was someone else. Someone I've never seen before. Her face was mutilated. Her name is Delphine. Can you help me find out about her?"

"Of course."

A heavy knock pounds the door. "Camellia," Madam Claire's voice calls out.

"I don't want to talk to Madam Claire until I find out what's going on. Tell her I'm a hard sleeper. One who doesn't wake easily once in bed. Blame it on the use of my arcana. Quick."

I slip back into bed and cover myself completely with the covers. Bree hustles forward to the door.

Bree and Madam Claire exchange a series of frenzied whispers.

I lie frozen as Madam Claire inspects me. I hold my breath until I hear the door lock again.

# 15

Warm days turn chilly, and the trees around the teahouse start to blaze in brilliant shades of gold and orange and red. Madam Claire is always fussing about money, and wanting to compete with the other teahouses for the most business. Clicks from her ivory and cardinal-beaded abacus fill the main hall each morning, and the banging noises of her spintria safes fill each evening. Yet the morning and afternoon ledgers stay impossibly full. She hosts late parties every night. Laughter coils around the chandelier-lanterns, racing along each balcony, only to be undercut by the melody of sobs and cries.

I ask Madam Claire about the other Belles at the teahouse at least once a day, and she sweeps away my questions like dust from a tea table. "Nonsense; you are the Belle of this teahouse." But the sounds of sliding doors, carriage wheels, and tiny footsteps drift through the house, and each time I leave my room to explore, a servant returns me to where I'm supposed to be.

I think about that Belle's face and wonder if she was really and truly a Belle. I wonder if Madam Claire is trying to deceive others besides just me. I wish my sisters were here to help me figure it out—especially Amber. If we were home, she would've launched a full-scale plan with lookouts and maps and secret meetings. I follow Amber in the papers to feel closer to her, but the stories are confounding.

FAVORITE DAZZLES COURT WITH HER MANNER ARCANA

LADIES COMPLAIN OF THE FAVORITE'S COLOR CHOICES

LADY AMBROSIA RESTORES A MAN'S
FACE AFTER PERILOUS ACCIDENT

THE FAVORITE CAUGHT CRYING AT A COURTIER LUNCHEON

NEED CHARM? THE FAVORITE CAN GIVE YOU
ANY DISPOSITION YOU'VE EVER WANTED

The tattlers and scandal sheets show pictures of a scowling Amber sitting beside the princess.

I think about her every day. I write her a dozen letters that I rip up after finishing, and prepare a dozen post-balloons that I don't have the courage to send. Stupidly, I wait for a palace post-balloon from her. I check the teahouse mailroom every day, hoping to see their lilac forms.

I receive post-balloons from all my sisters except Amber:

*Camille,*

*The new Belle babies are here. They have sweet little cheeks and tiny cries. You must come home and see them if you can.*

*Have you started in on our list? Seen all the sights we planned when we were little?*

*You're missed.*

*Love,*
*Valerie*

*Camille,*
*Amber's been writing to me. She's having a hard time. I hope you wrote to her, too. Or better yet, try to go visit her.*
*Love,*
*Padma*

*Camille,*
*One of the little Belle babies looks just like you. She even has the freckle underneath your right eye and the dimple in your cheek.*
*Their portraits are being painted tomorrow. I'll steal one of the duplicates and send it to you.*
*They're growing so fast. It's been a week since they were born and they already look like three-year-olds. Did you know we grew so fast?*
*Love,*
*Valerie*

*Camille,*
*Du Barry didn't tell us it would be this hard. I'm so tired. Madam Alieas works me for hours and hours. She won't even let me go into Laussat to explore or see any of the Fire Isles.*
*We are not blessed by the Goddess of Beauty. We are cursed.*
*I don't want to do this.*
*Edel*

*Camille,*
*I can't sleep. There are so many noises at the Glass Teahouse—crying and screaming late into the night. No one will tell me what's going on. I've*

*never wanted to go home so badly. We always wanted to leave Maison*
*Rouge de la Beauté, and now I just want to go back.*
*What's it like at the Chrysanthemum Teahouse?*
*Hana*

I write them back, and I tell Hana that I've heard the noises here too, and I've seen what looked like another Belle. I send magenta post-balloons out my window.

The days fill with the monotony of lonely work: breakfast, beauty appointments, lunch, more beauty appointments, dinner, dropping off spintria pouches to Madam Claire's office, a visit from the nurses with the sangsues, and to bed, only to listen to the late-night noises of parties and crying.

This morning the house buzzes with more activity than ever. Every house-lantern has been lit—morning, dusk, and night ones—every chaise and chair fluffed, every door opened to expose the currant red and fuchsia and rich butter yellow of the rooms beyond.

I lean over the balcony outside my room, peering down into the grand foyer. I tiptoe down the grand staircase unnoticed. The melody of preparation hides my footsteps: clinking glass, the jingle of silver cutlery, the clack of porcelain dishes, the grunts and whispers of the servants.

The breakfast veranda is open. Sunlight and a persistent breeze push inside. The golden noses of imperial carriages peek out of the trees surrounding the teahouse. Important people must be somewhere in the house. A servant ushers me to the only seat at the table. I long for the round table at home, complete with my sisters. Plates of petit-waffles, boiled eggs, tiny quiches, grape clusters, and sweet luna pastries are placed in front of me.

I pick over the food. Valerie would love these little waffles, and Hana likes anything and everything with eggs. Amber would've asked for a snowmelon. Padma would've frowned at the slices of steak shaped like stars. Edel would've been difficult and asked for something different—an omelet or sweet toast.

Newspapers rest in stacks. Their headlines pulse and flicker across the pages, calling my attention.

BEAUTY IS ALL THAT PLEASES THE GODDESS

WHAT IS FAIR IS EVER DEAR: NEW
SKIN-BRIGHTENING BELLE-PRODUCT

KING'S MISTRESS CAUGHT WEARING HIS ROYAL EMBLEM

NEW POLL SHOWS MANY HOPE PRINCESS
CHARLOTTE WILL WAKE TO TAKE THE THRONE

There is a shatter of glass, and a rush of pounding footsteps booms through the teahouse.

"Try to clear them out," a servant shouts.

"Grab a broom," another says.

"Close the doors," a third hollers.

I rush into the hallway. The foyer is filled with midnight-black gossip post-balloons. One after another, they swarm through the door like bees in a hive, zipping left and right, knocking into freshly lit chandelier-lanterns, staining the marble with their dark sparks.

I press myself against the nearest wall. My breath catches. "What's happening?" I say.

No one answers me.

"Seal off the courtyard," Madam Claire screams. She presses

the front doors closed, smacking away pairs of hands holding pens and parchment pads marked with the newsie house emblem.

Bodies thud against the doors. A chaos of men and women press against the glass, drumming and beating each window. I hold my hands to my stomach. My heartbeat overwhelms my entire body. Fists knock. Screams and shouts assault my ears. In one of the windows, a crack in the glass spreads out like lightning as the determined people try to get in.

Servants draw the curtains. Bree rushes to my side, her face pink and sweaty.

"What's happening? I ask her.

"Everyone's saying something's amiss at the palace," she whispers.

Madam Claire clicks a series of locks, and then topples over with exhaustion. Makeup runs down her face. A servant helps her to the nearest chaise.

"Madam Claire." I race forward, batting at black post-balloons. "What is all this?"

"I don't know," she pants, then motions to a nearby servant. "Use the circuit-phone to call for the guard."

"Madam, the queen's post arrived through the back entrance," a servant announces as she tugs the glistening ribbons of a gold-and-white post-balloon. It floats over Madam Claire's head like a small, glittering sun. She pulls it into her lap, removes a parchment scroll, and breaks the queen's seal. Her eyes flicker with excitement as she gazes from the page to me. "You've been summoned by the queen."

# 16

The dress Madam Claire picks out for me wraps my body in rich layers of cerise and coral. The six tiers of fabric are like different frostings of tulle and lace and silk. A sweetheart neckline scoops low above my bodice, and she decorates my neck with layers of diamonds. The waist-sash pinches around my center; its bow holds tiny embroidered Belle-roses.

I run my fingers over the dress to assure myself it's real. A tiny tremble quivers through me. Why would the queen want to see me? Why would the newsies attack the teahouse? My heart won't slow down. Should I be afraid or excited or hopeful or confused? The emotions crash inside me like a carriage accident happening over and over again.

I'm back in the queen's Receiving Hall. Its glass ceiling winks light over the queen's throne, making her glow. Du Barry and Madam Claire stand to my right. The Beauty Minister is at my left. The queen's court and ministers look on from plush high-backed chairs. I search for Amber. She should be standing to the left of the

Beauty Minister, but she's nowhere. I'm afraid to take my eyes off the queen, as if this whole moment might disappear. My stomach rises and falls like I'm on the tree swing at home.

"Your Majesties and Your Highness, allow me to present to you Camellia Beauregard once more," the Beauty Minister announces.

I curtsy and bow all the way to the floor. The queen's hot stare makes me sweat.

"Your Majesties. Your Highness."

"Up, my child. Let me have a look at you," the queen says.

I stand, head still bowed, but steal glances at her. The scandal sheets and tattlers call her icy and passionless. I swallow down the peculiar mix of dread and excitement bobbing in my stomach. She looks at me with cold eyes and an unsmiling expression, a gaze that sends a chill through me. Her dark skin glistens with powder, like she's covered in stardust. She clutches a small scepter.

As many times as I whispered to myself that this was a happy visit to the palace, one with the promise of good news, it doesn't feel like that. One question repeats over and over in my head: *What does the queen want with me?*

The king smiles at her and rubs his red beard. The princess sits on the very edge of her throne with bright red cheeks. She looks at me with eager eyes, like I'm a caramel crème-cone ready to be devoured on a warm day. Her teacup pets surround her—a monkey on her shoulder, an elephant in her lap, and a thimble-size rabbit perched on the tip of her scepter.

"I hope you don't mind me calling you back to court. Though the king says I'm behaving like a finicky cat, and I should be embarrassed."

The court laughs; the king chuckles, taking her jeweled hand and kissing it. I watch the way he looks at her, his eyes big, his mouth soft. I wonder if they're in love and the tattlers and scandal sheets are wrong about his countless mistresses and affairs.

"I'm happy to return, Your Majesty," I say. *And I want to stay forever.*

"Camellia, this is an important time in our kingdom. The marriage of my daughter is on the horizon."

The court calls out a wedding blessing. Everyone applauds.

"I want to ensure that Princess Sophia's marriage starts off properly, and that her eventual reign falls seamlessly into our legacy. House Orléans, as you know, founded our magnificent kingdom and created the great city of Trianon. My daughter must be outfitted with a look appropriate for the Orléans Dynasty. To fit seamlessly with the great queens and with her ancestors."

My heart thuds. I scan the room for Amber again, and search the crowd for a bright red Belle-bun. My hands knit in front of me. Trails of sweat inch down my back.

"Long live the queen," the crowd shouts out.

Kings and queens don't get to participate in the royal fad of changing their looks. Once married, it is customary to settle into one consistent appearance. According to Du Barry, it should be elegant yet regal, memorable but not eccentric, and most of all, fit for royalty.

"My daughter's been responsible for setting a few unnatural beauty trends among the younger courtiers. That terrible blip with the sea-blue skin tone, and the trend where courtiers matched their teacup pets." The queen shudders. "So unfortunate."

The princess scoffs, then glares at her mother, turning redder by the minute.

The women in the crowd nod their heads and whisper in agreement with the queen.

"And she's broken her fair share of beauty laws. However, with help, I have no doubt that she'll take this opportunity to refine herself and come into her life as a future queen, leaving behind the temperamental little girl."

Her words confuse me. My eyes volley between her and the princess, who squirms and fusses with the ruffles of her dress.

"Nothing about this year has been easy, Camellia. I thought my eldest, Princess Charlotte, would have woken by now. I thought my cabinet would have passed legislation to help make beauty treatments more affordable for the Gris." She sighs, and the king kisses her hand again. "I hope you'll be patient with me."

She rises. The entire court mimics her. My heart beats like a hummingbird's wings. The room becomes a swirl of colors with the queen at the very center.

"I am going to do something unprecedented in the history of our kingdom, and I hope you'll prove that it's the right decision."

I hold my breath. I don't take my eyes off the queen. I'm frozen.

"My challenge for you, Camellia, is for you to become the favorite, and teach my daughter. Will you?"

The word *favorite* ruptures through me.

My heart might stop.

"Yes," I almost shout.

Amber's face pops into my mind. My excitement tangles with a thread of sadness.

"Behold, Camellia Beauregard, our new favorite!" the queen announces. "May you always find beauty!"

Small chrysanthemum flower-lanterns are released in the air. Thundering cheers and high-pitched whistles roar through the room.

# 17

The Receiving Hall turns into a chaos of light. Newsies flood the room, flashing their light-boxes in my face. Black gossip post-balloons storm overhead, with their candles shining down on me. The windows open, and a kaleidoscope of congratulatory post-balloons pours in from every corner of the kingdom.

I search for Amber. A glimpse of red hair sends me snaking through the crowd. Where is she? Is she okay? What happened to her? Women squeeze my hands as I pass, and wave their beauty tokens in the air. Men tip their hats and wink. They say how excited they are to work with me. They ask my thoughts on the latest beauty laws. They swarm me with questions about my favorite arcana. I give quick answers and continue to search.

But I can't find Amber.

The Beauty Minister grabs my hand and kisses my cheeks.

"Where's my sister? Where's Amber?" I whisper to her.

"Shh," she says, like I've uttered a dirty word. "No talk of that. Enjoy yourself."

The night rages on in one continuous loop of laughter and dancing and questions and excitement until I'm brought to the Belle apartments right after the midnight star rises. The rich bed drapery now matches my signature pink camellia flowers. I think about the ambrosia-orange curtains that once hung here. A pinch burns in my chest, and I imagine Amber's Belle-trunk being packed.

I climb into the big four-poster bed and stare at the ceiling for an eternity until I fall asleep.

"Time to get up," a voice calls out. The bedcurtains rustle.

"But I'm not awake." I open one eye. "Who is it?"

"Ivy," she says. The favorite of the previous generation.

"You're talking, so you must be," she says, tugging at my sheets. "Always be up before they come in. So you can watch them and be aware of the things going on around you."

Ivy's veil reveals nothing. Not even an outline of her nose or mouth. The fabric completely hides her from view. I wonder how she can see through the shrouded layers. She wears a long-sleeved black day dress and lace gloves. Not one sliver of her skin shows. I touch her to make sure she's real and not some dark spirit. She removes my hand from her arm.

"Where's Amber?"

"Go on, freshen up. Questions later." A pitcher of steaming water sits beside the porcelain basin on my new vanity. She watches while I wipe the sleep from my eyes and wet my skin. "I need you awake. You'll bathe later."

"What time is it?"

"Just after the morning star."

I want to dive back into bed and tell her it's too early to be awake, but she knows what palace life is like, and I need to learn from her. While I clean my teeth and mouth, the silence extends to every corner of the room.

"Ivy, please. Tell me where Amber is? Is she at the Chrysanthemum Teahouse now? What happened?"

"These aren't questions you should be concerning yourself with." Ivy takes the wet cloth from me. How I wish I could see her eyes.

"But—"

"I will show you how to be the favorite. I'm staying in the room just down the main corridor. I will be with you during your initial beauty treatments to ensure all goes well. I will help you navigate the rules of working with the queen and the princess."

Ivy is all business, and I reluctantly accept that I'm not going to get any information about Amber. I'll have to find out about her some other way.

"Why do you and the other big sisters wear veils now? You never did when we were at home."

"Because it's protocol, and to signal to the world that our generation is over." She pulls one of the strings on the wall above the nightstand table, and a sleepy-eyed Bree appears.

"Bree!" I hug her.

"Congratulations," she whispers.

"Are you happy to be back?" I ask.

"Yes"—she leans in—"and away from Madam Claire."

We laugh.

"Breakfast," Ivy barks at her.

Bree slides out of my arms and scurries from the room.

"Time to check the morning ledger." Ivy walks to the main

salon. "Follow." She points to a board. Elisabeth Du Barry's cursive handwriting spells out the date: DAY 262 OF THE YEAR OF THE GOD OF LUCK. There are no appointments listed.

Moments later wheeled carts arrive, chock-full of pastries, eggs cooked in every way, grilled meat, petit-pancakes with sugar dust, and bowls of colorful fruit. Ivy doesn't touch the food, but I pick at it.

"We need to review a few rules for court life." Her words sound scripted and practiced. She clears her throat. "You are not to pursue anything other than your purpose. You are a Belle."

"Can we talk about what happened first?" I ignore her earlier warning and switch seats to join her on the couch. "Why was Amber dismissed? I need to know."

"You are to act as if you're an artist floating through this world. Your sole purpose is to beautify, and transform the Gris. You are a Belle."

I put my hand up, hoping she'll pause. "Ivy, can we—"

"You are to sell your skills—the arcana—not your body. You are a Belle."

My anger rises as she ignores my questions.

"You exist inside a secret world of beauty. You were born full of color, like a moving work of art. The Goddess of Beauty has given you responsibility. You are not to reveal the inner workings of your arcana. You are a Belle."

I touch her. Her whole body flinches and she stands.

"You are to respect your sisters—both past and present. You must respect those who are guardians of your kind. You are a Belle.

"You were cared for, and in return you must care for Orléans, the Land of Rising Beauty, and share your gifts. You are a Belle.

"You must vow to return home and continue the Belle line. These—"

"Just tell me what happened to my sister," I shout. "I don't care about these rules."

"These *rules* are to be adhered to and followed at all times. They have served your sisters and will serve you well," she says at last.

*Well, they didn't help Amber, the greatest rule-follower of us all.*

A wall panel shifts forward and Elisabeth Du Barry walks out. "Why are you yelling this early?"

"What happened to Amber, Elisabeth? Where is she?" I stand to face her.

Elisabeth flashes me the biggest grin I've ever seen. She presses a hand to her chest as if she's holding in the answer to my question.

"Please."

She sighs like I'm bothering her and it's an imposition for her to tell me, but I know she covets the attention. "Wouldn't you like to know?"

"This isn't a game," I snap.

"But it is, and you've won."

The word *won* hits me, and my stomach churns with the implication of it.

"I need to know if she's all right."

"What would you do for me? Give me an extra beauty treatment?"

I blink. Does she really want me to bribe her?

"I need you to fix me, Camellia. Mother is making me earn my own spintria now, just like everybody else, booking these appointments all day long." She turns to the large mirror over the hearth and examines herself.

"Yes." I take her hand, and the shock of it softens her. "Whatever you want."

Our eyes meet in the mirror, and I can tell she relishes the information she holds over me.

"Amber made one of Sophia's ladies translucent," she says. "You could see every vein and organ and blood vessel inside her. It was disgusting. And she gave Sophia a too-small waist that violated the beauty law. Then she covered another lady-of-honor in feathers. Like a parrot. They grew straight out of the woman's skin."

I gasp. "She wouldn't do that," I protest.

"I'm just telling you what I heard." Elisabeth smoothes her eyebrows, like we're merely discussing the weather.

"You must've heard wrong." I pace in a circle.

"I thought that, too. Amber was always the boring one. My mother's pet. It all sounded outlandish. But it was like she changed. Became a different person. More like you, and less like her." She inspects the breakfast cart.

"I wouldn't make someone see-through."

"Right, but you'd experiment." She grins at me, then pops a strawberry into her mouth.

The front doors open, and the Beauty Minister is announced. She strides in, her hair fashioned into a tower made of blond strands and blue flowers. She has to hold her head very still. "Good morning, Camellia. Glad to see you're already up," she says. "Good morning, Elisabeth." Attendants trail behind her, holding stacked towers of dress boxes. Her eyes flutter over Ivy as if she's a piece of furniture in the room. "Please set out the peach dress for Lady Camellia." She ushers the attendants into the apartment's dressing salon.

Du Barry is announced next. She rushes in like she's being chased. "Camellia." She wraps me up in a frenzied hug. She smells like home—Belle-roses and marzipan crème and the bayou. She leans close to my ear and whispers, "Now that Ambrosia has put us in a precarious position, you must fix it. You have to do what you're told. You have to be perfect." She pushes my shoulders back and stares at me with panic in her eyes.

Her words curl inside me and make my heart race.

"Tell me you'll do what needs to be done," she demands.

"Yes, Madam Du Barry."

The Beauty Minister returns. "Ana, let's have her bathed and dressed, then make introductions before she has her tour."

Du Barry squeezes my shoulder. She paints on a grin and turns around to face the Beauty Minister. "Of course, Madam Minister. As you wish."

The Beauty Minister steers me to the apartment's dress salon. Ivy's chair is now empty. "Where did Ivy go?"

"No need for you to worry about her, little darling. Go on and change. The staff await you in the bathing chamber."

"I've already washed up."

"You can never be clean enough, pretty enough, or smart enough." She pinches my chin and pats my back.

Servants draw me a bath. I soak in the steaming tub and close my eyes. Today is my first full day as the favorite. This is everything I've ever wanted. I wait for the excitement to fill me up, but all I think about is Amber. Her long lashes fringed with tears, her red cheeks flushed with anger and upset, the sound she made when she fell that night. Where is she? What did she really do wrong? Is she all right?

I dunk my head into the frothy water and try to let the warmth wash these thoughts all away. I wait until my lungs threaten to give out before surfacing.

"Camellia, time to get dressed," Bree calls from outside the bathing chamber door.

"Yes, just a second."

I step out of the bath and onto a prickly object. The rug is covered with thorny dead roses. Shriveled petals leave a rotten scent throughout the room. How did these get here?

An emerald-green post-balloon hovers in the corner. I grab a towel and wrap it around myself. I kick away the roses and make my way to the balloon. There's no house emblem or compass on the side of it. I snatch the dangling ribbons and fish out the card.

*Dearest Camellia,*
*Congratulations on being named the favorite.*
*I'm sure you deserve whatever comes your way now.*

I think of Amber's desk next to mine in our lesson room at home: her quill, ink pot, and handwriting ledgers. I think about the curling *g*'s and *c*'s she was so proud to mark on her pages and show Du Barry when we were little. In my mind, I see her clearly, sitting at a desk in her new room at the Chrysanthemum Teahouse, writing this letter.

I ball my hand into an angry fist, crumpling the note with it. I throw it into the tub and watch as the water eats away at the parchment, and the ink bleeds until it disintegrates into nothing.

"Lady Camellia." The door slides open. "Are you ready?" The servant looks at all the dead roses on the ground. "What happened in—"

"I'm fine. Everything is fine." I storm from the room.

# 18

Servants help me into a bustling day dress that is a creamy blur of whipped frosting and sweetened milk sprinkled with gossamer ribbons. My wet hair is sectioned and combed through with a cinnamon-scented hair cream before being twisted up into a Belle-bun.

I walk down the corridor to the main salon. Ivy steps inside from the solarium.

"Where did you go?" I ask.

"You look lovely," she says.

"Someone put dead roses in the bathing chamber."

Her nose crinkles. "Strange. Why would someone do that?"

"Is Amber still here? Please tell me the truth."

"She's been sent to replace you at the Chrysanthemum Teahouse. Stop asking about her."

"Why?"

"It's time for you to focus."

"She's my sister."

"She's your competitor." She pivots and strides toward the main salon.

I hurry after her.

A young man kneels beside the Beauty Minister, head down, sword at his waist.

"Camellia, the queen has assigned you a personal guard." The Beauty Minister reaches out a hand to me. "This is Rémy Chevalier, son of Christophe Chevalier, and a member of the Minister of War's First Guard."

He stands, towering over us with broad shoulders and muscles that strain the seams of his uniform. The hard angles of his face have the deep richness of a black calla lily. His lips don't betray the faintest hint of a smile; rather, they're frozen in a perpetual scowl. A scar hooks under his right eye like a crescent moon, and I wonder why he hasn't allowed a Belle to erase it for him. Dark hair is cut closely to his scalp with a single silver stripe down the very center, marking him as a soldier from the House of War.

I nod at him. He doesn't look me in the eye, choosing to stare at some point above my head.

"He's been trained to protect you. He is one of Orléans's finest soldiers. He graduated from the Royal Military Academy with the highest honors. First in his class. Rumor has it he's favored by the Minister of War himself, and might succeed him one day. He helped put down the Silk Rebellion, commandeered his own men. Very decorated soldier at such a young age."

He bows after the Beauty Minister's compliment, but still doesn't look at me.

"And now he's here to look after me like I'm a baby?" I say. "Don't you think it's a waste of his talents?"

The Beauty Minister laughs and touches my shoulder as if I'm purposefully being funny. "You're a very important person. Only a talented soldier would be entrusted with your care."

A muscle in Rémy's jaw clenches. I wait for his expression to change. Nothing.

"Now, Rémy will accompany you everywhere you need to go, and stand guard outside the Belle apartments at all times. Be sure to heed his instructions."

"I hardly find that necess—" I start to say, but Ivy reaches forward to squeeze my hand.

"The favorite is always given a proper guard, Camellia. It is tradition, and we are nothing without our beloved customs." The minister snaps her fingers at a nearby servant. The girl leaps into action. "By all means, move slowly. It's not as if I have a packed schedule." The woman rushes forward to drape a white mink coat around the minister, whose blue eyes burn into mine. "I'm not happy to be going through all of this for a second time, so please cooperate, will you? Ivy will give you a palace tour." She blows air kisses at me, then leaves.

"Come on," Ivy says.

We walk into the corridor outside the Belle apartments. The Beauty Minister heads in the opposite direction with her entourage.

I steal glances back at Rémy. Irritation and annoyance knot in my stomach. I don't want a guard. I don't want another person telling me what to do.

"Stop letting them know how you feel about things. No one cares," Ivy says.

"Them?"

"You let everyone *see* you so easily. No one needs to know that you don't want a guard. Nobody wants to be followed around all day. Not even the queen."

Her words feel like a scold. "I just don't—"

"You are now the kingdom's most important treasure. There are so many things you don't understand yet. But I will show you."

Rémy's heavy footsteps clomp behind us. Morning-lanterns drift through the halls, catching sunlight from long picture windows to carry through darker corridors.

"You are in the north wing of the palace. The Belle apartments face the morning star, the eye of the Goddess of Beauty," Ivy says.

The hall outside the Belle apartments stretches like a great river I never want to stop floating on. Colorful portraits of the Goddess of Beauty in her various forms cover the walls. Smooth marble floors spread out beneath our feet. The light from jeweled chandelier-lanterns dusts statues with beautiful silhouettes.

She leads me over a glittering walkway. Golden spindles curl into royal chrysanthemums. The palace floors below bustle with moving bodies. Balconies spill over with flowers, chatty men and women, and servants darting from one place to another. Royal vendors push pastry carts that leave buttery and sugary scents in every corner.

"Did you have a guard?"

"Yes. A soldier named Émilie."

"Where is she now?"

"Shipped off to the Spice Isles to protect the southern waters, now that I'm no longer such a valued asset," she says, then turns left.

We pass through a series of imperial guard checkpoints. Ivy salutes one of the sentries. He smiles at her. "They aren't so bad once you get to know them." She moves beneath a golden archway. "This is the west wing of the palace. The residential homes of the royal family are here."

Guards line the walls like statues.

"This is the Hall of Kings and Queens." She waves her hands at massive, gold-framed portraits of our many royals, from the very first ruler of Orléans, Queen Marjorie, all the way down to the current queen, Celeste.

We turn right. Walls sparkle with golden plaques that showcase the imperial beauty laws. "This is the Hall of Law and Justice."

We pass by thousands of plaques, each emblazoned with ornate script.

FINGERS AND TOES SHALL REMAIN AT A TEN-DIGIT
COUNT SO AS TO PRESERVE THE GODDESS OF
BEAUTY'S FAVORITE NUMBER. BELLES SHALL ADD
OR SUBTRACT TO MEET THIS DIVINE NUMBER.

BREASTS WILL BE LIMITED IN SIZE AND SHAPE—
NO LARGER THAN A SNOWMELON.

MIMICRY IS STRICTLY PROHIBITED.

Du Barry had tested us on these laws until we could recite them on command. *The flock must always be guided, and the laws keep their bodies safe. They are not to be questioned. They maintain a sacred order,* she'd said.

I stop to read more.

NO MAN SHALL BE TALLER THAN THE SITTING KING.

AFTER CORONATION, ROYAL MONARCHS
MUST SETTLE INTO ONE LOOK TO PRESERVE THE SECURITY
AND SANCTITY OF THE MAGNANIMOUS THRONE.

"Did you help pass the current beauty laws?" I graze my fingers across the cool metal and etched calligraphy.

Ivy turns around. "No, I wasn't consulted."

"I want to be part of it all."

"Why?"

"Why not?" I say. "I want to make the people of Orléans love themselves."

Ivy continues down the hall. "You are here to make things beautiful," she says.

"I know," I reply. "But—"

"The princess's chambers are ahead," Ivy says.

Servants move in and out of a set of doors carrying trays and baskets. The princess's emblem shines on the rich wood—a chrysanthemum blooming inside a jeweled petit-crown. Several other ladies hover outside.

The hall goes silent. Courtiers crowd on both sides of me. Ivy and I pass through the heavy silence like it's thick mud. Their faces are curious, and behind their smiles is a reminder: they all want something from me.

"I'm supposed to prepare you to serve Princess Sophia."

"I studied a lot about her, reading papers and beauty pamphlets, even the tattlers. I stole them from Du Barry's mail chest—"

Ivy presses a finger to my mouth.

"Not a single word you've read could prepare you for the real thing."

The doors open.

A trumpet flourish sounds. The princess saunters into the hall. Her day dress is buttercup yellow and perfectly complements her new skin color—a dusky light brown, like warmed milk with cinnamon and nutmeg stirred into it. A swirl of red hair sits atop her head like a tiered dessert stand.

"Do you still do her beauty work?" I ask.

"Yes," Ivy whispers while bowing.

"I heard the new favorite was outside of my boudoir," the princess calls out.

I join Ivy in a deep bow all the way to the floor. I lift back up. The princess takes my hands and kisses both my cheeks.

"Your Highness," I say.

"Call me Sophia." She smells like honey and anise.

A train of women cluster behind her. Newsies send navy story-balloons over our heads to try to capture any tiny bit of our conversation. Sophia's eyes scan my face, staring intently, like she means to memorize each part.

"I like the way you look," she says, reaching out to touch my cheek. "We will spend time together soon. I have so many questions."

An attendant approaches and bows before us. "Your Highness."

She turns to address him. "What is it?"

"The infirmary staff is ready," he says.

"Take her," Sophia orders before turning back to me. "Camellia, my mother's summoned me. And when the queen calls"—she sighs—"I can't ignore her, as much as I might want to." She touches my cheek again. "More soon. I'm very excited about you." Her eyes flash with eagerness. Her procession of women and attendants and newsies trails her down the hall like an army of ants.

The doors to her chambers reopen. Male attendants carry out a young woman on a stretcher. Her limbs flop like dying fish. Moans echo through the halls and scatter nosy women in a dozen directions.

"What do you think happened to her?" I ask Ivy.

She stiffens, and her gulp is so loud it almost echoes. "Princess Sophia," she says.

# 19

An afternoon fireworks display explodes over the Royal Harbor to celebrate the princess's birthday. The popping and crackling sounds boom through the apartment. I watch from the balcony. Colorful lightning spiderwebs across the sky; silver, white, and emerald green weave the most beautiful and terrifying exhibition to mark the hour of the princess's birth. The garden arcades and grounds are abuzz with movement as the palace prepares for the royal birthday party. A hopeful thought wells in my chest—my sisters will most likely be here for the party. It's an official kingdom-wide holiday.

I prepare two urgent post-balloons—one to Edel and one to Amber.

> Edel,
> Is anything better? Will you be at the palace tonight?
> Please come. I need to see you. We need to talk.
> Love,
> Camille

*Amber,*

*What happened to you at the palace? There are rumors, but I don't believe them.*

*I'm sorry. Please write me. I hope to see you at the palace tonight.*

*Love,*

*Camille*

I wait for a pause in the fireworks to send the two palace-official post-balloons off the balcony. An air-postman will check their compasses and sweep them to their destinations this afternoon. I just hope Amber will read the note and write me back, and maybe even come to the party tonight. I need to see her. I watch until their lilac forms disappear among the clouds.

A violet dress and a matching mask of sunbird feathers arrive in the main salon. The princess's masked garden party starts in two hourglasses' worth of time. I ring the bell near the Orléans tapestry.

"Yes, my lady?" Bree asks.

"Where's Ivy?"

"I'll—"

A heavy knock rattles the apartment doors. She scurries to answer it. Rémy's thick boots clomp against the wooden floors.

"Lady Camellia." His voice has a single, unaffected tone. The pitch of it booms in my chest like he's speaking into a voice-trumpet.

"You can call me Camille," I say.

"Lady Camellia," he repeats without making eye contact.

"Lady Rémy."

He clears his throat and sighs. "I'm here to discuss the plan for this evening's festivities, and review the protocol with you."

I sigh. "But of course."

He adjusts his uniform jacket. "When you go to the princess's chambers, I'll be stationed right outside. When you're in the gardens, I cannot allow you to venture more than fifteen paces away from me. At dinner, I'll be posted behind you with the other guards." He speaks as if I'm a child in need of a leash. And maybe I am.

"Will you come to the commode with me, too? Stand beside me while I use it?"

"I'll be outside the door."

"It's a joke," I say.

His eyes narrow. "There are risks at court."

The roses in the bathroom come to mind.

"Where's Ivy?"

"Her presence has not been requested," he says.

"Well, I'd like her with me."

He turns without another word and leaves. I bathe and get dressed, then return to the main salon. Rémy reappears with Ivy.

"Will you come with me today?" I ask.

"I wasn't invited."

"Why not?"

"Camellia, my time is up. I bring no more value, other than to do beauty work until you're trusted to do so, and train you to replace me."

The way she talks about herself reminds me of Du Barry discussing a worn-out pair of shoes. We learned that after our time is up at court or the teahouses, we train the next generation for a month before returning home to La Maison Rouge to become mamans and raise the next group of Belles. Maman once said that it went so fast she felt like she'd only been at court for a single turn of a télétrope.

"I disagree." I take her gloved hand.

"That seems to be a trend with you," she says, and if I could see her face, there might be a tiny smile playing across her lips.

"Will my sisters be here tonight?" I ask.

"All official Belles are invited."

"Official? What does that mean?"

"Just what I said."

Her ability to always use the fewest words infuriates me. She's like a locked door I can't pry open.

The Belle-apartment doors swing forward. An attendant announces: "The Royal Beauty Minister."

The Beauty Minister strides in. She wears a model ship inside her nest of hair. "Camellia, the princess has requested your presence while she dresses for her party. This is a great opportunity to get to know her and to learn her preferences."

"Yes, Madam Minister." Sudden nerves make my hands quiver. This is the first time the princess has asked to see me.

The Beauty Minister glances at Ivy. "What are you doing here?"

"Lady Camellia requested me," Ivy mumbles.

"It seems highly unnecessary. You won't be able to attend. They won't have a place setting."

Ivy steps back.

"Ivy must come with me to the princess's boudoir," I say. "I need her counsel."

The Beauty Minister sighs. "The *favorite* gets what the *favorite* wants." She leads Ivy, Rémy, and me out of the apartments, on the long walk to the princess's chambers. But the trip feels shorter this time. Servants move in and out of the doors, carrying trays and baskets. Laughter escapes into the hall.

"Sounds like she's in a good mood. This bodes well for the

day." The Beauty Minister checks her tiny pocket hourglass. "Her toilette ritual is set to begin in just a moment. You're right on time."

"You're not staying?" Panic crackles inside me.

"No, my dear. Not today. You must bond with Princess Sophia. Soon you will be completing all the beauty work for the entire family." She knocks on the doors. "Just be your charming self. And you have Ivy here to help, and Rémy will be right outside."

"Not that he's any comfort," I whisper.

Ivy thumps my arm. Rémy glowers at me.

"Now, now," she says. "That's not what he's trained for."

A servant opens the massive set of doors. I squeeze my hands together to keep them from shaking, and hold my head high.

The Beauty Minister steps inside. I follow, with Ivy on my heels.

The boudoir is a jeweled caisse: all pink, cream, and gold, with the scent of roses wafting through the air, and three crystal chandeliers. Jeweled beauty-lanterns sail overhead, dusting the room with the perfect amount of light. Courtiers mill in and out of an adjacent tea salon, loitering until the ceremony begins.

The details of a proper toilette ritual for a queen and princess took weeks and weeks of studying and endless days of exams from Du Barry. But the particulars of those lessons vanish from my memory as I soak in the enormity of this room. Alive with movement, teams of servants lug large sofas and toilette tables and gold-tiered stands of macarons and tarts. They arrange items on beautiful brocade cloths under the careful watch of a trio of well-dressed ladies. Lavish necklaces coil around their throats like collars, displaying their house emblems. Each emblem contains a chrysanthemum twisted inside the symbol of their high house to represent their relationship to the royal family.

They turn their attention to us. A flush climbs up my entire body. They whisper behind fans and glance at me. I tell my heart to slow down.

At the back of the room, a large screen is hooked around the silhouette of a claw-foot bathtub. A waist-high barrier isolates it from the rest of the space.

"Your Highness," the Beauty Minister calls out.

"Yes, Madam Minister," the princess's voice echoes.

"I have the new favorite, Lady Camellia Beauregard, here." She pulls me in front of her and drums her red-polished nails on my shoulders. "And the rest of the noble crowd eagerly waits outside your doors."

Water sloshes as the princess climbs from the tub. Servants rush to her. The screen is removed. Flushed pink and tangled in a web of towels, she's dressed in a bathing gown and doesn't look like the Imperial Princess, heir to the House of Orléans. She looks more like a little girl ready to play dress-up. Her appearance is different again—pale white as a snowflake, with hair almost a mirroring shade, and bright blue eyes. She smiles sweetly at me. I relax a little. Everything will be fine.

The princess waves me forward. I lean over the barriers and she kisses both my cheeks, leaving a warm wetness behind. "So nice to see you again."

I bow all the way to the floor. "Happy birthday, Your Highness."

"Thank you," she says.

The Beauty Minister clears her throat. "I will leave you here, Camellia, to get acquainted and witness the toilette ritual that only befits a princess and future queen. I'll see you later this evening for the royal games and banquet." The boudoir doors open, the Beauty Minister disappears, and a swarm of women floods inside.

I study them: most are princesses from the royal family—nieces of the king and queen—and a few girls and women from high houses. When courtiers receive their appointments, their portraits fill every newspaper and beauty pamphlet. The monarchs shower favored families with land, titles, gifts, and notoriety.

"Pay close attention," Ivy whispers to me before slinking backward into the growing pack of onlookers.

The women organize themselves by rank and wait patiently for their roles to begin. A few men squeeze into the group.

A massive vanity is carried into the center of the room. Large mirrors reflect the beauty-lantern light. Enameled caisses expose glistening Belle-products, crested with rich, sparkling Belle-emblems. Glass canisters hold colorful liquids. Golden pins poke out of a pink velvet cushion. Carts hold tiers of pastries frosted in rose-petal pinks and pearly whites and apple reds, flutes overflow with jewel-tone liquids, and sugar-dusted strawberries and pomegranates sit in glass bowls. Vases spill over with flowers in a rainbow of colors.

Sophia is led to a cushioned seat before the vanity. The towel on her head writhes. Out pops a teacup monkey.

"Singe," she cries out. "How'd you get in there?"

The tiny monkey jumps from table to table as servants attempt to catch him. The ladies-of-honor screech until he's safely returned to his small golden cage.

"Why must you have that creature with us in the boudoir?" one of her ladies says.

"Singe has a mind of his own," Sophia replies.

"The femme de chamber," an attendant calls out. A petite woman steps forward with an open book in her shaky hands.

Sophia gazes down into the pages of wardrobe choices. She plucks a sparkly pin from the cushion and pushes it into the pages. She does this three times. The group of women *oohh* and *ahh* at her selections. A maid shuffles in with a screen. Sophia steps behind it and disrobes, dropping the wet bathing chemise on the floor.

Servants bring in her garden dress, parading it in front of the onlookers, who fawn over it.

The attendant steps forward. "Lady Gabrielle, princess du sang, and first lady-of-honor to Her Royal Highness, please step forward."

Sophia's dress is handed to Lady Gabrielle, who ducks behind the screen.

"Camellia, my ladies will introduce themselves, won't you, girls?" Sophia calls out.

Lady Gabrielle steps into view once more. Her eyes are bright, her skin the color of the warm fudge my sisters and I used to steal from the kitchen.

"I am Lady Gabrielle Lamballe, a princess du sang, from the House of Orléans. Her *favorite* cousin." She throws the room a smile. "I am the superintendent and first lady-of-honor. I call myself Lady of All Things."

"A pleasure to meet you, my lady," I say as I curtsy.

From lessons on royal society, I know Gabrielle advises the princess and oversees the other ladies.

"Seeing you up close, you really are quite beautiful. The papers were right, for once." Gabrielle stares me up and down. "Most Belles are incredibly boring. Like the last one. What was her name again?"

"Her name was Ambrosia," I say. The words sound too hard. Too protective.

Gabrielle recoils like I've poked her.

"We call her Amber," I add to soften it.

"Yes. Amber. Dull as plain vanilla." Gabrielle smirks. "You look like you might be entertaining."

I can't tell whether she's paying me a compliment or an insult. I stutter out a thank-you.

The next lady-of-honor doesn't move from her spot, sprawled across one of the sofas. She barely turns to look at me, too busy pushing a strawberry crème tart into her mouth. "I'm Lady Claudine, Duchesse de Bissay," she grunts out, and waves a hand in the air.

"Mind your manners," Gabrielle snaps.

She flashes Gabrielle a smile full of food bits. "And Lady of the Dresses, though I haven't been helping the Fashion Minister with Her Royal Highness's wardrobe lately." Her hair is a frizzy nest haloing her plump white face.

"My lady," I say, with another curtsy.

"Don't mind her, she's just grieving the loss of her last marriage prospect," Gabrielle teases. "Though she might never get another one if she doesn't stop eating."

Claudine shoves two tarts in her mouth and licks her fingers loudly to make Gabrielle and the princess both cringe, as well as all the other people in the room. "I'll just have one of *her* people"—she points a sticky finger in my direction—"fix me right up. Slim me down even smaller next time, so I have more room to grow."

"Or we could just make curves a trend again. You have a beautiful shape," I say. "More women should covet your natural template."

Claudine winks at me. "I'd still like to see how small I could be."

Sophia steps out from behind the screen. The dress hugs her frame, a tornado of tulle and lace in emerald, turquoise, plum, cobalt, and gold. A mask of peacock feathers is fitted over her face.

Everyone applauds and whistles and shouts out compliments. I join in. She waves her hand and the room goes silent.

"Claudine, you know my mother has outlawed deep body restructuring," Sophia says. "Being too skinny is forbidden."

"But we all know you'll change that when you're queen," Claudine says, a satisfied smile spreading across her face.

Sophia's eyes narrow. A strange energy seeps through the room. No one speaks up until the last lady-of-honor pokes her head out from behind a high-backed chair. She's the youngest one, barely older than the little girl, Holly, from the carnaval night. She curtsies; her dress is reminiscent of a bluebell flower.

"I'm Lady Henrietta-Maria." She strokes the curls poking out of her long dark braid, and tucks a book into her dress sash. Her eyes glaze over with indifference. She's all freckled, and reminds me of a caramel drop cookie. She gestures toward a puffy chair in the nearby corner for me to sit on, before retreating back to her place near the window. "I'm in charge of nothing."

"That's not true, Henrietta-Maria. You are my beloved. Come here." Sophia reaches her arms out.

Henrietta-Maria scurries over to her. Sophia plants a kiss on her forehead. "Now, remember what I told you last week? You're going to be the Lady of the Jewels."

Henrietta-Maria's hazel eyes light up. "Oh, right, I forgot."

"Go fetch the jewelry boxes."

The little girl skips off.

"Camellia," Sophia says, turning to me. "I love my ladies and court so much. They've been so supportive and loyal. I like to reward those who are good to me."

Henrietta-Maria returns pushing a cushioned cart covered with tiered jewelry stands, each dripping with bracelets, earrings, and necklaces. The gems twinkle under the beauty-lanterns.

Sophia's court ladies remove their own jewelry. Servants mill around, collecting the pieces in velveteen boxes. The women clasp their hands in anticipation.

"Pick something new," Sophia says.

The women rush forward, swarming over the jewelry cart and fussing over who will get which piece. Gabrielle orders them around.

"Your Highness is too kind," one says.

"So magnanimous," says another.

"Camellia, would you like a necklace?" Sophia asks.

"You are too gracious, Your Highness. I couldn't accept," I say.

"You can, and you will." She has the cart brought closer to us. "Pick one."

My fingers glide over the glistening pieces as if they're petit-cakes ready for tasting. I choose a necklace with a cherry-size ruby. She helps drape it around my neck. The clasp pinches so hard it feels like the prick of a needle. I flinch.

"Sorry, favorite. My jewelry has a tendency to bite."

Her ladies-of-honor chuckle and swap glances.

"Out," Sophia says to the crowd. "Please leave me, now that you've gotten your gifts. I want a little privacy. It is my birthday, after all."

"Your makeup is not done, Your Highness," the attendant replies.

"Camellia will tell me if it's beautiful. I do not need all of your opinions today." She shoos everyone—except her ladies and a handful of servants—from the room. They grumble as they file out. "You, too, Ivy."

I'm not ready for her to leave me here yet, but she exits with the group. After the doors shut, the girls resume their conversation.

"You know Patrice is bringing her new lady tonight," Gabrielle reports to Claudine, who grunts in response.

"I hear she's a wonderful singer." Sophia makes a chirping sound. Gabrielle bursts with laughter.

"Are you ready to see her with someone new?" Gabrielle asks.

"Well, I have to be, don't I?" Claudine snaps.

Gabrielle plucks the tart from her hands, and they fuss back and forth until Claudine orders the servant to bring her another. "I'm grieving. Just let me be."

"You'll embarrass the crown. You're already embarrassing all of us in front of the Belle," Gabrielle says.

"It's Camellia," I remind her. "Or Camille, which I prefer."

She jumps back like I've hit her.

Claudine grins at her. "Forgetting names already, superintendent Gabrielle?"

"I don't forget anything." Her eyes hold annoyance. Sweat slicks my neck. Little quivers pulse through my hands. I hold my dress skirts and don't break eye contact until she looks back at Claudine.

Gabrielle orders the servants around, telling them how the princess will wear her hair for the evening—three single plaits twisted into a low bun—and she tells the other ladies-of-honor how to drape her with jewelry. Her slender brown arms wave about like wings as she doles out every command.

A body-length mirror is set before Sophia. She turns around and around, then slaps her hands against her legs. "I hate this look."

Her ladies-of-honor spring into action. They fuss over her like it's a competition to tell her how beautiful she is. Even the little one lingers at the edge, holding swansdown puffs, ready to spray Sophia with a perfume atomizer. Sophia's maids glue extra feathers onto the gown, creating trailing folds like a peacock's tail. They sew sparkling charms along the sleeves. A diadem is placed in her hair.

"I need to be the most beautiful girl at my party."

"Of course you will be," Gabrielle says.

"Why would you think otherwise?" Claudine adds.

"Henrietta-Maria, tell them to bring out the beauty boards," Sophia orders. Henrietta-Maria skips all the way to the door, then disappears into an adjacent room. When she returns, she's trailed by a team of servants holding canvas boards and easels.

"Camille," Sophia barks.

I leap up from my chair.

"What do you think of these? I had my beauty cabinet make them up. And my mother continues to meddle and edit them."

I circle the boards. They feature different looks—nose shapes, hair and eye colors, facial structures, hair textures, body shapes, and skin tones—matched with fabric swatches and rouge-stick smudges and nail lacquer.

"They're lovely," I say. And boring.

Sophia rushes up to me so fast, I take a step back. She cups my hand in hers. "I don't want to just be beautiful. I want to be the *most* beautiful." She doesn't blink, and her eyes stretch open so wide, it's as if she's trying to take me completely in. "I need to make the beauty-scopes this week. It's my birthday."

I've never seen her in the scopes. Not once. It's as if the newsies purposefully ignore her. But her sister, Charlotte, used to frequent them until she became ill.

"I have a secret for you," she tells me. She leans close to my ear. Her bottom lip grazes it. "I wanted you. My mother wanted your sister." Her words burn all the way down my neck into my chest like a scalding hot tear. "Your sister couldn't give me what I want, but I know you can. I knew from the night of the Beauté Carnaval." She pulls back and stares at me again. I feel frozen in place, like a butterfly pinned under a glass frame.

I open my mouth to ask her what really happened with Amber, but a chime sounds.

An attendant approaches. "Your Highness, your party will begin momentarily. It's time to go to the gardens."

She puts her hand up. "One moment." She turns back to me, touching my cheek. "Give me a type of hair no one has ever seen before."

Her challenge thuds in my stomach. Sweat creeps along my brow, and my cheeks flush. "Shouldn't we wait for our first official beauty appointment together?"

"No, I want this now, Camellia. Before my party. I have a feeling my parents are going to introduce me to suitors tonight. Everyone's gossiping about it." She bats her eyes at me. Her teacup monkey, Singe, starts to stamp his feet and reach his paw through the cage bars. "See, Singe agrees."

My stomach knots with worries. Ivy hasn't taught me what the princess likes yet. The word *no* bubbles up on my tongue. I think of Amber. I think of all I did to get here. I think of how much I wanted to be the favorite.

"Let's see if I was right about you," Sophia says. And the challenge—and threat—are clear in her eyes.

"I'll need my beauty caisse, Your Highness," I say.

"Gabrielle," Sophia says.

Gabrielle releases a deep sigh, then slides off her chaise and leaves the chamber.

Sophia sits at her massive vanity. Jeweled beauty-lanterns cluster overhead. I remove the diadem and set it in front of her. I undo her low bun and unbraid her three single plaits. Hair bounces around her face like a soft cloud of white-blond curls. I run my fingers through it. I feel her eyes watching my every move. I think about all the pictures I've seen of her. She always leans toward shades of honey and gold.

"Should I have Belle-rose tea brought out to you?" I ask.

"No, I'm trying to go without it. I like to be alert for small changes."

Gabrielle returns with Bree, who tows my beauty caisse. She winks at me, and I smile. Bree works quickly to unhook the hundreds of clasps and fan open the compartments. I run my fingers over hair-paste pots, letting the tiny clicking melody of their lids soothe my fears. I pluck a sunflower yellow and a silvery white from the tray.

"Bree, will you dust her, please?" I ask, trying to buy myself more time to make a decision.

"Yes, my lady." She takes a bei-powder bundle from a drawer and sprinkles it over Sophia's hair and scalp.

The latest hair trends are adding colored highlights, or mixing hair colors like black and red. I can't do any of those. They've been plastered all over the pamphlets. I look up into the skylight windows. The sun bleeds across the sky, leaving a garish trail of reds and oranges and yellows. An idea zips through me.

I use a brush to paint the roots of Sophia's hair with the golden color. It drips like honey down the length of her strands. I dip the ends of her hair into the silvery pot of color and spread the color upward toward the middle.

Sophia grins at me. She takes a deep breath and closes her eyes.

The arcana wake up inside me. I tug at the strands of hair, and they fall down to her waist. I twirl one around my finger to put a loose wave in her hair. The golden color fades into silver halfway to the bottom.

Her face is red and sweaty, and she pants.

"Your Highness, are you all right?" I ask. "Would you like tea after all?"

"No, no." She waves a hand in the air. "Continue. I'm fine."

I remove pots of ground graphite from my beauty caisse and embed the flakes in the shafts of hair, so now the strands almost shimmer.

Her breathing quickens.

"I'm finished, Your Highness."

Sophia opens her eyes and gazes into the mirror. A smile overtakes her face. Gabrielle's mouth hangs open. Henrietta-Maria drops her book. Claudine freezes, pastry hovering right at her lips.

"I've never seen . . ." Sophia starts to say, but stops to stand and admire herself. She twirls and lets her hair bloom all around her, then leans over to kiss my cheek. I jump back in surprise. Claudine, Gabrielle, and Henrietta-Maria rush forward.

I fill with satisfaction. "Let me also adjust your makeup to match."

"You can change someone's makeup?" Gabrielle asks.

"Well, I'm not supposed to, but I don't think any of you will tell Madam Du Barry." I wink, trying to get them to laugh. They simply stare at me with eager eyes and pursed lips.

I pull the head off a nearby rose. I stick it inside the soft belly of a cake of blush-crème on her vanity. The color drains from the rose as I add deeper red and white pigments to the makeup. I watch and wait for their reactions.

The girls applaud my tiny beauty enhancement.

"Splendid!"

"How clever!"

"That was beautiful."

I add the new powder to Princess Sophia's cheeks with a brush. When I am done, her eyes shimmer with delight. "May you always find beauty, Your Highness," I say.

The royal attendant returns to escort us to the gardens. Sophia slips her hand in mine. "We're going to be the closest of friends," she whispers. "I just know it."

# 20

Marble stairs lead down into the palace garden for Sophia's birthday game. Lady courtiers hand out beautiful masks. Party guests trample ahead, fixing the masks to their faces, each determined to be the first to win the treasure hunt. Sophia and her ladies stop to pose for portraits and talk to newsies. Young men and women mingle, eager to enter the labyrinth of hedges and begin the game.

I like watching how the people smile, touch, and laugh with one another. Garden-lanterns linger above the giant geometric hedges, and blimps carry small candles, gliding along the intricate maze. I put on my mask; the sunbird feathers protrude over my hair like ram horns. I gather up my dress and skip along. I need to find my sisters. I need to find Amber.

"Stay close," Rémy says.

"No." I duck into the nearest lane.

He grabs for my arm, but I slip out of reach. I like how his face twists with annoyance and his eyes flash with irritation. It's the most emotion I've seen from him.

"This is not a time to play," he grumbles. "Your safety—"

"But it is the perfect time. It's a game!"

I head for the thickest pocket of people as Rémy struggles to politely navigate through the crowd. He's big and broad and unable to slip through the small gaps in the crowd like I can. I make aimless turns until I can't see him anymore. Dark garden passages fill with revelers and laughter. I join them. I ignore the dangers of being separated from my guard. I ignore the fact that Maman and Du Barry would be upset with me for breaking protocol.

I imagine my sisters by my side: Edel, tasting the various treats offered in each pavilion and congratulating me on continuing to break the rules; Padma, collecting every interesting flower she comes across; Hana, talking to all the boys and interviewing the girls about falling in love; Valerie, dancing and singing until our ears can't handle it any longer; and Amber and I, finding corners to whisper in. I'd ask her what happened. I'd apologize for our fight.

Once I feel that I've thoroughly lost Rémy, I break from the crowd, heading in the opposite direction. Cool air finds its way into the fur bolero draped over my shoulders, and I squeeze it tightly closed. The promise of snowy months feels closer. I run my hands over orange and yellow leaves. They remind me of the color of Amber's hair, and little-girl memories of weaving flower petals into each other's braids. Twin feelings of anger and sadness flush through me.

I meander through the passages, turning left and right, right and left. Statues stand at sharp corners, and fountains spray rainbow-colored water in the air. Laughing ladies stream past with gentlemen trailing behind them. They smile and point at me, and whisper my name alongside the words *favorite* and *Belle* and *beauty*. Even with the mask, they recognize me.

Jeweled pavilions and gazebos dot garden lanes, serving different teas, coffees, and sweets. Music floats out of some, giggles burst from others, and the scent of sweet pastries mingles with the nectar of flowers. I scan pockets of people, looking for Belle-buns.

The sun sinks fully below the horizon. The night-lanterns are lit. I trample over a wooden bridge that crosses a small garden river, an offshoot of the Golden Palace River that runs the perimeter of the palace grounds. I make another turn and spot Sophia's dress. The jewels and feathers glow like fluorescent insects in the darkness, and her brilliant hair sparkles under the lanterns.

I crane my neck to see around the hedge. She's wrapped in the arms of a young man—legs, arms, and lips locked together. Their masks lie on the ground. The green trim of his jacket reveals he's from the mercantile House of Clothiers, and as such is ineligible to be her fiancé. He claws at her dress like it's a present he's desperate to unwrap. She directs his hands, moves his head from left to right, in complete control of his every touch and kiss. My fingers fly up to cover my mouth.

I'm careful to stay out of sight. Her ladies-of-honor fan out around her like a guard, surveying the area, running off people who wander by. Seeing his hands lifting her dress makes my body warm, like I'm preparing to use the arcana. The veins in my arms and legs rise. A curiosity inside me awakens.

I shudder from the ridiculousness of my thoughts. I turn to leave, but step on a branch. It cracks.

I freeze.

Sophia stops kissing the young man. She looks over his shoulder and motions to one of her ladies.

Gabrielle walks forward. "Who's there?" Her beautiful skin blends into the dark corners of the garden.

I take a deep breath, grab hold of my skirts, and run. I turn left and right and left again without a plan. I hear the girls shouting out behind me. I hope they can't tell who I am. I don't stop until my lungs threaten to give out. I might never catch my breath again.

My foot catches on a branch and I topple over in a heap. My legs ache, and sweat collects beneath my mask. I half want to cry, wishing my sisters were with me, but then find myself laughing instead—laughing at the craziness of it all. I think of Sophia's disheveled face, rouge-stick ringing her mouth and his; her hair, now a chaos of strands; of Gabrielle's angry expression.

"You've gotten yourself into a mess." A young man peers around the hedge. Tall and stately, with wavy dark hair, his mask is feathered and makes me think of the swallow birds that sailors paint on their ships. He reaches to remove his mask.

"Don't! You'll lose the game," I say. But he doesn't stop, and reveals his face.

It's Auguste Fabry. The boy from outside the gate.

"I'm not likely to win it at this point." He rubs along the beak of the mask and extends a hand to me.

I hesitate. The image of Sophia and the boy wrapped in each other's arms flashes in my head. I don't take his hand.

I remove my mask as well. He smiles with recognition, and his eyes pin me in place. A flush of nerves climbs from my stomach to my neck.

"You're looking at me like I did something wrong," I say.

"I'm just curious."

"Well, you shouldn't be." I try to get to my feet, further tangling myself in the bushes.

"Why not?" He extends his hand again.

"Do you always take such risks with your life?" I glance

around for Rémy or any onlooker before reaching for it, feeling like I'm reaching across worlds, oceans, skies, and realms. The warmth of his palm seeps through my lace gloves. My heart flutters like one of the nearby lantern candles. I will it to slow. Once on my feet, I drop his hand and wipe my palm on my dress as if I can be rid of that feeling.

"I'm not afraid of anything," he says.

"Neither am I," I say, even though that's starting to feel like a lie.

I brush myself off, but the train of my dress snares in the hedge. I work to loosen it, and he rushes to help.

"I'm fine," I say.

"You're stuck. And you'll rip your dress if you keep it up." I tense and shiver as his hand presses against the small of my back.

"Seems like you're afraid of me," he says, gently pulling at the folds.

"I'm not. It's just—"

"I shouldn't be talking to you. I know. We've established that fact." He frees the train of the gown from the hedge. "There's only a tiny tear. I don't know why you all wear these dresses. Too much fabric. Isn't it heavy?"

"You should try one on."

He laughs and tosses his mask into the hedge. Pieces of his hair fall along his face, and he tucks them behind his ear.

"I've seen a million articles about you in the papers. The *new* favorite. Your name is everywhere."

"You mean they have papers where you're from? Where was it again, the *Lost*?"

"It's the *Lynx*. Get it right, please. Do not insult her. She's sensitive."

I laugh.

"I just finished working on her. She's my first ship. Well, I don't count the little rowboat my father made for me when I was a child learning to sail. I was saying that the whole kingdom is in a silly frenzy over you."

"Silly frenzy?" I say.

He rubs his hand along the stubble on his face. "I meant, everyone adores you."

"Should they not?"

"You must love it."

"I don't know how I feel about it yet. Have they said anything about my sister?"

"Aren't you reading the papers?"

"I wouldn't be asking if I was."

He smiles back at me. "They're calling her the disgraced favorite."

The word "disgraced" thuds into my stomach. The pain of it shouts out in all directions. A determination swells inside me. I have to find her. She must be here.

"But the newsies don't know which way is up. They just want to sell papers." He pulls over a night-lantern and ties its tail ribbons to the hedge behind us.

"Afraid of the dark?"

"It's so I can see you better," he says.

"Oh," is all I can manage to say, and I look away from him.

He stares at me. I feel his eyes drift from my hair to my eyes to my mouth. I turn, ready to walk off and resume the search for my sisters.

"Does it bother you to be the runner-up, now that you're here?" he asks.

His question feels like a slap.

"I didn't mean to offend," he quickly adds.

"Then what exactly did you mean to say?"

He plucks a few leaves from my hair. The graze of his fingers sends a ripple through me, along with the realization that I've never been touched like this before. It softens the hard edges and fluttery nerves. "Is it difficult to be picked second?"

"This is all I've ever wanted."

He grins, as if what I've said is funny. "That doesn't answer the question, now does it?"

"Your question didn't deserve a response."

"That's not very nice."

"I never said I was nice."

"Women are supposed to be sweet. Belles even more so."

I make a gagging sound.

He laughs. "That's what my mother told me."

"And what do you know about Belles?"

"That they're magical."

I scoff. "Try again."

"That they have magical abilities."

"Try blessed blood."

"What does that mean?"

"That our arcana—not *magical* abilities, since there's nothing magical about them—lie within our blood."

"Oh," he says.

"Do they teach you about us?"

"A little . . . and if I were you, I'd outlaw that horrible trend of mosaic skin tones. It's all the rage in the Gold Isles. People are walking around looking like kaleidoscopes."

"Good thing you aren't a Belle."

He grins. "Do you have a hard time taking advice?"

"Do you always like to give your unsolicited opinion?" I try to sound exasperated, but the truth is, I like going back and forth with him.

"My mother would say so. I guess my father, too. My two older brothers tried to keep me quiet my whole life. I guess it didn't work. And are you saying that you don't like my opinions?"

"I—"

"Camellia!" Rémy races over. His brow is soaked with sweat. He stares at Auguste and brings his hand to the sword at his hip. "What's going on here?"

Auguste laughs. "An imperial guard to your rescue. You are quite important." He buttons the front of his jacket so Rémy can see his naval emblems. He puts his hands in front of him. "I'm without my dagger. No need to arrest me. I'm off."

He saunters away, leaving a trail of heavy laughter. Rémy waits until Auguste is out of sight, then turns to me with fire in his eyes.

"What were you thinking?" he says. "Running off like that."

"I just wanted to explore."

"Court isn't for fun. Not for people like you or me. You're here to do a service."

"I know."

"You don't seem to."

"I've never seen anything."

"Not all things are worth seeing," he says.

I let Rémy lead me forward. He takes sharp turns, navigating the maze with expert precision. Guests whiz past, their laughter a faint, distant echo. The white marble stairs glow through the darkness as we approach. A girl's giggle cuts through the garden.

Her hair is piled on top of her head with ribbons and jewels that sparkle in the darkness.

"Wait—" I touch Rémy's arm. "It's Hana!" My pulse quickens with excitement.

I chase after the woman, swelling with happiness by the second.

"Excuse me."

I duck past courtiers.

"Pardon me."

I call out, "Hana."

She doesn't turn.

I reach for her arm. She swings around.

"Yes, my lady, can I help you?" the woman says, her facial expression marked with confusion.

It's not her.

The disappointment makes me almost lose my balance.

Rémy puts a hand on my waist. "Your sisters declined their invitations tonight."

"What? Why?"

"It's not my place to speak for others," he says, ushering me away.

# 21

I soak in the Grand Banquet Hall: candelabras and centerpieces dripping with white and gold, animated ceiling frescoes of the royal family's bloodline, roses opening and closing to release their scents. The table is set for thousands, and enormous ballroom-lanterns flash so much light overhead that everything glitters. The snowmelons and strawberries in their bowls. The macaron towers draped with nets of sugar syrup and golden honey. The silver terrines filled with spiced soups. The ladies' hair-towers and hats. The men's cravats and suit jackets.

Du Barry and Elisabeth watch me cross the room as royal attendants ply the guests with wine and savory hors d'oeuvres. I lift my head and stand up straight, knowing I must impress.

Gossip flows faster than the water circulating through the room's centerpiece fountain.

*"One of the king's mistresses is in attendance tonight. She wears the emblem. Look!"*

*"I wonder if the new favorite is better than the old one. I liked the original."*

*"House Kent is falling apart, going bankrupt. Did you see Lady Kent's dress—frayed at the hem."*

*"I heard the princess ran the old favorite out of the palace."*

*"I was told Princess Charlotte will wake up any day now. The queen will announce it at the Declaration of Heirs Ceremony, you'll see."*

*"The queen doesn't really like the new favorite. If she did, she would've picked her from the start."*

I try to ignore the bits about Amber and me, and plaster a stiff smile on my face.

Guests are coaxed into their seats. Little handwritten labels tell us where to sit. Royal relatives, ministers, and titled courtiers from high houses and merchant houses crowd the table. I scan the names, looking for my sisters, hoping Rémy lied, but I don't see them.

An attendant approaches. "Lady Camellia, may I escort you to your seat?"

I nod, happy to be taken from Rémy's watchful presence and deposited between the Beauty Minister and the Fashion Minister.

Auguste enters the room. He looks up and catches me watching him. He winks. I laugh and look away, willing the flush rising in my cheeks to vanish. I find him absolutely ridiculous, and a little interesting, if I'm honest with myself. I glance around, worried that someone might've seen, and pretend to participate in the conversation at my end of the table. It's full of speculation about the queen's toilette-box allotments and new beauty laws. I need to be careful. I need to be perfect. Especially if any of that gossip about Amber is true.

"I heard the queen wants to extend royal beauty restrictions to high-house courtiers. All of us might have to settle for a single definitive look," one woman says.

"I think that's all newsie trash and gossip," another one replies.

"I'm just ready for her to announce the new toilette allotments. I'm excited to shop. The Pomanders will be releasing their new scents soon—and I don't want anything that's been picked over," a third adds.

The doors open, and the royal family emerges: the king, queen, and princess. The guests fall silent.

"We're so elated that you could join us in celebrating the birthday of our beloved daughter." The king speaks into a voice-trumpet, and his words echo from a sound-box peeking out of the flower arrangement on our table. It feels like he's standing right beside me. "My little girl is all grown up."

The applause is thunderous. I watch Sophia's eyes sparkle as she looks at her father.

He puts a hand on the queen's shoulder. "We will feast, have the presentation of the gifts, and conclude with much dancing and merriment. Bon appétit."

Servants release a set of sparkler balloons into the air. They glimmer above our heads, leaving glowing trails above the table, until they explode with color and light, and take the shape of Sophia's royal emblem. The brightness of the chrysanthemum blinds me.

"Happy birthday, my love." The king blows her a kiss. "Papa loves you."

He makes me wonder what it's like to have a father. As little girls, my sisters and I asked about ours, after being read stories full of mothers and fathers and their misbehaving children. We were told Belles had mothers. Several of them. We were told that Belles didn't need anything else.

The king and queen sit in their high-backed chairs. Sophia and her ladies are led to the opposite end of the table.

The queen rises again. Everyone stops talking. "My husband forgot to introduce another new member to court this season. Our new favorite Belle of this generation, Camellia Beauregard." My name booms through the sound-box like an explosion. Unexpectedly loud.

The Fashion Minister stands and pulls out my chair for me.

I flash them all my best smile and walk over to the queen. I execute a full bow before taking her hand.

"Your Majesty," I whisper. The queen's eyes remain cold, her face and words formal. I wish she'd look at me the way she looked at Amber after she named her the favorite. Elated. Thrilled.

My stomach tightens. Eyes are sweeping over me from head to toe. My knees shake, and I'm grateful for the thick layers of tulle.

I glance up and feel Auguste's eyes on my face. The heat in my cheeks threatens to melt my makeup.

Polite applause echoes through the hall.

I curtsy, keeping my gaze on the floor. I return to my seat. Sweat pools beneath my arms, and I use a lace handkerchief to blot my face.

The meal is served. I can't keep up with all the silverware and dishes appearing and disappearing in front of me.

A servant dips a spoon into the princess's bowl, tasting it. Sophia studies the girl's face as she swallows, then after a few moments waves her off. She spots me watching the exchange, and frowns. I drop my gaze and dig into the wedge of cheese that's been left beside my bread.

"Isn't that goat cheese just divine, Camellia?" The Beauty

Minister leans close to my ear. "Just keep smiling and pretend that I'm discussing the cheese. Be wary of staring too much. I know this environment can be shocking. I swear, Madam Du Barry shelters you Belles way too much for my tastes."

"But what was that woman doing with the princess's food?" I whisper.

"That woman was a food-taster. That young girl's tongue has been trained to detect over ninety-eight types of poisons to be found in our kingdom."

I try not to let the shock show on my face. Instead, I smile and ask another question. "Is it common to find poison in the palace food?"

"Poisonings have become more frequent than an assassin's dagger, my dear. The illness of Princess Charlotte makes the queen even more vigilant in taking care of her children."

With that, she turns her attention to another courtier. I remember the pictures of Princess Charlotte from our history books and the newspapers. Two years older than Sophia, she fell into a deep sleep after her fifteenth birthday, and hasn't woken up for four years. Periodically, the queen releases a new portrait of her—sleeping soundly in a four-poster bed—to assure the kingdom that their heir is still alive.

Another plate is put in front of me. I eat to distract myself.

"Camellia." The queen's voice travels through the sound-box again.

My fork clatters against my plate. People stare at me—eyebrows raised, expressions puzzled. My etiquette is usually impeccable. We had years of lessons on it. But now Du Barry glares at me, appalled.

"Pardon me, Your Majesty," I say.

"How are you enjoying your first few days at court?" the queen asks.

The Beauty Minister nudges me to lean closer to the sound-box. "Speak into it," she whispers.

"They've been wonderful, Your Majesty," I say. "Thank you for your kindness and generosity, and for this second chance." The noise of my voice drifts down the long table. Du Barry nods at me with approval.

The Fashion Minister draws the queen's attention away from me with a question about silkworm production and winter gowns. I exhale.

Auguste's voice travels as he tells a grand story about a sea monster he kept from capsizing the imperial fleet last year. The women don't take their eyes off him. Elisabeth puts an ear-trumpet up so she can hear every word.

"Did you capture the creature?" Sophia asks him.

"Of course," he boasts. "I'm quite strong."

"Did you cut its head off to make a trophy?" her lady-of-honor Gabrielle asks.

"I carry one of its tentacles in my pocket."

The ladies giggle and the gentlemen chuckle at his outlandish-ness. I hide a laugh with a forkful of salad. Waiters clear our plates. The fourth and fifth courses appear, and then the table is prepared for dessert. Three women wheel out a thousand-layer crepe cake with massive strawberries the size of snow globes. The princess and her ladies leave the table and pose in front of the cake. News-ies draw pictures for their late-night editions. The room's candles are extinguished. Sparklers blaze on each cake layer.

Everyone shouts "Happy birthday!" and Sophia blows out the hundreds of candles with help from her friends.

The cake is cut and served, and gifts are presented to Sophia. A royal attendant parades around an all-white teacup tiger with a jeweled collar from the royal House Lothair. The leash trembles in his grip as he walks the beautiful animal around the table. A display of plum-colored jewels and diamond necklaces comes from the mercantile House of Bijoux. A teacup dragon sails in through one of the doors with the House Glaston flag in its jaws.

Guests clap and comment as more gifts are showered on the princess. The treasures all seem to please Sophia and her ladies. Especially the dragon.

The king clinks his glass. The table falls quiet. "My darling girl," he says to Sophia, "dance tonight, for in the morning and the days to come, you will face more responsibilities as you take your place in this world. Your mother and I have also selected three suitors to vie for your heart. Marriage is on your horizon."

The crowd applauds. Sophia's eyes light up. Her ladies-of-honor perch in their seats, their mouths permanently fixed in smiles.

"On behalf of our entire family, Queen Celeste and I would like to extend the warmest welcome to Sir Louis Dubois and his son Alexander, from House Berry; Sir Guillaume Laurent, his wife Lady Adelaide, and their son Ethan, from House Merania; and the Minister of the Seas, Commander Pierre Fabry, and his son Auguste, from House Rouen." He raises a glass. "Thank you for being apt suitors for our daughter."

An unexpected knot forms in my throat as Auguste stands. He smiles and basks in the cheers and attention lavished upon him. My hand quivers as I grip the stem of my glass for the toast. Auguste is one of Sophia's formal suitors. The reality of that feels strange. He was just an insufferable, overtalkative boy before. And now he's someone important. Someone I have no business wondering about. I gulp down the fizzy champagne.

Sophia's ladies-of-honor whistle and clap.

Everyone drinks to the health of the suitors and the princess. The royal orchestra marches in with stringed misens and violins and cellos, and the first waltz of the evening begins.

The Fashion Minister presents his hand. "A dance with the favorite?"

"Is it allowed?" I tease.

"I am very important and have immunity from being jailed by the queen's court. I can risk it." When he smiles, the many freckles on his cheeks blend into one.

"I've never danced with a man before."

"I bet there's a long list of things you haven't done." He puts a hand around my waist and turns me. "I'm honored to be the first." Other couples steal glances at us. I watch them turn like colorful spinning tops. The Fashion Minister spins me as if we're on the Imperial Carousel. The room becomes a swirl of laughter and light and color. The rich dinner churns in my stomach.

"I have to slow down," I say.

"So soon?" He stops.

My legs wobble and shake. A sticky sweat climbs over my skin. People stare as they dance by. I press my hands to my mouth and vomit into them.

The Beauty Minister apologizes to the guests. She mentions the fragile constitution of the Belles. Du Barry gives servants instructions about me. Elisabeth laughs. Many people whisper about my soiled gown. Their faces blur, and their voices become one ambient hum like the noise of the bayou.

Bree rushes to help me clean off, but my gown is a wet mess. Remnants of the lavish birthday dinner stain its violet folds. I am disgusting.

The queen approaches, and I'm dizzy all over again.

"Camellia," she says.

"Yes, Your Majesty," I reply with a bow.

"I'm going to walk you out."

My chest flutters with panic. Her eyes burn into me. Giggles and whispers follow us.

She waves away her imperial attendant, and walks me into the long hall. Rémy and a member of the First Guard follow closely behind. Newsies maintain their distance but sketch pictures and send black gossip post-balloons in our direction. Both Rémy and her guard crush them like paper animals.

I worry that I look and smell terrible. I hate that she's standing so close to me. I hate that this entire thing happened. My stomach knots again, threatening to empty anything that didn't already escape.

The queen looks me over from head to toe. "Are you well, child?" She touches my cheek as if she's checking my temperature.

"I had too much to eat and drink. I've never really had champagne before."

"Can you do this?" she asks.

"Do what, Your Majesty?"

"Be who I need you to be."

"I will do whatever you want me—"

She puts a finger to my lips. "We will see. I am not yet convinced." She walks back to the Grand Banquet Hall.

I'm trapped by her words, each one a pin tacking me in place, until a pack of black gossip post-balloons swarms me like a kettle of vultures.

I sprint ahead.

"Slow down," Rémy calls out from behind, chasing me down the corridor. "You'll twist your ankle, and then I'll have to carry you."

I think he's attempting a joke.

I kick off my shoes and carry them so I can move even faster. The cold marble is a comfort to my swollen feet.

Rémy's boots pound the floors, and he catches me before I reach the staircase. "You're headed the wrong way," he says. "And you're too sick to run." It feels like he's poking at a bruise. "Your rooms are up the staircase to the north wing; this is the southern staircase." His forehead glistens over with sweat, the curve of it like a hazelnut.

"Show me, then," I snap, bunching the folds of my wet dress. I want to get as far away from the Grand Banquet Hall and the newsies and the embarrassing memory as possible.

He walks alongside me. "Are you feeling any better?"

"Why are you being nice to me?" I ask. "Up until now it's been nothing but instructions and protocols."

"My commander says I have to *shift my attitude*," he says, clearly repeating the instructions. "He believes my gruff demeanor is the reason you disobeyed orders in the garden."

"Oh, so it's not because you want to."

"That's not what I meant." He shrugs. "I'm not good with words. And I'm doing a terrible job at this. I've never done it before. My commander said the best way to protect a person is to start by getting acquainted with them."

"I don't feel like talking," I say.

"Well, I do," he says. "The third course was my favorite. Though the duck was a bit overcooked, in my opinion. And eating in the kitchen area isn't ideal."

I ignore his rambles. The embarrassment of the night hits me over and over again. I wonder if it'll land me in a tattler or scandal sheet or the late-night newsreel. I wonder if that is why the queen asked what she did; if she thinks I can't handle being the favorite.

The potential headlines scroll through my mind:

THE FAVORITE VOMITS ALL OVER HERSELF

CAMELLIA BEAUREGARD, NOT SO BEAUTIFUL TONIGHT

BRING BACK THE OTHER FAVORITE;
SHE DIDN'T SOIL HER GOWN

QUEEN OVERHEARD WONDERING ABOUT
THE FITNESS OF THE FAVORITE

I quicken my pace, knowing I'll need at least seven leeches tonight. Rémy makes three more turns, and my feet get colder and colder. "Are you sure you know where you're going?"

His back stiffens, and he turns to glare at me. "I won't dignify that question with a response."

We enter a small, well-lit foyer, and my surroundings start to look more familiar. Plush carpeted stairs lead up to the Belle apartments. Night-lanterns cluster above the doors, glowing with the Belle-emblem.

"Thank you," I spit out, ready to be rid of his company. I tromp up the stairs two steps at a time.

"I must check that your rooms are secure before you retire. New protocol after those dead roses were found in your bathing chamber."

"Spying in my onsen?"

"It's my job to know everything."

"I think the roses were from my sister Amber. She was upset," I say. "No need to check. I want to go inside, get out of this dress, and get back to the party."

"They said you are not to return."

This news hits me hard. "What?"

"Now, wait here. You can't be sure, and I don't take any risks."

I sigh, but stay near the doors. He doesn't light a single candle or release one of the lanterns strung up in a line beside the entrance. He skulks around in the darkness.

Servants rush down the hall.

"What happened, Lady Camellia?" one asks.

"The soup," I lie. She inspects the stains on my dress. They lift the fabric and frown. "Don't worry," I tell them. "No need to come in. I can undress myself." I don't want to be fussed over.

They look alarmed, but nod and curtsy.

I walk inside the apartments, impatient with standing outside. I want to get out of this dress. I want to forget this night. I hear the click of the locks on the solarium doors, then the ones in my bedroom.

Rémy returns with a satisfied look on his face. When he spots me, his expression morphs into a frown. "Why can't you follow directions?"

"People are always telling me what to do," I say.

"Do you feel safe here?" he asks.

"Yes."

"Wrong answer. You shouldn't." His brown eyes narrow. "As soon as you feel too comfortable, that's when you know things are bound to go wrong."

"Thank you for the advice." I sling my shoes in a corner. They thud against the wall, harder than I want them to.

He starts to smile, and it's a nice one. I wonder how many girls are running after him, a decorated military officer.

"You're not as delicate as you look. As all the Belles seem to be," he says.

"I'm not a flower."

"Well, they dress you up as one."

I clench my teeth.

"You look like you want to slap someone," he says.

"Yes, *you*," I say, and realize that it is untrue.

"I'm sorry I make you so angry. My sisters say the same thing, and also complain about the smell of my feet." His face droops a bit, and I can't help but laugh.

"Why are you telling me this?"

He shrugs. "To distract you from what happened."

I want to thank him, but the words won't form. "I'd wager nothing like this has ever happened to you."

"I've never thrown up all over my dress before, no."

I smile. "You know what I mean."

"The first time I met the Minister of War, I fainted," he says. "I was thirteen, and that morning I couldn't eat. The nerves made my stomach a mess. So when I marched into his office, I took one look at him and passed out."

I chuckle.

"I thought the minister would kick me out of the academy.

That I'd be sent back home. Dishonored. But he gave me hot choco-late and asked me to train under him—only if I promised to eat."

The more he shares, the more questions I have about his life before coming to the palace. Where did he grow up? How many sisters does he have? Does he have someone he loves? Someone he might marry? Did he always want to be a soldier?

I don't ask any of them.

"Now I have a piece of chocolate every day. To remember. He could've sent me home—called me too weak—but he didn't."

For a moment, the sword at his hip and the armor across his broad chest and the deep scar carved into his brown skin dissolve, and he's just a young man, trying to do his job.

A sunset-orange post-balloon putters into the main salon, glowing bright with the Fire Teahouse emblem. Its tails whip and snap. I rush to it, open the back, and remove the note. Edel's rushed handwriting races across the page.

*Camille,*

*Everything is terrible. I work from sunup to sundown. There's crying and screaming in the night. I can't sleep.*

*There are too many women. Too many men. Too many children. Too many appointments. I am exhausted all the time.*

*I can't do this.*

*Turn this over. You'll know what to do. Then burn it.*

*Love,*

*Edel*

I flip over the parchment and see rows of color smudges. It's the secret alphabet we made up as children, to communicate without

Du Barry and our mamans knowing. We'd slide notes under each other's doors or leave them in our desks, full of the colorful promise of mischief in the night.

Her secret message reads: I'M GOING TO LEAVE. I HAVE A PLAN.

I press the page to my chest and take a deep breath.

"Is everything all right?" Rémy asks.

"Yes." I don't look up from Edel's note. I need to see her before she does something rash. I need to know what's going on.

"I should let you get ready for bed." Rémy steps back. "I've done too much talking."

"You didn't." I pull a string on a nearby wall. A bell sounds, and a nurse appears from behind a side door.

"The sangsues, please," I say. "At least seven. And tell Bree I want to see her."

"Yes, Lady Camellia," she answers.

Du Barry would be proud. Maman would give me a nod of approval. I'm protecting my arcana. I'm making sure I get rid of unnecessary excitement and stress. I'm following their rules.

Bree appears. "What happened?"

"I ate too much and the Fashion Minister spun me around too many times." I shrug. "I need cold water and a new dress. Can you bring me parchment and pastels, too, please?"

She nods and exits.

"I'll be right outside the door if you need me," Rémy says.

"Don't worry, I won't," I say, and immediately want to take it back. "I only mean . . . that I'll be busy."

"I understand," he says.

The nurse returns, holding a porcelain jug.

"I'll be there just in case you do," Rémy says, and bows slightly before striding out.

As soon as he disappears, I use the pastels to write Edel a note in our secret code.

DON'T DO ANYTHING UNTIL WE SPEAK.

I slip it into a privacy case, tuck it into the balloon's interior compartment, adjust the tiny golden compass, and send the palace-official post-balloon off the balcony. I watch until its lilac body disappears in the darkness.

# 22

An early sun pushes its way through the gauzy canopy over the bed. I roll over, reaching for the bed warmer's rubber handle to pull it closer, but it's cold. I sit up. Sounds of the tide drift in through the terrace doors. I'm careful not to make noise and alert the morning nurses, who are waiting for me to wake. I don't mind following this advice from Ivy.

An edge of the bedcurtain lifts. "You awake?" Bree whispers.

"Barely," I reply.

"I have something for you." She fans out a spread of the latest newspapers, magazines, and pamphlets. "Look at the news," she says, climbing onto the bed.

My heart thuds. "Is it bad?"

She flips through the papers. Headlines scatter and reassemble—the animated ink scrambling—as she turns the pages too quickly.

She opens a tattler and points.

*   *   *

NEW FAVORITE A FRAGILE FLOWER,
MAYBE NOT STRONG ENOUGH

QUEEN RUMORED TO REPLACE NEW
FAVORITE WITH ANOTHER, AGAIN

My heart sinks. Last night's vomiting episode rushes back. The embarrassment feels like a fresh burn.

"By tomorrow, these will all be gone," Bree says. "But there's another one—about one of your sisters—that I thought you'd want to see."

"Where?" I perch on my knees now, hovering over the spread of papers and tattlers.

She opens the *Trianon Tribune*, the kingdom's most popular paper.

I scan.

She smoothes the page. "Here."

FIRE TEAHOUSE BELLE RUMORED TO
HAVE RUN AWAY IN THE NIGHT

I touch the words. She left already? "No, Edel, no."

Bree blinks at me. "I don't know, miss. It might not even be true, but I thought you'd want to see it."

"Thank you. There's only one way to find out." I put on my robe, take the paper, and burst into the main salon. Morning servants wheel in breakfast carts and set out tea and plates. I press my ear to the wall panel that hides Elisabeth's office. The tinny sound of circuit-phones echoes from the other side, and I can feel small vibrations against my cheek.

I knock. When there's no answer, I knock louder.

The door creaks open. A sleepy Elisabeth, still in her night-gown, stares back at me. "I'm barely out of bed and haven't had breakfast," she whines. "What is it?"

"Is this true?" I push the paper in her face.

She squints, then snatches it from me to have a closer look. She laughs. "Edel has always been so dramatic."

"Call the Fire Teahouse," I say.

"No. You sound ridiculous."

"Then I will." I try to brush past her and into the office.

She blocks me. "It's just a rumor. Clearly, you can't handle reading these"—she waves the paper in my face—"and take them *too* seriously." Elisabeth calls all the servants into the main salon. "Lady Camellia is not to have any newspapers or tattlers or scandal sheets brought to the apartments. Beauty pamphlets and beauty-scopes only."

"Don't listen to her," I say.

"Oh, but they will." Elisabeth grabs a luna pastry from a nearby breakfast cart and pops it into her mouth. "I am in charge here. And once I tell my mother, it will be as good as law." She turns back to the staff. "If any of you are caught bringing these contraband items"—she taps the paper—"you will be beaten or put in the starvation boxes. I will see to it myself."

"Elisabeth—"

"You, Camellia, should focus on being perfect so you don't lose the title of favorite," Elisabeth snaps before disappearing back into her office.

Hot, angry tears well up in my eyes. I bang the door again, but she doesn't answer.

\* \* \*

I furiously write letters. Five lilac post-balloons float to my left, waiting for messages, and to be set free off the balcony.

*Valerie,*

*Have you heard from Edel?*

*I hate Elisabeth Du Barry even worse these days. I didn't know that was possible.*

*I miss you and hearing you laugh. How big are the Belle-babies now?*

*Love,*

*Camille*

*Hana,*

*I haven't heard from you. Is everything all right? Have you found out about the noises? Or asked your mistress if there are other Belles at the teahouse?*

*Did you see that headline in the paper about Edel? Have you spoken to her?*

*I miss you. And you won't believe how Elisabeth Du Barry is behaving at court. It's worse than when we were at home.*

*Love,*

*Camille*

*Padma,*

*Has Edel written you? Or Amber, even? I can't get in contact with either of them.*

*Do you know if everything is okay?*

*Love,*

*Camille*

*Amber,*

*Please write me.*

*Did you see the headline about Edel?*

*I hope you're all right.*

*I'm sorry.*

*Love,*

*Camille*

*Edel,*

*There's a headline about you in the* Trianon Tribune. *Is it just a rumor?*

*Don't leave. Come here to see me first. I can help you.*

*Love,*

*Camille*

I roll up all the tiny parchments and slip them into privacy casings no larger than my forefinger. I tuck them into the compartments inside the balloons, light the post-charcoal, then close them again and tug the balloons out to the balcony by their ribbons. Below, ships dot the coastline. Waves crash against them.

I think about the lists my sisters and I made in our playroom as little girls, noting all the things we wanted to see when we grew up and left home: the spinning looms in the dress markets, cinema-graphs and avenue boards of famed courtier socialites along Trianon's promenade, the pet shops with teacup elephants and teacup tigers lined up in the windows like treats for sale, the patisseries full of tarts, cakes, and cookies, the royal beach with its grains of pink sand and white-sailed ships. I still wish we could do these things together.

I send the balloons off the terrace. They drift out over the royal sea, then turn in different directions, obeying the tiny compasses on their noses—southwest for the Bay of Silk to Padma, north to home and Valerie, across the Royal Square to Amber, west to the Fire Isles and Edel, and out to Hana in the Glass Isles near the barrier of Orléans. The sun lights a path for my balloons as they hover above the dark ocean, careful not to get swept into the masts of large imperial ships. Air-postmen glide about in open-top dirigibles with hooks and paddles to help guide the balloons along.

I watch until I can't see them anymore.

I unlatch my beauty caisse. The tiered compartments fan open, exposing a medley of beauty instruments tucked into nooks and crannies. I search for a place to store the pastels. I run my fingers along the ruby-red interior and discover a hidden drawer at the very bottom. A shiver of excitement rushes through my hands. How have I never seen this before?

I gently pull. It inches forward, and I wiggle it until the whole section is out. The tiny cubby holds a lace-wrapped book. I remove the fabric to find a portrait of my mother, who stares up at me from the center of the leather.

Her smile brings tears to my eyes. It's her Belle-book. I press it to my chest and wish that somehow I could bring her back, like she could be remade from parchment and sinew and ink and memory. The binding is frayed, and the rope around its center barely holds in the contents. Her signature flowers, linneas, are embossed in gold along its spine; the paired blooms curve upside down.

I used to catch her thumbing through the book late at night when I was supposed to be asleep. I remember finally getting the courage to ask her about it. "It's my beauty book." She'd rubbed her weak fingers across the rope. "It has all the notes I kept while at court. You'll start one as soon as you leave here. Never tell anyone you've seen mine."

The memory brings tears to my eyes. I set her mortuary tablets on the desk.

She's been gone for the entire warm season, and now the windy season is settling over us. We didn't get to take the rowboats out to see the dragonflies, or walk the perimeter of the dark forest as the Belle-rosés bloomed for the last time before the cold crested over them, or taste the mint from our chef's kitchen garden, or wait for the noses of imperial ships to show up in the bayou.

*Don't cry,* she'd said when the other mothers started to get sick and when a few of them died. *Everything will be fine. This is the way it has always been.*

I put my Belle-book beside hers. I rub my fingers across the etching of her face, then open her book. As I touch her scribbled handwriting, I imagine she's not really gone—that she's just out for a few days, visiting an old client that moved from court to the Gold Isles.

I close my eyes and see her before she got sick: rich, flame-colored hair; skin like dove feathers; bright emerald eyes; a tiny, mischievous smile.

I turn the page and discover a folded piece of paper marked with my name. I open it.

*Camellia—*

*My darling, if you're reading this letter then I know you've just started the most remarkable time in your life, and I am gone. Inside this book you'll find things to help you adjust to the new challenges. Guard it. You're not supposed to have another Belle's beauty book. Du Barry forbids* it. This was supposed to be burned along with my body. But I need you to have it. I wish my mother had given me hers. I would've known more. I want you to be prepared.

I have left you un miroir métaphysique, made from the magnificent crystal of the Glass Isles. It's a mirror that always tells the truth. At court and in the teahouses, you will find that what you see and feel and hear isn't always real. People aren't always who they say they are. This mirror reflects the soul. Use it when you feel lost. Prick your beautiful little finger and drop the blood onto the handle, and it will show you what you need to see.

I love you, ma petit. I'm with you always. The best part of my life was the time I had with you.

With all my love,

Your maman


I wipe away a tear and take the tiny gilded mirror from the inside crease of the book. I look at the glass, but it's blank, without a reflection. "Strange," I say.

Miniature roses are etched into the molding, and it fits in the palm of my hand. A thin chain loops through an opening in the handle. Grooved pathways and indentations travel up and around the glass like a series of streams and rivers.

I remove a needle from my beauty caisse, but hesitate to feel the sting. I brace myself for the prick of pain as I poke the needle into my forefinger. A small bead of blood oozes out. I push my finger against the very tip of the mirror's handle, and the blood pools inside an indentation. The liquid stretches into a long line, as if it's a rope being tugged forward. The streak courses through the gilded grooves, headed for the glass. It snakes along, climbing higher and higher. The red stream circles the glass and bathes the little roses. They redden, and their thorny stems lengthen and twist into words: BLOOD FOR TRUTH.

The glass fills with an image of me—perfectly applied makeup, Belle-bun without a single hair out of place, eyes that smile. The mirror fogs and empties again before a new image shows. Red-rimmed eyes full of tears gaze back at me. My mouth quivers like it's about to release a deep sob. Puffy brown cheeks are smeared with rouge and powder. My loneliness feels like a dark cloud that could be trapped and put in a jar.

I go to the vanity in my room and look in the mirror there. My makeup is intact. I gaze back down at the tiny glass and stick out my tongue, but the sad image of me doesn't change. I cover it with my palm, trying to get rid of this heartsick feeling. I read Maman's letter again, tracing my fingers along her words: *This mirror reflects the soul.*

I clean the blood from the mirror, and drape the chain over my head. The cool metal grazes my skin.

I continue to turn the pages of my mother's beauty book, devouring everything: ink drawings, rouge-stick color smudges, flower petals, and collaged petit-paintings; beauty pamphlets, spintria prices, diagrams of women's bodies. Well-organized hand-writing blocks note lady courtiers' names, their beauty services and secrets, and tips to tackling unforeseen treatment challenges, like stubborn moles and missing bones.

The pages make a lovely crackling sound as I study the treat-ment price list from her generation.

SURFACE MODIFICATIONS:

HAIR COLOR    45

HAIR TEXTURE    62

EYE COLOR RESTORATION    30

EYE SHAPE ADJUSTMENT    45

SKIN COLOR RESTORATION    40

ANTI-AGING SKIN TIGHTENING    55

DEEP MODIFICATIONS:

FACE:

     CHEEKBONE SCULPTING    3,000

     MOUTH PLACEMENT AND SHAPE    2,275

     EAR PLACEMENT AND SHAPE    2,275

BODY:

     LEG AND ARM SCULPTING    3,250

     STOMACH, BREAST, TORSO SCULPTING    5,100

     HIPS AND REAR SHAPING    5,000

     NECK AND SHOULDER SMOOTHING    2,107

     HANDS AND FEET ADJUSTMENT    1,200

Du Barry will release her pricing for the season soon. It will be printed in every newspaper, plastered all over every newspaper, tattler, and pamphlet. My nail circles the little spintria symbol, and I wonder how Du Barry and the Beauty Minister quantify the price of beauty. I remember eavesdropping as a little girl while the Beauty Minister and Du Barry spoke in her office about beauty trends and body parts, and how much the masses should pay to be beautiful.

My bedroom door opens. "Lady Camellia," a servant says.

I put the book back in the base of the beauty caisse. "Yes?"

"It's time for your first beauty session."

# 23

The morning appointment ledger shows:

*Princess Sabine Rotenberg, House of Orléans (du sang) 09:00*

*Lady Marcella Le Brun, House of Millinery 10:15*

*Baroness Juliette Aubertin, House of Rouen 11:15*

I pin my hair up into a Belle-bun and dress in a dark cotton work dress and apron. Bree ties my waist-sash on.

"Tighter," I whisper, wanting it to subdue the flutters inside my stomach. I drape the necklace holding the mirror around my neck, and tuck it inside my dress.

"What is that?" Bree asks.

The metal cools my too-hot skin. "Just something for luck."

"The God of Luck has already blessed you." She squeezes my arm. A pair of faded blue eyes stare at me. Dry curls peek out from under her hat. A gray tinge lingers just under the whiteness of her skin, and tiny patches of whiskers crop up along her cheeks.

I smile back at her, then touch her face. "I'm going to give you a few beauty touch-ups."

"I couldn't allow that, my lady. I don't have a beauty token. Plus, I have an appointment at the Silk Teahouse for late Saturday night. That's when they do servants."

"It can be our little secret."

Her eyes brighten. "I couldn't—"

"I insist. And you must do as I say," I tease. "Right?"

Her mouth fights away a smile. "Well, yes."

"So that's that. If there's any trouble about it, say I let you off early to go to the teahouse. Tell them I'm a tyrant about beauty."

She giggles. "I'll make sure you get the tattlers and newspapers."

"No. Don't risk the punishment. "

"I will. It's the least I can do." She hugs me, then pulls back. "I'm so sorry, my lady. I don't know what came over me."

I wrap my arms around her and hug even tighter. She lets go and still has the biggest grin on her face. "I'll see that the final preparations are complete." She curtsies and slips from the room.

I take one last look at Maman's Belle-book, reviewing her notes about her very first beauty session. *Be gentle and be quick.* I take a deep breath and put it in the hidden space at the base of my beauty caisse.

Ivy walks into the bedroom with an ocean-blue post-balloon. "This came for you."

I take the tail ribbons from her. I've never seen a post-balloon like this. Up close it's covered in tiny waves, and makes a sound like the tide.

"Are you ready?" she asks.

"Yes, I think so."

"I'll be in the main salon."

I open the back of the balloon, and fish the note from the compartment. My fingers tremble with curiosity, confusion, and excitement. I open the privacy casing, breaking the seal.

*Newest Favorite Belle,*
*Make sure not to turn anyone purple.*
*Good luck.*
*Yours,*
*Auguste*


I laugh, and read his words three more times. Bree returns to the room.

"Lady Camellia," she says. "What is so funny?"

"Nothing," I say, holding the paper to my chest.

"Her Royal Highness Princess Sabine has arrived. She is in the main salon."

I turn around. "Then let's go."

I tuck the tiny paper inside my Belle-book, then press a hand to my chest, trying to get my heart to slow. The cool surface of the mirror brushes against my skin. I take a deep breath, hold it, then walk to the main salon.

*I am ready.*

Ivy sits at the edge of the room. She almost blends in with the room's trappings, like a flower arrangement. On a puffy cream settee is Princess Sabine Rotenberg. Gray and white strands snake through dark hair. An attendant announces me. The woman whips around and leaps off the couch.

"Lady Camellia." She takes my hands and sweeps me into a hug. She smells of rose water.

"Your Highness." I pull back, then discreetly wipe my arms and face. Powder covers my hands.

"My apologies. I've been waiting so long to see you, I had to resort to covering my skin to hide the gray, and I'm even wearing eye films. They're so painful, you know. I almost broke down and went to the Chrysanthemum Teahouse. As I've gotten older, it pushes through so much harder." She pats her forehead with a handkerchief. "It's disgusting, like in the old days. People would walk around court looking like rotten chicken ready for frying." She thrusts the beauty key into my hands. "And this, before I forget."

"Yes, and thank you."

Bree approaches, takes the key, and fits it into a slot on a velveteen board.

Princess Sabine is strikingly beautiful, despite the tiniest hints of gray. Sand-colored skin, a perfectly sloped nose, and a rosebud mouth. She's wearing one of the Fashion Minister's new "vivant" day dresses that vary their color every few seconds. Hers changes from gossamer to quicksilver to a stormy blue. She motions at one of her attendants, who sets up an easel with a beauty board on it. The surface is covered with courtier portraits and tiny beads from broken beauty-scopes. I run my fingers across the color swatches she's tacked onto it, and the rouge smudges smeared at the corners.

"I want you to combine a few looks," she says, settling back on the settee. Bree brings out the tea tray, and she takes a cup. "My beauty consultants mocked this up. They are certain the next beauty trend will be textured hair-towers, heart-shaped faces and lips—like a matched set—and freckled skin. Don't you just love freckles? And I want my waist as small as possible within the queen's limits. After my last child, deeper body work around my middle just doesn't settle for long. One slice of bread too many sends me back to the Belles quite often."

I nod, my head filing each request into my memory. "I plan to bring round waists back into fashion as they were last year."

She bites her bottom lip. "I'll try that next time. For now, more freckles. Did I say that already? They're so youthful. On my nose, especially, like little ants on a log. Could you get rid of some of these wrinkles, too? And I'd like my nose smaller this time around. Don't overdo it. One time, last year, a Belle made my nose so small I could hardly breathe. I should've never gone to anyone other than Ivy, but I was in a pinch. I had a gala. I felt light-headed for a whole week. I had to be carried around in a palanquin. I got so tired of hiring the man power to lift me." She giggles.

"Your nose shape fits well with your face. The heart shape—"

"You're so kind." She pats my hand and gulps down the rest of her tea. "Do they train you all to lie so well?" She waves the empty teacup in her hands for a servant to take away. "So, I'd like to use my beauty token for the waist adjustment, and I'll pay spintria for the other services. I'd like an eye color close to yours. I know it's impossible to have your amber-colored eyes, but let's try, shall we? And let's start my blond transformation. Dark blond, then I'll go gradually lighter to white as the snow comes—yes, yes—that's what I'll do. My ladies will be amused. The newsies might enjoy the transformation. I'll get more press. Maybe another feature in the scopes—or better yet, a scope *and* a profile in the *Dulce* pamphlet. My husband likes darker hair, but I don't care." She stands, and marches over to the wall mirror. "Also, if we have time, could you fix my lips? They're looking very fishlike today."

"Are you sure you want all of these things done at once? What about the pain?"

"Of course." She scoffs, then eyes me. "If I could have you rebuild me from the bones out, I'd do that as well. I can tolerate it. I'm strong." Her eyes glaze over with tears. "I'd do anything to be beautiful."

Her statement thuds inside my chest. Heavy. Maman's words echo inside me: *The people of Orléans hate the way they look.*

She takes a deep breath and the tears vanish.

"We won't need all of that. We could just touch up your skin and—"

"Stop lying to me," she shouts. "I know what I look like."

Movement in the room freezes. I bristle and look over at Ivy. She clutches her hands together in a tight, tense squeeze. I don't take a breath. Why did I question a client again?

The princess places a hand on my shoulder. "I'm sorry to yell. It's just, when I don't look my best, I don't feel settled inside or like my true self." She sits up straight. "You can soften my temper while you're at it, too. I need to become nicer. Sweeter. I'm a hard edge these days." She lets out a sigh. "I'm ready. I'm looking forward to our time together." She snaps at her attendants, and they lead her off to the bathing onsen. Nerves flutter inside me like bayou fireflies.

"Just do what you're told," I whisper to myself, "and everything will be fine."

# 24

I flip over the one large hourglass on the mantel in the treatment room. Sand swirls from one end to the other, keeping track of the beauty-treatment time.

I take deep breaths. Princess Sabine lies underneath a lace cloth. The House Orléans crest is all she wears—a tiny emerald serpent swallowing a chrysanthemum over her identification tattoo. This indicates she's a direct relative of the queen. The pendant sits on her bare collarbone.

Sabine is the first of many. There will be more men and women waiting to be changed, anticipating perfect results. There are expectations: to be better than Amber, to please Sophia, to satisfy the queen despite being her second choice, to make the kingdom fall in love with me. The pressure curls around me like the serpent on Princess Sabine's emblem. I gaze down at her body. Her desires parade through my mind like a series of télétrope images—each more complex than the next.

Servants wheel in tiered trays bursting with skin-color pastilles and rouge pots, brushes and combs and barrel irons, tonics and creams, bei-powder bundles, waxes and perfumes, measuring rods and metal instruments, and sharpened kohl pencils. My beauty caisse is set up behind me, fanned open so the medley of instruments inside twinkle in the subtle light. I think of Maman's Belle-book in its base, comforted by the thought that a piece of her is nearby.

Tiny clusters of beauty-lanterns drift over the princess like night stars. Perfect beads of light reveal the cherry red of her fluttering eyes and the gray of her skin. They highlight what needs to be done.

I look at the beauty board sitting on an easel. Color smudges streak across it and display Princess Sabine's chosen skin, hair, and eye color palette, and bodily proportions.

Ivy watches my every movement. I try to be perfect.

"Princess Sabine." I lean forward. "Are you ready?"

"Yes," she says. "Yes, yes."

I fold back the lace and expose her graying legs. Their bodies always fade before their faces. At the end of each month, the skin color drifts away like dust caught in the wind.

"Please remove the hair from the princess's legs," I direct a servant.

"Yes, miss," she replies, coating Sabine's legs with honey-scented wax.

After my client is hairless, I glide a kohl pencil over her skin like it's parchment. Lines of symmetry run through the body like the architecture of beautiful buildings. It creates the perfect harmony preferred by the Goddess of Beauty.

I mark Sabine's breasts so they will be enlarged to the size of snowmelons, and move the pencil down her stomach, making a series of hachure lines so as to smooth out the small depressions. I draw circles on her waist and legs to indicate spots to polish. I place a measuring lace on her face, and my hand shakes as I draw contour lines along the fabric onto the woman's nose and forehead and cheeks.

I take bei-powder bundles from my beauty caisse and shake them over her. The white flakes coat her like flour. I use a paint-brush to spread the powder, a trick Maman taught me, to coat it evenly.

"Very nice," Ivy whispers.

Her compliment spurs me forward.

The deep lines of the kohl pencil on Sabine's stomach show beneath the powder like avenues covered with snow. I step forward. I pull out her arms and cross them over her chest. The empty weight of them feels like Maman's did before she died.

"Pastilles, please," I say.

Bree wheels over a cart of chafing dishes. Triangular color blocks sit on tiered trays like a series of sugary petit-cakes. They melt in glass skin-tone pots creating every pigment imaginable: ink black, sandy beige, eggshell white, desert brown, lemony cream, soft sable, brown sugar syrup, and more.

I use a flat blade from my beauty caisse to cut a slice from the ivory-white and sandy-beige blocks. I also take a wedge of the soft sable for the freckles. Bree hands me an empty pigment pot. I swirl the colors together until they blend into a richness that matches a sliced almond. I spread a smudge across her arm. It seeps into the dry and wrinkled folds.

I identify all the smaller pigments—the rich browns and tans and whites—that help make the hue bright and uniform. Maman used to make me tell her all the pigments that made up the deep red of an apple, or the brown of a peanut. It was her nightly test for me while I was studying skin transformations. While the other mothers forced my sisters to trace their cursive letters, I worked on shades and spectrums. *The core of beauty is color,* Maman used to remind me when I complained about her exercises.

All three arcana wake up inside me. I soften her temper. I push the color down into her skin. I smooth away the tiny wrinkles.

The woman's soft moans echo off the walls.

I wipe off the paste. The color climbs over the woman's body, changing it from pale gray to soft beige with yellowy undertones.

Ivy circles me and watches over my shoulder. "Ask her if she's all right," she whispers.

"Princess Sabine, how are you doing?" I say close to her ear.

She grimaces out a reply. "I'll be fine."

I use another flat blade over her stomach.

She shifts a little. I close my eyes, picturing her body. I think of her hips as a pair of overly frosted crème-cakes. The tool scrapes away the layers. She squirms and sighs. I lift the blade and start to ask her if we should leave her natural shape intact. But Ivy's hand finds mine. "Keep going," she whispers.

I rub the instrument across her stomach again, and it flattens with each stroke, the extra skin and bulk beneath it melting away, her waist growing smaller.

She grips the edges of the table. Her knuckles whiten. I quicken my strokes. I chip away at the pelvic bones, just a pinch on each side.

She cries out. "It's much more painful than usual. I can't tolerate it."

"More Belle-rose tea should help." I wave for Bree. She approaches with a cup and helps to sit Princess Sabine up. Her stomach and hips glow red in the subtle darkness. She lifts the facial mesh and gulps down the tea. "Why can't the Royal Apothecary give us something stronger to withstand it?"

My brain is a fog of nerves and worries. "I...I—"

Ivy steps forward. "Princess Sabine. It's me, Ivy."

"Oh—Ivy."

"Yes." Ivy's soft voice puts Princess Sabine at ease. "Anything stronger than Belle-rose numbs the blood, Your Highness. The arcana will not work." She holds the base of Princess Sabine's teacup, helping her take larger sips. "I put Belle-rose elixir in this pot. It'll be a bit stronger for you."

The princess's eyelids droop, and her mouth softens. "Yes, I suppose that worked. I feel much better." Bree helps her lie back down.

"Quickly now," Ivy says to me. "You're taking too long—hesitating and perfecting too much. They can't tolerate the pain in long increments, and it isn't good for you, either."

"But she said she wanted it all at once."

"They always want it all at once, but we have to guide them. We have to be wiser."

I nod and look up at the hourglass. Almost time for my next appointment.

In my head the rest of her beauty requests arrange like a checklist:

*New nose*
*Smooth wrinkles*
*New eye color*
*Brighten skin color*
*New mouth shape*
*Freckles*

*Smaller waist*

*Lighten the hair*

*Soften the hair texture*

*Sweeten her disposition*

Sweat drips down my brow. I promised Sabine I'd get it all done. My heart accelerates. My hands wobble. She clenches her teeth. The grinding is loud enough for me to hear.

I rush through the changes to her face. My eyesight is blurry from fatigue. I try to hold myself still, but my legs start to give. I drop a metal rod, the room swirls into a kaleidoscope of colors, and then—darkness.

"Camellia!"

"Camellia!"

"Camellia!"

My arms shake, and I open my eyes. Ivy stands above me. "You've done too much all at once."

Princess Sabine is craning over the edge of the table, vomiting into a bucket. She screams and cries as she spews. Her skin is an angry red, like she's just stepped out of a scalding bath. Two servants drape a lacy covering over her naked body. Another holds her new honey-colored hair up above her head. Bree tries to hold the bucket steady.

"I'm s-sorry." My head feels like it might float off, like one of the beauty-lanterns.

"Princess Sabine, our apologies," Ivy says.

Servants help Sabine back into the bathing chamber for an ice bath. Ivy reaches for me before my eyes close again.

# 25

The gentle warmth of a damp cloth wakes me. For a moment, I'm back at home. The bedcurtains fluttering across an open window. The bayou birds' morning melody, floating through the room. Maman leaning over me. Her fingers sweeping back my curls. A kiss on my forehead. *You'd kill yourself to be the best*, she whispers in my ear. *You always do too much.*

I reach for her hand, but my arms feel pinned to my sides.

"Camellia, wake up. Can you hear me?" a voice calls out. "Camellia."

Maman's face fades away like dust. My eyes startle open. Ivy's dark veil frightens me. I try to sit up, but needles are sticking out of my arms, and tubes snake through the blankets.

I panic and try to rip them out of my skin.

Ivy stops me. "Don't! You're getting fluids."

"What happened?"

"Be quiet," she whispers, then looks behind her. "I don't want the nurses knowing you're up yet." She climbs onto the bed and closes the curtains. We're bathed in darkness until she lights a morning-lantern and sets it afloat above us. It blinds me.

"What's wrong?" I ask.

"I need you to pay attention."

The beauty appointment with Princess Sabine floods back with a hot wave of embarrassment and shame.

"Is Princess Sabine—"

"She's fine. In one of the recovery chambers. You pushed yourself, and the arcana, too hard when you tried to rush," she says. "You can't do those treatments all at once. You must learn to refuse. You should only do three at a time, especially when you have back-to-back appointments. Your arcana levels took a massive dip."

"Why didn't you tell me this when Sabine was making her demands?"

"I thought you knew better."

"How low were my levels?"

"Three point five for Manner, three point two for Age, and two point four for Aura," Ivy says, and it's a punch to the stomach. "You've been asleep all day and night because of it. You missed your other two appointments."

All day and night?

"I completed them for you."

"Thank you," I say. Edel's face unexpectedly pops into my head. "And have you heard anything about my sister Edel?"

"It was just a rumor. She's fine. I overheard Du Barry talking to Madam Alieas at the Fire Teahouse. She said it was pure fabrication."

A sense of relief washes over me, but questions remain. Edel told me in secret she was going to run away, and then there was the headline about it. What are the chances of that? Perhaps someone overheard her saying she wanted to leave—and a newsie got wind of it? I hope she'll be more careful.

I try to sit up again, but I'm weak and shaky.

"Don't try to move. If you're too loud, the other servants will alert the Beauty Minister immediately. We don't get much time"—she leans in—"away from others."

She's close enough for me to see underneath her veil a little, and she lingers there, as if she wants me to. Tiny creases ring her eyes and mouth. Why would she have wrinkles? We don't age the same as the Gris. Maman had very few, even up to her death.

"You must pace yourself. You haven't been here a whole week yet," she says.

I rest my head in my hands. "I wanted her to tell the court that I gave her everything she'd asked for," I admit. "I wanted to prove that I should've been the favorite from the start."

"You'll burn out if you overexert yourself, and you'll end up like Ambrosia."

"What actually happened to her?"

Ivy hesitates, then lowers her voice to the quietest whisper. "Princess Sophia had—"

The bedcurtains snap open. The morning-lantern zips out. One of the Beauty Minister's servants stares at us.

"Oh, you're awake?" The Beauty Minister peers in. "And Ivy, what in the name of the gods are you doing in bed with the favorite? Now, what if this hit the tattlers? It'd be an incest scandal."

Ivy slinks out. "Just checking on her, Madam Minister."

"Well, go tend to something else. The nurses are here to look after her. She doesn't need additional fawning." She shoos Ivy off with a flick of her delicate wrist. "How are you feeling, darling?"

"A little tired, but better."

"Get her up on her feet," she orders her servants and mine. "And have tea and a late lunch brought to the main salon. She needs her strength."

Bree rushes forward with a smile. She removes the needles from my arms and helps me out of bed. I slip on a fur robe. My legs feel soft and rubbery and unable to support my weight. Bree holds me up. "I've got you," she whispers.

"Thank you," I reply. I find my footing and walk behind the Beauty Minister into the main salon. We sit in a pair of matching chairs.

"You did splendidly with Princess Sabine. She's been raving about you." She leans over and kisses my clammy cheeks. "You now have a month-long waiting list."

"Really? I didn't think it went so well."

"You gave her everything she wanted. She can't wait to have another session with you."

Relief surges through me.

"And look! There's a congratulatory post-balloon from Madam Du Barry, and another from the princess. They've left a trail of glitter throughout the chambers." The post-balloons spit out little fireworks, one crimson and the other rose-petal pink and cream. They dance around the room like children. Their ribbons swish and sweep the floor. I think of the one Auguste sent, and the memory of his words makes me smile—a shimmer of light in all this darkness.

Servants park lunch carts beside us brimming over with cheese towers, spires of tomatoes, and piles of sweet rope bread and sliced meat. The minister nibbles, and I eat ravenously.

"When will I get to work with the queen?" I want to show her what I can do and prove to her that I can be who she needs me to be.

The Beauty Minister stifles a laugh, then looks up from her

teacup. "Eager mouse, aren't we? You have much more work to do before that."

"But I have a waiting list."

"Patience, little love." She smiles indulgently. "Eat up. You have another beauty appointment this afternoon."

"I do?"

"The princess has requested you." The Beauty Minister taps my arm. "Even though she usually waits to see how the favorite settles in. The new hair you gave her for her birthday party was quite impressive. Very inventive. Landed her in the scopes for the first time. The press corps loved it."

"Thank you," I say, filling with equal parts excitement and worry. "I wanted to please her."

"I hope you can continue to do so," she says.

After lunch, Bree and Rémy walk with me to the princess's chambers. Bree pushes a trolley with my beauty caisse. Courtiers point and whisper as we pass through the palace corridors. I square my shoulders and try to feel less exhausted. A newsie post-balloon hovers overhead. Rémy pushes it away.

"I hate these things," he says.

"Not exciting enough for you?" I ask.

"Newspapers are pointless."

"Not all of them."

"Most of them spread lies."

"Some lies are delicious," I say.

He doesn't laugh. "Lies are as dangerous as a sword. They can cut to the bone." Rémy posts himself beside the princess's doors like a statue. He's back to his old self, the cold Rémy I first met, instead of the one who tried to make poor jokes and ask me questions the night of Sophia's birthday. I sigh at him. His expression remains fixed.

Bree lifts the brass knocker. Its heavy booms radiate through the chamber. A servant cracks open the door.

"Lady Camellia, welcome," she says. "We're just about ready for you."

The servant scurries to an adjacent room, leaving us alone in the chamber foyer. The jewel-box room is no longer pink, cream, and gold. Cerulean walls hold golden fleurs-de-lis and the princess's royal emblem. Frost-white chairs and chaises crowd around tables like swans floating on a serene pond.

The servant returns for us. "She is ready."

Fear settles under my skin, and my hands quiver. But I know I can do this—I can impress her. I have to. We follow the servant into a massive treatment salon. Golden walls hug around us like we're trapped inside the sun. Cabinets burst with so many Belle-products, it could be the storeroom at home. Dozens of jeweled beauty-lanterns leave the perfect amount of light in each corner. One can't help but be beautiful in here. Tiered trays of rouge-sticks, complexion crème-cakes, skin-tone pots, and hair-color creams wink like diamonds beneath the light.

"Camellia." Princess Sophia rushes forward, wearing a sheer bathing gown. She slips her hands in mine. "I need you."

Her words sweep away the worries.

"My parents scheduled dates with my suitors, and I don't have the right look. I don't know what to do." She clings to me like I'm her last hope of survival. "The first one is tonight with Alexander Dubois from House Berry."

"I'm here, Princess. We'll find the right look for you."

She leans away and beams at me. "I knew you'd be perfect."

Sophia skips over to a cart of tiered vials. "The way you changed my hair for my birthday party was just the start. You're clever. You passed my first little test."

That was a test?

"Thank you, Your Highness," I say.

"I want to become a beauty tastemaker. A queen who sets trends, unlike my mother. And it's no secret that I haven't been featured in a single beauty-scope. At least not until you came along. I swear, it's like the newsies have a vendetta against me." She runs her fingers across the vials, plucks one filled with violet liquid, and yanks out the stopper with a loud *pop*. "I brew my own Belle-rose elixir and mix it with other medicinal plants. The elixirs Madam Du Barry supplies aren't strong enough to withstand the types of changes I want." She drinks the entire vial, then wipes her lips.

She pulls down her bathing gown and stands naked.

I quickly turn around. "Your Highness."

"Oh, don't be shy. You've probably seen countless bodies before."

"Well, yes, of course, but—"

"How does mine match up?"

My stomach churns. "What do you mean?"

"As my body returns to its natural state, I wonder how it stacks up against others. I'm too scared to let it turn fully gray and see exactly what I was born with. So tell me . . ."

"It would be inappropriate to compare, Your Highness. Plus—"

"Look at me," she yells, then softens. "Just look."

Her command jolts through me. I slowly pivot. She jams her hands to her hips. Her breasts are small apples, and her stomach is smooth.

"Don't you quantify us? Break us into parts? Tabulate what features are more beautiful than others?"

"Yes, but—"

"Then you must have an opinion."

"I don't see you that way."

"How noble of you. I bet Du Barry taught you to say that. To make us feel better."

"I don't listen to everything Du Barry says."

She smiles.

"I shouldn't say that—"

She raises a hand and wipes away my apology. "No need. I won't tell her." She uses a footstool to climb into the treatment bed. Servants tuck her in. "I'm ready. Come."

Sophia reaches her hand out to me. I take it. She squeezes. "Make me the most beautiful," she says, then closes her eyes.

Bree drapes her face with the measuring lace. The cloth drifts up and down as Sophia takes deep breaths. I shake out the nerves in my fingers. Bree nods encouragingly. I press my hands to my stomach, then run them over the mascara cakes and pastille waxes and hair-color pomades and texture wands.

Sophia's breathing slows. It's so quiet in the room I can hear each inhale and exhale. I cover her with bei powder and brush it into her hair. The two-toned hair color I gave her still shines brightly. My hands tremble. I'm caught off guard. If I'd known I would be working with Sophia today, I would've planned out every single moment.

*Make her beauty mean something.* Maman's wisdom echoes inside of me.

"Are you going to begin or just play with my hair?" Sophia says.

"Yes, Your Highness." My mind whizzes through dozens of looks like the spinning of a roulette wheel. Pictures of her from the tattlers, the scandal sheets, the newspapers, and the beauty magazines. I strike certain color schemes and hair textures from consideration. I want to do something original.

I close my eyes.

My nerves tingle with power. The arcana stir inside me like flickering candles. The warmth moves from the bottom of my toes to the crown of my head and the very tips of my fingers. Bree helps me paint her hair with oil-black hair cream, then streak it with red. I plunge my hands into the strands, pushing the color through it. I wrap a tendril around a rod to give her the perfect coil, and mix two skin tones together—seashell white and a dark citrine brown. The skin colors her parents each chose for themselves.

Not a drop of sweat appears on her face. Kohl pencil marks map the changes I'll make: higher cheekbones like her mother's, a button nose like her father's, and deep sloping eyes. I resist the urge to do more, remembering Ivy's warning and what happened last time.

"Your Highness," I whisper.

"Yes," she replies.

"I'm finished."

"So quickly? You didn't do any body work."

"I wanted to be sure I was headed in the right direction first."

Sophia springs up. "Bring the full-length." She slips back into her bathing gown.

I wait for her praise, craving it like a hot luna pastry.

Three servants march forward with a gilded mirror. She eyes herself, running her hands through her hair and over her skin, then leans close to the glass, inspecting her new cheekbones and nose. She bats her eyes, then pivots to see her profile. "I look too much like my mother."

"I did that on purpose, since the queen is incredibly beautiful." I search her face for any trace of happiness.

"I know she's *beautiful*. But I don't want to look like anyone else. I want to look like no one in the entire kingdom." She studies her naked body. "Try again, favorite. And give me larger breasts. The size of grapefruits. They always seem to shrivel down by the middle of the month. Also, a creaseless eyelid. Those are trendy now."

The air streams out of me like a crumpled post-balloon.

She gulps down another vial of Belle-rose elixir. Her servants help her back onto the treatment bed.

I take a deep breath. Bree hands me a square of chocolate and whispers, "For strength." She winks. "And patience."

I smile at her. "Thank you."

The chocolate dissolves on my tongue, and I think about the pounds of the stuff we devoured in the lesson rooms. I remember when Du Barry paired us up to change our very first person. In our lesson rooms, we'd stood beside the beds, and Penelope the kitchen sous chef had lain across mine. Hana and I held hands as we gave her a new hair color, eye color, and skin tone. But it all turned out brassy orange, and took three more tries to get it right. Du Barry had fed us chocolate squares to help us maintain our stamina.

I erase Sophia's new skin color and make her beige as a crepe. I use a hand-iron to press out the coil in her hair and give her strands as straight as a board. I add a teardrop curve to her eyelids, and take away the crease. I add thirteen tiny freckles to a new, slenderer nose. I use metal tongs to pull at her skin to add volume to her breasts and curvature to her waist.

She looks like Hana. It makes me miss my sister.

Sweat drips down my cheeks. Bree hands me a glass of water, which I drink down in one gulp.

"I'm finished," I say.

She jumps out of bed and goes straight to the mirror again, examining herself from all angles. "The breasts are perfect. And I like the hips. But"—she pivots to face me—"I've never liked dark hair." She fingers her waist-long strands. "It was always my mother's—and sister's—preferred shade." Sophia kisses my cheek. "You are strong, yes?"

"The strongest," I say.

She giggles. "Let's try again. I'm not quite satisfied."

I force a smile and turn my back to her, pretending to rifle through a cabinet of Belle-products. Sophia gulps down another vial of Belle-rose elixir and climbs back onto the treatment bed. I press a hand to my stomach, trying to slow my breathing. Exhaustion seeps into every part of me.

I wave Bree over. "Bring me my leeches, please, and quickly."

"Yes, my lady." She scurries off.

I run my fingers across glass pots, opening and closing compacts as if I'm preparing, until Bree returns moments later. She opens the porcelain jar, flashing its slimy contents. I reach my fingers in and grab a leech. It writhes within my grip. I hook the creature around the back of my neck. Its tiny teeth bite the skin. I wait to feel the tingle of its secretions pumping into me.

I steel myself and return to Sophia's bedside. I mix a new skin color—rich pearl white and buttermilk. I recreate the same two-toned hair color with a deep scarlet and ash blond. I give her my mother's face—thin sloping nose, light brown freckles, a pink bow of a mouth. In my current state, my mother's visage is all that will come to me.

"Done," I say, almost out of breath.

"A looking-glass," Sophia says. Her attendant holds the hand mirror over her and she smiles. "This is perfect for now. A good start." Sophia's eyes bob open and shut. "I've had too much Belle-rose elixir to do this anymore."

Her attendants help her shimmy into a robe and out of the room. When the doors close behind her, I collapse forward onto the treatment bed.

"Are you all right, my lady?" Bree asks, but my mouth is too tired to open. She helps me into a chair.

The overuse of the arcana dulls my senses; the room feels thicker around me, and I feel too thin to be part of it. My legs shake and coat with sweat. My limbs are light as feathers, ready to drift off in the wind.

She hands me a cup of spicy cayenne tea and another sliver of chocolate, and adds a leech to each wrist. I close my eyes and sink into a nap.

Bree jostles my shoulder. "Lady Camellia, it's time to go. Do you feel better?"

I stumble awake. "Yes. How long was I asleep?"

"An hourglass's worth of time."

We walk out of the treatment salon. My legs are more like putty than bone. Bree's cart rattles behind me. I have to think about each step, willing my feet to move.

The boudoir doors snap open. Rémy is waiting in the same spot I left him. His dark eyes hold concern. "Do you need help?"

"No, I'm fine." The edges of the hall fade into a haze.

Bree hands me another square of chocolate. "I'll meet you back at your room," she reassures me, then heads off in the direction of the servants' lifts.

Rémy offers me his arm.

"Where are you running off to?" a voice says.

It's Auguste.

# 26

Auguste leans against one of the marble columns, thumping at a dying night-lantern. His hair is out of its usual knot, in a mess around his shoulders. Freckles create a trail across his cheeks. He wears a betrothal pin on his lapel—a reminder that he's one of the princess's suitors.

An unexpected shiver rushes through me. I pull my shoulders back, open my eyes wide, and try to feel—and look—less exhausted. He smiles and stares as if he's waiting for me to say something first. I bite the inside of my cheek and fuss with my hands, if only to have something to do.

"What are you doing here?" is all I can manage.

"I can't be in the hall?" he replies.

"I meant—"

"You thought I was waiting for you," he says.

"I didn't say—"

"I'm not tracking you, if that's your concern." He shifts position, moving closer.

Rémy steps forward, his jaw clenched. His hand goes to the dagger at his side.

"Not to worry," Auguste says. "I don't plan on harming her."

I scoff.

Auguste smiles. He points at Rémy. "Serious, this one is."

I stifle a laugh.

"Maybe *she's* following *me*," he tells Rémy.

Rémy doesn't laugh. His grimace deepens.

"I just came from a session with the princess," I say.

"Well, aren't you lucky."

"Tired is more like it." I move closer to Auguste, away from Rémy. It feels like I've stepped into a bubble with him. The hall's grand staircase and white marble columns vanish. Nearby courtiers melt away. Rémy turns into a statue. The rules Du Barry made me swallow down about fraternizing with men and boys outside of beauty work vanish. It's just the two of us talking, and it feels both deliciously terrifying and fascinating. I am a tangle of giggles and distractions and delirium. I should be back in the Belle apartments. I should be checking my arcana levels. I should be resting after hours of beauty work.

"Did you get the post-balloon I sent?" he asks.

"Oh, yes." That memory is still warm.

"Well, aren't you going to say thank you? Or send me one in return?"

I snort and immediately feel my cheeks redden. "You sent it yesterday morning, so you haven't given me much time."

"Take a walk with me."

I fight back a smile and try to frown. "Why should I?"

"Why shouldn't you?"

"You're a stranger. And—"

"You know my name. I'm Auguste Fabry, dreadful son of the Minister of the Seas. We've met before. We're best friends, even though I suspect you don't like me much. Plus, I sent you a post-balloon."

"I've received many post-balloons. Am I supposed to walk with every single sender?"

"Aren't you popular?"

"I am. Didn't you hear?"

"Hear what?"

I lean in and whisper, "I'm the favorite."

"Is that so?" His mouth breaks into a dimpled smile. "I hadn't heard. I must be living at the very edge of the world."

"You must be," I say, "at the kingdom's rock barrier, for sure."

He laughs. I laugh. Our eyes meet for a brief second, and then I look away. Excitement bubbles up in my chest like I'm an over-flowing champagne flute. My mouth, once tired, now can't stop moving.

Rémy clears his throat. The bubble pops. Well-dressed court-iers step out of the glittering chariots that lift people from one palace floor to another. Imperial servants carry trays in and out of rooms. Newsies send their black gossip post-balloons and navy story post-balloons through the halls, hoping to catch a snippet of something for the newsreels and tattlers and scandal sheets. People lift spyglasses to their eyes and slide ear-trumpets from their pockets.

"Take a walk with me," Auguste asks again.

And even with the world come to life around us once more, I nod. I can't seem to help myself.

"You're easy to convince."

"I can just as easily return to my apartments."

"No, come." He offers his arm, but I shake my head. "Right. Those *rules* again. I thought you said you didn't follow them."

"I don't, but just because I don't want to take your arm doesn't mean I'm following protocol. Maybe I'm worried you're carrying sickness. Or maybe you don't smell very nice."

He sniffs himself. "I'll be sure to wear cologne next time so I won't smell like sea and the pier market."

"You don't smell like—"

"I didn't want to take your arm anyway." He smirks.

I roll my eyes, and we walk out of a smaller palace exit. Rémy trails us. The burn of his gaze on my back is like the warmth of a candle too close to your skin.

One of the topiary arcades that leads to the palace gardens holds peek-a-boo flowers that wink light. Night-lanterns shine bright as the watching moon; the glow clings to the curved hedges arched over us, and skims the surface of the palace river ahead. Gem-bright birds perch in dangling cages and lend their sweet songs to silent garden nooks.

"How does it feel to be back at court?" His questions always feel like challenges.

"It's great," I say, but Amber's face flashes in my head.

"I've never liked court much. I was lucky to be at sea with my father most of the time. He's grooming me for a boring life on a boat."

"Is that not what you want?"

"It's what my father wants," he says. "Did you always want to be a Belle?"

"Yes. I don't know what it would mean to be anything else."

"Didn't you ever wonder?"

"No."

He frowns, as if that's an incorrect answer to his question.

"What else is there?" I say.

"Ordinary life."

"What is that?" I say with a laugh. "And who would want that?"

"You could be a famed courtier. Only having to worry about dresses and gossip and landing in the scopes and papers."

"I'd rather have the responsibilities that I have," I say. "The duty."

"What if someone found a way to cure us?" he asked. "An elixir that could be bottled and could make everyone beautiful. Wouldn't your life be easier?"

A searing anger fills every part of me. "What I do—what my sisters do—could never be bottled!"

"I didn't mean to offend. It's just, I like to lead a carefree life. I suppose being on the water fosters that sort of temperament. The God of the Sea has no allegiances."

"You shouldn't assume everyone wants that," I snap.

"You're right."

Then his eyes narrow and he leans toward me. "There's something on your neck." Auguste touches a forgotten leech. He jumps back with a shout. "What is that disgusting thing?"

"Hah. It's just a leech. Are you afraid?" I tuck it back into its hiding place beneath a neck ruffle on my dress.

"Why do you have that?" He looks a tad green.

"Another secret of the Belles."

"A horrifying secret."

"They help reset our arcana and purify our blood. And don't insult the sangsues."

His eyebrows lift with curiosity. I realize I've said too much.

Du Barry's voice thunders inside me: *Don't reveal the secrets of the Belles.* The heat of my mistake lingers in my stomach.

"Clear the way," an attendant calls out. Four imperial servants carry a windowed palanquin. Its golden edges shine like a trapped sun in the early evening darkness. Inside rests the sleeping Princess Charlotte on an embroidered pillow. A veiled woman wearing a crown walks alongside the palanquin with her hand resting on the glass. A group of newsies trails closely behind.

"Where are they taking her?" I ask. "And who is that woman with her?"

"The princess is—" Auguste starts to say.

"Princess Charlotte takes the air every evening around this time. That's her Belle, Arabella," Rémy interrupts. "We should be going, Lady Camellia. I've received word that dinner has been served in your apartments, and Madam Du Barry awaits."

Reality crashes back in like a heavy ocean wave.

"Thank you for the walk," I say to Auguste.

"I'm sad it's over so soon." He smiles handsomely.

My cheeks flame again. "Good night."

"Good night," he says, "and don't forget to write me back. I'm waiting. I expect a response."

"Yes, all right."

I follow Rémy back inside. His footsteps clomp. I start to thank him for not insisting I return immediately to the Belle apartments. I know it can't be exciting to follow me around all day. Not when you're used to defending a kingdom or training for battles. But the words get stuck, and by the time we're back and he's taken his stance outside the doors, the moment seems lost.

Dinner carts sit in the main salon, chock-full of steaming hot food.

Bree greets me. "Where have you been?"

"I went for a walk." She removes the leech from my neck and helps undo my waist-sash.

"You're blushing, and your skin is all warm." She smiles. "Also, a post-balloon arrived for you several hours ago from the Chrysanthemum Teahouse. I tied it to your desk."

I leap toward my bedroom.

"Your dress is half unbuttoned," she yells out with a laugh.

A magenta post-balloon floats over my desk. The Chrysanthemum Teahouse emblem glimmers on its side. I open the back and fish for the letter inside the compartments. My fingers fuss with the fold. My heart thuds. I drop the note, then scoop it back up.

*Camille,*
*I'm sorry, too. And I'm all right.*
*I miss you.*
*Be careful.*
*Amber*

I turn the letter over. Pastel colors make a series of lines.

Another message reads:

I THINK EDEL HAS ESCAPED. AN IMPERIAL INVESTIGATOR CAME TO THE TEAHOUSE LOOKING FOR HER. BUT SOME OF MY CLIENTS TOLD ME THAT BEAUTY WORK CONTINUES THERE. DO YOU KNOW WHAT IS HAPPENING?

# 27

The bedcurtains snap open. Night-lanterns float in, their light glaring down on me. I cover my face. After tossing and turning, worrying about Edel, I feel as though I've just now fallen asleep and it couldn't possibly be morning.

"What is it?"

A sleepy-eyed Bree stares back. "You've been summoned."

"By whom?" I rub my eyes. "What time is it?"

"Her Highness, Princess Sophia." She pulls back the blankets. "And it's two hours after the midnight star."

"Why?"

"Her first servant, Cherise, didn't say." Bree drapes a fur-lined robe over my shoulders, and I step into slippers. "She said the princess wants you to come as you are."

I fuss with my hair, removing the silk scarf and trying to pull the mess of frizzy curls up into a Belle-bun.

"Come, quickly. She's in a foul mood and does not like to wait." Bree rushes me out of the Belle apartments, where Rémy awaits me.

"Good evening," I say.

"Actually, it's good morning," he corrects.

I sigh. "Do you know how annoying you are?"

"My older sister told me often." He walks ahead. I've memorized the way to Sophia's apartments, but we go in the opposite direction, toward the south wing of the palace. We pass grand ballrooms and glass solariums and ornate parlors.

"Where are we going?" I ask Rémy.

"Where I've been instructed to take you."

"And you wonder why I don't like having you around."

He stops, and faces me. "I was trying to joke with you."

"Well, you're terrible at it."

"I'll try harder next time." He stalks ahead again. "The princess requested you come to her private workshop."

"Do you know why?"

"They don't pay me to know, just to follow orders."

Thick black doors shine bright with the House of Inventors emblem—a chrysanthemum growing out of a stacked tower of cogs and gears. A trio of imperial guards block the entrance. Rémy salutes, they step aside, and he takes his place beside them.

The doors open. Enormous shelves scale the walls and split into hundreds of balconies. Books choke every spare place. Silver-gray work-lanterns dangle over long tables. Their surfaces are scattered with beakers, tubes, droppers, spoons, a set of mortars and pestles, and graters. A caged catlike animal with blond fur and black spots purrs. There are baskets full of flower petals, and a monstrous stove in the corner releases tiny clouds of steam. The shelves are lined with apothecary bottles that twinkle like jewels, as well as clear jars and magnificent flasks containing resins, balms, waxes, and oils made from flowers, plant secretions, and

extracts. Powder puffs, brushes, and pots of rouge sit like macarons on a sweets tray.

Sophia is peering into two flower terrariums, tapping her fingers against the glass. One contains bloodroot, a flower with white
petals and a yellow center. The other holds pale pink and white
blooms in starry clusters—mountain laurel. She coos at the flowers as if they're teacup pets. Her hair is a static-filled cloud around
her shoulders. Her pale skin is flushed pink with anxiety. She still
looks like my mother, and I regret the decision. It turns my stomach.

"Camellia." Sophia rushes forward. Her nightgown sweeps
behind her like a tail. "I want to show you something special." She
smells like sweat and salt. The whites of her eyes are bloodshot.
"My favorite." She takes my hand and drags me merrily forward,
like she's one of my sisters and we're headed to lessons, or breakfast, or to sneak off someplace we aren't supposed to go. "I need
your help again."

A part of me is thrilled to be the one to help her. This is what
I wanted.

We pass the terrariums. "Do you know much about plants?"
she asks.

"Yes. We mostly study them for shading, pigment work, and
for Belle-products."

"Flowers are so underrated." She gazes up at the ceiling. "Only
coveted for their beauty, when they can help solve so many prob-
lems." She tugs me forward to a large table overflowing with piles
of tattlers, beauty pamphlets, and scandal sheets. Torn-out pictures
are pinned to boards. Eyes, legs, breasts, hair, body shapes, faces.
Beauty caisses sit in rows, their contents on display.

Sophia leads me to a beauty board on an easel. Two identical
women stare back—white-blond hair, pear-green eyes, dark brown

skin, and sweetheart mouths. "These are my cousins—Anouk and Anastasia." She runs her fingers over their faces. "They only allow themselves to have tiny differences between each other. You have to search for them."

"They're beautiful," I say.

"Exactly the problem."

I bristle.

"I've been watching them these last few days. Tracking their beauty work. They've just come from a vacation in the Silk Islands, and from seeing your sister Padma."

"Tracking their beauty work?"

"Oh, I haven't shown you my masterpiece." She tugs a series of braided cords that dangle along the wall, and a tapestry lifts back, revealing a complete wall of rose-porcelain portraits set in a curling network of brass tubing. Every spot and corner is filled. Each one is labeled with a titled name and royal emblem.

The gentle whoosh of liquid snakes through the tubes. A few of the portraits change—hair grows shorter or longer, noses shrink, skin tones flush over with enhanced or brand-new colors, hair textures morph, mouths plump up.

I reach for one.

"Don't touch," Sophia warns. "They're very sensitive."

"What are they?"

"It's how I see everybody." She admires them. "How beautiful my court is."

"But how?" My stomach clenches.

"It's a secret." She takes my hand and squeezes it. "Can I trust you?"

"Yes." My heart gallops.

Sophia returns to the table and opens one of the beauty caisses.

Velvet boxes hold ornate bracelets and teardrop earrings and necklaces dripping with gold and gems. "One of my royal inventors made these for me. Remember when you first came to my toilette ritual—on my birthday—and I handed out jewelry?"

I nod, recalling how her court ladies had clamored over the jewels.

"They draw the tiniest bits of blood. I only need a little. And when mixed with your blood, Belle blood, remarkable things happen."

"My blood?"

"Yes. I have your leeches drained, and sometimes the ones from your sisters at the teahouses, too."

I try to keep my disgust from showing on my face. "Why?"

"Oh, don't let it bother you." She pats my shoulder. "I discovered it long ago, when I was a child and my mother's favorite, Arabella, used to change my hair and eye color in the playroom. She's still my favorite Belle, too. Though you might be able to continue to win me over." She bats her eyes at me. "I used to bite Arabella playfully, and tiny drops of her blood stained my little day dresses and pinafores. I'd have my nursemaid cut out pieces of the bloodstained fabric and save it. A strange keepsake, I know. But I was fascinated by what you all can do."

I step back from her. I search her face and eyes, and wonder if she's serious. She beams at me. Pride oozes out of every corner of her. Does she want me to be honored that she's fascinated by Belles?

"That's when I made the discovery. That's when I began to understand the power of it. If Arabella's blood touched my skin, it would restore the color momentarily. Imagine! I thought Belles had more power than queens. I wanted to be like that." She runs her fingers over the jewelry, tracing her fingertip across the tiny places where needles poke out, and the hidden chambers tucked inside the crested jewels. "I sucked the fabric and sometimes stole Arabella's leeches to eat. I thought if I ingested the blood, I'd become like you. Like Arabella. Like the Belles I saw in the teahouses. But it didn't work. It just made me sick."

Discomfort settles into my stomach.

She returns to her wall. "As I got older, my sister, cousins, and friends became prettier and prettier than me. My mother wouldn't let me do deep body work. She started enacting laws and shying away from radical changes. I felt ordinary. Forgotten. Plain. My sister made it seem so easy to be beautiful. The colors she chose and her subtle changes made her look extraordinary—more lovely after each appointment with Arabella. I needed people to pay attention to me like that. I needed to be better than everyone. I needed to have the same style and beauty instincts."

She leans close to one of the morphing portraits. "Look!" She pulls me forward. "Lady Christiana just had her hair color changed from brown to a plum purple. Hideous color. And at this hour. I wonder which teahouse she's patronizing."

We watch the image change. The nose transforms from a slender-tipped point to more of a cute button. Her cheekbones lift higher and her jawline smoothes out. Her skin darkens from ivory to honey brown. It's like watching a télétrope reel of minute-by-minute changes.

"Your powerful arcana connect them to my wall," she says. "It's more immediate with yours than your sisters', or even Arabella's. Even with only a few drops of their blood mixed with yours, I can see what they do."

"I don't understand." And I don't know if I want to.

"I change the jewelry every week to always have a fresh supply of their blood. And for some reason—it even evades my scientists—your blood allows me to watch them."

"I don't know what to say."

"Be excited. You are strong." She clasps my wrist. "And you will be the one to help me achieve my goals—finally. I want to be the most gorgeous woman in all of Orléans, and the world."

"But you are already stunning."

"You lie so easily, it makes me wonder what else you aren't telling me." The pitch of her voice sends a skitter of nerves through me. Her eyes burn into mine.

"I'm not ly—"

"I know that I'm not the most beautiful. I come here twice a day. And I'm reminded when I see pictures of my sister in the royal halls. When I see the looks your sisters create. When I see my mother. I know I'm average at best. I wasn't blessed by the Goddess of Beauty with a superior natural template. I don't have a good base to work with."

She reminds me of myself—wanting to be the best, researching and plotting and planning to make sure I am ahead of everyone.

"But how can you tell who is more beautiful? They all look different," I ask.

"Do you understand what I want?" She raises her voice.

I start to sweat. She steps closer to me. Her heavy breaths are coming out in pants.

"You want to be the best," I say, and somehow it's too familiar—like I'm talking about myself. *I might do the same thing if I was preparing to be queen.* The dark realization sinks down inside me.

Sophia grins. "I knew you'd understand." She takes my hand and kisses it. "We must become friends. Best friends. After all, I wanted you. Always. From the first time I saw you in your Beauté Carnaval carriage." She heads toward the door. "You will do whatever it takes to help me, right?"

"Yes, Your Highness," I say as I curtsy, but I don't know what it will cost me.

# 28

Ivy waits for me in the main salon the next morning, and rushes to me as soon as I step into the room.

"I need to speak with you." Her nervous energy radiates out like the rays of a too-strong sun.

"And I have a question for you. Why didn't Arabella return home?" I ask, before she can lecture me about whatever it is.

Ivy bristles. "How do you know about her?"

"Is she one of your sisters?" I say. "I saw her."

"No, she's from the generation before me. She's the queen's favorite Belle. She kept her at court to work with Princess Charlotte."

"She's been at court that long? Du Barry allowed it?"

"The queen gets what the queen wants," Ivy says.

Servants push in breakfast carts overflowing with hard-boiled eggs, grilled-meat and fruit tarts, pastries, fried bacon, and sweet toast, but Ivy shoos them out, then races to Elisabeth's office door. She knocks three times and presses her ear against the wall. The door doesn't swing open.

"Good, she's gone." Ivy hovers over me. "What happened last night?" she asks. "With Sophia?"

"How did you know about that?" I pluck a cheese tart and plate from the cart and sit on a chaise.

"I'm supposed to know all things when it comes to you and your transition to court."

"Like a spy?" I tease, trying to make her smile and relax a little.

"Like an older sister." She sweeps the plate from my hands and sets it on the table. "I need you to focus and tell me exactly what happened." She furiously knits her lace-gloved hands.

"Sophia brought me to her workshop. I saw her—"

"The portraits." She flattens her hands on her waist-sash as if she's nursing a stomachache. "It's starting again."

"What is?" I reach for my plate.

She slams it to the table.

I jump.

"I need you to focus right now. Her issues. Her obsessions. I thought she'd gotten better. I thought I'd helped her," she says.

"You talk about her as if she's ill."

"She is unhinged."

"A bit, yes. She's pressured, anxious. She wants to be the most beautiful," I say. "I think I can help her, too."

Ivy freezes. Her stare burns. "I thought that, too. Foolishly. You can't tell? You don't sense it?"

"Sense what?"

She squeezes down next to me on the chaise, so close I catch a scent of the lavender cream she wears. "I'm not supposed to poison your thoughts. Du Barry and the Beauty Minister gave me strict instructions not to tell you things." Her voice quivers. She pauses as doors open and shut in other parts of the Belle apartments.

"Tell me what?" My pulse flutters.

Ivy glances over her shoulder. Breakfast attendants fill teapots with piping-hot water, and set down carafes of snowmelon juice. "Wait," she whispers to me. "Leave us, please," she tells them. "I'll ring the bell when you can return."

They scurry out.

"Sophia has dark impulses." She is as still as stone. "When I was named the favorite, she had just turned thirteen. One of the queen's ladies-of-honor gave her a teacup crocodile. It was a tiny little thing named Pascale, with sharp teeth and a long tail that dragged behind him like a train of pearls. But Sophia had had her heart set on a teacup dragon. Those had become increasingly rare a few years earlier. Royal breeders couldn't get one to survive beyond a few hours after hatching." Ivy takes a deep breath. "Sophia forced me to do beauty work on Pascale."

"We worked on our teacup dogs and the stray teacup cats at home," I remind her.

"Yes, but we only changed the color of their fur, for arcana practice." She eyes the front salon doors. "Sophia made me break his back"—her voice cracks—"and refashion the bones into a pair of wings."

My hand goes to my mouth.

"I had to snap his neck and stretch it out so he looked more like a dragon than a crocodile. Then she tried to make him fly."

I raise my hand. "I don't want to hear any more."

"She dropped him off a balcony. She killed him."

"Ivy, I told you I didn't want to know." I leap up from the chaise.

"You have to know."

"She was just a child."

"This was only a few years ago. What if those impulses have grown with her, rather than diminished?"

"I don't want to talk about this anymore." I storm out of the main salon.

"Camille," Ivy calls out. "Camille."

Inside my bedroom, I slam the door, then step onto my terrace. A cool breeze carries leaves across the floor like a prism of windy-season makeup colors—marigold, chestnut, scarlet, apricot. I wish the breeze could sweep away what Ivy just told me. Whisk it off to some other place.

A bright leaf gets caught on the abacus on my desk. I rescue it and rub it between my fingers. I smell it and I think of Maman. When the warm months turned windy, she would take me around the edges of the forest that surrounded Maison Rouge de la Beauté, and we'd hunt for leaves, collecting only the most beautiful, the brightest, still rich with color. Back in our room, she'd show me how to use them to make natural-looking pigments and mix hair shades, and we'd press them between tomes of fairy tales to keep them as records of our adventures.

I open her Belle-book. A frayed scandal sheet called *Madam Solaina's Secrets* is tucked between two pages. The headline:

LADY SIMONE DU BERTRAND OF HOUSE EUGENE DIES WHILE
HAVING HER SKIN COLOR RESTORED BY THE FAVORITE

*What?*

Maman's frantic handwriting accompanies it.

*Date: Day 53 at court*

*She wanted the whitest skin in the whole kingdom—pure as fresh milk and a newborn daisy, she kept saying. Her attendant held a mirror above her body the entire session. I would press the chalk-white color down into her skin, and it would sour, mixing with stubborn shades of radiant gray. She would sit up, slap me, and make me do it again.*

*I got so angry, I couldn't hold on to the picture of her in my mind. The arcana didn't work properly. She kept slapping me harder and harder, and threatened to use a belt if I couldn't deliver the right color. I felt a pinch inside me and couldn't stop myself from imagining her flesh covered in wrinkles, her heart slowing. When I opened my eyes again, her eyes were bulging and her mouth was slack. Her heart had stopped. I didn't understand what had happened at first, but then I realized—it was me. I'd done this. The Minister of Justice ruled the case accidental—her private doctor confirmed she'd had health challenges before having beauty work done.*

I suck in a sharp breath. Maman killed a client? The arcana betrayed her? How could she have kept this a secret? Could the same thing happen to me?

I slam the book shut and tuck it back into its hiding place in my beauty caisse.

Two post-balloons zip inside, trailed by more leaves.

The first: a crimson one, burning bright with Maison Rouge de la Beauté's house emblem.

The second: a silvery white one covered with a twinkling collage from the Glass Teahouse.

I tie their ribbons to the balloon hook on my desk. I cut open the one from home first. I pluck out the parchment.

*Dear Camille,*

*I haven't heard from Edel. I asked Du Barry, but she just keeps saying everything is fine and to focus on my own work. Is everything all right? What have you heard?*

*The babies have grown even more. Du Barry had us celebrate their* sixth birthday two nights ago. I don't quite understand how it all works. Did we grow this fast, too? The nurses hum them songs and call them rose babies. I've included a drawing of the one who looks like you. She could be your twin—dimple and all. I keep accidentally calling her Camille, but she doesn't mind. She wants to be just like you when she comes to court. Her name is Belladonna. We call her "Donna."

Love,
Valerie

I unfold the second page and see a portrait of a smaller version of myself. Bright eyes. Warm brown skin. Dimple in the left cheek. Curly hair with a pile of frizz. Why would the Goddess of Beauty create another Belle who looked like me? Du Barry gave us pamphlets about our births. She told us Beauty had sent each one of us to our mothers. That we'd fallen from the skies like shooting stars. That she'd handpicked all of our features. That we were all flushed and warm with blessed blood. What isn't Du Barry telling us? And what about the Belle at the Chrysanthemum Teahouse with the deformed face? Did Beauty send her, too?

I open the second post-balloon—from Hana.

Camille,
I've been staying up late at night, trying to find whoever keeps crying. My Madam, Juliette Bendon, says it's just overly drunk courtiers at her late-night parties. But I don't believe her. I think there are other women here. But I can never search for long. I'm so tired these days. I don't have a moment's rest.

I haven't heard from Edel, but I saw the headline, too. She won't answer my post-balloons.

Hana

I pace the room. Where are you, Edel? Why haven't you written back? Amber might be right. Maybe she did escape. But if so, how is she surviving? Where did she go? How is the teahouse continuing to operate without raising alarm?

"Lady Camellia." Bree interrupts my thoughts.

I tuck the letters away and join her in the main salon.

"What is it?"

"Come, have a look." She waves me to the Belle-apartment doors. "Rémy is with his sisters."

We peek through a space in the door. Rémy holds the hand of a little girl a quarter of his size while two others fuss over him. The little one's hair is a dark cloud of coils and glitter, complete with metallic threads reminiscent of lightning streaks. They all share his rich midnight coloring, and standing together they look like a bouquet of black calla lilies.

"What's she like?" the little one asks. "You promised to tell me everything about the favorite, and you've only sent two post-balloons. How can you fit *everything* in only two letters?"

He smiles down at her with an easy demeanor that I've never seen.

"You haven't told us anything," the tallest one says. The silver color of her gown makes her skin glow and hugs her curves like silk around an hourglass. "Even Maman's been asking."

"She's nice," he says.

His compliment warms me.

"That's it?" the third one replies with a stamp of her foot. She shoves his shoulder and pouts, her lips a brilliant shade of coral.

"She's a little stubborn."

I smile.

"Can be a bit impulsive or reckless," he adds.

I scoff. Bree chuckles.

"That's why I like her," the tallest one says. "She does what she wants. Or that's what it seems like."

"I bet you just love that, Rémy," the third one replies. "She's probably not listening to you at all."

They all laugh together, their voices at a similar pitch. A set of warm-toned pavilion bells. A family. It makes me miss my sisters.

"Have you rescued her? Protected her from evil?" the little one asks, like this is all some fairy-tale adventure.

"More like escorted her places and followed her around," he says, picking the girl up. "Mirabelle, you are missing nothing. I promise you." He presses his forehead to hers and they rub their noses together.

"I'm missing everything." Her bottom lip quivers, and tears well up in her eyes.

"Shall we sing our song?" he says.

"Yes," she whimpers.

He hums, the deep baritone of his voice rippling through the hallway, resonating inside me. She sings a little tune about a yellow frog and its lily pad and pond. He kisses her cheeks and she bursts into laughter. It makes me wonder about his life before the palace. It makes me wonder about how he might be, if he wasn't my guard.

"Can we meet her?" the tall one asks.

"No," he says with a frown, and now I recognize him again.

"But please," little Mirabelle begs.

"Soldiers of the Minister of War aren't supposed to use their positions to seek special treatment or favor. It's against the code."

"Everything is about rules with you," the middle one says.

"Always has been," the tallest one adds.

"It wouldn't be appropriate," he says. "You three shouldn't even be up here, and I've indulged you already too long."

"We were just passing through," the tallest one says.

"No one just *passes through* the residential parts of the palace."

"We were invited to court to see the princess's wedding dress," Mirabelle says. "I saw the invitation."

He pinches her cheeks. "I don't doubt you. But I suppose your sisters *invited* themselves up here?"

"Why would you—" the middle one starts to say.

"I admit, we did," the tallest one says. "We just missed you."

"That's a lie," he says.

"Fine. We just wanted to know more about her. The papers say she's stronger than the other favorite. And the *Trianon Tribune* said she might have a fourth arcana."

I glance at Bree and mouth, *Really?* She nods with a smile on her lips.

"You know how I feel about tattlers, scandal sheets, and newspapers. And you can't just use my name to come up here. It's not—"

"Appropriate," the three of them say in unison.

Bree and I exchange a mischievous grin. I smooth the front of my dress and make sure all the curls in my Belle-bun are neatly in place. I yank open the door.

The girls gasp.

"Rémy?" I call out, as if annoyed.

He steps forward at attention.

"Oh, there you are. I was looking for you."

Mirabelle has her hand cupped over her gaping mouth. The other two are statues, frozen in place.

"Hello," I say. "Did I interrupt?"

"No, Lady Camellia, they were just leaving," Rémy says.

"Not without a proper introduction. Rémy, where are your manners?" I say, loving the twist of horror present on his face. "Who are these beautiful girls?"

"My sister, Adaliz."

The tall one curtsies.

"Odette."

The middle girl bows.

"And Mirabelle."

The little one barrels into me, wrapping her pudgy arms around my waist.

"Mira—" Rémy reaches for her.

I sweep her out of his reach and kiss her. "It's fine."

I talk to them about court, and their home in the Spice Isles, and how insufferable Rémy can be. Their eyes grow wide, and smiles spread across their faces. His mouth finally softens again. They wave good-bye and disappear down the long staircase. I watch Rémy watching them, and think, Maybe he isn't so terrible.

# 29

In the Receiving Hall, the queen's court is called together for a presentation of Sophia's possible wedding looks. Chrysanthemums and Belle-roses adorn the welcoming foyer, creating garlands around marble pillars. The din of gossiping voices fills the room. I sit with the Beauty and Fashion Ministers in chairs near the throne platform. Rémy stands behind me.

The queen raises her scepter. Imperial guards labor to bring out massive gold-framed portraits of the princess the size of wall tapestries. The frames are numbered and labeled PRINCESS SOPHIA'S WEDDING LOOKS. In each one, Sophia is painted with a different look. Hair textures range from loose curls to needle-straight to corkscrew curls to waves to zigzag coils, and the styles showcase each new hair-tower trend. A smiling version of her face is presented in an array of skin tones. Her dresses vary—from gold brocade with cream lace ruffles, to a pink bustle gown with silk rosebuds and beige lace, to a dark peacock blue–colored silk embroidered with a sequined trim, to an all-white A-line covered in seed pearls.

Sophia squirms on her throne.

The queen stands. "My wise and loyal court. Please join me in helping to decide the princess's wedding look. Besides becoming a wife, my daughter will also step into her 'forever' look, as tradition demands of the royal family."

The crowd applauds.

"But first, I want to hear from the favorite. Camellia, please join me," she says.

I jump at the sound of my name.

The queen leaves her throne. Her fur robe trails her as she points at the portraits.

I proudly stand and walk over to join her.

"These were put together by my cabinet, but you and your sisters hold the secrets to the art of beauty. I want to know what you think."

"Yes, Your Majesty," I say.

"What look would you give my daughter? Which would you choose?"

My hands knit in front of me. The questions she asked me at Sophia's birthday banquet compete with her latest challenge: *Can you do this? Can you be who I need you to be?*

I comb over the portraits. I want to show her that I belong here.

The sound of whispers and the whoosh of newsie post-balloons echo. My brain struggles to puzzle out which one would be best. In our lessons, Du Barry gave us beauty templates to work with— skin and hair colors that complement each other, the most balanced shades and pigments, symmetrical facial structures, dresses for specific body types, Belle-makeup colors for every color palette. But I never wanted to use them, always preferring to create my own looks from scratch. My mind is a well of doubt.

I glance up at Sophia. Our eyes meet. Deep-green eyes stare into mine. Her hair falls into her lap, swirling into a pile of ringlets, and her tiny teacup monkey plays hide-and-seek within the strands. I wonder if she wants to pick her own look. I wonder if she has an opinion or was given a choice. Her dress begins to rustle.

The crowd snickers. Out pops a tiny teacup elephant, its trunk longer than half a peppermint stick. The monkey jumps from her lap and chases the elephant around the throne. Sophia leaps forward and scoops both of her teacup pets into her arms, giving them a flurry of kisses.

The queen waves her hand at one of the imperial guards. He wrenches the creatures from Sophia's hands. The animals cry out.

"Zo! Singe!" she says. "It's all right. It's just for now."

"My daughter has an unnatural fondness for animals," the queen says.

The crowd laughs. The distraction buys me some time to think.

The queen turns her attention back to me. "Now, shall we begin?" She walks back to her throne.

I circle the pictures. All eyes are on me. I chew on the inside of my cheek. Du Barry would want me to do something simple. Pick a portrait. Make a few suggestions. The Beauty Minister would say to discuss what I like about each one. The Fashion Minister would want me to highlight which dresses best match each particular look.

I snuff out their voices like candles.

I want the queen to see what I can do, to see that I can be the person she needs, to know that I can help her daughter.

Sophia has patterns—always returning to blond hair, no matter if her skin is a warm hazelnut or paper white or a deep inky black, or if her hair texture is a frizzy cloud or deeply wavy or shaved to the scalp.

I run my fingers over one of the portraits, feeling the lumpy paint beneath my fingertips. These pre-approved looks aren't enough. I can't tell what she would look like from the back, or whether her profile would suit.

I turn to the queen. "Your Majesty, would you indulge me if I experimented a bit?"

Her mouth is a straight line. "As you wish."

I close my eyes. The room dissolves around me: the women and their flapping fans and raspy whispers, the queen's strong gaze, Sophia's frustrated sighs, the noise of the newsies' pens, the gentle flutter of post-balloons and lanterns, the roiling boil of anticipation.

I think about what I'd do if Du Barry had assigned us this task. I return home to the lesson rooms. I'm with Maman at a worktable. Her hands on my shoulders. Her laugh ringing in my ears. Her voice drifting over me: *You know what to do. Make beauty mean something.*

There are no grades. There is no commentary from Du Barry. There is no competition from my sisters. Just me. And the arcana.

I can see the princess in my head.

My body warms.

Beads of sweat dot my neck.

My heart pounds.

My blood races through me.

The arcana awaken.

I fix my gaze on the portraits. I pull the paint from the canvases. It circles around me like a colorful tornado.

The court erupts in *oohs* and *ahhs*.

I push myself further. I want to show them that I am unforgettable. So unforgettable that the queen realizes she should've chosen me first, that she won't ever let me go.

I rip the canvases into shreds, breaking them into parts— cotton, linen, glue, and aged hemp. They add to the windstorm. I use the Age arcana to smooth the hemp, bringing life and moisture back to the material, then form it into legs, arms, a torso, and a head, like I'm a little girl playing with papier-mâché. I give her my sister Valerie's gorgeous voluptuous shape.

I use the Aura arcana to extract the paint and coat the new body-shaped canvas, coloring it the same shade as the sand that lines the royal beach. I make her eyes the color of a stormy gray sky to honor the people of Orléans, but add tiny golden sunflowers around the middles to mirror the royal chrysanthemum. I tug the silk threads from a nearby tapestry. They crawl along the floor like golden and white snakes. I fashion them into a blond halo of tight curls, and create a cream wedding dress.

The final product stands like a life-size doll beside me. Women cover their mouths with gloved hands or lace fans, and the men's eyes bulge. Many stand motionless.

No one speaks.

My legs threaten to give out. My eyelids droop. I inch down into a bow, waiting for the queen's reaction, and to hide my utter exhaustion. I try to stop panting.

Sophia claps furiously and races down the throne platform. She pulls me up to my feet, hugs me tightly, and whispers, "I knew you were the best." She links her hand in mine. "Together we're going to be more powerful than any queen and favorite."

The queen starts to clap, followed by the rest of the court.

Sophia releases me. I bow again, but struggle to push up from the floor. Rémy's hands find their way around my waist, lifting me like a baby that's fallen from a chair. The words *thank you* catch in my throat.

The queen leaves her throne. She descends the stairs and admires the statue I've created.

"Camellia, very lovely," the queen says, giving me an appraising look. My heart races. Another wave of exhaustion hits me. "I've never seen anything like it."

The court gives me a standing ovation.

"It's more than lovely, Mother," Sophia says. "It's spectacular." The princess turns me away from the queen. She hugs me again and whispers close to my ear, "I made this happen, you know. I got you back here. And now you've proven I was right all along."

Sweat drips down my back.

"What do you mean?" I stutter out.

She flashes me a smile, and the world spins—chairs stretch into colorful putty, laughter crescendos in peaks, and the floor beneath my feet wobbles like the land is melting out from under me.

# 30

After Sophia's wedding-dress presentation, the newsies go wild with their headlines:

NEW FAVORITE TOPPLES QUEEN'S CONCERNS WITH HER SKILL

PRINCESS SOPHIA ECSTATIC ABOUT THE NEW FAVORITE

SOPHIA'S WEDDING LOOK TO BE THE
MOST COVETED IN THE KINGDOM

CAMELLIA IS RUMORED TO BE THE MOST
POWERFUL FAVORITE THAT EVER EXISTED

THE BELLES' ARCANA MAY BE ABLE TO DO MORE
THAN THE GARDIENS HAVE REPORTED

My days settle into an ebb and flow like the crystal-blue waters of La Mer du Roi crashing onto the beach below the Belle apartments. I become stronger, pacing myself and using the sangsues to keep from fainting. Sophia doesn't invite me to her workshop again.

The morning appointment ledger is usually only filled with lady courtiers from all over Orléans.

But today it shows:

*Auguste Fabry, House Rouen (son of Minister of the Seas) 09:00*

*Duchess Midori Babineaux, House Helie 10:00*

*Countess Anzu Charron, House of Bowyers (Favored Bowmaker) 11:00*

*Lady Daruma Archambault, House of Spice 11:30*

I run my finger across Auguste's name, believing Elisabeth's handwriting might disappear. I count the letters in *Auguste*. Seven. A number loved by the God of the Sea. Did his parents do that on purpose? I can feel his sly smile, almost as if he's in the room with me. A tiny flutter flits in my chest.

Bree opens my bedroom door. "Treatment salon four is ready."

I gaze down at my teal work dress and apron. "Bring me a day dress instead. The lavender one. No, the buttercup yellow with the ruffled sleeves."

"But it's against trad—"

"Please, Bree." I add a smile. She leaves for the wardrobe room.

I pace in front of my desk. I think about sending my sisters post-balloons. I think about telling them more about Auguste. I think about asking for their advice: Is there anything wrong with being nice to him? Is there anything wrong with being friendly?

Edel's face flashes in my mind. She would tell me to flirt and let myself laugh.

*Answer a post-balloon, Edel.* My worry for her piles on top of itself. She has to be at the Fire Teahouse still. There would be more headlines if she wasn't. Maybe Du Barry sent one of our older sisters back there? But Du Barry wouldn't do that. When a Belle leaves court, she is to return home and remain there. Or what about the Belle from the Chrysanthemum Teahouse?

I lift my pen from its inkpot, but my hands feel too light to hold anything. I shake them out.

Bree returns with the day dress. "Is everything all right?"

"Yes, fine." I change, then drape my mirror around my neck. Its cold glass presses against my too-hot skin.

"Your client is in the salon with Ivy." Bree opens the bedroom doors.

"He's here already?"

"Yes, my lady. It's almost time to begin his treatment."

I walk down the hall. I try not to break into a run. I pass the wall of favorites and stop in front of Maman's portrait before entering the main salon. Her eyes twinkle. I hear a memory of her voice: *Don't be silly about meeting boys and girls at court. Keep focus on your arcana, your strength, and your sisters.*

"Camellia." Bree touches my shoulder.

I startle.

"He's waiting," she says.

I take a deep breath before stepping through the entryway. I let it out slowly, like the air in a post-balloon. Auguste stands beside the fireplace, his eyes fixed on the tapestry above it. Elisabeth fires questions at him, but he doesn't answer. Attendants buzz in and out of the room, and servants carry supplies and push golden carts. Ivy sits in a nearby chair.

Bree announces me.

Auguste whips around with a smile.

"Have a great session," Elisabeth says, trying to attract his attention. He glances around her. She pouts, then retreats into her office, closing the door behind her.

I fight with my lips, trying to press them into a serious and professional frown rather than the grin that threatens to overtake them. "Hello, Mr. Fabry."

"So formal now? Are we not friends?" He steps forward.

"Friends?" I say with a laugh, then swallow it. Standing with him feels like we're exchanging a secret in front of everyone.

Ivy clears her throat.

"Have you had tea?" I ask.

"Yes, and it's awful." He lifts off a teapot lid. Hot vapors drift up like smoke. "Couldn't you slip honey or sugar into it? To make it more pleasant?"

"That dulls the Belle-rose effects, unfortunately," I say.

"Or fortunately, if you like pain."

"Who enjoys pain?"

He starts to push his finger into the teapot, as if he's going to plunge it into the hot liquid.

"No, don't." I reach for his hand.

"Are you worried about me?" he asks.

I pull back. "If you want to burn yourself, go ahead."

He does, and I try not to gasp. "I don't mind it. Sometimes it reminds me that I'm awake." He flashes the now-red finger at me.

"You are odd," I say.

"The good kind or the bad kind?"

"I don't know yet."

Ivy taps her hourglass. "It's time," she whispers to me.

"Are you ready to begin, Mr. Fabry?"

"Only if you stop calling me that. I'm not my father," he says with a smile.

"Are you ready, Auguste?"

"Yes, now that you've asked me nicely." He winks before his attendant leads him to the bathing chambers.

I return to the hall that leads to the treatment salon.

Ivy rushes behind me. "Camellia"—she grabs my arm—"how do you know him?"

"We've met before," I say.

"When?" Her voice turns serious. "Where?"

I'm overwhelmed with the need to lie and withhold the details of how I know Auguste, like hiding a rare and expensive gem in a secret pocket. "Just around—at court."

"You aren't supposed to be friendly with young men."

"What about old ones?"

I feel her scowl beneath her veil. "You need to be careful."

"I know. I am."

"It is forbidden." She clicks her teeth. "And besides, he is one of Sophia's suitors!"

"I know."

"The passion between two people can ruin the arcana. Poison the blood with toxins."

I touch her shoulder. "I'll be sure to use more leeches. On the hour."

"Camellia."

"I'm only teasing. I was just being nice to him."

"Too nice," she warns.

"I'll work on being mean." I leave her standing there, and walk to treatment salon four. Roses sprout out of jeweled vases. Beauty-lanterns drift overhead like small suns, shining perfect beams of light across the treatment bed. Auguste steps from behind an ivory screen in a silk robe. I blush at the sight of him.

"You sure know how to take your time," he says. "Are you trying to run up my bill?"

"I'm certain you can be patient," I say, just before Ivy enters the room behind me like a dark cloud. I move a cart of bei-powder bundles, just to pretend to have something to do.

His eyes are on me. It sends a warm flush across my skin. "I did a lot to get onto your schedule. After your latest feat at court, my attendant said you were booked for ten months straight."

"What did you have to do?" I find his gaze.

"Kiss three different women, plus send them flowers and love-themed post-balloons. The expensive kind, from Marchand's shop."

"Can't you get in trouble for that? You're one of Princess Sophia's suitors."

"I swore them to secrecy. I could be the future king, and they think all kings need mistresses. It's made me more popular."

"Disgusting."

"I try not to disappoint."

"Aren't you humble." I laugh, then turn my back to him. I light tiny tea candles beneath a chafing dish to start melting a skin-color pastille.

"I went to a lot of trouble to get here."

"It sounds exhausting."

"It was. Backbreaking work."

I stifle a laugh. Ivy groans.

"What services would you like?" I ask.

"Make me look as handsome as I already am."

"Who said you were handsome?"

"The women I had to kiss in order to take their appointments. Also, I was featured in last season's male beauty-scope."

"Good for you."

"Are you not amused?"

Ivy clears her throat again.

Auguste turns to her. "Are you sick, miss? Because I cannot afford to catch a cold."

"No, sir, I'm not—"

"Well, then, perhaps you should leave us anyway. I'm feeling a bit shy with all these people in the room," he says.

I feel Ivy's stares through her veil, no doubt waiting for me to ask her to stay. I press my lips together until she rises from her seat.

"If that's what you wish," Ivy says.

"It is," he replies.

She curtsies and saunters out. The air in the room thickens like pudding now that she's gone.

"You lied. You aren't shy," I say.

"Not in the least," he says. "I just wanted to be alone with you. Or as alone as is possible, within the rules."

My cheeks warm. I glance away. "So, what services do you want?"

"I hate that I even have to do this."

I frown.

"I didn't mean it like that. It's just, I dislike"—he waves his hand around—"the fact that I *need* to be altered. The ship had to dock every month for us to have this maintenance done. It always felt so ridiculous. Unnecessary."

I don't know what to say to him. I don't know how to process his distaste. I thought everyone loved changing the way they looked. I thought they all coveted it. "Then let yourself be gray."

"Then no one would want to look at me."

"You'd be rid of all of this." I wave my arms around.

"But now I think I'll like these treatments more, because I can have them done with you." He stares at me.

I fiddle with metal instruments on a nearby cart. "I might not be available next time."

"I'll do what it takes. I'll find a way."

"Why would you go to this trouble?"

"I don't know, really," he says. "I went to the Chrysanthemum Teahouse two days ago and didn't like—"

"You saw my sister?" My heart skips.

"I did."

"How is she?"

"A little grumpy. She wasn't amused by my charm."

"I don't think many people are."

His mouth drops open. "Ouch."

"How did she *seem*?"

"After I tried to flirt with her, lighten the mood, she refused to speak to me."

I imagine Auguste on Amber's treatment table and almost laugh. His antics definitely would have gotten under her skin.

"We should begin," I say.

"Yes." He starts to disrobe, and servants rush forward to help. I whip around.

"Are *you* shy?" he asks.

"No, but it is not customary for me to see you nude. You should've waited until I left the room."

"I don't care much for customs." The bed groans as he climbs onto it. "Plus, I'm not naked. Not to worry. You don't have to be afraid."

"How many times do I have to tell you I'm not afraid?"

"A thousand."

"You're harmless."

"I'm quite dangerous, actually." He playfully grazes my arm. The touch of his fingers sends a warm ripple through me. I slip out of his grasp.

"Do you behave like this with all women?"

"No, just you."

"I find that hard to believe."

"You don't trust me?" he asks.

"I don't know you."

"What do you want to know?"

"Nothing." *Everything*. Bree lifts one of the hourglasses on the table, showing me I only have a few more minutes left in his session.

"It's almost time for my next client."

"Well, you've done an awful lot of talking," he says. "So I should get more time. You haven't given me my spintria's worth."

"You're the one who's been asking questions. And you haven't told me what you want."

"You choose. *I*, at least, trust *you*." He closes his eyes.

I dust his face with bei powder and put some up his nose to make him sneeze. I only have time for a quick treatment. I paint tiny freckles across the bridge of his nose and cheekbones, like caramel raindrops. The arcana wake up inside me.

I brush my fingers over his face: his skin is soft and warm, his breath hot on my hands. His pale white face appears in my mind. I add the freckles one by one, like I'm painting delicate flowers on a canvas.

I close my eyes.

He moves. Bree gasps.

My eyes snap open. A grinning Auguste covered in bei powder sits inches from my face. The heat of his skin warms mine. I smell the strawberries he ate before the appointment. The softness of his breath lands on my cheek. I can almost taste him.

He kisses my cheek and says, "For luck. I trust you won't tell anyone." Then he disappears out the door.

# 31

After my morning appointments, Rémy walks Ivy and me to the queen's sitting room for a private meeting. Ivy fusses about Auguste the entire walk. But her words can't erase the dangerous feeling of his mouth against my cheek. Even though they should. The thought of him almost distracts me from the fact that I'm about to have my first semi-private audience with the queen.

The large doors open for us. The red damask walls of the queen's tea salon display her royal emblem—a six-pointed crown with a glittering ruby and chrysanthemum in the center. Chafing dishes melt medicinal pastilles, and steam vases release vapor into the room. A fireplace hisses and crackles.

Rémy posts himself near the door with the other guards.

"Your Majesty—Lady Camellia, the favorite, here to see you as requested," her attendant says.

The queen stares out an arched window. Wrinkles mar her rich brown forehead. "Sit with me, Camellia." Her voice is soft and reminds me of my mother's.

I ease into the chair beside her. A teacup and saucer find their way into my nervous hands. I take small sips, wondering why she wants to see me.

"I'm very impressed with the strength of your arcana." She finally looks up.

"Thank you, Your Majesty," I say.

"You do things with them that I've never seen before," she says. "I wasn't sure about you. I think you know that." She pats my hand. "I thought you'd be as reckless as my daughter."

I gulp.

"But ... I think you will be the one to help me. After all this time. You might just be strong enough." She rises. "Come with me. You, too, Ivy."

I stand, then stare back at Ivy. She shoos me forward and follows behind. We navigate a series of hallways in silence. We pass an indoor garden, a marble bathing onsen, and a series of offices, until we stop before a white door marked with a white rose snaking through a four-pointed crown.

The servants stand aside, and the queen herself pushes this door open. I have no idea what to expect.

Cerulean light escapes the healing-lanterns drifting through the chamber. The walls are papered with thick lines of black and cream. A fire roars in the hearth, warm and bright and comforting, splashing coppery beams across a large, gauze-draped bed. The wood crackles as it burns, providing the only sound in the room. A beautiful, dark-haired woman stands beside the bed, her light brown hands knitting a scarf.

The queen smiles at her. "How is she?"

"The same," the woman replies, walking over to kiss the queen on the mouth.

"Camellia, this is Lady Zurie Pelletier."

I bow. Her lover.

Servants and nurses curtsy to the queen as they scurry around as quietly as mice.

"May I introduce you to my firstborn, Princess Charlotte," the queen says, "heir to the kingdom of Orléans." She goes to the bedside and lifts the whisper-thin curtain.

I step lightly forward, peering in. A sleeping young woman is propped up on silk pillows stuffed with feathers; a quilted blanket laced with thick gold ribbons lies over her. She looks like a perfect blend of the king and the queen. Her ponytail is a long rope at her side, with tiny frizzy curls that blend the color of the king's currant-red and the queen's midnight-black coils. A jewel-encrusted hair comb winks in the light. Her skin is a warm bronze dotted with freckles.

The queen rubs her daughter's hand and hums a song.

Newsies have speculated about Princess Charlotte's condition. Some reports say she was born frail and unable to fend off disease. Others say she suffered from a broken heart after her childhood sweetheart and betrothed died in a freak accident.

I have never known what to believe, but one thing is clear—the queen loves Charlotte with all her being.

"Isn't she beautiful?" The queen sweeps a loose curl from Charlotte's forehead. Weary creases ring the queen's eyes, and sadness slopes her shoulders forward over the sleeping princess. She looks up, and our eyes meet. I'm seeing Her Majesty for the first time. I glance away, feeling like I've discovered something hidden, something not meant for me to see.

"Yes, she is," I say.

"She's been asleep for four years." She kisses her daughter's cheek. "And I make sure she never fades to gray." She waves me forward. "Come closer."

I ease into my question. "May I ask what happened to her?"

"You may, but I have no answer for you." She strokes Princess Charlotte's cheek. "And that's why I've brought you here. I need you to make her well. The royal physicians haven't been able to awaken her. Even my Belle, Arabella, has been unsuccessful."

"I don't have the power to heal." I bite the inside of my cheek.

"But you must be able to do something. I need her awake. Even if she's no longer beautiful. It's too early for her sunset. You must find a way to help me. To help your people."

"Your Majesty, I don't understand. How does healing Charlotte help my people?"

The queen grasps my hands. Her own are cold and clammy. "The Declaration of Heirs Ceremony is coming in eight days' time. I will have to tell the kingdom that I'm sick, and designate who the crown will pass to. Sophia cannot become queen. She must never have the throne."

Her words send a tremor through the room. I remember Sophia in her workshop, her eyes wild and frantic.

"Sophia isn't fit. She's the way she is because I didn't give her enough of myself. I didn't have enough to give her after Charlotte became ill. And if I'm honest, she's too much like me. Full of the temper I had in my youth. The one that had to be leeched out of me by Belles every month." She coughs. Attendants rush forward, bringing her medicinal chafing dish closer. Her coughing subsides. "I tried to do the same with Sophia, but it didn't work." She sips hot tea. "I pray to the God of Life every day that Charlotte wakes up before I die so she can take her rightful place as queen. To be at my side when I announce my illness."

I can't imagine the queen and Sophia being anything alike.

"I must tell my people. The newsies are starting to speculate. They've been ruthless with me as of late. The sicker I get, the more the gray seeps to the surface, it seems. The more I return to my natural form." She takes a deep breath. "Orléans will not survive having Sophia as its queen. I need you to wake Charlotte. Use the arcana in any way you can to heal her. Experiment. Do trials. Something. Anything. It would be a sacrifice, I know, but you would save us."

I open my mouth several times. The words stick at the back of my throat.

"Your Majesty," Ivy says, stepping closer, "Camellia will die if she attempts this. The arcana aren't—"

The queen puts her hand in the air. Ivy swallows the rest of her sentence.

"I need you to consider doing this for me. I'll need an answer and a plan in eight days' time. By the Declaration of Heirs Ceremony, Charlotte must be awake. We must try."

My heart leaps with each beat. "But—"

"The kingdom needs you. I need you." She leaves me at Princess Charlotte's bedside. "Ivy, come with me."

They leave me alone with the servants and nurses and their charge. I'm a mess of worries and questions. Princess Charlotte's soft breaths hum. Her chest lifts and falls. I touch her cheek. She doesn't react. Her skin is warm to the touch.

"What happened to you?" I ask her. *What if I can't help you?*

I watch her lying there. I wonder what Maman would do: risk her arcana to help her country and queen, or refuse. What if I fail?

How terrible of a queen would Sophia be? Why doesn't the queen trust her own daughter?

I crave the way the queen looked at me—her eyes full of admiration and confidence. I want to be able to meet every challenge she gives me.

I slip the chained mirror from around my neck, then take a pin from my Belle-bun and stick my finger. The seed of blood climbs through the mirror's ridges. The roses twist and reveal their message—BLOOD FOR TRUTH.

I place the mirror before Charlotte and wait for the fog to reveal her true reflection.

"What are you doing?" a voice says.

I scramble to shove the necklace down the front of my dress. A round veiled woman stands behind a screen; only her silhouette shows.

"Who are you?"

"You know who I am."

"Arabella."

"Yes." She steps from behind the screen and joins me at the princess's bedside. She's reed-thin and tall, her limbs swaying as she walks. Her unusual veil is the entire length of her gown, giving away nothing of her outward appearance.

"What happened to Princess Charlotte?"

"One day she wasn't feeling well, and she went to bed, and never woke up."

I glance over her again. "Have you tried—"

"I've tried it *all*," she whispers tersely. "Nothing I've done has worked. My arcana cannot fix her."

"Then why does the queen think I can help?"

"The papers speak of your legendary feats," she says with

curiosity. "And I saw what you did in the Receiving Hall with Sophia's wedding looks. Your arcana are more powerful than mine. They're like nothing I've ever seen before."

Her compliment surges through me with a mix of excitement and nerves and concern. I've always felt the same as my sisters— the only difference was that I liked to experiment with my arcana, even if it landed me in trouble.

"She thinks you can do miracles. She takes your power as a sign that the gods haven't forsaken her child." Arabella sits on the bed and rubs a gloved hand along Charlotte's cheek. "Maybe they're right. You might be the only one who can save her."

# 32

I chase Maman around the perimeter of the forest behind Maison Rouge de la Beauté in my nightmares. She's a dream specter racing past the naked trees, her red hair a flame against the darkness. My bare feet find every discarded twig and branch on the forest floor.

"Maman!" I shout behind her. "Wait for me."

She looks over her shoulder and smiles, leading me farther in.

I ask her what to do about Charlotte and the queen. "I need help."

She stares back at me.

"Tell me what to do. They say I can use my arcana to heal," I shout.

"What do you think?" Maman asks without turning around but instead ventures deeper into the forest, dodging massive roots poking out of the dark soil.

"I don't know," I say, almost catching up, but she turns left, just out of reach. "I need you to tell me what to do."

"I can't. You have to decide for yourself."

"But what would you do?" I stop to catch my breath.

"It doesn't matter."

Her words dig under my skin like pinpricks.

"You have to decide for yourself. It is you who must live with the outcome."

"What if I die?"

"Do what is right. Always."

*Camille.*

"Camille."

A hand jerks my shoulder. I startle awake and jump at the sight of Ivy's dark veil leaning over me.

"I need to talk to you. Get up, quickly." Her whispers are panicked.

"What is it?" I rub my eyes. "What time is it?"

"Just after the midnight star. The staff have gone to bed."

I sit up. Ivy hands me a fur-lined robe and points at satin slippers on the floor. She lights a heat-lantern and tugs its thick ribbons. My nightmare still hums through me.

"Come."

"Where are we going?"

"Shh." She takes my hand in hers. It trembles. I squeeze it tight to keep my own hand from quivering. We tiptoe down the hall. Dim night-lanterns float overhead, bathing our footsteps in light. The marble floor holds the cold, pushing it up through my slippers.

Ivy eases open the solarium door. A garden of Belle-roses reaches up toward a dark sky, their petals large and rich as sunshades, their thorns glistening like arrows. We step into the chilly garden crusted over with a layer of frost.

"Why—"

"Whisper, so your voice doesn't carry." She takes a deep breath. Rose vines push from their pots, curling and lengthening to create a thick and thorny arbor over our heads. Ivy is manipulating them. The Belle-rose petals bloom so big we're now inside a pavilion of flowers, shielded from the solarium's glass walls. The heat-lantern bobs between us. I warm my hands under its fiery belly.

"You can't do what the queen asked. It's too much," she whispers.

"I didn't say yes."

"You have to say no."

"I thought ... maybe ... I should try." The queen's desperate voice is a sharp memory alongside Maman's dream advice.

"Do you understand how our arcana work?"

"Yes, of course. We study—"

"If you truly did, you would have said no immediately. This could warp your blood proteins. The arcana are meant to beautify. The Goddess of Beauty blessed us with them to help enhance people's natural templates. The template she gave them, buried deep below the gray. They are not meant to heal like medicine."

"What if I worked on her organs? Made them youthful again. Perhaps there's some failing within her body that keeps Charlotte in this sleeping sickness."

"You think Arabella hasn't tried that already? The queen is looking for more from you." Ivy starts to pace. "Your showing off made her think you're a miracle worker. Made her think the arcana can be used in unintended ways. But only the God of Life can control sickness and death. Not us."

I think of how Maman accidentally killed a woman. If we can bring about death, then why not life?

"But what if it can? The queen thinks Sophia will destroy the kingdom. Ruin lives. Is my life not worth the lives of so many others? Don't you think we should find out?"

"No, I think you should leave."

The word crashes through the garden like a bolt of lightning.

"Leave?" I stare at her, unsure if I understand exactly what she means.

"Yes."

"I can't leave. Where would I go? I worked so hard to get here. All I ever wanted was to be the favorite. I'm supposed to be here. I'm supposed to help."

"I thought the same thing. It's what Du Barry wants you to believe. It's what the world tells us we should be." She puts a finger to her lips and turns to the solarium door. "I hear something."

My heart pumps hard, each beat fueled by panic.

When Ivy faces me again, she lifts her veil, and I take a step back, holding in a gasp. Her skin is a patchwork of colors—gray, white, beige—and wrinkled like a paper sack. Her lips resemble two leeches puffed up from gorging on blood. Her eyes have drifted toward the corners of her face, giving her the appearance of a fish. "Some days are better than others, and my arcana can repair it. But tonight is a bad one."

"What happened . . . ?"

"Sophia," she says, biting back tears. "I overused my arcana to please her. Now they are forever unbalanced. The proteins are unable to regenerate and keep me beautiful. Our arcana help us maintain ourselves, too. They keep us alive."

I touch Ivy's cheek. The skin feels like clotted cream. "Can I fix it?"

A tear escapes one of her eyes. "Not without damaging your own gifts." She drops her veil. "But thank you. And it's not always this bad. Only after I've used the arcana. My eyes will drift back into place after a few hourglasses." She touches my shoulder. "You can't let this happen to you. You have to get out of here."

"Where would I go? Back home? And even if I did, the queen would just bring one of my sisters to court to try to help Charlotte. I have to find another way."

Ivy clenches her fists. "You're not listening." She storms toward the garden door, shrinking the Belle-rose stems and returning the swollen petals to their original size.

"Ivy," I call after her.

She doesn't return. I linger in the garden alone. My thoughts are a tangle of Ivy's words; the queen's request; Sophia's tinkling laughter and her worries about being beautiful; how the queen spoke about Sophia as selfish, jealous, and spiteful; and the ways in which Sophia and I are alike. The reasons line up next to each other like matching pairs of earrings—both of us want to please our mothers, both of us want to be the best, both of us want respect and adoration.

Maybe if I can't heal Charlotte, I can help Sophia be a better version of herself. Maybe that's the answer. Make her a better future queen.

"I can't give up!" I call out, hoping Ivy is still somewhere near.

"What are you doing out here?"

I whip around and find Rémy in the solarium.

"I couldn't sleep," I lie. "And what's your excuse?"

"My nightly security round." He holds the door open as I step through toting the heat-lantern.

We stand in the hallway. I'm buzzing with questions and indecision. I'm not ready to go back to bed. "Have tea with me?" I ask, then immediately want to take it back. "If you're busy, then never mind. I can just..."

He pauses. I wait for him to say no. He opens and closes his mouth two times before saying, "Yes, all right."

"Meet me in the tea salon."

He nods.

I take the heat-lantern and go to a smaller room beside the main salon. I pull three night-lanterns inside; their light illuminates two low tea tables and mauve-papered walls and cream floor cushions. I tug a string on the wall, and a woman appears from behind a panel. "Yes, miss."

"Could I have tea? Enough for two. And would you mind lighting the fireplace?"

"Yes, of course." She bows and disappears.

Rémy returns. His boots clomp against the floor as if he's stomping bugs.

"You're quite noisy for this time of night," I say.

He grumbles and sits on the floor pillow across from me.

The woman returns with a tea cart and pours us both a cup.

"Thank you," Rémy and I say in unison.

I laugh. He fights away a smile. She lights a fire, and the bright flames cast shadows across his deep-brown skin.

We sip tea in long stretches of silence. Whenever one of us can't bear it any longer, we ask the other a question: *What is your favorite season? Do you miss home? Do you have a favorite sister?* If I was sitting with Auguste, the conversation might never stop.

But when the quiet expands and the tea grows cold, my thoughts return to the queen and Princess Charlotte, and Ivy's fears. This is the time of night when I miss my sisters the most. Whenever one of us had a problem, we'd wait until our mothers were sound asleep and Du Barry's snores roared through the belly of the house; then we'd slip out of bed, sneak onto the veranda, and climb up on the roof. We'd lie there lined up like snow owls, staring into the heavens and talking out whatever trouble Edel had gotten herself into, or Valerie's newest upset about being left out, or Amber's anxious nerves over her lessons. We'd entertain Hana's latest fantasy of kissing someone, or Padma's worries about the babies in the nursery, or my daydreams of seeing the world, or what might be in the dark forest behind our house. They'd argue back and forth about what I should do.

But I was never alone.

I steal glances at Rémy. The silver streak down the crown of his head almost glows as the night-lanterns sail over us. I remove the small mirror from beneath my gown and finger it. I wish I could find a way to use it—to see what his reflection holds, to see if I can trust him.

"What's that?" He points to the mirror.

"Nothing." I take a chance. "Actually, can I ask you a different kind of question?"

"It depends on what kind."

I force a laugh at Rémy's attempt at humor. "How would you respond if someone asked you to do something dangerous?"

He sets down his teacup. His eyes narrow, and somehow his perfect posture becomes even straighter. "Dangerous how?"

I search for the right word. "Something that could make you sick."

"Why would anyone ask you to harm yourself?"

"What if it could save a life?"

"Is the person being asked *you*?"

"No," I lie. "Of course not. I need to . . . I need to advise one of my sisters on whether she should complete a specific beauty request for one of her clients."

He nods, but I can't tell if he believes me.

"Clients ask Belles to do many things," I add.

"I suppose."

"What would you do?"

"People have duties. She's been tasked—like you—with a massive responsibility, and has vowed to fulfill a specific obligation. But none of those obligations require risking one's life. That is the role of a soldier. Is your sister changing professions?"

"Of course not."

"Then she can set boundaries," he says.

"That's another way of saying no. Can *you* say no to the House of War?"

"Soldiers take a vow to protect Orléans to the death. I can't, but your sister can."

I want to tell him that refusing Du Barry, the Beauty Minister, clients, and most of all the queen or Sophia, feels impossible.

"No one is a prisoner." He takes a sip of tea. "Even you have the power to make your own choices."

His words burn and crackle like the logs on the hearth.

# 33

Today is Maman's birthday. All the mothers' birthdays. Forty days after the last warm day, deep into the windy season. I set her mortuary tablets on my vanity. I place her Belle-book beside them and trace my finger over her portrait on the cover.

"Maman, what would you do?" I whisper. "Help the queen?"

I wait to hear her voice.

Silence.

I open her Belle-book and comb through entries that mention the queen. It's so strange, knowing that my mother dealt with the same queen every day that I deal with now. I wonder how Maman felt about Her Majesty. I wonder if the queen liked her.

*Date: Day 96 at court*

*The queen was angry today. More than I'd ever seen before. The newsies buzzed about her inability to get pregnant. When I went to her chambers she had all the papers strewn over her tables, the ink scattering and reassembling, hollering their scandalous headlines. The tattlers and newspapers had released cameo portraits of the queen's sisters and their newborns. They say she is desperate to birth an heir. The worst of them claims she might replace the king, or use another man to father her bloodline. Everyone at court knew that she preferred the company of her lover, Lady Zurie Pelletier, but securing an heir had become her cabinet's top priority. She felt the pressure.*

*I sat in the corner of her chambers for three hourglasses. I waited for her to tell me she was ready for beauty work. She paced so furiously I thought she might put a hole in the fur rug beneath her feet. She threw vases and Belle-products and her own shoes. When exasperated and out of things to pummel against the wall, she turned to me and said, "Get rid of my anger. Make it go away. He won't lie with me. He says my temper is too much. He says I lack patience with him because he's not Zurie."*

*She yanked me from my chair and dragged me to her treatment salon. I pressed my fingers along her spine, pushing my Manner arcana deep inside her. For hours and hours she had me drain her temper from her, like how the leeches remove the toxins from our blood. She never felt like it was gone. I worked on her for three days straight. She wouldn't let me stop for meals or to rest. Leeches crawled over my limbs to help me push through, and I had to eat pastille cakes and skin-color pastes to quiet my stomach.*

This can't be Queen Celeste. It doesn't sound like the person I know. Her gentle brown eyes and slow smile flicker in my memory.

I reread the passage twice.

Bree tiptoes up to my desk. I press Maman's book to my chest.

"Didn't mean to startle you." She sets down a fresh stack of newspapers, scandal sheets, and tattlers, plus a shiny beauty-scope. "These just arrived."

"Thanks." I smile at her. She rushes off.

I thumb through the papers. Headlines pulse and flash.

PATRONS LEAVE THE GLASS TEAHOUSE WITH
GILDED HAIR AND PERMANENT MAKEUP

BEAUTY LOBBYISTS MEET WITH THE QUEEN TO
PETITION FOR AN EASE ON BEAUTY RESTRICTIONS
AND TOILETTE-BOX ALLOTMENTS

MAKING ORGANS MORE YOUTHFUL TO BE OUTLAWED
BY THE QUEEN IN FAVOR OF NATURAL DEATHS

WILLOWY FRAMES AND DAINTY HANDS,
THE MOST REQUESTED LOOK

FASHION MINISTER'S NEW DRESS COLLECTION BOASTS NEW
VIVANT DRESSES MADE OF LIVING THINGS LIKE BUTTERFLIES

QUEEN CHANGES LAW: ALLOWS BOY TO
REVEAL TRUE SELF AND TRANSFORM INTO A
GIRL AT MAISON ROUGE DE LA BEAUTÉ

"Camellia. Correspondence is here." Bree guides a massive rose-petal-pink post-balloon into my bedroom. The princess's royal emblem blazes brightly on its side. Two cream-colored ribbons hold a dress box.

I open the back of the balloon. Sparkles rain down at my feet. I slip out a sealed letter and read aloud.

"Your presence is requested by Her Royal Highness Princess Sophia in her chambers in an hourglass's worth of time."

I open the dress box. A windy-season tea dress stares up at me with a handwritten note that says WEAR ME. The plum silk and tulle are the shade of a fresh bruise.

"What is it, Lady Camellia?" Bree asks. Her voice squeaks

and she clears her throat before continuing. "Do you not like the dress?"

"No, it's beautiful," I say.

She takes it out of the box and holds it up. "The princess has excellent taste."

"What do you think of her?"

"Who, my lady?"

"The princess. Sophia."

She shudders. "I—"

I take the dress from her. "What is it? Tell me."

"I'm not supposed to have opinions of royalty. I'm supposed to do my job." She turns to fuss with the dress and make sure it doesn't get a single wrinkle while draped across the bed.

"But if you did. What would it be?" I step closer to her.

"The servants call her 'la chat,' my lady," she whispers.

"Why? Cats are sweet."

"Not always. At least, not the teacup ones. It's just that Her Highness loves you one day and hates you the next."

"Temperamental," I say.

"Worse. Cats cuddle you when they want something and will scratch your face when you don't give it to them."

"Give me an example," I say.

"Last year one of the servant girls, Aria, was put in a starvation box by the princess. She had been a favored servant of the royalty. She got to wear that purple pin on her uniform. The princess would shower her with extra gifts—beauty tokens, food—and allow her to travel as her companion on trips to palaces in the other isles."

"And? What happened?"

Bree sighed before continuing. "One day the princess said Aria's eyes were too beautiful for a servant girl. Even though Aria maintained the beauty restrictions for servants. She accused her of getting additional work done, and put her in the box for three days. She had her eyes pecked out by birds. She almost died."

My stomach lurches. A chill settles over me.

Sophia cannot become queen.

Bree slips her hand in mine. "Please don't ever tell anyone I told you that. I could be—"

"Don't worry." I stare into her eyes to reassure her. Tiny hints of red push against the warm sepia brown of her irises. A gray tinge lingers beneath her pink-white skin and more stubble dots along her chin.

"Let me refresh you." I touch her face lovingly.

"I couldn't—"

"You will." I lead her to my vanity and force her into the seat. Her mouth fights away a grin. She sinks into the high-backed chair. I grab a pot of Belle-rose tea from the tearoom and bring her a cup. She sips and smiles.

"Close your eyes." I open my beauty caisse, remove a bei-powder bundle, and find a skin-pot color that matches hers. I cover her face with the skin paste. I slip my mirror from inside my dress. I quickly push the pin into my finger and wipe the blood on the base of my mirror. I watch it climb, willing it to go faster. The rose turns red and twists into its message—BLOOD FOR TRUTH.

I examine her. The glass fogs, then it reveals her smiling face bathed in a halo. Her loyalty reflects in the glass like a warm sun. The confirmation surges through me.

I restore her skin color, add more freckles to her nose and cheeks, and deepen the brown of her eyes. I touch the light stubble on her chin and cheeks.

"Do you mind..." she starts to ask.

I smile at her and touch her face, pulling the short hairs out and killing the roots of them.

"Those hairs won't come back again," I say.

"Thanks," she whispers.

I add a small dimple—like mine—to her cheek as a bonus.

"Do you like the new dress?" Sophia asks as she flits around her boudoir in a sheer bathing gown. Her legs and hands twitch, and she fights to keep herself still. Wire-rimmed glasses sit on a wide nose, and her deep-set hazel eyes are two pools of sadness. She reminds me of a flower that's lost all its petals. Her hair-tower is a frantic mess of tangles and jewels. Old makeup rings her eyes and lingers on her cheeks.

"It's pretty," I say.

"Spin for me."

I do a careful turn. Unease fills me.

Sophia cannot be queen.

Sophia is unfit.

Sophia is temperamental.

The dress folds release a tiny melody each time I move.

"Isn't it a lovely sound?" She leaps around to the beat of it. "I'm working with the Fashion Minister to make a line of dresses that sing. This is my first attempt."

"Very clever." I don't tell her Rémy teased me on the entire walk to her chambers, calling me a pavilion bell.

"I need to make sure I take fashion to a new place, too. My mother is not a very fashionable queen. Her dresses are always rather dull. I will commission gowns the likes of which the world has never seen." She digs into her vanity, throwing creams and puffs and tonics and perfume vials. Glass shatters.

I step back as some of the objects fly over my head like shooting stars. Servants rush to clean, but more hit the floor and splatter their contents before the servants can catch them. I shift my weight and try to find the right moment to interject.

"Will we be having lunch, Your Highness?" I ask tentatively.

She pauses. "I've planned a windy-season picnic. It's partly a date with another one of my suitors."

I wait for her to say Auguste's name.

"Ethan Laurent from House Merania."

I smile with strange, unexpected relief.

She returns to lobbing beauty products. "But I just can't find..." She jerks upright. "Hmm, I can't seem to remember what it is I was looking for." She stares at the ceiling.

Servants duck and dart around her, trying to sweep up her mess.

Sophia steps in front of her vanity. "I look horrendous, favorite. I need you. I was up too late." She reaches out her hand. I hesitate before taking it. "Fix me."

"I must change into my work dress."

"No, I want you as beautiful as possible while you work on me. Perhaps it'll inspire you."

We go to her treatment salon.

"Can we send for Bree? I need my beauty caisse."

Sophia snaps a finger at a nearby servant. The woman ducks out of the room. I call out a *thank you* behind her.

"I will go bathe while you set up," she says.

"Yes, Your Highness."

I double-check the treatment room: adequate beauty-lanterns floating about, a servant setting Belle-rose tea on the table, pastilles melting on chafing dishes and filling the room with a lavender scent, another servant draping a large bed with pillows and linens,

Belle-products sparkling on tiered trays. I trace my fingers over the fleur-de-lis Belle-emblems etched onto each item.

I remember the first time Amber and I sneaked into the Belle-product storeroom. After the house had gotten quiet, we stole night-lanterns and dragged them to the back of the house. The room's wonders had unfolded to us for hours: perfume atomizers and color crème-cakes and rouge-sticks and powders and kohl pencils and golden vinaigrettes and pastilles and potpourri and oils and sachets. The room had smelled heady and sweet, and we'd fallen asleep there after powdering ourselves all night. Du Barry made us write fifty lines each as punishment.

I wish Amber was here now. What would she tell me to do?

Bree arrives with my beauty caisse. "I thought you were headed to a luncheon," she whispers.

"So did I."

Bree sets it up on a nearby cart and begins the process of unhooking its compartments. Servants usher Sophia back into the room. She guzzles a vial of her specially made Belle-rose elixir and climbs onto the bed.

I pace around, trying to figure out what look I'll give her. An idea wells up.

"Facedown, please," I say.

"Why?" Her eyebrows lift in surprise.

"I need to get a good look at your hair," I lie. "I want to experiment."

Sophia claps giddily. "You know how much I love to toy with things." She turns over.

I stand at the top of the treatment table. Bree and I work to cover her with bei powder. The weight of my plan is like a solid-gold spintria block, heavy with risk. Doubt curls into my stomach, souring it with anxiety.

I brush her hair down her back. I lighten the strands to the color of snow and add streaks of silver and embed diamonds. I paint her in a new skin tone, the color of freshly laid eggs. The second arcana awakens. I freckle her body with beautiful beauty marks. Goddess-of-Beauty kisses.

She grunts, and sweat dots her skin.

"Are you all right, Your Highness?" I pretend to fuss with the metal rods used to shape the contours of the face and body.

"Yes, proceed," she whispers.

I motion to Bree to lift her hair. Bree's shaky hands gather the new strands. Sophia's spine curves beneath her skin, visible on her skinny frame. The first arcana awakens inside me at the sight of it. I think of Maman's entry about the queen. A poor manner can be leeched out of anyone.

I take a deep breath. I nudge my fingers lightly into the back of her neck. Her soft skin warms beneath my fingertips. I push out her temper, plucking it from inside her like a weed in a garden, and plant the virtues of patience and serenity.

Sophia screams out and leaps up. Her sudden movement knocks me to the floor.

"Are you in pain, Your Highness? Is everything all right?" I scramble to my feet.

A servant hands her another vial of her elixir. She brushes it away. "I'm just..." Her eyes blink, and her head moves left and right as if she's having some sort of conversation with someone who isn't there. "I'm done for today. You can leave." She doesn't look at me. She doesn't even ask for a mirror.

"But—"

"Good-bye, favorite." Servants sweep me out of the room like dust. My pulse races with panic and worry and fear.

She knows what I was trying to do.

# 34

The next day, the salon doors burst open with a flourish. I brace myself for the Beauty Minister, Du Barry, or even Sophia herself, with a reprimand for trying to soften Sophia's manner without her consent.

But the Fashion Minister barrels in, followed by his team of dandies and a wardrobe closet with massive carriagelike wheels. Its white birchwood sides remind me of my Belle-trunk, but its gilded edges and damask pattern allow it to blend in with the rest of the luxurious room.

"My little doll," the Fashion Minister cries out. He lifts me out of my chair and twirls me around and around, no doubt inspecting my day dress. His false hand presses into my back.

"Not too fast," I say.

He chuckles. "Yes, no more losing your stomach. And, hmmm, looks like you've missed me. At least, your body and sense of fashion have."

I smile. "Where have you been?"

"Locked in a tower. Forced to make dresses for the rest of my years." He kisses my cheek. "I've been at the Dress Bazaar, trying to settle on the proper fabric for Princess Sophia's wedding gown. I have to match your glorious feat from that day in the Receiving Hall somehow." His team wheels the wardrobe closer.

I blush at his compliment. "Perhaps I can help you."

He blows me a kiss. "Firstly, I have a few special gifts for you."

"For what occasion?"

"No need for an occasion, doll. You are *the favorite*. It's an honor to dress you." The wardrobe doors open and the interior explodes with color. Dresses with full skirts, A-line cuts, empire waists, sheaths, long sleeves, cap sleeves, no sleeves, V-necks and scoop necks and plunging necklines. Dresses made of brocades, laces, velvets, glass beads, cashmeres, silks, and pastel satins in every color and pattern. Special carts follow the wardrobe, carrying vivant dresses inside large glass bell jars. These are dresses made of living things. Butterflies open and close their wings, exposing their dress's inner rib cage. Honeybees buzz in and out of a honeycomb-shaped gown. Roses of every color wave their petals.

Elisabeth slips from her office and approaches the wardrobe jars with widened eyes. She stretches out her fingers, mesmerized.

"Don't touch, little Du Barry," the minister says, bopping her hand lightly. "Those are not for you."

I can't help but laugh at her pinched expression.

"Show some respect. Those are for the *favorite*. They are gowns and dresses befitting the most important person in the kingdom ... aside from the king, queen, and princesses, of course." He bows and then shows me each frock one by one, much to Elisabeth's chagrin. She scowls as they're presented like delectable pastry treats.

"What do you think?" he asks.

"You've outdone yourself."

His eyes light up. "I know."

We laugh.

"You must wear one tonight." He pulls an invitation from his pocket. A mix of gold and black calligraphy announces: SOPHIA'S CARD PARTY. Glittery stars gleam on the parchment, holding the promise of excitement. He takes my hand and twirls me once more. "You won't get sick again, will you?"

"No. I've learned my lesson," I say, blushing.

We dance, swaying back and forth to the noise of people moving in and out of the apartments. He leans close to my ear, whispering, "I've been hearing good things about you, favorite. You are loved by our princess. She believes you can do anything and everything. That you could possibly bring the Goddess of Beauty herself down from the heavens."

"I—"

"Don't give me any flowery excuses." He smiles. "You've been giving the princess just what she wants. Wise plan, for now. But don't let your flame burn out, little beauty. You'll be in trouble." He turns me once more, taps his cane on the ground, and then kisses me good-bye. "Time to go."

Rémy walks Elisabeth and me down the six flights of stairs and through the Grand Entry Hall to the south wing. I'm wearing one of the Fashion Minister's latest creations—a honey-and-marigold bustle dress with a waffle texture and a waist-sash of striped fur. My Belle-bun is adorned with snow-white pearls to complement it.

The halls hold decorations for the upcoming Declaration of Heirs Ceremony. Cameos of Sophia's face mark night-lanterns. Her favorite flowers have been made into garlands. Vendors sell dolls in her likeness, fitted with a tiny version of the queen's crown. Five days until the kingdom-wide celebration. Five days left to decide how to answer the queen.

Newsies are swarming the halls, sending out black post-balloons full of gossip. Sparklers are bursting overhead. Night-lanterns oscillate with bright colors. Courtiers are wearing cold-themed headdresses and hats, adorned with snow-flecked branches and holly berries, owl feathers and foxtails. Everyone is eagerly anticipating the first snow. Bubbly, jewel-toned liquid fills their glass flutes and tumblers. Some lift up ear-trumpets to listen to the conversations happening in the halls. Men chase women down corridors, and laughter and spirited chaos ensue.

Rémy grumbles and then guides us through the pockets of people. "This way." He pushes aside an eager newsie wanting to sketch my picture. "Not now. You know the rules."

The newsie ignores his request. He moves one pen on his small pad, and three others sketch alongside it. The picture is complete before I can take two steps forward.

The doors of the Royal Game Salon open for us. The ceiling arches in jutting curves and slopes. Night-lanterns rub along its surface, bathing the enameled décor in light. The room spills over with sounds of clinking glasses and tumbling dice and whooshing table-lanterns and hissing candles and laughter. So much laughter.

Plush tabletops display porcelain boxes studded with gold and diamonds and precious gems. Game chips line a wall behind a kiosk labeled BANKER. Chaises and high-backed chairs and claw-footed sofas circle the game tables, which spill over with candles, desserts, and pastel-colored gambling chips. People stuff their mouths with treats, and blow onto game pieces for luck.

"Keep up," Rémy says over the din.

Women smile and coo and wave their fans in my direction. "I guessed it would be you," one calls out. "So happy to win, even if late."

"I made back my forty leas in the lottery now that you're here. I picked you from the beginning," another calls out.

I smile and wave. Elisabeth giggles beside me. "We're going to make a ton of spintria, Camille, and Mother will be proud of me." She grabs for my hand, and I jerk away.

"*I* will make a ton of spintria," I say.

A cold wind follows courtiers through the doors leading from the Royal Game Salon dock. The moon winks light across the golden pier. Canal boats float like jewels on the dark water. Men and women from merchant houses enter, displaying their families' wares on their clothes, in their hair, or even embedded in their skin. Women wearing House of Spice dresses leave tiny trails of cinnamon and anise and saffron, and those from the House of Inventors are outfitted in gowns covered with silkscreen pictures of their newest products. Men are donning House of Bijoux top hats, indented with chambers to display pearls and rubies and sapphires.

Princess Sophia's game table sits dead center in the room. Hand-painted plates boast a kaleidoscope of patisserie and petit-cakes pierced with flaming sparklers. Champagne bubbles over a tower of stacked glasses into a small golden well. Courtiers dip their flutes into it. Sophia bounces up and down in a high-backed chair, sipping from two goblets while a woman fans her. Her teacup elephant, Zo, sits in her lap, stealing sips from her glass and nibbling the strawberry on her petit-cake. Sophia laughs and directs her teacup monkey, Singe, to roll the die for her on the circular board that hooks around the champagne-flute tower. Hand-drawn boxes circle the center of the board and hold brilliantly colored numbers, one through seventy.

"Your Highness," Elisabeth says, bowing. "I have the favorite, Camellia Beauregard, here as requested." Elisabeth pulls me forward. I lower my head.

"You look well," Sophia says.

"As do you." She's changed her look from the one I gave her. A halo of tiny blond corkscrew curls bounces up and down on her shoulders. I push down worries that she knows what I tried to do in our last beauty session.

Her ladies-of-honor stare. Sophia waves for a chair to be brought for me. "Sit, sit. And watch. I'm on my second official date with suitor number one—Alexander Dubois from House Berry."

He nods. He is feeding Singe grapes, and grins at Sophia with a gap-toothed smile. His hair almost matches hers tonight—long and blond, with a hint of a curl. But his skin is the same warm brown as mine, and Sophia is as pale white as the porcelain die she clasps in her hand.

Gossip swirls around me: Lady Hortense Bellaire is rumored to have fleas and mice living in her dreadful wig, while Countess Isabelle Favro has no beauty tokens, so she's taken to kissing Fabian, a well-known dandy, for spintria. Gabrielle lifts a smelling box to her nose when a courtier woman comes to say hello to Princess Sophia. She shakes it to release some of its lavender and lemon scent. The woman scampers off, near tears.

Princess Sophia claps her hands to gather the attention of her game table. "Singe is the banker. Place your bets."

Courtiers slam colorful gambling tokens on various numbers. The teacup monkey stamps his tiny feet and points at the velvet bag beneath them. Hands move even more quickly, tossing chips on the game board.

"Singe, all bets are placed." Sophia sits back with a smile. Singe unclasps the bag's strings and disappears inside of it. The players await his return. The woman to my left holds her breath. The bag rustles; then Singe's head reappears. He flashes all of his teeth and leaps forward onto the ledge in front of Sophia.

"Zo, take the ticket," Sophia commands the teacup elephant in her lap. Zo drops her strawberry and trundles forward to the edge of Sophia's voluminous gown. She reaches out her tiny gray trunk. Singe hands her the ticket. "Good girl, Zo. Such a good petit," Sophia says. "You follow directions so well."

She smiles at me as she takes the ticket.

"Number twenty-six," she announces. "Whoever bet on twenty-six receives sixty-four times their stake."

"That's my number," a young woman shouts from the far end of the table.

Singe dances along the table's edge.

The young woman barrels through the thick crowd. "Excuse me. Pardon me."

"It's one of Madam Pompadour's triplets. I should've been able to smell her coming," Sophia says to Gabrielle and others nearby. Courtiers chuckle. The young woman bounds forward with an eager smile. A perfume atomizer sits atop her brunette head like a grand hat. It spits perfume every few moments. A person behind her sneezes. Pomander perfume beads coil around her corset like interlaced chains, and her waist-sash is swallowed by a stitched advertisement: VIVA LA POMPADOUR. She's from the mercantile House of Perfumers, affectionately called Le Nez.

Sophia fans her nose, and Singe covers his. "My, my, Astrid, aren't we smelling lovely this evening."

The group laughs.

"Mother says she wanted the whole court to preview our new line of scents, just in time for the queen's presentation of toilette-box allotments for the new year." Astrid blushes and jumps with excitement, seemingly ignorant of Sophia's jokes. "She will be so pleased to hear your compliment and to hear about my winnings. How much? How much?"

Nearby ladies cup their hands to each other's ears and whisper and giggle and frown at Astrid Pompadour. My stomach squeezes.

"A question first," Sophia says.

"Anything, Your Highness," Astrid replies with a bow.

Sophia turns to me, then touches my hand. The unexpected touch makes me leap. "Do I frighten you, Camellia?" Sophia smiles—a slow, teacup-tiger reveal of teeth.

"No, Your Highness. I just..."

"Just what?"

Everyone listens and watches.

"You startled me."

Her lady-of-honor Gabrielle whispers something in her ear. Her gaze fixes on me once more. "My favorite, I have a question. What do you think of Astrid? Her looks, that is?"

I turn my head like it's on a slow swivel.

Astrid grins at me. Bright pink rouge-stick stains her teeth, and the face powder she has used doesn't mask the tiny gray tint in her skin. Gray strands streak her hair, though she's cleverly tried to cover them with beeswax and pomatum.

"She's lovely," I say.

Astrid squeals with delight. "Thank you, thank you, thank you, favorite. Blessings to you. I do try very hard with limited—"

"Silence!" Sophia commands.

Astrid swallows the last bit of her sentence and her happy giggle. Laughing courtiers button their lips. A hush falls over the entire game room. Hands freeze over tables, mouths are afraid to chew their contents, dice and game chips dig into palms instead of being placed on lucky bets.

"Have a closer look, Camellia. You must be too far away to judge her beauty accurately," Sophia says.

I search Sophia's eyes, trying to understand why she's making me embarrass Astrid in front of all these people. Is this retribution for attempting to change her manner during our session?

She waves her hand, pushing me to scrutinize the poor girl.

A servant lifts the seat under me. I almost topple forward. Her ladies-of-honor Gabrielle and Claudine snicker at the mishap. My feet fill with lead, and moving each one forward feels like it takes an hourglass's worth of time. The mirror hidden deep in my corset warms against my skin. I'm face-to-face with Astrid. She smiles again. My own smile in response is weak.

"What do you see, Camellia?" Sophia says. "It can't be anything lovely. Not in the least."

Astrid's face crumples. Her mouth pulls down with sadness. Her eyes dart around. Courtiers whisper their agreement with Sophia's statement. "Your Highness, I hope I have done nothing to offend you, but if I have, my sincerest apologies," Astrid stammers out. A deep sweat rushes down her brow, taking her face powder with it. The tinge of gray in her skin is more visible now.

"You *have* offended me," Sophia declares.

Gabrielle hands Astrid a scandal sheet called *Sir Daniel's Dastardly Delights*. The vulgar words race along the page as if they're afraid of all the candlelight in the room. The pictures morph into a dozen lurid scenes, and capture the salacious rumors circulating the kingdom this week.

"Extinguish a few of the candles so the ink will settle," Sophia says.

Servants reach long-handled douters overhead and snuff out a few flames. Others herd night-lanterns into faraway corners. A candle is brought right beside Sophia. She places it on the game-table ledge. It illuminates her face but casts shadows in her eyes. She clears her throat. She's terrifying. "Your offenses, Astrid Pompadour, are enormous. There's the slovenly way you—and your sisters, I might add—carry yourselves, and embarrass Orléans, and your merchant house, Le Nez. And there's the fact that your mother is rumored to be my father's latest mistress."

A roaring gasp rushes through the room. My hand cups my mouth.

Astrid shakes her head. "She is not."

"Your mother is quite glamorous. I don't know why she lets you parade around court looking a mess. Maybe all the family spintria are spent on her."

"She isn't—"

"Your assurances and promises mean nothing to me. I've heard it on good authority that she is." She reaches for a platter of strawberries and dips one into the bubbly liquid in her flute. "Camellia, she must have a new look. To match her harlot of a mother."

She waits for my response. Fear flashes in Astrid's eyes. The words stick in my throat.

"Don't you agree?"

I want to walk away. I will my legs to move. They shake instead, remaining fixed in place like deep roots. Astrid stares at me, her pupils dilated, tears brimming over at the edges.

"I'm waiting," Sophia says. "I demand an answer."

"Of course she does," Elisabeth blurts out. I glare at her, and her eyes plead with me. Astrid's breathing accelerates.

"If you say so, Your Highness," I say.

Her mouth curves into a grin. "Yes, I do say so. I do." She pops up from her chair and hands Claudine her teacup elephant. Claudine keeps her gaze low. Singe leaps from the game table and onto her shoulder. Sophia circles Astrid and waves the scandal sheet in the air.

I spot a few words and phrases:

MADAM POMPADOUR

MISTRESSES OF THE KING

SHAMEFUL

DISGRACE ON LE NEZ

Sophia takes a deep breath and beckons for us all to mimic her. The room sucks in a collective breath. She exhales. The whole room sighs.

"I smell a . . . PIG! That's what." She touches my shoulder. "Give her a face befitting one."

Astrid cries out. "Oh, please don't," she begs, cowering. "Please, Your Highness." Guards lift her arms and force her upright.

"Your Highness, I couldn't possibly. I don't have my caisse, the Belle-rose tea, my accoutrements," I say in a panic.

"She's right, Princess Sophia, Your Highness," Elisabeth adds. "Beauty work must never be done without those items."

Sophia whips around. "It can, and it will."

"Please," Astrid cries out again.

"SHUT your mouth!" Sophia says.

Astrid bites her bottom lip, desperate to hold in the sobs. Rouge-stick is smeared over her mouth.

"Now, Camellia, *my favorite*, do it," Sophia says, returning to her seat to watch. "And not in an hourglass's worth of time, but now."

I purse my mouth to keep it from quivering. I take deep breaths. I search Sophia's face, waiting for her to shout out that this is all a big joke.

"Do it," Sophia hollers. "I order you to. Now."

The conversation in the room halts. Eyes settle on me. No one dares to move or talk or take a breath. Sophia's eager stare burns.

I close my eyes. "I'm sorry," I whisper.

"Don't, favorite. I beg of you, don't," Astrid pleads.

Astrid's face appears in my head: her close-set eyes and graying skin and too-small lips and beaky nose. The arcana awaken. A rush of heat flashes through me. The veins in my hands swell. I open my eyes.

I stretch out the hump on the bridge of her nose like it's a clay model. I dig out more space in her nostrils. I force her bones to twist and the cartilage to fill in.

Astrid screams.

I stop. I can't do this. I can't.

The guards hold Astrid still.

"Keep going," Sophia snaps. "Do as I say, Camille."

I shape Astrid's flesh into a snout. Tears fill my eyes as she wails.

"Add hair. Add hair," Gabrielle shouts.

"Yes," Sophia demands. "Bristly hair."

Some in the crowd laugh. Others grimace, no doubt thankful

that this isn't happening to them. A few look away. I thicken Astrid's nose hair, and lengthen it so it pokes from each nostril like the stubble on a man's chin.

Astrid screeches and drops to the ground, slipping from the guard's grasp like a piece of silk. She's a pile of sobs and moans. The guards hustle her back up onto her feet. She presses her hands to her face. A favored lady courtier yanks them away to reveal her new nose. The snout glistens with snot.

"Well done, Camellia. Beautiful. May you always find beauty, Astrid." Sophia waves the guards forward. "Let's go see what the newsies think. Give them something for their late-night papers." She leads Astrid, her ladies-of-honor, and a train of eager courtiers out of the room and into the Grand Entry Hall. She announces that everyone should follow and head for the Receiving Hall for a night-parade.

"You must go with them," Rémy says, unsticking my feet.

"I didn't want to do it," I say.

He is silent, but disappointment is reflected in his eyes.

"What was I supposed to do?"

"None of it is my business," he says, escorting me at the tail end of the group.

In the Receiving Hall, Sophia marches Astrid up and down the long entryway from the door to the throne platform and back. She commands the musicians to play and that Geneviève Gareau, the most beloved opera singer in the kingdom, be brought in to sing. Geneviève is taken from bed, and shows up in her nightgown. Misen players pluck their instruments, and Astrid is forced to perform peasant dances. Sophia drags in Astrid's two sisters to watch. After three hourglasses pass, Sophia's ladies-of-honor are splayed out on plush kneeling-pillows at the base of the throne, and their snores add to the misen players' song. My stomach is twisted into a knot that might never uncoil.

Can this be real? Is this how Sophia treats people? Is this how she will lead? Will she force me to torture her people for the rest of my life?

The queen's words echo in my head again—*Sophia cannot be queen.*

I have to stop her.

# 35

Rémy deposits me in my apartments and takes his nightly seat outside the door. He doesn't say good night. He doesn't offer to have tea with me, which I was hoping would become a habit. He won't even look at me. I pace the perimeter, circling all six apartments at least twelve times with my hands on my head, squashing the top of my Belle-bun. Flower petals and jewels tumble out. I yank the ornamental combs from the top and unpin the curls. The nest of hair grows around me like a frizzy cloud.

I step out on the windy terrace. The cold nips at my shoulders. The scent of snow is in the air.

Bree pokes her head out. "It is time for bed, my lady."

"In a few minutes." I slip past her, down the hall to the very last apartment. I knock on Ivy's door. I wiggle the door handle. It's locked. I knock again.

"Ivy," I whisper hard, hoping it will somehow travel all the way inside. There is no reply.

I go back to my room to a waiting Bree. "Can you wake Ivy?"

Bree looks startled. "But it's time—"

"Please," I say softly.

"Wait in your room, and at least dress for bed. Also, there's a post-balloon hooked to your vanity."

"Thank you." I undress and put on my sleeping gown. An orange post-balloon floats above my caisse like a flame. It's from the Fire Teahouse.

Edel.

I rip the back open and grab the note.

*Dear favorite, Lady Camellia Beauregard,*

*Your sister Edel Beauregard is not presently at the Fire Teahouse. If you have any knowledge of where she might be, please send me a personal correspondence. I have been able to keep the ledgers full and the customers happy, but if Edel doesn't return soon, I'm afraid everything will unravel.*

*If you hear from her, tell her she should return to the teahouse immediately; otherwise, she will be treated as a fugitive, subject to punishment in accordance with the laws of our great queen and country, and held in contempt by the Minister of Law.*

*I do not want this to happen. I just want her back.*

*A Goddess-of-Beauty blessing to you. May you always find beauty.*

*Sincerely,*

*Madam Alieas Saint Georges, House Maille, Mistress of the Fire Teahouse*

My heartbeat quickens.

How is Madam Alieas keeping the newsies from finding out? How is she keeping business going?

Where are you, Edel?

I write Amber a letter. My handwriting is a frantic scribble across the page:

*Amber,*

*I need to talk to you. It's about Edel and something Sophia made me do. Can you come to the palace? Or I'll try to come to the Chrysanthemum Teahouse.*

*Edel's in trouble. I think I might be in trouble, too.*

*Camille*

I send the post-balloon off my balcony edge.

"Camille." Ivy stands in the doorway. Her voice is thick with sleep.

I rush to her. "Sophia made me do the most awful thing, and I..." My voice trails off.

Ivy closes the bedroom doors and sends the servants away, suddenly alert.

"What happened?"

"She made me give a courtier a pig nose! In front of everyone in the game room." I can't stop pacing.

Ivy gasps. "It's starting all over again. She did this with Amber, too. Oh, this is all my fault."

"Did what?" I ask. "What's your fault?"

"I told Ambrosia to do everything Sophia said," Ivy says. "I told her it was her job to please Sophia. And Sophia began asking her to do unreasonable and ridiculous things."

I remember what Elisabeth said—that Amber gave one of Sophia's ladies-of-honor translucent skin, covered another in feathers, and gave Sophia the smallest waist possible. I hadn't believed it at the time—couldn't believe Amber would do such things. And now I had ruined a girl's face.

"It's going to get worse. She's going to ask you to do more. She's testing your loyalty." She takes my hand. "I already tried to tell you. Nothing will stop this. It's just the beginning. We have to go."

"If we run, Sophia will just drag Valerie, Hana, Padma, or even Edel here to be the favorite. It will never end."

"None of this is supposed to end. We are *supposed* to do as we're told and go along with it. I can't any longer."

"We have to *do* something."

"There's nothing—"

"I'm going to help the queen," I almost shout.

"But you could die."

"Yes, but maybe I won't." I take a deep breath. "And we don't have any other choice."

# 36

The next morning, I pack a small satchel with bei powder, two smoothing instruments, and a few color pots. I tuck it into my fur waist-sash, then go to treatment room four.

Servants are tidying the room. I pay them each a pouch of spintria and leas coins and ask them to help me mess up the room. I put leeches into the Belle-products. They stare at me with puzzled expressions, but aid in the destruction. I add one beauty token to each palm, with an instruction to keep their mouths shut.

I hustle back to the main salon and knock so hard on Elisabeth's door that it rattles.

She snatches it open. "Who the—" She swallows the curse on the other side of her sentence. "What is it? I'm busy. The phones won't give me a moment's rest since the card party."

"Leeches got into the Belle-products in the fourth treatment salon, and the room is in shambles. Maybe someone broke in?"

"What? How?"

"I don't know. You need to hurry. It's a mess," I say. "I would hate for word to get to Madam Du Barry. We'll both be in trouble."

Her mouth goes slack and her face pales. She races off, leaving her office door ajar.

After she disappears, I slip in. Circuit-phones line every inch of the walls like floating candlesticks. Cone-shaped receivers rattle left and right on top of each one. Their ringing pierces the room. I don't know how Elisabeth can tolerate it. A rolling ladder scales the wall, giving access to the phones that nearly kiss the ceiling. Iron spintria safes sit like a stack of blocks beside the door.

I bolt to the corner desk. It's covered with beauty-scopes, spyglasses, appointment ledgers, spintria pouches, post-balloon letters, and beauty pamphlets. I open each drawer, searching for an address book. One is cluttered with newspapers and tattlers and scandal sheets, another with petit-hourglasses and abaci. The last one is packed with unused post-balloons and parchment. I dig under them and discover a royal address ledger.

Thank you, Goddess.

I scour it for the address of the Pompadours from Le Nez, House of Perfumers. I use Elisabeth's quill to write the information on my hand, and step out from the office just in time to hear her angry voice echo from the hallway. I race back to the bedroom and pull the string for Bree.

She steps out from behind the wall. "Yes, my lady?"

"Bree, pack the bed with pillows, tightly, and draw the bed-curtains as if I'm in there. If Elisabeth asks, say I'm not feeling well and went to rest. Tell no one I'm out. Will you do that?"

Her brown eyes grow big. "But my—"

I press a few leas coins in her hand. She shakes her head and pushes them back at me. "Go, and hurry back."

I hug her. She helps me into my traveling cloak and gives me a veil; I tiptoe back through the main salon and out the front apartment doors. Rémy stands at attention as soon as he sees me.

"I need to go to the Rose Quartier," I say.

"Has the travel been arranged ahead of time?" he asks.

"Of course," I lie confidently.

Rémy marches forward. I'm careful to keep my head down as courtiers pass by. I search for signs of the Beauty Minister or Du Barry. We leave through the northern gate. The sky is a snow white, with the promise of ice-flakes and wind at any moment. A line of rickshaws sits, ready to carry important passengers into Trianon or beyond. Glamorous courtiers climb in and out of private carriages. Imperial canal boats load and unload people onto gilded docks beside the Golden Palace River. Heat-lanterns trail behind pedestrians to add warmth.

He pauses and looks around. "Where's your official carriage?"

I scurry to the nearest rickshaw and tell the man the address. He helps me up into the seat.

Rémy runs behind me. "What are you doing?"

The man holds up the canopy's thick brocade curtain so I can speak to Rémy.

"Get in," I say. "I'll tell you."

He looks pained. "This isn't protocol."

"You can either come with me or stay."

"Or I can take you back to the palace."

"Please. I need your help." I pat the place beside me. He stalks forward and climbs inside.

I peek through a small window that gives me a view of the front of the rickshaw. Two imperial runners take their places. Their graying hands stand out in contrast to the black lacquered finish of the rickshaw handles.

"Where are we going?" Rémy asks.

"To fix the mess I created last night."

He doesn't respond. The rickshaw bumbles forward. The runners' braids slap their backs as we race across several Golden Palace River bridges. The wheels thunder over the cobblestones. I clench my teeth until the palace gates open, and we zip through the Royal Square and past the giant Orléans hourglass, waiting for the Beauty Minister or Elisabeth or Du Barry to appear and stop me. My heart races to the rhythm of the rickshaw's movement.

Rémy drums his hands against his thighs. I steal glances at him. The silver streak in his closely shaven head glows in the subtle darkness, and the crescent-shaped scar under his right eye looks deeper. He even has a freckle on his left eyelid. The Belle who created his look paid attention to small details, made him unique. I want to ask him if he chose his look. I want to know if he cares about his physical appearance, or only about his duty. I can hear him saying, *I have no need for beauty.*

I laugh to myself.

"What's so amusing?" he asks.

"You seem nervous," I say.

"I don't like breaking protocol."

"I know."

"But you do," he replies.

"Guilty." The pink brick of the Royal Square gives way to white limestone mansions and townhouses adorned with quartz roses and blush-pink lanterns above their entryways.

"Number thirteen is on the right," the rickshaw driver hollers back. He brings the foot-carriage to a stop. I hand him a few coins.

"Thank you," I say.

We climb out. The House of Perfumers' Le Nez emblem shines brightly on the door—a bouquet of flowers tickling the underside of a nose.

I lift the heavy brass knocker. Its echo booms. A stout woman answers. "Can I help you?"

"Is Astrid Pompadour available?" I ask.

"Is she expecting you?"

"No, but—"

"She's not seeing anyone today." She starts to close the door. I put my hand on it and wedge myself into the doorway.

"Tell her it's Camellia Beauregard. Please. And if she still doesn't want any company, I will leave."

"This is highly inappropriate and irregular. Just who are you?"

I lift my veil. She gasps when she sees my face. "My lady. I'm so sorry, le favori. I did not recognize you," she says, giving a little bow. "Come into the foyer and out of the cold."

I wave away her formal apology. She disappears farther into the house. The foyer spreads out like the base of an hourglass—open and round—and a gilded balcony juts out overhead. Countless vases sit on every surface, holding snow-season flowers—tangerine calendulas and creamy candytufts and crimson cyclamens.

"Camellia!" My name is screamed from the balcony. Astrid races down a plush spiral staircase. She wears a jeweled veil over her face. Two sad brown eyes stare out of it. She swallows me in a thick hug. I almost topple over. "I can't believe you're here." She pulls back. "I'm so sorry. I'm a mess. I'm suffocating you."

"It's all right." I remove my veil. Her house servant takes my coat from my shoulders. "I wanted to apologize for the other night."

"It wasn't your fault." I spot tears brimming in her eyes through her veil. "Sophia forced you."

"I'm here to fix it." I take her hand and squeeze it. Rémy smiles at me, but it's so quick it could've been imaginary.

"Really?" Astrid squeals. "But what about—"

"It will be fine," I tell her, sounding much surer than I feel. "Where can we be alone?"

Astrid squeezes my hand in return. "We'll go to my bedroom." She turns to her house servant. "Carina, bring me Belle-rose tea. We have a few leaves in the tea closet. Top row. Left-hand corner."

"I'll wait here." Rémy stations himself beside the front door.

Astrid's bedroom feels like a gigantic flower. Heather walls wrap around us. A domed ceiling holds golden lanterns that drip with light like raindrops made from the sun.

Astrid sits at her vanity. "I went to the Chrysanthemum Teahouse early this morning, but Madam Claire turned me away. Princess Sophia alerted all the teahouses to refuse service to me."

"It's going to be fine." Sophia will be furious with me if she finds out.

Her house servant knocks, then enters the room with a tea tray. She pours a hot cup for Astrid. "Thank you. Thank you, Carina."

"You must still wear this veil, and you can't let the princess know you've changed your nose. Nor can you tell her it was me who did it."

"Or course not, Lady Camellia. I wouldn't dare. I'm so grateful."

"It should've never happened."

I pull the satchel of tools from my waist-sash. I examine her nose. The snout juts out of her face. My shame and disappointment overwhelm me.

I cover her nose with bei powder and dip one of my metal instruments into the pot of steaming water.

"Ready?"

"Yes." Astrid nods and closes her eyes. She takes a deep breath.

The arcana ignite inside me. I feel the warm hiss of their movement through my veins. I sweep the broad-sided metal instrument across the bridge of her nose. The excess skin melts away. I sculpt it back to its original shape—high bridge, long slope. I shrink the nose hairs. The former snout now curves into a slight upturn at the tip. I touch up the gray in her hair and skin as a bonus.

"It's finished," I say.

Her eyes pop open. She exclaims, touches her face, then bursts into tears. "Thank you, thank you. I just…can't…thank you enough."

I rub her back.

"It's the least I can do."

I leave Astrid in front of the mirror, examining her new nose. Rémy and I walk out into the late morning sun, out of the Rose Quartier into the Market Quartier to hail a rickshaw back to the palace.

"That was nice of you," he says.

"Nice?"

"I mean, I'm glad you did it," he mumbles.

"Even though it wasn't on the official agenda? And the princess will probably be upset?"

"Yes. It was the right thing."

"So, do you break the rules for noble reasons?" I ask.

He grunts in response. A poor version of a laugh.

We navigate the bustling corridors of the Market Quartier with their cobalt-blue lanterns and clogged shops. Representatives of merchant houses parade their wares. Women wear dresses covered in products for sale: pearls, perfume bottles, spice pouches, and more. Men shout from their tents and lure customers with promises of what's inside. I lift my veil to get a better look at it all.

"Can I trust you not to run off?" Rémy asks.

"Yes," I reply.

"Stay right here, I'm going to get us a rickshaw." Rémy trudges ahead to a carriage-and-rickshaw pavilion. Courtiers haggle over prices and admire trinkets. Rickshaws empty passengers full of happy laughter and gasps of excitement.

A royal carriage pulls up across the street. The emblem of one of Sophia's ladies-of-honor winks in the sunlight. I move into the shadow of a nearby pavilion as the door opens.

It's Claudine. She steps off the carriage and reaches a hand back. Out climbs one of the servant girls I've seen tending to Sophia. Her uniform peeks out from under a luxurious fur coat. Claudine opens a parasol over their heads, and they disappear under it like a pair of gossiping courtiers.

They giggle, exchange glances, and head into the market. I watch and follow them. They stop to admire baubles and necklaces, then enter a dress shop. The owner fusses over them with silks and brocades and taffetas. The woman pulls out a dress for the servant girl. When the owner turns her back, Claudine leans in, kisses the servant girl on the mouth, and runs her fingers through her cropped brown hair.

"You told me you'd stay put." Rémy startles me.

I crash into the shop door. The owner turns around. The girls look at me and scamper away from each other.

Claudine stomps forward. "Who's there?"

"Rémy, let's go, quickly." I try to hurry away.

Claudine snatches the door open and catches my arm.

My heart bubbles up into my throat. "Lady Claudine," I say with a bow, and lift my veil.

"Camellia." She stares with a terrified look in her eyes. Rouge-stick rings her swollen lips. "And just what are you doing here? Does Sophia know?"

"Pardon, Duchesse de Bissay." Rémy bows. "It was my fault entirely. I was giving her a tour of Trianon."

"Well, I was just looking for dresses," Claudine says. "With my attendant." She points to the servant girl, who stares at the floor. "I wasn't doing anything." She wipes a handkerchief across her mouth, fusses with her hair, trying to pull herself together. Tears shimmer in her blue eyes. She fans them away. "Violetta, go prepare the carriage. We'll return to the palace."

The girl rushes off.

A heavy silence expands among the three of us.

"Camellia, can we talk in private?"

"Yes."

Rémy walks a few paces ahead.

Claudine takes my hands. "Please don't say anything. Even if Sophia asks about me being in Trianon."

"I—"

"Sophia can't know." Her bottom lip quivers and her hands shake. "I'm in love with Violetta, Camellia." She gulps. "And I know I shouldn't be because she's without status. I'll be ruined.

311

Sophia is trying to secure a marriage for me. Someone suitable. Titled. Someone my father would respect and want for me. Someone who would help him settle his debts. And I know I need to tell her about Violetta. But—"

"I won't say anything, my lady." I hug her to get her to stop shaking. "I promise."

Claudine takes a deep breath. We stand there until her body stiffens and she pulls away.

She steels herself. Wipes away falling tears, shakes out her arms. "I will marry the next person she proposes."

Her words feel empty and practiced.

"Why not just tell her, and marry who you want?"

"As you are well aware, Camille, you don't say no to Sophia." The servant girl reappears. Claudine gives my hand one last squeeze, then gathers up the voluminous layers of her dress and leaves.

I'm numb as Rémy and I walk back to the market entrance, where a rickshaw awaits.

Once the curtain drops, Rémy whispers, "Be careful about carrying other people's secrets at court."

# 37

That night, light filters in through a slit in my bedcurtains.

"My lady..." Bree's voice slips in. "Are you still awake?"

I set Maman's book to the side.

"Yes."

"A post-balloon just came for you." She releases the canary-yellow balloon. It glows like a sun inside my dimly lit bed canopy, and knocks around the night-lantern.

"Thank you," I reply, and close the bedcurtains again.

I tug the tail ribbons and open the back to retrieve the note.

> C,
> *I'm safe.*
> *More soon.*
> E

I turn the page over, and the words SPICE and PRUZAN are spelled out in pastels. I'm not sure what these coded words mean, but at least she's safe. I press the tiny paper close to my heart, and a rush of relief surges through me. I blow out the night-lantern and drift off to sleep.

A rough shove awakens me. "Lady Camellia. Get up quickly."

Shouts and yells ring through the apartment. Feet tromp along the floor.

I sit up and rub my eyes. The scent of burning feathers, parchment, and wood stings my nose. A pair of strong arms pulls me out. Flames rush up the left side of the bed. The curtains flap and hiss.

Smoke fills the room.

"Wait! My Belle-book." I try to turn back.

"The bed is burning," Rémy yells.

I snatch at the curtains. He grabs my arm, but I struggle away. "Don't touch me." I lunge at the bed again.

He throws me over his shoulder like a satchel. I kick and punch at him. It makes no difference. "I'm supposed to protect you."

"I don't need your help. Put me down." He totes me into the main salon and puts me on a couch.

Elisabeth paces in front of her office, her cheeks flushed, a hand in front of her mouth.

"I have to get back in there. I have to get my Belle-book," I cry out.

She looks at me like I've just said I have wings and can fly. "I can have Mother send you another one."

"But—" I race forward and try to go back inside my bedroom. Servants block the doors. Rémy sighs.

"It's not safe, miss," one says.

"The fire will be out soon," another assures me.

I start to cough. More servants wheel in breakfast carts with carafes of snowmelon juice and water.

Rémy hands me a glass. I reluctantly take it and gulp down the cool liquid.

The bedroom doors snap open. A servant wipes soot streaks from her cheeks. "The fire's out. The bed will be replaced."

"What caused it?" I ask.

"The bed warmer, my lady. There was a book inside it."

Every muscle in my body clenches, and I rush forward into the room. No one stops me this time.

Servants break down the burnt bed, carrying off bedposts scarred by the fire. The sheets are charred black and eaten away. The metal bed warmer lies open like a pie without a crust. The remains of Maman's Belle-book are inside it. How did it get in there? The scent of fire brings back Maman's funeral and the flames that engulfed her body, smoldering the bed of Belle-roses, tearing first through her silk dresses, and then her skin and body. When I think too hard and my eyes get all blurry, I still see those tiny sparks flickering off the pyre like fireflies as Maman's body disappeared, and my old life evaporated.

The loss of her Belle-book feels like the last piece of her is gone. I sit at the edge of the burnt bed with my head in my hands until men come to tear down what's left.

I don't move from the spot for hours. Not even when Elisabeth tells me I have beauty appointments. Not even when Bree brings me a cart of food. Not even when the men return to construct a new bed.

I rest my head on my knees and listen to the thud of my heart.

"Will you just stay there all day?" a voice says.

I look up. Arabella stands over me. Her long veil dusts the floor and her crown glitters.

"Get up," she orders, grabbing my arm and pulling me to my feet.

"What are you doing?" I yank away from her.

"Checking for burns. Do you have any?"

"No."

"In any pain?" She lifts my arms and inspects my hands, her touch rough.

"No."

"Then you need to focus on helping Princess Charlotte before the queen's Declaration. It's in three days' time. The palace grows more dangerous every day, and Sophia will only get worse. You weren't hurt this time, but—"

"Sophia had something to do with this?"

Bree walks through the door holding newspapers.

"Sophia is involved in everything, and the sooner you realize that, the better." Arabella rushes away.

Bree bows at Arabella as she passes. The doors close with a thud behind her.

"Are you all right, miss?" she says.

I can't answer her question. My eyes fill with tears. My skin prickles with goose bumps. Rage thunders in me like a great storm. The heat of it warms my blood more than the arcana. The hairs on my arms lift as if lightning is near.

Sophia took away the last thing I had of my mother.

# 38

I go to the Imperial Library to find out if there's any record of Belles having an ability to heal. The space could fit all four wings of Maison Rouge de la Beauté and the surrounding forest and gardens. The shelves are mountains scaling the walls, tapering toward a sky of stained glass. Balconies split the room into levels. Ladders click along poles and hold servants squeezing books into nooks. Spiral staircases and tiny lifts connect to the very top. Maps of Orléans stretch along the walls, showing the kingdom's growth over time. A wall of royal emblems illustrates the tiers of the high and middle houses. Velvet armchairs and puffy couches are scattered around small tables. Reading-lanterns are clustered near visiting patrons.

This place has to contain an answer to my questions about the arcana. The things Du Barry never told us.

Rémy waits for me at the door.

"I'll only be a few minutes. Maybe a full hourglass?"

He nods.

I walk through the aisles, letting my hands drift over the spines. I pull a book from the shelf and open the pages just to smell them. When I was little and in trouble with Du Barry, I'd hide in our library. Maman would find me curled up behind a shelf with a reading-lantern and a book of fairy tales. I'd make a little tent out of my traveling cloak. She'd hunker down with me and read one of the stories with tough words in it. I was much more interested in falling into stories than completing Du Barry's assignments.

The scent of oil lamps and old paper and leather circulates. It makes me miss the tenor of Maman's voice and the perfume of her skin and how her arms made me feel like I'd never fall. The thought of Maman's burnt Belle-book brings tears. She'd want me to help Charlotte. She'd want me to do what's right.

Glass cabinets line a wall, displaying newspapers from various years. I gaze into them. The headlines are sluggish, showing their age. I'm drawn to the ones about Princess Charlotte.

PRINCESS CHARLOTTE HASN'T AWOKEN FOR A MONTH

THE QUEEN ISSUES A PALACE LOCKDOWN
AFTER THE PRINCESS FALLS ILL

IMPERIAL SERVANTS PUT IN STARVATION BOXES
AFTER THE PRINCESS REFUSES TO WAKE

THE FALLEN PRINCESS RUMORED TO BE NEAR DEATH

ROYAL POISONMASTERS BROUGHT TO THE PALACE
TO TASTE THE BLOOD OF THE SLEEPING PRINCESS

Her portrait is printed in the paper. Cameos sit side by side, showing what she looked like before—big hazel eyes, a freckled nose and round face, a small forehead like her father's—and after the sleeping sickness. She's still beautiful, even when asleep. Soft mouth, curls draped around her shoulders, a jeweled hair comb instead of a crown.

Articles boast different theories: imperial doctors blame sleeping draughts and poppy illness, tattlers and scandal sheets speculate about love sickness because Princess Charlotte's favored suitor, Ren Fournier, accidentally drowned days earlier, and many courtiers believe that someone tried to kill her because she was just too beautiful.

"Interested in royal history, Lady Camellia?" a voice says. I turn, and a pair of piercing brown eyes stares back at me. Deep wrinkles rim her mouth and eyes. Her hair frizzes around her head in a lovely disc shape. "I'm the royal librarian. Can I help you with your selections?"

"Actually, I'm interested in Belle history."

"Right this way." She leads me through countless aisles, snaking left and right. Spines show titles like *The History of Orléans* and *The Policies of Queen Marjorie II* and *Imperial Laws Throughout the Verdun Dynasty*, and so on. There are art books and romance novels and children's tales and thousands of rows I can't see.

She pulls back a gauzy curtain and ushers me into a small alcove. These shelves hold books bound with red leather. Tables hold maps of Maison Rouge de la Beauté, newspaper advertisements for the teahouses, and imperial beauty law ledgers. Display boxes feature first-edition beauty-scopes, framed pictures of gardiens, Belle-cards from past generations, and ancient beauty tools marred by age. Small beauty caisses, ranging in size and age, sit in the corners.

"We should have everything you're looking for. Otherwise it's in the library at your home." She lugs heavy tomes from the shelves and sets them on a nearby table. They have titles like *A History of the Goddess of Beauty and the Belles*, *The Very First Belles*, *The Mythos of Belle Origins*, *Belle Beauty Trends*, *Queens and Belles—the Most Important Royal Relationship*, and more. "Here are a few to get you started."

"Thank you."

I circle the alcove, admiring all the bits of Belle lore. I open gardien journals, scanning the text for any mention of the arcana and their healing powers.

One is written by Du Barry's fourteenth great-grand-mère:

*Day 12 of the Philippe Dynasty, the Year of the God of the Sky*

*One of the little Belles doesn't have a Manner arcana. Every time the girls are tested, she cannot soften a temperament or bestow talent. Instead, her subject's skin warms and their spine begins to protrude from their back, as if it might actually push through their skin. She won't be viable. I must reexamine how she became damaged.*

Another is from her sixth great-grand-mère:

*Day 274 of the Clothan Dynasty, the Year of the God of the Sea*

*I have to keep one Belle from the latest generation home. She has a darker side to her arcana. Her gifts behave erratically. Almost backward. Instead of removing wrinkles, she creates them. Instead of softening one's manner, she worsens it. Instead of making her clients beautiful, she distorts them. She killed a teacup house cat yesterday by slowing its heart. And the day before, she froze the blood of a bird.*

*I will work with her to reverse this. Or to control the manifestation of the dark side. But it troubles me. Something went wrong during her birth. I force her to pray to the Goddess of Beauty each night and leave candles at an altar. She's been cursed.*

Maman's arcana accidentally did the same thing. But a complete reversal of the arcana? I cup my wrist and trace the veins there, wondering if I can do the same. If the arcana can kill, surely they must be able to heal? But how?

The librarian returns with open scrapbooks. "I thought you might find these interesting. Mostly reputable, but there are a few tattlers and scandal sheets in there, too. They often hint at the truth at times, but never tell anyone a librarian told you that," she says, setting down three in front of me.

"Thank you," I call out as she leaves.

The pages crackle like the ones in Maman's Belle-book as I turn them. The pinch of the loss comes back again. Many of the headlines are so old they no longer flash on the page.

GODDESS OF BEAUTY PUNISHES THIS GENERATION
OF BELLES WITH FAULTY GIFTS

BEAUTY CARNAVAL WILL LAST TWO MONTHS THIS YEAR
WITH A WHOPPING 212 BELLES TO BE PRESENTED

COURTIER STUCK IN PERMANENT GRAY
STATE NO MATTER THE WORK OF THE BELLES
BECAUSE OF CONTAMINATED BLOOD

I shove the scrapbooks away. I'm no closer to finding what I'm looking for. The pieces to this puzzle seem too fuzzy and too out of reach.

"Researching yourself? Isn't that a bit narcissistic?"

A smiling Auguste slips into the alcove. Each time I see him feels like it's the very first time. His scent finds me from where he stands—salt, sand, and the seas: the comforting scents that waft inside my windows in the morning when I open them.

"I'm looking for information to help the queen. What are you doing here?"

"I'm looking up something for my father, if you must know," he says.

My heart hiccups as he approaches. "You shouldn't be here."

"I thought we were done with your warnings."

"Are you following me?"

"Yes, I saw you." His eyes twinkle. "And I *had* to come bother you."

"Is that what you're going to tell the Minister of Justice? When you're arrested, don't come crying to me for help." I hide my smile by looking at another gardien's journal. In the silence I hear him lick his lips and take small breaths and swallow. I try to focus on the words. They blur on the page.

"If someone wanted to change every single part of themselves—including the shape of their fingernails—could you?"

"Tired of the way you look?" I tease.

"No," he says, and toys with a beauty-scope.

"You ask a lot of questions."

"Some women find it charming." His gaze is so intense it sends a shiver through me. "I guess not you."

I laugh.

"I just like to know things," he says, and puts the scope down with a thud. "And I know a lot about you."

"Like what?"

He moves beside me. "That you have three gifts from the Goddess of Beauty."

I nod, unimpressed. This is something widely advertised.

"That you, obviously, can change a person's outward appearances, their manner, and age."

*Also, make someone ugly. Also, stop someone's heart.*

"Did I lose you?" He fishes for eye contact.

"No, I was just thinking about the other night. The card game."

"I heard about that. But you shouldn't feel bad. Sophia is..."

"Frightening," I whisper.

His eyebrows leap up in surprise. "She's misguided."

"That's what you call it?"

He shrugs and runs his hands through his hair. Its brown waves tumble right back to his shoulders.

"I shouldn't have said that," I say.

"You aren't shy."

"I'm not afraid, either," I say, thinking about the person I was before I was named the favorite—before I came to court, before I met Sophia.

"And she's my future wife."

I flinch. The words unexpectedly sting. "Has she made her choice? I hadn't heard."

"It's inevitable," he says cockily.

"Is that so?"

"Wouldn't you choose me?"

I laugh.

"I'll take that as a yes. But I don't know if I want to be married to her. We're just so..."

"Different."

"You could say that." His eyes drift over me. "I guess I'm looking for something else."

I reach for a newspaper to distract myself. He intercepts my arm. "You know what else I know about Belles?"

I should yank my arm away, but I let him hold it. His warm fingers press into my wrist. He turns it over, tracing his fingers along the path of my veins. An urgent knot ties in my stomach, and it only uncoils as I realize that I wanted him to touch me. I wanted to know what that felt like. "Your power lives inside your blood."

He shouldn't know these things. I shouldn't talk about what Belles can do. It breaks all the rules Du Barry taught us. But his curiosity about me, about Belles, is flattering.

His thumb makes its way to the puffed cuff of my dress, then back to my palm. My heart races and I'm worried he can hear it. I swallow. A deep flush snakes through me like the arcana. He twirls his fingers in mine. The pad of his finger traces shapes along my wrist and palm. A star. A square. A circle. A triangle.

"Would you ever give up your arcana?" Auguste whispers.

"No," I say, pulling my wrist back.

"I meant no offense."

"You never do." I return to my search, and hope this buzzy feeling dissipates.

"What are you looking for?"

"None of your business." I don't look up at him, for fear I might smile.

"Maybe I can help—"

"Help my favorite with what?" Sophia's voice cuts through his. My heart all but stops. Her teacup pets bound into the alcove with a series of noisy squeaks.

"It's nothing, Your Highness," I say with a deep bow, trying to hide my panic. Alone with one of her suitors. What will she do to me for this offense?

"It can't possibly be nothing if you're here in the Imperial Library and surrounded by so many books. I dropped by your apartments, and your staff said I could find you here. They said nothing of my suitor Auguste being with you, though." She bats her eyelashes, and I can't tell if she's upset or teasing.

"I escaped a cabinet meeting with my father and found her on my way out." Auguste moves to her side. He kisses her hand and whispers something in her ear. She giggles, and Auguste slips out.

"I came here for you, Your Highness." I show her scrapbooks and newspapers. "It was supposed to be a surprise. I was searching for vintage styles to present to you," I lie. "Ideas for new trends and unexpected looks for you to try. Especially one for the upcoming Declaration."

Her lips part in a wide smile.

"People who always aim to please me will be treasured."

She steps closer, and I am suddenly aware of how very alone we are. Her teacup monkey, Singe, jumps from the table and onto my shoulder. I'm frozen. The nails on his little feet dig into my skin. He pets my hair and leans close.

"But those who cross me..."

Singe hisses, his sharp teeth grazing my ear. I flinch and he leaps into Sophia's arms. She strides away. Her laughter echoes after her down the hall.

# 39

When I return from the Imperial Library, I find the king's nephew, Prince Alfred, sitting in the main salon, ready for his appointment. Several female attendants flank his sides. Newsies have filled their papers, tattlers, and scandal sheets with Alfred's exploits— gambling losses and several marriages and expensive tastes. He's notorious.

"Lady Camellia." He lumbers over to me. "Pleasure to make your acquaintance."

"Welcome," I say with a small curtsy. His musky scent fills the whole room. "Your Highness."

He goes to kiss my hand, then pauses. "Am I allowed to?"

"I'm afraid not," I say.

He grins and kisses it anyway.

I pull my hand away. My cheeks warm.

"I need a new wife, and I figured the best Belle in the kingdom would help me attain a look that women enjoy." He releases a deep laugh that makes my stomach knot. "I think I need more charm, too. It wears off too fast, and they leave me."

His female attendants release a series of fake chuckles and coo over how amusing he is. Servants help him into a seat and yank off his thick boots.

"What number are you on now?" I ask.

"Four, but who's counting?"

Disgusting.

"The servants will take you to a bathing chamber," I say. "Then we'll be ready to begin."

He insists on undressing in the main salon. A privacy screen is brought out. Every undone button and opened zipper echoes. I fixate on a spot on the wall. His female attendants ogle me. One holds a teacup tiger. It purrs quietly. Another gawks through a spyglass.

"This way to the bathing chambers, sir," says a servant.

Instead of listening, Prince Alfred marches out from behind the screen. His robe hits the tops of his gray feet. "How do I look?" he says to me, and turns.

"Just fine," I say.

The servants shower him with compliments and affection.

He finally allows himself to be led from the room. I find Bree stocking a beauty-cart. "Where's Ivy?"

"She's been summoned by Du Barry today," Bree whispers.

"Why?"

"I don't know."

We walk to the treatment room. The bed is dressed with warm towels and pillows. "Light more beauty-lanterns, and melt the pastilles early. Is the Belle-rose tea brewing?"

"Yes, my lady." Bree brings the teapot over, lifting the lid to show me the swirling rose petals in the hot water. I give her a nod of approval. Anxious nerves drum through me. They've prepared the room several times before. It's always been perfect. But being alone without Ivy, and with this prince, makes me feel uneasy. The memory of Auguste distracts me, untethering my mind and setting it afloat like a post-balloon.

Bree wheels out trays that hold hairbrushes and combs, hot irons and steam curlers, rouge-stick canisters, tiny pots of skin-tone paste, paintbrushes, and various kohl pencils. I take deep breaths, and I hope I can calm the too-fast beat of my heart.

"Set up chairs with pillows for his attendants."

"Yes, my lady," she says.

The man thunders into the room and guzzles two cups of Belle-rose tea. His female attendants take their places at high-backed chairs set in the corners of the room. I look away as the servant women disrobe him. He climbs onto the table. They drape his naked body with towels.

"Like what you see?" he asks one of the servant women.

They don't answer. One giggles. I flash her a look and she quiets.

I try to avoid squirming as I approach him. I place my fingers on his temples.

"Your hands are very soft," he says.

"Thank you, Your Highness," I whisper. "No more talking now. Let the Belle-rose tea start to work, and relax your mind."

"It's hard to stay relaxed around all of these beautiful women."

His attendants release approving chirps.

"Add the charm last. I like to be my true self through the process."

"Yes," I reply.

"I'm very curious about Belles, and—"

"In order for me to concentrate, and let my arcana work, I need complete silence. You understand, don't you?" I say with a purring voice he seems to like.

"I do." He turns his head so his cheek lands in my palm. I re-center his head and move to the side of the table.

I fold over the towels to reveal his legs. The sickly gray skin resembles an elephant's trunk with thick hair poking out. I grab for a charcoal stick. I draw lines along his thighs, then move to his stomach. The women study every movement I make. All four of them inspect my lines. I cover him with bei powder.

Bree presents a tray of tiny skin-tone pots. I pluck one that matches his royal look. Its rich yellowy hue reminds me of smashed bananas. I finger the round bulb in my hands. I mix a little russet brown in to deepen the color and add several undertones.

The women inch out of their seats. Servants usher them back.

I use a paintbrush to finish coating the man's skin with the paste, like sticky marmalade on toast.

I close my eyes and focus on the man's arm. I rub my fingers along the skin. Sweat coats my forehead. The beat of the man's heart, and the noise of his blood as it circulates through his body, grow louder and louder. I mix the pigments.

I open my eyes and wipe off the paste. The color climbs over the man's arm, changing his skin from pale gray to a warm color with yellowy undertones.

The women gasp with awe and approval.

"How's the pain, Your Highness?"

"Just fine. I'm like a thoroughbred," he says. I motion for a servant to blot his sweaty brow.

"I'm moving on to the deeper work you requested now." I run my finger over his stomach.

He squirms a little. "Give me muscle definition."

I close my eyes, picturing his body. I push a metal instrument along his belly.

He grimaces and grunts. Muscles appear. His skin tightens and reddens. He winces with pain.

I wave the servants over. "Sit him up. Give him another full cup of Belle-rose tea. Add a drizzle of elixir."

I do exactly what Ivy did with Princess Sabine. They lift his head and place the cup to his mouth. He thanks me. "Also, prepare an ice bath for him."

Bree scampers out.

"Are you all right, Alfie?" one of the attendants calls out.

He puts his hand up and flicks it to the right. The women stand on command and file out the door.

"Where are you going?" I say.

They don't answer, and close the door behind them.

He sits up.

"Sir, please lie down. I'm not finished."

He grabs for me—one hand closing on my wrist, the other pawing at my dress and neck. His mouth presses against my face. Panic tears at me.

"Your Highness." I push him away.

"I want to know what you taste like. If being born with color changes the way you feel." He rips one of my skirts and tries to untie my waist-sash. "You must all be different. I visited one of your sisters. The white-haired one—Edelweiss, yes, that was it—and she was lovely."

I scream out.

His hands find their way under my skirts. We knock into the trays, scattering Belle-products across the floor.

"I like screaming." He hisses at me like an animal.

I kick him and escape to the opposite side of the treatment table. He jumps at me again and presses me against the wall. He kisses my neck and smells my hair. I reach for the tools in my belt, grab a metal smoothing rod, and stab him with it. The rod pierces his belly. He grunts, but still pushes forward, trying to sandwich me between his body and the treatment table. I shove the rod in harder and finally make the space to slip away.

"Get back here!" he bellows. "Just one kiss." He yanks the rod out of his flesh and tosses it aside, like it's nothing more than a splinter.

He chases me around the table and catches me by the waist. I use my arcana to call the Belle-roses in the teapot back to their younger forms. They surge; the teapot explodes. The porcelain shatters. Liquid splatters all over, and he flinches as the hot droplets sting his back. I uncoil the flowers, stretching out their petals and stems. They bloom into thorny chains that I use to press Prince Alfred's arms and legs against the wall. He fights against the restraints.

"I like you. You're feisty," he says. Blood trickles down his arms and legs. I push the thorns deeper into his skin, then let a vine hook around his neck. He makes a kissing noise at me.

Anger pushes my arcana further. The sound of his heart pounds in my ears. Its fleshy red shape sears through my mind. Its erratic beat is a drum.

I slow it down, beat by beat.

The color drains from his face.

I tighten the rose thorns around his throat. They dig deeper, drawing more blood. His eyes bulge. He chokes and coughs and sputters.

The door bursts open.

Rémy bounds in. "Camellia!" He grabs me. My concentration breaks. I release the roses. Prince Alfred collapses forward, crashing into two carts. Belle-products shatter everywhere. The female attendants flood inside and cry out with concern.

I almost hit the floor, too. Rémy catches me, sweeping me up in his arms. I curl into him, arms tucked under his, legs pulled up, my head against his chest.

# 40

I'm immediately taken to see the queen—still covered in Prince Alfred's blood and Belle-rose tea, still angry from his disgusting advances, still shaky from almost stopping his heart. A veil covers me, an attempt at protection against the ever-present newsies and courtiers in the palace halls.

"What will Sophia's forever look be?" many shout out as I pass, ready to cast another wager in the newest palace-wide game. They flash animated cameos at me.

"What about this one?"

"No, this one."

"Will she be a blonde?"

"Freckles?"

"Will she take the coloring of her mother or father?"

Rémy blocks them from getting too close. I don't look up from the ground. The buzz in my head and heart and body make it impossible to think of anything else. We take a palace lift to avoid more courtiers.

Rémy posts himself outside the queen's door.

Chafing dishes melt medicinal pastilles, and steam vases release vapor into the room. The fireplace burns brightly.

"Your Majesty. Lady Camellia, the favorite, here to see you," her attendant says.

She sits beside an arched window. The Beauty Minister and the Minister of Law flank her sides.

"Sit with us here, Camellia." Her voice is soft and reminds me of my mother's.

I take the seat across from her.

"Let me see you." She motions for me to lift my veil. A nearby servant helps me remove it. She *tsk*s at the bruise on my cheek left by Prince Alfred.

A teacup and saucer find their way into my nervous hands; I take small sips.

She rubs my cheek. "I heard about the unfortunate incident with Prince Alfred. We've called you here to let you know what we're going to do about it," she says. "First off, let me apologize for his terrible and ungentlemanly behavior."

"I don't want an apology. I want him to be punished. I want it to never happen again. To anyone." The rage inside me flares and leaks out. I think about how he mentioned going to see Edel. Did he do this to her, too? Is that why she ran?

The Minister of Law twirls a black mustache between thick fingers. "Camellia, we're issuing his estate a fine of several thousand leas."

"And he will never be able to book an appointment with you again," the Beauty Minister adds.

"What about my sisters? Can he see them?"

"He is a prince, Camellia," the Beauty Minister reminds me. "He will need to maintain himself."

It feels like she's slapped me. "He shouldn't be able to."

"We'll make sure to have imperial guards in any treatment room with him in it from now on," the Beauty Minister adds.

"We'd rather not turn this into a scandal," the queen says. "If the newsies got wind of it . . ." She shakes her head and sighs. "We've paid the attending servants in your apartments for their discretion."

"So you want me to lie about it?" I grit my teeth.

"No, that isn't the case," the Beauty Minister says.

"Just be discreet," the queen adds.

I want to see Prince Alfred embarrassed. I want to see Prince Alfred lose his adoring flock of females. I want to see the kingdom ostracize him.

"He will be sent away. Banished to the Gold Isles," the Minister of Law declares.

"He should be put into a starvation box," I say.

The Minister of Law clears his throat and loosens his cravat.

"If that is what you wish," the queen says.

Her answer takes me by surprise. "It is."

"Very well, then." The queen motions to the Minister of Law. "William, see to it that the first few days of Alfred's banishment to the Gold Isles are spent in a starvation box. Make it a little too snug for him. I'm tired of his antics." She gives me a grim look.

"But, Your Majesty, don't you think it's a bit harsh?" the Minister of Law says.

"Not at all. Belles are not toys to be played with or abused," she says.

The Minister of Law opens his mouth to protest further.

"I'd like time with Camellia alone." She turns to the Beauty Minister and the Minister of Law. "If you would excuse us for a few moments."

The Beauty Minister squeezes my shoulder before leaving the room.

"Have you made a decision about my request, Camellia?" the queen asks as soon as the door closes.

I fuss with the rim of the teacup. The bruise on my cheek still throbs.

"I believe you've had an opportunity to witness just how wild Sophia can be. I saw her handiwork with one of the Pompadour twins. And I take it she's shown you her portraits? Her obsessions."

"Yes," I say.

"I take full responsibility for her actions." The queen reaches to her side and lifts an album. She shows me sketches of Sophia as a child with Charlotte. "She misses her sister. The illness has taken a toll on all of us." The queen circles their faces with her fingers. "I apologize for anything she might have done to hurt you. She's just broken." She takes my hand and looks me in the eye. Her fingers feel frail and bony, like Maman's did. The wrinkles around her eyes have deepened.

"She cannot be queen. What is your answer? Will you help Charlotte now? The Declaration Ceremony is coming swiftly in three days' time." She coughs. Attendants rush to bring her chafing dish closer. They hold it near her until her coughing subsides.

I don't want to disappoint the queen. I don't want to tell her no. I don't want to admit that I may not be able to help Princess Charlotte. I haven't found the answer yet.

"I still have three days to decide, right?"

"Yes, that's correct. I figured since you saw for yourself why Sophia is unfit, you'd be ready to help."

"I did, but . . . I need more time."

"That is fair," she replies. "Camellia, would you do me a favor before you go?"

"Yes, Your Majesty."

"Freshen my face up a bit so I don't look so sick. The world will soon find out, but I'd like a little more time. Just as you do."

"Should we go to your treatment salon?"

"No, no. Do it here." She pats my arm. "I don't have the strength."

I wonder if I can add youth to the queen's organs, so she can live forever and Sophia will never have to become regent queen. "I could help you reverse some of this. Maybe you could rule for years more—then Sophia won't have to be queen at all. Or at least we could give her time to grow into it."

The queen's mouth pulls upward. "Yes, you could, but I don't want it. Plus, one could have young organs, but still be sick. Illness cares nothing of age. One of my newest beauty laws will forbid the practice entirely. When my sunset comes, I'll be at peace with it. We all should be."

"But—"

"And I don't think Sophia will ever grow into it. Some people can change, while others can't. They're just insects stuck in amber." She touches my cheek. "Just take a few of the wrinkles away. Make my skin a little darker and richer. Like molasses. The sicker I get, the more the gray seeps to the surface and spoils the color, it seems." An attendant serves her a cup of Belle-rose tea in the most beautiful garnet-red porcelain cup.

"Is there bei powder available?" I ask one of the servants.

A lovely caisse is placed on the table between us.

"Leave us," the queen tells the attendants. She finishes the cup of tea and sinks back along her chaise. Her eyes close, and her breath is soft. We are alone again.

I close my eyes and picture her face. My pulse accelerates to the beat of her unsteady heart rhythm and the slow chugging of her blood moving through her veins. I use the Age arcana to smooth the deep crevices around her eyes, like rubbing a wet finger across dried-out dough. I deepen the brown of her skin. The queen's light snores and wheezes fill the room.

While she rests, I slip my mirror from inside my dress. I take a pin from the caisse and stick my finger. The seed of blood climbs through the mirror's ridges. The roses twist and reveal their message: BLOOD FOR TRUTH.

A fog appears in the glass, and then clears. I study her true reflection. The deeply wrinkled face of a sleeping woman looks back at me, alongside her grace, fragility, and her sadness. Tears streak her cheeks, following the deep creases in her skin. The queen's image holds all the weight of her title and the worries she carries. I feel them all like heavy bags.

I slip the necklace back down the front of my dress.

Her eyes snap open. "Please help Charlotte," she says. "You have three days until I need an answer. Until it's too late." She squeezes my hand. "I felt like the answer you were about to give me wasn't what I wanted to hear."

"I—"

"Please, Camille. Don't make me replace you, too."

My hands freeze.

Her eyes close before I can answer her.

"It's time to leave, Lady Camellia," her attendant says.

I stand and leave the room, quiet as a mouse, the queen's threat stinging like a fresh cut.

# 41

The next day, the Fashion Minister waits in the main salon for me after my first beauty appointment. "Well, good morning, little doll."

"What are you doing here? Have more dresses for me?" I kiss both of his powdered cheeks.

"No, and aren't you spoiled." He takes my hand. "Today, you are coming with me and the princess to the Dress Bazaar."

"But I have more appointments." I point to the wall ledger.

"And this is your most important one. We have yet to find a suitable fabric for her wedding gown. Nothing compares to the look you created. She says she needs you there, and future queens get what they want. Or have you not learned?" He waves the latest scandal sheet at me. "Come along," he says, sensing my hesitation. "You never know what mischief one can get into. You might have fun. The Trianon Dress Bazaar is the largest in all of Orléans."

Hearing the full name strikes something in my memory. A sign from the carriage ride on my first night as an official Belle.

"The Trianon Dress Bazaar. Isn't that near the Chrysanthemum Teahouse?"

"Why, yes, it is," the minister says, and winks as if he knows what I'm thinking.

Amber.

I race to get dressed.

The minister smiles. "Now that's more like it."

After lunch, we ride in a procession past the royal hourglass. It wears a coat of ice and snow, its diamond-like sand swirling inside like an impending storm.

"More tea," the Fashion Minister orders the carriage servants. Bree stokes the small fire and places more pots of tea on the iron rack. This is the largest carriage I've ever been in—like three regular-size ones put together.

I press my nose to the window. Sophia's royal carriage glitters like a sun ahead of us. My breath makes tiny flat clouds across the glass. A plan to slip away and see my sister buzzes through me, alongside my ever-present fear and panic. Rémy sits beside me on high alert, as if he can sense I'm up to something.

I laugh and join the conversation, hoping to quell his suspicions.

We pass through the Market Quartier. Blue lanterns fight the wind, clutching the hooks above their stalls. Vendors stand before their pavilions and shops, hawking their wares.

"Silkworms—finest quality!"

"Cravats that change color!"

"Best brocades in the kingdom!"

"Glass beads from Savoy—this color is *made* for you."

"Dresses that light up the night!"

Shoppers carry heat-lanterns over their heads like parasols

to keep warm. They drift over high hair-towers and hats like tiny stars tied to ribbons.

The carriages snake through the narrow passageways as they enter the Garden Quartier. The stores are piled on top of each other, like gift boxes in all the colors of the rainbow. Emerald lanterns shine above doors and inside windows. Golden lifts and spiral staircases take passengers up to the highest stores—some are hidden by the thickening white clouds. I spot the Chrysanthemum Teahouse in the distance, its turrets shining like the wings of bright bayou fireflies in the dark of night.

The carriages park. We step out onto the street. Sophia's ladies *ooh* and *ahh* at the sights.

"Isn't it beautiful?" Sophia says to me.

"Yes, Your Highness." I paint on a smile.

She hands me a heat-lantern. Its warmth heats my Belle-bun. Part of me wishes it could lift me away into the clouds.

Imperial guards clear the shops Sophia chooses to visit— Prima's Petticoat Palace, Gascon and Duhart's Fichu Forge, Lady Cromer's Brocade Bonanza. The Fashion Minister guides her through the complex vertical network of stores. Gabrielle, Claudine, and Henrietta-Marie saunter behind her. People bow and shout wedding blessings. Newsies sketch pictures and swarm us with gossip post-balloons.

The Fashion Minister's dandies comment on the best shops to visit: where to get the richest silk, which shopkeeper gives customers the best-quality champagne, what dressmakers have the keenest eye, which of the owners are favored by the queen and the Fashion Minister himself.

We take one of the golden lifts up. The glass windows boast advertisements: vivant dresses that shift color every ten seconds,

cravats that release cologne so a man always smells his best, matching outfits for teacup pets and their owners, hats and headdresses
as tall as the ceiling, lace shoes that jingle pleasant tunes.

I try to imagine when I will be able to slip away. With seven
guards around us and Rémy behind me, it's going to be difficult.
My head rattles with possible escapes. Maybe I can accompany
Sophia into a dressing room and slip out a back exit? Maybe I can
use the commode and sneak out through a window?

I try to keep track of the staircases, lifts, and shop names, but
the corridors twist and turn with no orderly pattern. It's a maze.

Sophia volleys in and out of several shops. Tailors, dressmakers, and merchants try to woo her with free gifts for her ladies, or
offer pastries and champagne. The princess's voice drifts down
the passageways as she speaks with the Fashion Minister and her
ladies.

"What do you think of this fabric?"

"I can't decide, Gustave."

"Beadwork or not?"

"Sleeves or no?"

"I haven't liked anything you've showed me, Gustave. You're
the Fashion Minister. Find me something the world hasn't seen yet."

I slow my pace between the sets of guards and glance into a
nearby shop called Shurette and Soie before we're rushed along.
It's lined with shelves of twinkling apothecary bottles, and smaller
tables hold even more. They contain animated dyes for vivant fabrics. The jewel tones shift from ocean blues to cobalts and magentas, from crimson reds to sunflower yellows. Others change from
pastel pinks to sky blues to lemony creams.

It would take several days to examine each one, to watch for
each color. There are thousands of them.

"Finest silkworms in the whole bazaar," the owner says, motioning at the opposite wall. Live silkworms stretch across gently turning rods. Silk eases from their bodies onto a spoke-wheel. "Perfect for any dress. Can be dyed with animated ink."

I nod my appreciation as I glance around for an exit.

"Camellia." Rémy rushes me along to rejoin the tail end of the royal group, and I lose my chance. In the next shop, I stand alongside Sophia and her ladies while vendors parade around her with fabrics and dress samples. Again, I search for exits. There are two: the entrance we came through, and a door in the back.

"I don't know about this dress." Sophia examines a gown Gabrielle holds out for her. "But it could be the start of something. It would have to be altered, of course."

"Try it on," Gabrielle urges. "Let's just see the cut to find a starting place."

"Yes," Claudine adds. "You won't know until you see how it fits."

"Wait, wait, I want Camellia's opinion on all of this. She's been awfully quiet," Sophia says. Her ladies chuckle and hide whispers behind fans.

"What would you choose if you were getting married?" she asks me.

"I can't even conceive of the thought, Your Highness," I reply.

"Of course you can. Weren't you with one of my suitors the other day?" The left side of her mouth curls up.

A cold stone drops into my stomach.

"He interrupted me. I did not welcome his company," I lie. "I find him to be insufferable and cocky."

"Is that so?" she says.

"Yes—I'm grateful I never have to marry."

My answer seems sufficient.

"Well, if you did, what kind of dress would you wear?" She stares straight into my eyes, as if she's searching for the answer somewhere deep down inside me.

I don't think of my preferences, but of Sophia's. How she changes her look almost daily—how she detests the idea of choosing one royal appearance for life.

"I would consider a dress that would change throughout the ceremony and reception. Not just in color, but in shape. Something that will morph into all your favorite dress cuts. A ball gown for the ceremony, a slim silhouette for the receiving line, a flounced skirt for dancing—but without you ever having to leave the party."

Sophia's eyes widen. "Do you think it's possible?"

"It could be. We could work with animated ink, and experiment with silkworms," I say.

Sophia winks at me. "You know how much I love to test things. I knew I wanted you around for a reason." She steps behind a screen.

Her attendant prepares to dress Sophia by removing her coat and gloves. Gabrielle lifts the hanger and carries the dress back to her. For a moment there is nothing but bustling and murmured compliments—and then Sophia screams. The sound pierces through me.

Guards rush forward. Rémy moves me aside as he helps to remove the screen. Sophia is crouched on the floor. Attendants flock to her. They rip the gown from her body. Ugly hives and burns mark her arms and chest. Tears course down her face, taking her makeup with them. Her body is racked with sobs. She suddenly seems so small and vulnerable.

"It's poisoned," someone says.

"I didn't do it," the shopkeeper says. "I swear."

The guards turn to arrest her. She runs off. A few chase her out of the store. Bodies swarm inside—newsies with post-balloons, nosy courtiers, passersby. Rémy and the remaining guards work to establish order and clear out inquisitive onlookers. Voices ping like sparklers around me. Flurries of hands reach for the princess, trying to comfort her.

More guards flood the space. In the chaos, I let my heat-lantern get too close to one of the hanging dresses and it ignites. Adding fire to the chaos only draws a greater crowd. Rémy whisks me out of the shop.

"Stay here," he says.

"I will," I lie.

The moment he turns to put out the fire, I flee down the winding corridor. I fight through the crowd to get to a set of staircases. I jump down three at a time and almost fall.

"Is this the way out?" I ask someone.

"Yes, three flights down. Or the lift is faster, miss. Oh, wait, aren't you..."

I don't wait for her to finish. I'm spurred on by fear, trying to apologize as I knock into shoulders and purses and small children. I make my way out of the maze and onto the street. I step out into the path of an approaching rickshaw and wave my hands.

The man halts. His fur hat flies forward. A woman snatches the privacy curtain back and screeches at the man and then at me. The woman sitting next to her joins in the barrage of insults until she sees me.

"Viola!" She slaps the woman's arm.

"Oww," Viola says.

"That's the favorite." She points.

"No, it isn't. Couldn't possibly be." She leans forward. Her nose scrunches as she inspects me. "Oh my!" She clutches her large bosom.

"Are you going to the teahouse?" I ask. "Can I have a ride? I promise to give you both a beauty token for your troubles."

"We aren't, but we'll take you there. Get in." She waves me forward. "Help her," she hollers at the driver.

"I can get in myself." I gather up my long skirts, step up on the footstep, and slide between the two women.

The squeeze is tight. The man races forward.

"What were you doing, Lady Camellia?" one asks.

"Yes, where is your carriage, my lady?" the other adds.

"I got lost inside the Garden Quartier," I lie.

"Well, that's easy to do. It's quite a mess. All those stores scattered here and there and on top of one another like a messy closet of hat boxes."

"Yes, it was my first time," I say.

"Not to worry," one says. "We've rescued you, the loveliest of favorites."

The women tell me all about the card game they're about to attend in the city of Verre. They kiss my cheeks and hold my hand and tell me how they won money in the kingdom's lotteries by betting on me to be named the favorite.

The rickshaw pulls up to the Chrysanthemum Teahouse. I press two beauty tokens into their hands and thank them as they whiz away, full of laughter.

My heart thuds.

I pull my jacket closed to block the wind. I avoid the entrance and walk around the side of the teahouse to the gardens near the veranda. I take off my coat and throw it up over the small railing, then lift my skirts to climb up. A buzz hums under my skin like the arcana.

I duck as servants set the veranda for afternoon tea. I wait until they disappear into the kitchen before darting into the hall. Day-lanterns putter overhead.

I climb the stairs. Madam Claire's high-pitched voice rings out, so I hide in the nearest room and press my back to the wall.

"Is Ambrosia still resting?" she complains.

"Yes, my lady," an attendant answers. "She always rests for an hour before tea."

"I lose three possible appointments in that time. Who said she could continue to do so?"

"She's slow to rebalance these days."

Their voices taper off as they move farther into the house.

I inch forward and check the hall, then race up the last set of staircases to my old bedroom on the third floor.

I turn the knob and sneak inside. The room is outfitted in deep reds and oranges like a phoenix's feathers. Ambrosia flowers wink and bloom from animated wallpaper. The bedcurtains are drawn.

I rush forward. "Amber?" I whisper.

No answer.

I say her name again and open the bedcurtains.

The bed is empty.

Disappointment floods every part of me. I'm near tears. On Amber's nightstand sit little mortuary tablets for Maman Iris.

"What should I do, Maman?"

I wait for an answer. I run my finger over the mortuary tablets.

*Search.*

The word drums through me.

I go back to the bedroom door. The noise of the servants in

the hallway sends me to the wall. I run my fingers over it, waiting to feel air. Then I push. Bree's old servants' quarters are empty. I slip out and up the servants' staircase. I search every room on this floor, then go to the next and the next until I'm at the very top of the teahouse, the tenth floor.

Madam Claire's apartments are on the right. Each door is locked but one.

As soon as I open the door, the sound of soft crying greets me. The room is pitch black, aside from one single day-lantern tied to a nearby door hook.

"Who's there?" a sniffly voice calls out.

I untie the lantern and walk forward.

"Amber? Is that you?" I say.

Something metallic drops with a clatter.

"There's no Amber here," a second voice cries.

The soft light of the day-lantern spreads.

A girl leans forward. She has one eye and half a nose. I startle and fall backward with a thud. Another girl reaches for me. The light hits her. Hair grows down the left side of her head—only the left side.

"Help us," she says.

I scurry away from her as more voices join hers like a chorus.

# 42

The day-lantern illuminates the faces of the women. Broken. Disfigured. Injured. Silver chains loop around their wrists like bracelets, and jeweled collars tether them to high-backed chairs.

"Who are you?" I say.

A parade of names hits me: Kata, Noelle, Ava, Charlotte, Violaine, Larue, Elle, Daruma, Ena. And Delphine.

Her face is seared into my memory. That night she fixed the woman mauled by a teacup bear.

"We're Belles, too," Delphine says. "Madam keeps us locked up here." She leans into the light; her eyes are lined with dark shadows.

"What happened to you? How did you get here? I don't remember you at home—"

"She works us all night."

"The crying," I say.

"We cry because they force us to take appointments until it hurts to use the arcana."

Delphine jerks forward. The chains clatter against the floor. "Help us."

"Please," another one says.

"Wait!" Delphine puts her hands up. "Shh."

They all go quiet. The melody of their tense breaths echoes.

I release the day-lantern. It putters to the middle of the room. We all hear the approaching footsteps.

"Hide," Delphine says.

I tuck myself behind one of the high-backed chairs and burrow inside thick drapes. I press my back against the wall, as flat as can be.

The door opens.

"My little darlings," Madam Claire coos. Her heels click against the floor as she approaches the floating day-lantern. "Hmm."

The girls start to whimper and cry.

"It's time to work." She walks a lap slowly around the room. "Larue, I think I need you today." Madam Claire unhooks one of the women. Larue's wails and protests bounce off the walls. "Please don't ruin my day," Madam Claire says impatiently. "Just come, will you?"

Larue digs her feet into the ground, but Madam Claire drags her like a stubborn teacup dog. The door opens and shuts.

I take five deep breaths, then leave my hiding space. "How many of you are here?"

"Thirteen, I think," Delphine says. "But I can't always be sure. The numbers change. Girls go missing."

Where did these girls come from? How can I help them? Only one answer comes to mind.

"I have to get you out of here." We can figure out the rest later.

"You'll need to get the keys," Delphine says. "From her waist-sash."

"You won't be getting anything." Madam Claire's voice booms through the room from another entrance. She releases four day-lanterns, the light so bright it's blinding.

The girls scream, the sound cold and sharp.

Madam Claire *tsks*. "I knew something was wrong when I came in here. The day-lantern wasn't tied to the hook, and I could smell you."

Smell me?

"They always put lavender in your soap. It's the queen's preferred scent."

"You must let these girls go," I tell her. "You can't keep them chained up like this."

Madam Claire laughs. "Oh, but I can. They are in the employ of the Chrysanthemum Teahouse." She turns her back to me. "Guards!"

Madam Claire's guard tails me up each flight of palace steps. I wouldn't be able to run again if I wanted to. The Belle apartments whirr with activity as palace guards swarm the halls, and post-balloons whiz in and out. Inside, Rémy is pacing. Du Barry is wringing her prayer beads, and Elisabeth has bitten her lips raw. The Beauty Minister is tapping her foot to an erratic beat but freezes when I enter.

"There you are!" Du Barry hollers.

Rémy lets out a deep sigh.

"I've returned her safely," Madam Claire tells her sister.

Du Barry clutches my shoulders, her red-tipped nails digging into skin and bone. "Where have you been?"

"Are you all right, little darling?" The Beauty Minister rescues me from Du Barry's grip and inspects me. "All in one piece?"

"Yes, I'm fine. I got lost in all the chaos after what happened with Sophia," I lie. "How is she?" I add a thick layer of concern.

"She's on the mend," the Beauty Minister says. "Quite scary. You must be rattled." She lays a hand on my cheek, then motions for a servant.

Rémy clears his throat. The rumble is deep and cuts through the room. "Madam Minister, let me express my sincerest apologies. Protecting Camellia is my responsibility. I failed you and my queen." He bows.

The Beauty Minister puts a hand on his shoulder. "You secured the princess. You did what was needed. Plus, it seems our favorite knows just where to go when lost. She ended up in the right hands." She smiles at Madam Claire. "Now that you're home safe and sound, I take my leave. I need to report this to the queen and check on Sophia." She kisses my forehead, leaving behind her deep plum rouge-stick color.

Once the doors close, Madam Claire says, "Ana, you've lost control of the favorite. She's been snooping around in my teahouse. She found the others."

Du Barry turns to me. "You saw them?"

"Yes, I saw *them*. The *other* Belles you keep in the attic."

Du Barry flashes her sister a look of annoyance and purses her lips. With a tilt of her head, she dismisses Elisabeth, who for once goes without an argument.

"What's wrong with them? Why does no one know about them?"

"You should be grateful to them, and to us for raising them, and to the other teahouse madams for caring for them," Du Barry says.

"Grateful?"

She takes a slow sip of tea. "You'd all expire much sooner if it weren't for those girls."

Expire? "You lied to us."

"Lie? No. I did not tell you things that aren't your business. This is gardien territory. My duty. But yes, since you've seen them, I suppose there's no use in trying to keep the secret any longer—there are more Belles in this world than you knew of. I didn't want you to find out this way. Actually, I never wanted you to find out at all." She glares at Madam Claire. "They aren't as strong as you, but they are necessary to address the growing needs of the kingdom."

"Why didn't you tell us? What did you do to them?"

"Caring for Belles is an imprecise art, Camellia. You will one day see, when you return home and raise a daughter of your own. Some turn out whole, beautiful, and obedient. While others are broken and rebellious."

"Were they born that way? Or did you work them so much that their arcana couldn't function anymore?"

"Both," she says.

The faces of those Belles flicker before my eyes. The faces of my sisters follow. We're all going to wither like flowers on a vine if we work the way they want us to.

"She chains them." I point at Madam Claire.

Madam Claire trembles. "Ana, you must understand—"

"Claire, you will not be entrusted with them if you cannot care for them properly," Du Barry barks.

"But they get unruly."

"Find a better way to maintain control and order. Otherwise, I will replace you at that teahouse and appoint another. Mother always said you didn't have what it takes." Du Barry wags a finger at Madam Claire, then sighs. "I'm sorry you saw that, Camille. It's not customary. But you must understand—"

"I will never understand," I spit.

"One day, with wisdom and age, you'll see that I've done what was necessary for the survival of the art form. For the goddess. For all of us."

I let out a guttural scream.

Du Barry laughs. She snaps an order at a servant, who produces a stack of newspapers. Du Barry reads aloud:

PRINCESS SOPHIA ALMOST KILLED WITH A POISONED GOWN

BEAUTY WORK SURGING TO A NEW HIGH—RUMORED TO
BE A BIGGER EXPENSE FOR HOUSEHOLDS THAN FOOD

OWNER OF GERALD'S GOWNS NOT COOPERATING
WITH THE QUEEN'S GUARD

A PLOT AGAINST THE PRINCESS FOILED—
THE REGENT HEIR STILL LIVES

THE FAVORITE CHOOSES A NEW WEDDING
LOOK FOR THE PRINCESS

"Do you know which of these headlines I care about? *Rumored to be a bigger expense for households than food!* Can you imagine?" She tosses the papers aside. "Spintria and leas and the longevity of Maison Rouge de la Beauté and Orléans. That is what I care about. To do my mothers' and grandmothers' and great-grandmothers' work. The teahouses will continue to run as they always have: with order, grace, and dignity. There will be a favored set of Belles, and a secondary set to ensure that the needs of the kingdom are met. Basic supply and demand. That is the way it's always been. And I hope I will be able to have even more Belles. In my mother's time, there were a hundred per generation. I haven't gotten as lucky, but I will change that soon. The God of Luck will bless me as I do this divine work."

I seethe with anger.

"And if you or anyone else gets in the way of that, you will be repurposed," she threatens haughtily. "Now, go to your bedroom. The nurses are waiting with the leeches. You've had enough excitement for a week. The toxins in your blood must be high. It's what makes you behave this way."

And with that, I am dismissed with the wave of a hand.

# 43

The next morning, I dress to see the queen. There are no beauty appointments this week. The Declaration festivities start today, and I sent word to Her Majesty that I've made my decision two days early.

The queen's gold-and-white post-balloon sits tied to my vanity. The note is pressed flat on the lid of my beauty caisse.

*Dearest Camellia,*
*I look forward to your decision.*
*Sincerely,*
*HRM*

Fireworks illuminate the snowy clouds outside the windows. The kingdom of Orléans will learn of the queen's illness and will have an heir announced this week, either Sophia or an awakened Charlotte. My stomach erupts just like the sparklers in the skies.

My angry thoughts hiss and pop like lightning. My heart thunders in my chest. My hands tremble with rage. Every thought of Du Barry and Madam Claire and the other Belles and my mother's Belle-book sends another surge through me.

"Tighter," I tell Bree as she ties my waist-sash. I have to keep it all in.

"Where do you think you're going?" Elisabeth strides through my bedroom entry with her arms crossed and her signature pinched expression.

"Ivy and I have an important meeting with the queen."

"Ivy has been sent home."

My heart plummets. "Why?"

"My mother doesn't like the influence she has over you. And I agree. I never really liked Ivy either. She wasn't very nice."

"Where is she?" I rush out to the hall and head off in the direction of Ivy's bedroom.

"She's already gone."

I pivot to face her. Elisabeth has a smug grin on her face.

"Why wouldn't you let me say good-bye to her?"

"So she can tell you to escape again? Or so you two can attempt to go together? Oh, yes, my mother knows Ivy told you to run, and the fact that you did—to the Chrysanthemum Teahouse—disappointed her even more. She thought you wanted to be the favorite so badly."

I open my mouth to lie. The sense of dread wraps itself around me. There isn't a private place in these apartments. They could know everything I've ever discussed with Ivy or Bree.

"Don't even try it." She waves her hand at me. "But Ivy will be punished for it. As she should be. Meddling in our business and making things more difficult."

"She didn't *meddle*. She warned me."

"That was not her purpose. That's not what big sisters are supposed to do. She was supposed to prepare you."

"She did," I yell.

"Soiled you, is more like it. And you better get back to work, before Mother sends you home, too."

Rémy and I walk to the queen's chambers. His strides are heavy blows against the floor.

"Are you still angry with me?" I ask.

He steps ahead of me. His jaw clenches. "This way."

"I'll take that as a *yes*."

He turns a sharp left.

"I needed to see my sister. Surely you understand that."

"I don't *understand* many things about you. Or your choices," he says.

Two guards and an attendant step into our path.

"Lady Camellia." The attendant bows and presents a rose-petal-pink post-balloon.

Sophia.

"You've been requested by Her Highness, the princess."

"I am headed to see the queen."

She thrusts the post-balloon's tails into my hands. I open the back of the balloon and remove the letter from its compartment. I open the privacy casing.

*Your presence is requested by Her Royal Highness Princess Sophia in her tea pavilion immediately. My mother says you can come see her afterward.*

I glance at Rémy. He glares straight ahead.

Does she know the reason I'm meeting with the queen?

"You are to come now."

In the gardens, a tea pavilion shimmers: a thick white-fur canopy draped over a beautiful low table, set with flowers, pastel teacups, and flickering candles. A cold wind loosens the curls from my Belle-bun as Rémy and I follow the attendant, weaving through the maze of winter shrubbery. A shiver races across my skin, and I'm not sure if it's a reminder that more snow is to come, or if it's because anger rattles every part of me.

Sophia's ladies-of-honor sit on plush cushions and feast on petit-foods. Heat-lanterns float overhead, casting a copper glow and warming the inside of the tent.

The attendant announces me. "May I present Lady Camellia, the favorite," she says with a curtsy.

I bow my head, then look up and spot Auguste sitting to the left of the princess, feeding her grapes one by one.

The sight of him makes my breath catch. He winks.

"How are you feeling, Your Highness?" I pretend to show concern.

"Much better. The rash is gone. The poison is out of me. I'm back to feeling like myself."

"And now you're ready to play," Auguste adds, which makes her giggle.

"I am." She feeds her teacup elephant, Zo, a carrot and pets her head. "Come sit. We're having a debate." If it weren't for the royal Orléans emblem hanging around her neck, she'd be unrecognizable. Her hair is like Hana's—bone straight, black with golden streaks, and soaring down her back.

I stare for a second too long.

"Don't be jealous, Camellia," she coos. "I had to get one final look out of Ivy before she was sent home."

"And she knew I preferred brunettes," Auguste adds. "Curly-haired, but—"

"No one cares what you prefer, *Auguste Fabry*," she says with a laugh. "A newsie challenged me to do something different—to not have blond hair for once. I rise to every challenge given to me." She fixates on me, waiting for me to meet her gaze. "But don't be jealous, you're still my favorite." She blows me a kiss. "For now." She pats a nearby cushion. "Come, sit beside me."

I ease down beside her like I'm getting used to hot water in a bathtub.

She gives me a playful shove, and I topple over.

Gabrielle and Sophia laugh. My cheeks flush, and I worry my anger will explode out of me any minute.

"Be careful. You almost sat on Zo." Her teacup elephant peeks above the cushion.

"My apologies," I say.

She eyes me. Zo rubs her tiny trunk along my dress ribbons. I catch the warm little trunk like a worm, and it wraps around my finger. Her gray color is beautiful, unlike the Gris. Rich and deep, like ocean stones. The teacup elephant scratches her blue-painted nails on my dress, and flashes me the chrysanthemum flower on her belly. I rub it, and she makes a happy sound.

"Zo," Sophia calls, and the little pet turns away from me, stretching her trunk in the opposite direction. "Leave Camellia alone. She has to join the glorious conversation."

The little creature flops down on a nearby cushion, her legs splaying in all directions.

A strong wind whooshes against the canopy. The heat-lanterns hiss and crackle and send the scent of woody charcoal through the pavilion. Gabrielle steals Claudine's pastry, poking at her waist. Henrietta-Marie sits in the far corner with her nose in a book. Singe bats the heat-lantern ribbons.

"We were just arguing about whether I should have you change Auguste's dreadful manner if I decide to choose him," Sophia says.

He laughs, then looks at me, trying to make eye contact. I stare into my lap.

"You could do that, right?" she asks.

"Yes, Your Highness," I say, keeping my answers clipped.

"Could you make him into a bumbling fool?"

"I gather you already think I am that," he teases.

"Maybe." Sophia turns back to me. "Could you make him obey my *every* command?"

"Our aim is to enhance, Your Highness. The first arcana is meant to refine one's natural disposition, or help one develop his or her talents, so that he or she may meet their goals." I sound exactly how Du Barry wants me to. A parrot. A tool, ready to be used. "Sometimes one's demeanor can become an obstacle for them."

Our eyes meet. Hers grow wide with a mix of curiosity and intrigue. Maybe if I had been successful in changing her manner, her mother would trust her to be queen.

"What type of disposition should I choose for him? Definitely get rid of the ego. The arrogance—though cute at times—must be lessened." She ticks off each thing on her fingers. "Girls, what do you think?"

"Camellia could make him humbler," Gabrielle says.

"Sweeter," Henrietta-Marie offers, barely glancing up from her book.

He wiggles his cravat as if it's too tight around his neck, then smiles at each girl.

"Claudine?" Sophia says.

She glances up from a tray of tarts. Her eyes are puffy and bloodshot. "No opinion."

Sophia scoffs.

"She's in a bad mood," Gabrielle says, rolling her eyes.

"Shut up, Gabrielle," Claudine snaps.

Gabrielle continues: "The second suitor you set her up with has refused to go on a date with her. She's been eating her feelings all morning."

"I will outlaw bad moods—especially for my official ladies-of-honor—when I am queen." Sophia picks over the trays of cherry puffs, honey tarts, macarons, and petit-cakes.

I glare at her. *You'll never be queen.*

"Regent queen," Claudine corrects.

Sophia's hand freezes before her mouth. A peach macaron falls into her lap.

"Completely unnecessary," Gabrielle says. "And rude."

"Well, won't you just be a regent queen? Will you get to change laws?" Claudine softens her voice. "I wasn't trying to be rude. I was just saying . . . Ignore me. I'm having a bad day. . . . I misspoke."

The tent goes silent, the kind of quiet that's laced with lightning and heat and thunder.

"Thank you for reminding me that I will never be queen on account of my sister," Sophia snaps, her voice booming.

"I'm—I'm—" Claudine stammers out, a deep blush climbing through her entire body.

"Why don't you leave, Claudine?" Gabrielle says.

"Fine." Claudine stumbles to her feet. "Sophia, I didn't mean to be..."

Gabrielle puts a hand in the air. "You're making it worse."

Claudine storms out. I wish I could leave with her. Gabrielle reaches over to Sophia and strokes her hair. "Now that she's gone, maybe we can all actually have some fun."

Sophia's frown softens. Singe kisses her cheek and feeds her a grape. Zo lets out a little trumpet noise.

"Could you make someone ugly?" Gabrielle asks me, which brings a sick smile to Sophia's face.

"That was my next question," Sophia says.

"You made me give Astrid Pompadour a pig nose. I think that was rather ugly."

The table bursts with laughter. Except for Auguste. He tenses.

"It wasn't that bad," Sophia says. "And I hear that she's had it corrected."

"Oh, has she?" I ask.

"Yes, even though I gave instructions to all the teahouses to refuse treatment to her. Someone has disobeyed me."

"Maybe she went to La Maison Rouge," Henrietta-Marie suggests tentatively. Servants rush in to clear plates and refresh drinks and set down more savory bites and sweet treats. Sophia grabs the arm of the nearest servant. The woman is startled and drops a glass. It shatters on the ground.

"Leave it," Sophia says. "It's fine." She turns back to me. "What if I wanted to test it? See if you can land this woman in the tattler *Ugly Papers* at the end of the year."

The servant squawks with fear.

"Wouldn't that be wrong, Your Highness?" I say.

Sophia lets the servant's hand go, and the woman races from the tent. "You must be very tired, Camellia. Maybe that's why you're not in a pleasant mood either." She glares at me. "We should all retire to our rooms."

I stand, more than happy to make my escape.

"Not you, Camellia, not yet. Linger behind a moment."

I freeze mid-step.

Auguste hovers in the tent's doorway. His eyes find mine, finally. They hold questions and concerns. I glance away.

"Will you walk with me, Your Highness? Another snowstorm is coming in a few hours. I'd love to catch the first flakes," Auguste says.

"No," she snaps.

He looks crestfallen.

"Leave. Camellia and I have business to attend to."

"As you wish." He bows, looks at me one last time, then ducks out of the tent.

The table clears, and her ladies-of-honor kiss her and exit. Sophia rises from her seat and plucks one of the cream tarts from a tiered dessert platter. She takes small nibbles. Just like her teacup monkey, Singe. The cherries stain her lips red.

Sweat slicks my skin. I gnaw at my bottom lip. Anger bubbles up inside me, threatening to boil over.

"I am a princess," she says. "I will be a regent queen." She fixes her gaze on me. "Did they teach that to you?"

I don't answer. I don't look at her. I stare straight ahead.

She walks over and stands so close to me that with each breath I take, I inhale a mix of her flowery perfume and the tart she just consumed. "You are to answer my questions," she spits.

"Yes, Your Highness. I know you will be queen."

"Did they teach you what queens do?"

"Yes, Your Highness."

"What did they say?"

"The kingdom of Orléans is ruled by queens; the crown is passed down through the women of your family. Queens ensure the proper governance of the kingdom and maintenance of its well-being."

She leans in so close she could kiss me if she wanted to. "Wrong!" The word pelts my face. I refuse to move a muscle. "Queens do whatever they please."

Singe dances along the ground, then climbs up her skirts and perches on her shoulder. He pets her now-flushed cheeks and kisses her several times. She blows him a kiss in return.

A servant enters the tent toting a clearing-tray. "Leave at once," Sophia barks. "And do not come in again until you're sent for."

The servant cowers away.

I maintain a blank expression.

*I'm not afraid of you.*

Singe covers his face with his hands.

"Did you see how quickly she followed orders? How she didn't question me? They were supposed to teach you that. Du Barry was supposed to teach you to have reverence and respect for your queen."

"But you aren't the queen," I say. "Not yet."

*And you won't be if I have anything to do with it.*

Sophia rushes close again. "What did you say?"

I crane my face away from hers. She takes hold of my chin, forcing me to look her in the eyes. Her pupils flash with rage. Singe peeks out at me from behind her towering hair. She runs her fingers over my face.

I clench my teeth and scowl.

"Don't move." She continues over my lips, down my neck, my chest and arms. She lifts my right hand in the air. "You really should have a moon manicure. I'll have my nail attendant do one for you. When I am regent queen, I will mandate it. Even for Belles. Everything about a person should be beautiful." Her grip tightens around my hand, and her jewel-tipped nails dig into the skin.

I cry out and try to pull away.

"I told you not to move." She grits her teeth. "Don't move, *Belle*, or I'll break your hand. A Belle with a broken hand won't be a very good Belle. Certainly not the *favorite* Belle. Perhaps I'll tell my mother that we need to name a new favorite again. Just like I did with Ambrosia. I bet one of your other sisters would gladly take your place. Hana, perhaps? Or Valeria? She cried after the Belle assignments were announced. Maybe I'll choose Ambrosia again. Bring her back for another round." She tightens her grip on my hand.

I double over in pain. The pressure. Heat. Swelling. A popping sensation. My other fist balls up. I try to shove at her. She's a solid block in front of me and just squeezes harder.

Sophia turns her head but doesn't loosen her grip. "Zo, dear."

The little teacup elephant peeks out from beneath the thick tablecloth. Only her trunk shows.

"Zo, my sweet dear, come out."

She inches forward, eyes down and little feet twitching. Even she's afraid.

"Please leave. I don't want you to see this. Wait for me near the tent."

The elephant turns and trots off.

"Singe." Sophia looks up at him. "You too. Stay with Zo." Singe leaps down from Sophia's shoulder and scampers off. Sophia smiles at me with soft lips, the corner of her mouth lifting. It's the smile from every single portrait, painting, newspaper, tattler, and scandal sheet. "See, even they know how to obey."

I seethe.

"Don't ever disobey me."

I clench my teeth.

"Did you hear me?"

I press my lips together. She clamps down harder until I cry out again.

"Yes, I heard you."

"Yes, what?"

"Yes, Your Highness."

She twists my wrist even tighter. "You owe me an apology. Princesses aren't treated in this way."

"I'm sorry, Your Highness."

"I don't believe you."

"I swear, Your Highness. I'm sorry."

Finally, she releases me. I stumble back, cradling my hand. Sophia leans in and kisses my nose, then calls for servants.

"Summon her personal guard. Tell him there's been a small accident. That poor Camille must be taken to the Palace Infirmary at once. Alert the royal doctor."

"Yes, Your Highness," the woman says and disappears.

Another servant drapes Sophia's shoulders with a white floor-length coat, and she's led from the tent. I cradle my hand. The pain is unbearable. Rémy appears, and I've never been so glad to see him. Behind him, a servant wheels in a rolling chair.

"I can walk," I say.

"You shouldn't," Rémy replies, surveying my hand. "We'll get there faster."

He lifts me up and deposits me gently in the chair.

"What happened?" he asks.

A hood lifts above my head: a privacy canopy, shielding me from view. Unruly tears fall down my cheeks. I'm too upset to answer. I don't want him to know I'm crying. Rémy walks beside the chair as it tramples over lightly frosted ground.

"They said you lifted your caisse by yourself and hurt your hand, but you didn't have it with you. I brought you there empty-handed."

"I don't want to talk about it," I say.

"I can't protect you if you don't start telling me the truth."

*You can't protect me from her. I have to protect myself.*

We reenter the palace. Whispers follow us. Rémy shoos away trailing newsies trying to figure out how the favorite landed herself in a rolling chair. We take one of the golden lifts to a higher floor.

The journey to the Palace Infirmary feels long. I'm pushed along winding corridors and balconies. The doors of the Palace Infirmary glow bright with lanterns, the royal apothecary emblem burned into their sides. Their light pushes through the privacy curtain.

Rémy shoves the doors open. I'm wheeled inside. The attending nurse lifts the hooded veil and helps me up.

"My goodness, what happened?" She shepherds me into a private area. "We must also check your levels. The doctor will be in soon." She fills a tray with needles and takes out the arcana meter from her pocket. "It looks like you've broken those fingers. The last two. Treacherous work, being a Belle at court, isn't it? Fixing up spoiled little girls and boys."

She tries to make me laugh.

I can't. My thoughts storm and the pain throbs.

"Her Royal Highness sent word that you were trying to lift your beauty caisse. Du Barry warned that you were stubborn and a bit unruly. But doing the servants' work, young lady?" She pats my arm. "You shouldn't have. Rest now, and the doctor will have these bones reset in no time. Your arcana will help them heal quickly."

"The arcana don't heal," I grumble.

"Aye, but their proteins can refresh, and that speeds the healing."

*The arcana refresh.*

*The arcana rejuvenate.*

*The blood proteins.*

*Princess Charlotte.*

"Where is my personal servant, Bree?" I ask.

"I will send for her."

I sink back into the chair. I'm leeched, stuffed with food and two pots of Belle-rose tea, and my fingers are set and wrapped in a splint. Rémy takes his place outside the doors, and I close my eyes to drift in and out of a fitful sleep.

"Camellia."

"Camellia."

I wake to whispers, then Bree's concerned face.

"What happened?"

"Sophia."

She runs gentle fingers over my hand.

"I need you to find the queen's Belle, Arabella. Tell her to come to me."

"Yes, of course."

"As quickly as you can."

Bree nods, then scurries off. I watch an hourglass on a shelf. It expires before Arabella arrives.

She rushes to the bed. Her veil blends into the darkness of the room.

"Are you all right?" she asks.

"As well as I can be."

She examines my hand, then scrunches back the ruffled sleeves on her dress to expose a series of scars that look like quill scratches and bite marks. "Sophia's anger can bite."

"Tell the queen I'm ready to help Charlotte. I'll do whatever I can." I lift my cast. "Broken hand and all."

"Thank the goddess," she whispers.

# 44

I pace my bedroom, waiting for Arabella or the queen's post or her guards. I cradle my splinted hand. The day dims into evening, and evening fades into night, and an open window carries the symphony of laughter and cheerful voices into my room. I step onto the balcony and look out on the imperial carriages clustered down below. The moon burns dull white and winks light over their gilded frames. Sophia must be having another party.

Bree opens the door.

"Is she here?"

"Who, my lady?"

"Arabella?"

"No, my lady, just the dinner cart." A flurry of post-balloons trail her.

"What are all of those?" I ask.

"The newsies found out about your hand," she says. "And thus, the entire kingdom."

The main salon is filled wall to wall with post-balloons.

Currant red. Emerald. Dark plum. Onyx. Cerulean. Saffron. Primrose. Jade. Quicksilver. Elisabeth complains and grumbles, smacking them left and right. They dodge her angry swings and drift higher toward the ceiling.

One catches my eye. It's shaped like a black ship in the Royal Harbor. I reach for it. My heart is starting to beat faster. I remove the note from the back.

*Camille,*

*Lifting heavy objects doesn't seem like it suits you. Please stop.*

*Feel better. Write me. But most likely, you won't, because you're very important and will receive a dozen of these or more. Nonetheless, I challenge you to write me back.*

*Yours,*

*Auguste*

A smile warms my entire body. The only bright moment of today.

The Belle-apartment doors snap open. I fill with sudden relief. Arabella.

I rush forward.

"Her Royal Highness, Princess Sophia, House of Orléans," an attendant announces. "Followed by her ladies-of-honor and the Royal Fashion Minister, Gustave du Polignac."

I freeze, then slip the note down the front of my dress.

Does Sophia know about my message to the queen? Has something happened to Arabella?

Sophia runs over to me. "How are you, my little love?" She bats her long eyelashes and purses her lips. Her mouth is like a miniature pink sweetheart pastry from one of the patisserie windows in Trianon. There isn't a single trace of our earlier fight.

I step back, shielding my hand. "I'm fine."

She smiles. "I've brought you dinner. It's the least I can do. I was angry earlier. Claudine provoked me. Forgive me, will you?" She turns to Claudine. "Apologize for provoking me, Claudine," she hollers.

"I'm sorry, Your Highness." Claudine curtsies. "I take full responsibility. I'm sorry, Camellia. It's all my fault."

Servants flood through the doors, pushing steaming carts and carrying heavy trays. An entire feast is laid out before me in seconds. Beautiful flowers adorn the platters—roses, edelweiss, bloodroot, violets, laurels, and tulips. Her ladies-of-honor find seats, eyeing the army of post-balloons overhead.

"Does it hurt?" Gabrielle asks.

"Yes," I say.

Claudine plucks a strawberry from one of the dessert carts.

"Don't eat that food," Sophia barks at Claudine. "It's for Camellia only."

Claudine flushes the color of the strawberry in her hand, and drops it. Henrietta-Marie skips around the room, inspecting each corner. The Fashion Minister picks at invisible lint on his pants. He's unusually quiet. I wait for him to say something lighthearted, make a joke, even look at me, but he stares into his lap.

"You didn't have to interrupt your busy schedule to bring me dinner and come talk to me. I'm fine," I say, hoping Sophia and her ladies will leave. I watch the door, anticipating Arabella's arrival.

"Oh, but it's not just a social call. Right, Gustave?" She turns to the Fashion Minister.

"Her Highness has had me attempt to make several vivant dresses based on the one you created as her wedding look." His voice is flat, eyes glassy. "We'd like your opinion on them."

He snaps his fingers.

The Belle-apartment doors reopen, and his dandies push in massive bell jars that hold three dress stands. Three different gowns glitter beneath the glass. The first one blooms bright with the color of fresh blood, then turns snow white and back again. The second has the texture of a honeycomb; the fabric is cut in sharp angles, hugging the mannequin like it's the queen of the hive, as the color oscillates like the sunrise from rich oranges to bright yellows to soft tangerines. The third is feathered and covered in seed pearls that shift into various gleaming shades of white—cream and milk and lily and ivory and bone.

I do a lap around each one. They change as I pass. "They're beautiful," I tell the Fashion Minister.

"But still not quite right." Sophia joins me, slipping her hand into my good one. She strokes it like I'm one of her teacup pets. I flinch at her touch, but she tightens her grip. "I need your wisdom. I need you to help Gustave make these even better."

I pull away. "Of course, Your Highness."

"That's what I like to hear." She returns to her seat, a triumphant look on her face. "Tell me your ideas."

"Perhaps the fabrics can transform the length and style of the dress throughout the ceremony," I say.

Sophia leaps with joy. "That's right. That's right. It would be so unexpected." She turns to the Fashion Minister. "Can it be done?"

His eyes are wide with panic, but he says, "I will do my very best."

"You never disappoint. I will keep you in my cabinet forever." She kisses him. "Now, come eat, Camellia. I've brought this just for you."

Bree makes me a plate, collecting different meats and vegetables from all the carts. Sophia sprinkles the plate with flowers. "Don't forget these. They're popular now. The Minister of Health says we all should ingest colorful vegetables and even flowers. It's beneficial, supposedly."

I eat as the others watch. The food has a peculiar smell. Pungent. Flowery. Strange.

Sophia smiles. They discuss the coming Declaration and what Sophia will wear. The Fashion Minister suggests several looks.

I fade in and out of the conversation. Their voices turn muffled, their words drifting off like they've been set afloat. A shiver floods through me, both hot and cold at once. The room spins around like a télétrope reel. My stomach turns.

"Are you all right?" Sophia asks.

"I don't feel . . ." I mumble as the food starts to come up and out and all over my dress.

Bree rushes to my side. "What is it, miss?"

"Don't touch her," Sophia commands.

Bree jumps back.

"Didn't you serve her?" Sophia accuses.

"Yes, Your Highness, but—" Bree stammers.

"Did you put something in the food?" Gabrielle adds.

The room rocks left and right like a boat. Sweat races down my cheeks. I can't speak. I can't defend Bree. I can't stop vomiting.

"Call the guards," Sophia says. "Take her. She's tried to kill the favorite."

Sophia's guards drag Bree kicking and screaming and crying from the room. I want to stop them, but I can't form the words. She becomes a tiny pinprick before everything goes dark.

The hours tangle together, a mess of night sweats and medicine and not being able to keep anything in my stomach. The poison chokes my veins like a vise. It dulls and mutes the arcana. I can't feel my gifts anymore; the gentle hum of power just beneath my skin is gone. My connection to my sisters and the Goddess of Beauty is lost. The drowsiness is too heavy to resist. My eyelids fight to stay open.

Someone touches my wrists. There's a pinch as needles push into my skin.

"Low blood pressure."

"Extreme drowsiness."

"Dilated pupils."

"Very low arcana."

"Deep sleep. Almost coma-like."

"Poison for sure."

"But her blood is clean."

"How is this possible?"

"We may never know."

# 45

Three days pass, like sand falling from one side of an hourglass to the other. A new imperial servant—Marcella—helps me dress. It's my first day out of bed. The queen's post-balloon floats from my vanity hook. Her note—telling me to come immediately to her chambers when I am strong enough—is tucked into my dress. The Declaration of Heirs Ceremony has been postponed until both the queen and the princess can be prepared by the favorite.

The main salon is a flurry of chaos. Battalions of gossip post-balloons swarm the solarium as the morning-lanterns are lit. Their black noses click and clack against the glass, begging to be let in. I know they're full of parchment that hold questions and tattlers replete with speculation about what happened to me.

Knocks rattle the Belle-apartment door.

"Lady Camellia isn't seeing anyone yet. Please make an appointment," Elisabeth shouts from her office. The circuit-phones blare.

Rémy's powerful voice blasts through the doors. "You can leave get-well flowers, but you must clear the hall."

Newspapers sit on tea tables flashing their headlines:

FAVORITE ALMOST KILLED BY THE JILTED EX-FAVORITE

POISON HAS BECOME MORE DEADLY AT
COURT THAN AN ASSASSIN'S DAGGER

PRINCESS SOPHIA OUTRAGED AT THE TREATMENT OF THE
FAVORITE AND JAILS AN ENTIRE STAFF OF SERVANTS

IMPERIAL SERVANT RESPONSIBLE FOR THE
FAVORITE'S POISONING PUT IN STARVATION BOX

"My jacket, Marcella," I say, my words clipped. I want Bree back.

She drapes it over my shoulders. I open the Belle-apartment doors. Claudine stands there with her attendant.

"I didn't even get a chance to knock," she says.

"I'm leaving. I have an appointment." I step out. Rémy gathers flowers and cards and post-balloons left along the hall.

"Wait. I need to talk to you. I have to tell you something."

"If it's about what I saw in the Market Quartier, don't worry, I haven't told anyone. I promised you I wouldn't."

"I know you haven't," Claudine whispers. "And I'm so, so grateful." She takes a deep breath. "Are you feeling better?"

"The poison has left my system, thanks to the leeches." I don't mention how it took a full day for my arcana to return.

"And I'm sorry about your imperial servant. What was her name? I saw the headlines about the starvation."

"Bree." I bite back tears.

"Can we go inside for a moment?" She looks all around as if we're being watched. "It'll only take a moment."

I sigh, then return to the main salon.

Claudine licks her bottom lip. "Actually, can we use one of the treatment rooms?"

"Claudine, I must go."

"Please." Her eyes are desperate.

I lead her to a treatment salon and close the door behind us. "What is it?"

She leans in and whispers, "Don't react to what I'm saying. We're always being watched. The servants. The attendants. Make sure to laugh as if I'm telling you something ridiculous, so they don't pay attention." She waits for me to nod. "I'm almost certain Sophia was the one that poisoned your food that night. She told us not to eat from the carts. She made it seem like it was a special treat just for you. But I knew. I suspected."

I cover up my anger with a laugh. "I knew it was her. Bree would never harm me."

"When we were younger, Sophia would hurt us. If we didn't do what she wanted—even if it was to play a different game in the gardens or playroom—she'd get angry. And if we spent time with people other than her, she'd punish us."

"How?"

She pauses as we hear someone pass outside the door.

"She would slip draughts into our tea, or lace our rose creams with something to make us sick so we wouldn't spend time with other people or go places she didn't want us to. She always gets what she wants." She pauses and fakes a giggle, so I mimic her. "And I've always obeyed."

"She can't get away with this anymore," I say.

"She can, and she will. She's just started manipulating you, Camille, and the more you fight back or resist what she wants, the worse it will get." Claudine drops her head. "I'm not strong enough to fight her."

"I won't let her get away with it."

"She's talking about how she'd like to be able to change her look with the snap of a finger if she steps into a room and sees someone more beautiful than she is. She's trying to figure out how to make this possible. She's experimenting—"

"We have to stop her."

"I don't have the courage." Claudine shakes her head. "I'm leaving. After her wedding. I just wanted to tell you to have Madam Du Barry hire a taster for your food. You've been kind to me, and I wanted to return the favor."

"Where will you go?"

"I don't know. Just away from here."

After Claudine slips out, I slam skin-color pots and pastilles on the table. I throw one at the wall. It shatters, leaving its gooey contents behind like a spatter of blood.

"In a bad mood?" a voice says from behind.

"Auguste?"

I whip around. He stands beside the dressing screen.

"How did you get in here?"

"I have my ways," he says, closing the gap between us. His jacket and shirt hang open, his cravat is a loose tangle, and his sailor pants are worn at the knees. He smells like cologne and champagne. Stubble peppers his jaw, and his eyes look tired, like he's been up all night. He removes his jacket.

"You got past Rémy." The thought both thrills and terrifies me.

"And Claudine. I saw her in the hall," he says. "The first time I visited you, I figured out there were ways in and out of these apartments without being seen. There would have to be. Gods forbid if there was a siege. There would have to be some way to get valued people out secretly." He lifts his hand to touch my cheek. "Are you all right? I read in the papers about the poisoning."

I let his hand rest there for a moment too long before stepping away. The softness and the heat linger. "I'm better. I'm fine."

"I sent you a post-balloon. You never answered."

"I've received over four thousand letters and balloons. I'm still opening them."

He touches my shoulder, the pad of his thumb grazing where the fabric meets the skin.

"I'm very busy, Auguste. I have an appointment with the queen."

"Maybe I should leave, then." He sounds disappointed.

There's a pinch in my stomach. "You don't have to just yet." I can spare a minute. Just one.

"No. I should go." He gives me a sheepish look. "Truth is, I'm a little afraid of you," he says.

I laugh, presuming he's joking. His expression tightens. A wrinkle furrows his brow. "I'm afraid of this." He motions his hand between us, like he's running it along a ribbon that connects the two of us.

I turn my back to him. "I'm not sure what you mean." I clutch my skirts to stop the tremors in my hands. I feel each one of his footsteps as he nears. I feel the warmth of him like a heat-lantern, the sensation pushing through the back of my dress. I feel his breath hit the top of my Belle-bun.

"Have you ever wondered about love?"

"Love?" I say, barely able to get the word out.

He rests his hands on my waist and pivots me around. The scent of him wraps around me, and I inhale. I let him pull me forward. He places his fingers right above my breast. His thumb presses into my skin. He takes my hand and puts it to his chest. "You feel that?"

"Yes." His heart is racing.

"Love is when hearts beat together."

I pull away. "I have that with my sisters."

"Have you ever wanted it with someone other than them?"

"I'm not allowed to entertain that idea. It would be dangerous."

"Another rule?"

"A reality."

"I'm going to leave," he says. "Leave court, I mean."

My heart plummets, even though it shouldn't. Is Sophia chasing everyone away?

"Why?"

"I'm taking myself out of the running to be one of Sophia's suitors."

"Why would you do that?"

He touches my face. Fingertips drift over my forehead, down my cheeks, and across my lips.

My pulse races. A blush rises in my cheeks. The warmth of the heat-lanterns and his body are making me sweat. He presses the answer to my question against my lips, and I taste it, wrapped with the faint flavor of the rose pigment I smeared on my mouth and the cinnamon he must've taken in his tea. The kiss is soft at first, then harder. He opens my mouth with his tongue, and I let him.

My heart flutters. All of the things Du Barry warned us about—our blood, our arcana, our gifts—are forgotten. There's

me. There's him. There's a meeting of our mouths, our skin and
bodies. He pushes deeper. His hands drift up and down my back.
I tug his hair. The world is this room around us, and all I want to
do is feel this over and over again. I could kiss him for a thousand
hourglasses. Even if Du Barry says it will damage my arcana.

I pull away to catch my breath.

"I've wanted to do that since I first saw you," he says.

I tap my fingers over my puffy lips. They tingle. I don't want
to lose that feeling.

"I know," I say, still breathless. "Me too."

"You should leave with me," he says, kissing my forehead,
then nose, then mouth again. The heaviness of his words settles
into my shoulders.

"Where would we go?"

"To the edge of the world, beyond the barrier."

"They would hunt us. Sophia would—"

"I don't want to marry her. She's a—"

"Monster," I say, and he smiles.

"So leave with me. It would be an adventure. We'd be together."

"I would get sick. I'm not supposed to love. I'm a Belle."

"But you can." He traces a finger along the rim of my mouth.
He lifts my chin and kisses me again. I imagine what it might be
like—us in a boat, leaving Orléans and seeing the world, kissing
him every day, learning what it's like to be loved by someone other
than my sisters.

I sink deeper into his kiss. I float alongside the fantasy, giving it
breath and flesh and bone. It could happen. I could leave with him.

Maman's voice whispers: *Do what is right.*

Charlotte's face flashes in my mind.

The promise to Arabella and the queen.

I place a hand to his chest and slide my mouth off his.

"I can't." I whisper so softly, maybe he won't hear; maybe it won't be true.

"Is it because you love all of this too much?" He steps away with a frown. The warmth of him is lost, and a sudden chill settles in.

"No. Auguste—"

"I should've never come here." His expression hardens. I reach for his hand. He yanks away.

"Auguste."

Without another word, he storms out. I follow him into the hall. Tears well up in my eyes. There's no trace of him. Just Marcella standing there holding the golden tail ribbons of the queen's glittering post-balloon.

I snatch it from her and retrieve the note.

*Camellia,*
*Sophia is visiting her sister today. I'll send an escort tomorrow.*
*HRM*

# 46

The next day, bells chime through the belly of the palace in honor of the queen. In preparation for the Declaration Ceremony, she's announced her sickness. The court sent out mourning post-balloons, complete with the queen's joyful miniature portrait, and words about all she's done for the kingdom during her reign. They putter along in the halls and corridors, and leave a sad trail of tear-shaped glitter and the noise of tiny wailing cries. The court is called to prayer in the Receiving Hall at different intervals of the day. Today will be marked as a day of mourning.

I wait for word from her but instead receive a dress and a summons from Sophia. I walk to the princess's chambers with Rémy at my side.

Sophia's private dining room sparkles like a diamond. Cold-season flowers burst from every surface. Goblets, champagne flutes, and tumblers boast jewel-toned liquid. Towers of silver-flecked macarons sit like snow-covered trees on the grand table. Heat-lanterns add their warmth and light over us like stars.

I am announced to the room, the last guest to arrive.

"So glad you could make my spontaneous feast," Sophia says. She wears a black mourning dress and a black diamond draped around her neck. Her blond hair-tower features a cameo of her mother.

"May I express my sincerest apologies for the illness of your mother, our queen," I say with a bow, and kiss two fingers to place at my heart. The whole table mimics my gesture to show respect for the dying.

I will play this game with her tonight.

She nods and motions for me to join them. Rémy joins the other guards fanned out across the room. Auguste sits to Sophia's left, along with a beautiful redheaded woman. Prince Alfred sits to her right with a greasy smile on his face. I startle at the sight of him.

He was supposed to have been banished.

He blows me a kiss when I pass by. Every part of me clenches. Anger sits just beneath my skin, mingling with my arcana. I spot Elisabeth at a separate child's table, glaring down into her lap with a scowl. Sophia's ladies—Gabrielle, Henrietta-Marie, and Claudine—sit to her right. The rest of the courtiers present are strangers.

Singe dines with us, and Sophia presents her new, tiny teacup giraffe to the group. A gift from her mother. The animals eat from porcelain plates and stalk along the table.

"Camellia?" Sophia calls. "Have you met Lady Georgiana Fabry, my suitor Auguste's esteemed mother?"

"No, I haven't," I reply. "A pleasure to meet you, my lady."

Her mouth is a straight line. She gazes at me and nods, before turning to whisper something to Auguste. I try to make eye contact with him. He avoids my gaze.

"Where's the food?" Claudine jokes, and taps her knife on a plate.

"Oh, do have manners," Gabrielle says.

"We're waiting for one more guest," Sophia reveals with a smile. She turns around and waves a hand at her guard. A new place setting is added to the table.

Whispers about the mystery guest ripple down the table through the voice-boxes.

"Any guesses?" Sophia says. "I'll gift a beauty token to anyone who gets it right."

Gabrielle and Henrietta-Marie bet on a famous singer. Others list beautiful courtiers who have landed in the beauty-scopes this week.

"She's here," Sophia says.

The doors creak open.

We all turn.

My jaw drops when Amber strides in. A jade-green gown blooms around her waist like flower sepals stitched all together. "Ambrosia Beauregard," the attendant announces. "As you requested, Your Highness."

"Amber!" My heart fills instantly, and I realize just how alone I've really been without her. I leap up, run across the room, and hug her. "I've missed you," I whisper into her neck and hair.

"Me too," she replies. It's so good to hear her voice after all this time that I almost burst into tears.

"A nice surprise, right, Camellia?" Sophia says.

"Yes, Your Highness," I say.

Amber sits beside me. I have to let go of her hand as the food appears, but I don't want to. I'm filled with all the things I want to ask her, all the things I need to tell her.

The courses appear in rapid succession—savory rabbit and roasted duck and fish, platters of vegetables and salads. I'm careful to only eat after the others have taken bites, and tell Amber to do the same. Amber and I slip into our own bubble. Conversation swirls around us but we only whisper to each other.

"What happened while you were here?" I ask.

"I'll tell you later," she replies. "Have you heard from the others?"

"Not for a few days," I say. "But Edel—"

She nods and lifts her eyebrows with acknowledgment.

Sophia taps a champagne flute. "I have an announcement."

Conversation at the table stops. All eyes turn to her.

"My dearest lady-of-honor Claudine will be married."

Claudine drops her spoon in shock. My heart instantly goes out to her.

"I can't have my ladies rotting on the vine," Sophia says. "So I've decided to arrange suitable mates for each of them before my own nuptials."

"Who is the lucky person?" a guest calls out.

Sophia clasps her hands together over her chest. "One of my very own cousins. Prince Alfred."

I grip the fork in my hand so tightly it leaves a chrysanthemum-shaped imprint in my palm.

Sophia puts her hand up. "No need to thank me, Claudine. He noticed how beautiful you are, and we've been discussing it. I thought you'd make a lovely match. I did think about arranging you with Lady Walden's daughter Rebecca from House Lothair, but she was already betrothed to another."

Prince Alfred stands. He walks to Claudine's side and drops

to one knee. "I'm certain I can make you the happiest woman in all of Orléans."

Claudine's cheeks flame red. Sweat dots her brow.

"But—"

"You're so welcome. You'll be a princess du sang. We will be cousins." Sophia pulls Claudine from her seat and hugs her. Claudine is like a statue. Her lips quiver.

"I don't think I'm ready for marriage, Sophia," Claudine says when the princess finally pulls away.

"Oh, don't be silly. You were so devastated by the last person who dumped you. I thought I'd spare you the further humiliation. This way you're all settled."

"But, please, Sophia. I need to tell you—"

"Not another word. It's time to celebrate. I have chosen for you. That is my divine right."

I spot Claudine's attendant in the far corner. She stares forward, glassy-eyed and near tears.

"Now, my cousin Alfie can be quite particular about the way his wife should look. He's been through quite a few."

Alfred chuckles. The whole table laughs.

"But since we have another Belle in our midst, I figured I'd give you the opportunity to try on a new look. Feel more confident. Have you both choose your forever look together. And for my closest friends to see, in the open, more displays of our lovely Belles' talents. We should have more exhibitions like the Beauté Carnaval on a regular basis to remind us of their talents." She rests her hands on top of Claudine's now-slumping shoulders. "Stand for me."

"Sophia, I'm happy with my look," Claudine says. "I'll just settle into this one."

"But I'm not," Prince Alfred says. "I think you could be a bit bigger in your middle section. I like women with curves."

The table laughs again. Panic shines in Claudine's blue eyes.

"Let's be a little adventurous, shall we?" Sophia says. "After all, I'm in mourning from the news about my mother, and I need cheering up."

"Sophia, please," Claudine begs.

"May you always find beauty, Claudine." Sophia pivots back to the table. "Ambrosia and Camellia, please join us."

"Your Highness, this is highly irregular." Elisabeth stands. "We cannot have beauty alterations done like this. So exposed. So out in the open."

Sophia eyes her. "You are dismissed. I didn't ask for your opinion."

"But . . . but, Your Highness . . ." Elisabeth stammers.

"Escort Miss Du Barry out of my chambers and back to her office," Sophia demands.

Elisabeth stares at me as the guards flank her and lead her out. I try to control my breathing.

"You and I didn't get along when you first came to court," Sophia says to Amber. "I didn't understand you. I thought you were a little boring. All rules and order. But now I think I want both you and Camellia here. At least for a little while. This whole process can cause such tension between the Beauregard sisters. So much pressure being the favorite, isn't it, Camellia?" she asks. "And so much upset over not being the favorite anymore, Ambrosia?" She claps her little hands together.

Amber balls her fists. The warmth of her anger radiates like a high-noon sun. A little hiccup escapes her mouth when she opens it to speak, but she, as always, says the right thing. "Thank you for this honor and opportunity, Your Highness."

Sophia lays one hand on each of our shoulders. "I'm desperate to see your different styles in action."

A cold sensation drops into my stomach.

"We're not different," I say. "We don't need to put on a show."

"I agree," Auguste chimes in. "This is a party, Sophia. The Belles shouldn't have to work."

"Auguste, hush," his mother says. "Let them show us their divinity, their connection to the Goddess of Beauty."

"She's my sister. She's talented. You experienced it for yourself when she was first chosen," I say. "There's no need for further comparison."

Sophia grins at her, then turns to me. "Camellia, you must really love Ambrosia so much to tell that lie. You were thrilled to take Ambrosia's place at court. You believed you should've been chosen from the very start."

Heat flushes through me by the minute.

"I won't participate," I say. "This is ridiculous."

My words set off a firecracker in the room. The guests gasp at my insubordination. Sophia's face turns an embarrassed shade of red.

I think of Ivy.

I think of Astrid.

I think of Arabella.

I think of all the pain she's already caused.

Claudine exhales, a sound like air whooshing out of a post-balloon.

"You *won't participate*?" Sophia laughs in my face. "What do you mean? I command you to help Claudine."

Amber squeezes my hand and leans in to whisper, "Camille, please. Play along so we can get out of here." Her eyes flash with worry.

"Well, favorite?" Sophia says, crossing her arms over her chest.

Amber releases me and rises to her feet. "I'm game. Let's see who the better favorite is," she says.

Courtiers nod and clap, ready for a show. Sophia jumps up and down with excitement.

"Amber, I'm not going to do this," I say.

"Are you scared?" Amber garners a laugh from the table. Her words bite. She stares at me, begging me to play along.

"No," I say.

"Ladies, please. This is outrageous," Auguste shouts.

"We don't need your opinions, Auguste," Sophia snaps. "Camellia will do it because I want her to." Sophia looks me dead in the eye. "She knows what will happen if she doesn't." She plucks a strawberry and flower from one of the fruit baskets and saunters over to Amber. "Do you like strawberries, Ambrosia? Or flowers, even?"

She rubs the strawberry across Amber's lips, then tickles Amber's cheek with the flower.

I jump forward. "Don't eat that, Amber."

Sophia strokes Amber's head and adds the flower to Amber's Belle-bun. "Why?" Amber asks me. She opens her mouth to eat the strawberry.

I slap it from Sophia's hand.

Sophia leaps back. "You act as if it's poisonous," she adds with a giggle. "And if you had struck me, even by accident, you could spend twelve years in the dungeons. Did you know that?"

"Fine!" I say. "I accept your challenge."

Sophia plucks another strawberry from the basket and bites. Its flesh stains her teeth red. "It'll be a friendly game. And Alfred will pick the winning look. Any wagers?"

A woman takes bets at the table and collects spintria and leas coins in her pouch.

"Bring me a mirror!" Sophia calls out.

One appears moments later and is set against a nearby wall. Servants bring carts holding our beauty caisses. Sophia walks Claudine before the mirror. "Three tries. Whichever look Alfred likes best wins."

Claudine bursts into tears. Sophia uses her handkerchief to wipe them away. "You'll thank me." She kisses Claudine's cheek. "You can even take your servant with you after you marry. I know how fond you are of her. I just want us to be sisters in the eyes of the gods."

"Oh, goodie. How I love this!" someone at the table says.

"Do you understand the rules?" Sophia asks.

I stare at Amber. Her brow furrows. The is no game.

"Yes," I say.

"Yes," she answers.

Sophia stretches out Claudine's arms before stepping out of the way. Amber coats bei powder on Claudine's face and then gathers supplies from the drawers. I order a servant to bring Belle-rose tea. My hands shake with nerves as I offer it to Claudine. She takes only a few too-hot sips. Her eyes brim over with tears. I squeeze her shoulder in the hope that it consoles her.

"Aren't you going to get supplies?" Amber asks me.

"No, I don't need them," I say.

Her mouth drops open with annoyed surprise. "Well, then. You first, since you're the favorite now and all." Her eyes narrow.

I move to the other side of Claudine. My body warms like the roaring hearth at our backs. The veins in my body swell. They rise in my hands.

Claudine appears in my head: doughy gray flesh, beautiful round frame, dull brown hair, big eyes.

I touch her hair. The strands darken and fall down her back in ribbons.

I touch her eyelashes. Her irises lighten to dove gray. Brown shades of eye shadow appear on her lids, and mascara elongates her lashes.

I touch her lips, painting them to look like a flower in bloom.

I run my fingers along the edges of her body, smoothing her legs and hips to make her thin and willowy like the imperial dancers on their tiptoes.

Claudine wipes her forehead with a handkerchief. Her breathing accelerates and she grimaces a little.

I stop. "Are you all right?"

"She's fine," Sophia interjects. "Continue. It's beautiful."

I make her breasts larger.

"I'm finished," I say.

The table claps.

"Don't get excited, Camille. My turn. Step aside." Amber takes a hot iron from its caddy. She wraps a strand of Claudine's hair around the barrel, and it turns white-blond and twists into tight corkscrew curls. Soon her hair halos her head.

The courtiers at the table *ooh* and *ahh*.

Amber wipes a pecan-brown paste over Claudine's skin in quick strokes. Claudine's face comes out a little darker than the rest of her. But I don't point that out. Amber changes Claudine's eyes back to hazel.

"Lovely," I say. Amber's mouth tightens.

Claudine's knees buckle. Sophia's attendant sweeps in behind her before she falls.

"We should stop," I say.

"Not yet," Sophia replies. "Look how beautiful she's turning out. She'll be fine. Right, Claudine? You're just fine."

"I . . ." Her voice trails off. Her eyes flutter and fight to stay open.

"More tea," Amber says.

I gaze up at Amber and wonder if this is really just a ploy to help get us out of here. If she's just playing along, or taking this seriously. Her eyes are steely and cold. "Let's stop now, and the table can be the judge of it," I suggest.

"No," Amber and Sophia say in unison.

"It's your turn," Amber states.

I close my eyes and think through what to do next. I don't touch Claudine this time. I let my mind randomly fill in the details. The corkscrews Amber placed in her hair shrivel down into a thick fish-tail braid dangling below her waist. Her hair color darkens to a pale gold the color of spintria coins. I reshape her body again, stretching her limbs like sugar-sticks, cinching her waist, and making her a whole four inches taller.

Her skin lightens to the color of whipped butter and cream. I use her dress to create a new one, stretching it over her frame and letting it bell out at her waist like a parasol.

Amber scoffs.

I open my eyes and admire Claudine. She could sit atop a royal wedding pastry.

Claudine gasps for breath and bites down on her bottom lip. Her head bobs toward her shoulders. "I didn't know it would hurt so bad," she mumbles.

"We need to stop," I say.

"Not before I get a second chance. You're trying to cheat me," Amber says.

"Can't you see she's hurting?" I yell.

"Just give her some tea. She'll be fine." Sophia snatches the teacup from the tray and forces Claudine to drink it all. The scalding liquid dribbles down her chin, leaving two pink burns behind. Claudine cries out.

The room sits in stunned silence.

Auguste stands. "I've had enough." He strides toward the door. Sophia motions to her guards. They step into his path. He tries to move around them.

"Have a seat, Auguste, or the guards will force you to sit, like a baby."

"Sophia, this is ridiculous," he protests, and my heart swells. At least he is on my side.

"The show has just begun. Enjoy it." She winks at him.

His mother leaves her seat and leads him back to the table. Each breath I take catches in my throat as I watch.

Amber steps forward. "My turn!"

Guards hold Claudine up. Amber draws black kohl lines over Claudine's chest and arms and face, making a beauty road map. She changes the contours of Claudine's body, shrinking her down and erasing the height I'd given her but making her round as a ripe apple. She uses a kohl pencil to mark Claudine's face. Amber chisels out higher cheekbones and a more pronounced forehead.

Claudine puts her hands to her cheeks. She flushes crimson. The blood inside her is aggravated, trying to get out.

I reach for Amber to stop her.

Amber moves away and paints a sapphire-blue smudge

on Claudine's gown. It changes to match the color of Auguste's mother's gown. Claudine's limbs whiten like rice grains, and her hair explodes out from the braid I put in, hitting the floor in one cascading wave. Amber uses a hot iron to start straightening it, then changes her mind and grabs a steam-roller for curls.

Claudine jerks forward.

"Amber, stop," I yell.

"No, you won't win." Amber continues to work. "I'm not done yet. I'm not done."

Claudine's body morphs so quickly I can't identify all the changes. Her skin shifts into a mosaic of colors. Mahogany brown. Sandy brown. Midnight black. Creamy white. Her hair alternates its texture and length. Her breasts balloon and shrink and balloon again.

"Amber!" I grab her arm.

"Get off me, Camille. You're not going to cheat. I'm going to beat you." She clamps her eyes shut and pushes forward. Makeup races over Claudine's face.

I close my eyes and see Claudine there again. Amber's beauty work zips over Claudine's body like a télétrope reel. I try to counter it, to block her from making any more alterations. I feel Claudine's heartbeat and it's not normal. It's so very far from anything I've ever heard before. I can't let this happen. Not now.

A loud cry pulls me out of my focus. I open my eyes to see Claudine topple to the ground like a branch that has fallen from a tree. Blood pools in her mouth, then drips down her chin. Her eyes bulge open, then dim. Her heartbeat, so frantic a moment ago, is gone.

# 47

Claudine's attendant screams. The courtiers sit, eyes glassy, hands shaking. Auguste stares into his lap. His mother holds a handkerchief to her mouth.

I sway with exhaustion, guilt, and regret. I drop to my knees and press my ear to Claudine's chest. I search for a pulse, even the faint beat of her heart. I close my eyes; the arcana wake again. I try to find something inside her that is alive, but there is only emptiness.

A palanquin is brought in, and her body is removed. Servants wheel in dessert carts spilling over with trays of luna pastries and snowmelon tarts and petit-cakes.

"We will have dessert. It will rejuvenate us after such a competitive game," Sophia announces, taking a sip of champagne.

I'm frozen in the place where Claudine's body was. Amber trembles beside me. Tears stream down her cheeks. She mutters the word *sorry* over and over again.

"Have a seat," Sophia orders. "Now!"

"Don't you care about what just happened?" I say to Sophia.

"Dessert is here." She sweeps away my concern.

"She's dead," I say.

"Come." Sophia motions for me to return to my seat. "And I will tell you a story."

I hobble back to my chair; my legs are iron.

The guests try to bite into their sugary treats. No one looks up.

"There was this girl at court. She was one of the best liars. It was a practiced skill. She made me believe that she would help me. That she enjoyed our time together. That she would make me into the best queen I could be. All the while, she actually hated me. She even called me a *monster*." She takes a sip of her champagne.

Her eyes settle on me. My heart trips over the word.

"Anyone here think I'm a monster? That's such a strong word. Usually reserved for creatures in fairy tales. Not princesses. Not future queens."

I take deep breaths. I look forward, remaining expressionless.

"Is that what you really think of me, Camellia?"

"Excuse me, Your Highness?"

"I've been told you think I'm a monster. That you called me that, in fact."

My eyes volley between Rémy and Auguste. Neither of them look at me.

"I said—"

"Do not lie to me." Sophia pounds her fist on the table. The whole thing shakes. "You've been talking about me. And calling someone a monster isn't very nice. It's dangerous, actually. I cannot have anyone in the kingdom saying those types of things about me." She drums her fingers on her plate.

No one breathes.

"I also can't have you sneaking around with one of my suitors."

"I haven't—"

"Another lie."

Auguste's face turns scarlet.

"You insult me even further the longer you keep up this deception. You make it seem as if I'm unintelligent. As if I can't see your affection for Auguste." She leaves her chair and walks behind mine. Her perfume gets caught in my throat. "You thought, *Oh, poor Sophia, she doesn't know anything. She's pitiful. Regent queen. Second best to her older sister.* But I've gotten smarter. I've learned to pay attention to the little things—to who looks at whom when they enter a room, how one's voice changes when they talk about a person, and more." She cranes down, getting close to my ear. "You've been a naughty girl."

My hands curl into heavy fists, nails digging into the flesh of my palms. A rage simmers from my heels to my head, tinged with sour fear.

"But I have something to tell you." She cups her hand to my ear and lowers her voice. "Your lovely Auguste—well, *my* Auguste—was responsible for every bad thing that has happened to you. The dead roses in your bathing chamber when you first arrived, the fire in your bed, the poisoning of your food."

Her words are whisper-soft, but they hit me in my chest and in my heart like heavy punches.

I gaze up at Auguste.

"Did you tell her?" Lady Georgiana asks.

"I did. I did." Sophia jumps up and down and claps wildly.

Lady Georgiana sighs. "It's all my fault, really, Camellia. And I'm so sorry to tell you all of this the first time we're meeting. I will be replacing the Beauty Minister when Sophia is queen. And I sent my very handsome and charming son to ascertain the secrets of the Belles. The Du Barrys have had a monopoly on the trade for too long. Change is coming."

The betrayal feels thick and hot in my chest. Like my heart is on fire. My stomach roils with shame and embarrassment.

Sophia snaps her fingers. An adjoining room opens. Servants wheel in a contraption. Clear vats shaped like cradles hold floating babies. Golden tubes connect them to arcana meters and large vessels filled with blood.

Amber gasps.

Sophia stands beside it proudly. "Isn't it beautiful?" She kisses one of the glass cradles, then wipes away the smudge left behind by her rouge-stick. "You really are the roses of our kingdom. And you can be grown like them. Planted like flower bulbs to germinate in the blood of dead Belles. Then you just spring up."

The meager food I've eaten rises in my throat.

"Your blood truly is divine," Sophia continues. "And now, I'll be able to grow as many of you as I wish. I could even sell you. Build a golden auction block in Trianon—or better yet, in the Royal Square in front of the Orléans hourglass."

"You can't do this," I say, shaking.

Sophia laughs.

"The things you told Auguste made it possible. He got more out of you than we've ever been able to get out of the Du Barry family. They're quite loyal to your kind. Taking the whole divine-appointment thing very seriously."

Amber dissolves into tears.

"I will stop you." I rise to my feet.

"I'm not sure how that will be possible, since you will be rotting in jail for the rest of your days." Sophia's eyes are like pinpricks of ice as she addresses the guards.

"Arrest both of them for the death of Lady Claudine, Duchesse de Bissay, beloved lady-of-honor to the princess."

# 48

Rémy and three other guards cart Amber and me through halls thick with courtiers. Whispers explode. Many pull monocles and eyescopes from their pockets. Others lift ear-trumpets. Newsies sketch pictures. Gossip post-balloons swarm over me like dark storm clouds.

I fight against Rémy's grip. I thought I could trust him. Angry tears rush down my cheeks. I trip over my dress skirts as he drags me forward. He shoves me down a long and narrow staircase. I push back, jerking against his hold, wishing I could claw his face. My shoulder shifts in and out of place, dislocating each time I jerk and try to free myself. The pain rushes through me.

"Where are you taking me?" I shout.

He doesn't answer.

"Let me go." Amber tussles with the guard restraining her.

I try to run. Rémy grabs my waist and tightens cuffs around my wrists. A dark bag is put over my head, stamping out the light.

Then he flings me over his shoulder like a potato sack. I'm carried for a long distance. Every time I squirm or fight, his grip tightens.

He walks down another set of stairs. My injured shoulder hits a cold wall. The click and clack of metal sliding on metal echoes. Cries and moans pierce through the space.

The bag is snatched off of my head. I'm tossed on the ground. The hard surface knocks the air out of my lungs. The floor is gritty and wet under my hands. My eyes adjust, and bars sharpen into view in the dim light. The ceiling hangs heavy and low, and drips with foul water. Amber curls into a ball at my side.

Rémy closes and locks the gate.

"Why are you doing this to me?"

"I do what I'm told," he finally says before stomping off.

I run to the bars and shake them. They rattle but don't give. I trace my fingers over their cool surface. I push my finger in the lock over and over again, thinking I can somehow get it to open.

Amber bursts into a thousand sobs. "What are we going to do?"

"Maybe we can use the arcana?" I pound the bars again, even though I know that force won't help. All of the air shoots out of me, and I'm dizzy. I sink to the floor, weary with defeat.

Sophia tricked us.

She forced us to murder Claudine in front of everyone. She could leave us locked down here forever.

My head spins like a top. I close my eyes. The cold in the stone floor seeps through my gown. I rest my head on my knees and concentrate on the arcana.

I picture the bars like a body or a canvas or a candle. My fingers tingle as the arcana wake up inside me again. They're dull and weak from overuse on Claudine. Sweat skates down my back, and a headache floods my temples. I shake and tremble.

"It's solid metal, Camille. We can't manipulate it." Amber's cries turn to hiccups.

I sigh and crumple forward. If the bars were made of wood, the planks would soften and become malleable; when I opened my eyes, the wood would be nothing but chips in a pile, to be used for kindling. *Your gifts are useless when it comes to metals and gemstones,* Du Barry had told us. Punishment because the Goddess of Beauty chose the God of the Sky to love over the God of the Ground.

"Take a pin from your hair," Amber says, ruining her Belle-bun as she extracts her own. I fish one out of my curls, my hand trembling. "Help me."

"It's no use," I say.

"We have to try."

We twist our hands through the bars and jam the pins into the lock.

"Try pushing to the right."

She grunts and twists hers.

"Harder."

"It won't give. The bolt's too thick."

I push harder. My hand grows fatigued, my fingers slippery with sweat, and I drop the pin. It flies out of reach.

She slumps back with her head in her hands. "Pointless."

I run my fingers through her hair. It used to shine the color of rich autumn leaves, but now it is dull. Her eyes are ringed with yellow. Her skin is paler than a white privacy screen. "I'm sorry," I whisper. "For everything."

"I'm sorry, too," she says. "I was so stupid. I walked right into her trap."

I wrap my arms around her and we're little girls again, two

spoons side by side in a drawer. I feel her breathing, her heart beating.

"What happened when you were the favorite?"

Amber gazes up. Kohl lines streak her pale cheeks. She wipes her nose. "She made me do horrible things."

"Elisabeth told me some of it."

"She fired me after I refused to kill Lady Ophelia Thomas of House Merania."

"Kill?"

"She wanted me to age her. Reverse the arcana. She said she read somewhere that we could do that. Make her so old she'd die quickly."

"But why?"

"Because Ophelia was too beautiful, she claimed." Amber begins to cry again, softly this time. "I wouldn't do it. So she threw me out."

I hug her tighter.

"Did she make you do that, too?" she asks.

"She would have if we'd had the time."

"How . . . are we going . . . to get out of here?" Her head sinks into my shoulder. "How . . . will we reset our levels?"

"She's not going to win. We won't let her. We need a plan."

"Might as well go on to sleep, little ladies," someone calls out from a cell. "'Cause there isn't a way out of here. The dungeon bars never break."

Amber and I curl up even closer. Tears stream down my cheeks, and my shoulders shake as we sob. I cry for all our sisters. Padma, Hana, Edel, and Valerie. I couldn't save any one of them. I can't even save myself.

# 49

It's impossible to tell how many hourglasses have passed. A girl with a bucket, a ladle, and water comes five times a day. Guards walk the perimeter of the space twice a day.

The queen should be looking for me. What happened to her? Why hasn't she come? Doesn't she know?

A guard passes a bowl through the metal bars. The meat is rotten and the vegetables moldy, but they haven't fed us since we got thrown in here. I take the bowl to Amber.

"What is it?" she asks.

"I don't know. We have to eat it to balance our levels. We have to get our strength back."

She takes a bite, then spits it out and coughs. "It's disgusting."

I swallow some of it. The flavors are rancid on my tongue, but the sustenance is welcome in my stomach. More hours pass and it feels like we've been down here for an eternity.

"Well, aren't you two pretty?" Sophia presses her powdered face against the bars.

I rush at her. "Let us out of here."

"All right," she says with a smile.

My heart flutters as the guards unlock the gate. What is happening?

I step out, then Amber follows.

"Oh, not without chains."

Guards clasp metal cuffs around our wrists and tug us forward.

"Make them tight, so she can't try anything."

One guard drags me forward. His thick hands squeeze my arms and leave behind more bruises. A second guard grabs Amber.

"Where's the queen? Where's Du Barry? I demand to speak with them."

"You don't get to make demands. You are a criminal now." Her golden dress makes a tiny tinkling melody when she moves.

"The queen wouldn't allow this," Amber yells. "Nor the king."

"How nice of you to ask about my mother. She's grown even more ill. I've stepped in to help while she rests. I have been named regent queen by her cabinet, as I was supposed to be at the Declaration. She will make it official any day now, when she has an upsurge of strength. And my father is in the south at the winter palace, his favorite retreat after the first snows." She motions the guards forward, and we're marched through the dungeon.

I push and pull and kick, but my strength is no match for theirs.

"Still fighting?" Sophia laughs. "I thought we'd starved that out of you."

They cart us upstairs and through cold hallways. My weak legs can't keep up with the guard's pace. I trip and stumble.

The doors of the Receiving Hall open. Obsidian mourning-lanterns leave their sad and solemn light throughout. Wellness candles burn. Black calla lilies and roses burst from pots and line trellises that ring the room. The queen's cameo is prominently displayed, along with messages wishing her good health.

A sleeping Princess Charlotte sits on her throne. Sophia strides up the staircase to sit beside her. Auguste's mother, Duchesse Georgiana, readjusts the crown on Charlotte's head and admires the glittering scepter in her lap. Sophia's teacup pets parade up and down—Singe and Zo are leading her new giraffe and three teacup dragons.

"Bring them here," Sophia yells out.

The guards slam me to my knees on the stairs leading up to the thrones. Amber is deposited beside me. Sweat drips down her ruddy cheeks. She pants and can't catch her breath.

I reach for her. The guard steps on my hand.

It feels like my heart is threatening to jump through my mouth, along with everything else inside me.

Sophia slowly descends, letting her little heels click against the floor. "You've never been that pretty, Camellia, not without help. And certainly not after a few days without bathing." She leans down and sniffs me. "You smell revolting." She waves a hand before her nose. "Stand her up," she tells the guards.

She circles me, then cups her hand around my ear. "I win. I win. You should've just been loyal to me. You could've been by my side."

I jump at her. Guards catch my hands before I can wrap them around her throat.

Sophia scoots back, turning to inspect Amber. She lifts Amber's chin and *tsk-tsk*s. "So weak. The lesser Belle."

Amber bares her teeth.

Sophia slaps her. "I don't want to hear it." She goes back to her throne, sinking into the plush red high-backed chair.

Lightning crashes overhead, followed by claps of thunder that vibrate through the room. Rain beats against the glass ceiling.

"Don't you just love storms? Especially ones with snow? The God of the Sky helps us cleanse the land. Rid the kingdom of things we don't need. It's fitting for tonight." She claps her hands together.

"I have to make my first hard decision as regent queen. My first trial. You're going to be tried and imprisoned for the murder of my beloved lady-of-honor, Claudine."

I fight against the guard's grip. He holds me firmly in place.

"That's the only way House Maille will forgive you. The city of Bissay, her hometown, is very upset. Justice must be served. But instead of sentencing you to the starvation box, or death by hanging in the Royal Square, or throwing you off one of our great rock barriers in the southern part of the kingdom, I'll spare your life. Isn't that kind of me?"

I glare at her.

"Show me your gratitude."

My guard forces Amber and me down in a bow. "Thank Her Majesty," he orders. I say nothing. Amber refuses, too. He jerks my arm. Sharp, hot pain blasts through me. "I'll snap it clean off."

Another guard kicks Amber in the side. She coughs and cries out.

"Thank you," I mumble. Amber parrots me.

"What was that?"

"Thank you, Your Majesty," I yell.

"Oh, but maybe you shouldn't thank me yet." She motions at a nearby attendant. "Bring me little Du Barry."

A side door opens. A red-faced and sniffing Elisabeth is dragged out. She stands beside me. Her eyes spill over with tears, her fear palpable.

"Elisabeth Du Barry, you haven't been paying enough attention to the favorite. She's been spending time with one of my suitors—breaking our fraternizing law. She ran away to the Chrysanthemum Teahouse under your watch. And worst of all, she called me a monster."

"I'm sorry, Your Majesty," she stammers out. "Won't happen again."

"You're right, it won't." She stands again and reaches for a long golden staff. A fat glittering diamond the size of an ostrich egg sits atop it. She lets the bottom hit the ground several times, reveling in the echo it sends through the room. "Elisabeth, you'll be jailed alongside Camellia."

Elisabeth bursts into a sob.

"You will bleed her every day, collect every drop of her blood, and we will create an elixir from it. I will test it myself."

"That will do nothing," I shout.

"But didn't you tell Auguste the arcana live in the blood?"

His face burns in my memory. Our conversations. The touch of his fingers.

A collar of fear tightens around my throat. Tremors work their way through every part of my body. The memory of him is like a poison masked in a beautiful glass.

"Did you think he liked you, or better yet, loved you? Did you think he'd keep your secrets?"

The words sting. A dead, haunting silence stretches. The word *love* bounces off the walls, only to slap me in the face and explode inside my chest.

Georgiana saunters forward with a perfectly proportioned smile on her face. "Out of my three sons, I made him the most handsome because, coupled with how naturally charming he is, I knew it would make him powerful. He cracked you open like an egg, and the secrets of your arcana poured out into trusted and loving hands."

Sweat races down my face, like the rain across the glass above our heads.

"Anything to say, Camellia? You're usually never at a loss for words," Sophia taunts.

Duchesse Georgiana Fabry claps her hands. "With your blood, Camellia, we will usher in a new form of beauty work that will make the kingdom millions of leas and billions of spintria."

"And the best part," Sophia says, "is that Ambrosia will be our new favorite until I'm ready to reveal our newest and most potent Belle-product, the Beauty Elixir. Yes, that's what I think I'll call it." She waves her staff in the air.

The guards start to drag Amber from the room.

She screams out.

"Didn't you always want to be the favorite?" Sophia says before waving her good-bye.

A hard knot of anger churns in my stomach. My heart beats to the sound of the quickening lightning outside. The veins in my arms rise like angry snakes. I feel the pulse and blood flow of every person in the room. The rushing and churning and simmering grow louder, like a river swollen by a storm.

The arcana wake up inside me. I stretch the black roses from the pots behind the throne platform. I use their thorny stems like a set of chains. The vines grab the sleeping Princess Charlotte from her throne chair, lifting her high above us all. The thorns push into her unblemished skin. Rivulets of blood skate down her limbs.

Sophia screams. Her teacup pets scatter in all directions.

"Let Amber go, and you can have me. All my blood."

"Put her down," Sophia cries out.

The guards pin me to the floor. I curl a stem around Princess Charlotte's throat. She starts to cough. Other guards hack at the vines with their swords, but it only makes them grow back thicker and bolder.

"Make her stop," Sophia commands the guards.

The guards kick my sides and slam my head into the staircase, but I hold tight, pushing my arcana further. Blood trickles down my nose. I make the stems recede. Charlotte's body plummets toward the ground like a star falling from the heavens.

Sophia hollers, "Charlotte!" She opens her arms to try to catch her.

The black calla lilies balloon to the size of a carriage and catch her limp body. I close the dark petals around her, squeezing her into a cocoon. Guards try to yank the calla lily down, but I push it to grow higher toward the glass ceiling.

"Give me Amber."

"No," Sophia yells.

"I can stop her heart, you know."

"You let her out," Sophia screams.

I collapse the calla lily petals more, shrinking the space inside. Thunder clatters.

"I will suffocate her. You will be queen. Not just regent. Don't you want that?" I shout.

413

"I want my sister. I get to decide her fate. Not you."

"And I want mine."

"Pearl! Sapphire! Jet!" Sophia hollers. Her teacup dragons flutter over her head. "Burn her. Eat her flesh." They elongate their wings, hiss and hiccup, then fly toward me. Tiny fireballs ignite my clothes.

"No, stop!" I scream as the burns scorch my arms. The scent of my burning flesh chokes me. The black calla lily starts to shrink. I can't focus on two things at once.

"Put her down," a voice commands. A deep stab pierces my side. Rémy holds a bloody knife. My blood.

My strength fades. I lower the cocoon in front of Sophia. I peel back the petals to reveal her unharmed sister. Sophia touches Charlotte's sleeping face.

"Dragons!" she calls out. They turn their attention to her. "Enough. No need to waste her." She calls for a palanquin to take Charlotte back to her chambers.

I stare at Rémy. "How could you?"

He snatches me from the other guard. "I'll take her."

# 50

Rémy drags me down the hall. My wound leaks, but slowly my arcana start to heal it.

"You're a liar," I say, and spit at him.

He tightens his hold.

I pummel him with insults:

"I hate you."

"I wish I never met you."

"Your sisters would be ashamed of you."

He shoves me through dank passageways and down slippery staircases. His hands blend into the darkness. We pass dungeon cells and watchful guards. He tells one, "I need the keys. I got orders to lock this one up again."

The man grumbles and hands him the key ring. He knocks me forward. This tunnel is darker than the others. My pounding heartbeat stamps out the noise of our footsteps and the hiss of the dungeon-lanterns.

"Was anything you ever told me true? Were we ever friends?" I say.

"I don't have friends," he says, and his voice is a firecracker in the underground corridors.

I fight with the cuffs again. I fight with the memory of the times we talked, the times that I actually liked him and wanted his advice.

The passageway opens up into a trio of cages. Amber lies in one. "Camille," she says, her voice rough as sandcloth. She reaches her hands out and presses her dirty face to the bars.

"You're all right."

"I'm in one piece," she replies.

"When are you going to learn to shut your mouth?" Rémy says, turning me around to face him.

The keys jingle in his hand. Then, a click. And my wrists are free. Rémy glares at me. "Help Amber out of the cell." He tosses another key at me.

I'm frozen. "Rémy."

"Hurry up." He startles me out of it. "You can thank me later."


Rémy leads Amber and me down a dark passage. He makes a series of sharp turns. Amber trips over the cobblestones.

"I'm sorry I stabbed you," he says.

"I might be able to forgive you."

"Where are we going?" Amber asks.

"For days, I've been testing this path out of the palace. It'll lead us to the eastern gate—the quietest pier—so we'll easily be able to take a boat. I'll navigate it out to the harbor instead of going into Trianon."

His plan fills my weak muscles with strength they don't have.

"The Golden Palace River empties into the harbor. We can escape that way."

I stop. "Wait! We can't leave."

Amber crashes into me.

"We have to go," Rémy urges.

"We can't. I need to help Charlotte," I say.

"This is our chance to get out," Amber says.

"I made a promise. I have a duty."

Rémy's eyes widen and he smiles. "You can't even follow my directions after I save you," he says.

"No. And we can't let Sophia remain in power." I look Amber in the eye. "Not if there's something we can do."

Rémy considers this, then nods. "We can take the queen's passage."

The queen's private passageways snake from the piers back into her chambers, which are connected to Charlotte's room. Medicinal pastilles burn on chafing dishes surrounding Charlotte's bed. Healing-lanterns drift over her like sun-filled clouds. The fireplace roars and hisses. Nurses move in and out of the room with trays of vials and powders. Arabella stands at Charlotte's side, veiled, shoulders slumped, holding and stroking her frail hand.

The princess lies there, hands crossed over her chest. There is no sign of my earlier attempt to smother her.

"Arabella," I whisper.

She swivels around. "Oh, Camellia." She rushes to me.

Rémy and Amber step out of the passageway behind me.

"I heard what Sophia did. I couldn't get to you. I'm sorry." Arabella hugs me.

"It's all right. We're all right," I say.

"Where's the queen?" Amber asks.

"She's very ill," Arabella reports.

"You have to tell her what's going on. You have to wake her," I say.

Arabella nods, motions to a servant, then says to me, "Hurry. Sophia probably knows you've left the dungeons."

I look at Amber, my eyes saying: *Can you do this? Are you strong enough? Are we strong enough?*

She nods.

"We need leeches, and a needle," I say.

Servants disappear and return quickly with a cart of supplies.

"What's wrong with her?" Amber asks.

"I'm not sure, but I have a theory."

A side door opens, and in hobbles the queen with Lady Zurie at her side. She uses a cane, and her back curves into a question mark. Gray hair falls down it in a large wave. Her once-brown skin is now almost completely gray. "Camellia, you came." She barely makes it into a nearby chair. "Help my sweet girl."

"We will," I say.

Arabella hands me a needle herself. I pull the mirror from beneath my dress.

"What's that?" Amber asks.

"A miroir métaphysique," Arabella says. "It only shows the truth."

"My mother left it to me." I prick my finger and let the blood race up the little handle. The roses and stems uncoil, and the message appears: BLOOD FOR TRUTH. I gaze at the glass, waiting for the fog to clear, and to see Charlotte's reflection. Her eyes fight to open. I feel her will to live and her anger. A red glow circles her image.

"See?" I show Amber.

Amber leans in to look, and gasps. "I don't understand," she says.

"She's trying to wake up."

I study Charlotte's reflection. *What are you trying to tell us?*

I glance up at the queen. She's rocking in her chair, hands pressed together, prayer beads looped around her palms.

"Take Charlotte out of these garments," I say.

The servants remove her dress, the corset and crinoline, and stockings and gloves. She's stripped down to her dressing gown, which makes her seem even more frail.

"The jewelry, too."

Rings are pulled from her fingers, bracelets unclasped from her wrists. Her royal emblem is taken from her neck, exposing her identification ink.

She looks ordinary. Like a woman from Trianon's market, or the Achillean Alps.

"And the hair ornaments."

A servant reaches to remove the comb from the crown of Charlotte's head.

"Wait," the queen says. "She's never without her favorite comb. Her grandmother gave it to her a year before she grew ill. She wore it everywhere. Even in the bathing tubs." Her tired mouth lifts in a half smile. "I never let them take it off. I feel like it gives her strength. And Sophia adds flowers to it weekly."

"We must, Your Majesty. I want her as bare as possible."

"I just"—she starts to cry—"hate to see her like this." She totters over to the bed, touches the comb, then pulls it from Charlotte's hair and squeezes it. She waves to a nearby servant, who steps forward to remove large sections of Charlotte's hair. The pieces of wig are set on the nightstand. The princess is almost bald, with only a few tendrils growing limply from her scalp. Lady Zurie starts to sob.

"The hair wouldn't grow back. No matter how many times I tried," Arabella says.

Amber and I climb onto opposite sides of Charlotte's bed.

Servants return with the porcelain jug of leeches. I dig my fingers in the damp jar, retrieving two—one for me and one for Amber. I loop the creature around my wrist. Amber mimics me. The leech's tiny teeth bite into the vein, and its secretions start to flow.

"We have to work together." I reach my hands over Charlotte's body. Amber holds them tight.

"The last time we did this, we killed someone," she whispers.

"We won't change her at the same time. We just need to see her natural template and find out what's wrong."

Amber gulps, then nods. "But neither of our arcana are balanced."

I squeeze her hand. "As long as we stay connected, we'll be all right," I say, even though it feels like a lie.

We close our eyes.

A knock rattles the door. "Your Majesty," a guard calls out.

Amber jumps.

"Go on," the queen says. "Ignore it."

Arabella takes a sharp breath. I shake Amber's hands. She

closes her eyes again. In the darkness, I see Charlotte's body. She's thin, down to her bones. Almost a skeleton. I find every imperfection: her wispy hair, her hollow cheeks, her sallow skin, the too-slow beat of her heart. Her veins have a yellow tint beneath her skin. Her blood pressure is low. It reminds me of how I felt after being poisoned.

My eyes snap open. "Your Majesty, can I see the hair comb again?"

She hands it to me.

I turn it over and examine it, then wrench it open. The comb breaks. The queen gasps. The comb's teeth release a clear liquid. The scent is familiar. "It's poison. Just like the one that was used on me. It's made from the pollen of bloodroot flowers."

"We had her blood tasted." The queen rushes to my side. "When she first became ill."

The door vibrates again.

"Your Majesty!" the guards shout. "We will take down these doors."

Lady Zurie rushes to press her back against them.

"Yes, but this poison smells and tastes like flowers," I say to the queen. "I didn't recognize it either."

"How did the doctors not catch this?"

"It's untraceable," I say. "I overheard the nurses saying my blood was clean as well. But I know this smell now. I will never forget it."

Amber touches Charlotte's head. "It's coming from her scalp. Look where the bald patches are. They're oozing. The comb's been piercing her."

The queen rubs her fingers over Charlotte's scalp. She sinks back. Arabella leads her to the chair, then scoops up the broken comb and holds it under a night-lantern. She sniffs. "There's definitely something on the teeth."

The door jolts forward.

"I don't know how long I can hold them," Lady Zurie calls out.

"She needs to have her blood cleaned." I remove the leeches from my wrist and Amber's, and pluck out the others in the jar. I hand a few to Amber. We lay them on Charlotte: on her wrists, beneath her neck, and on the top of her head near the small wound. The leeches turn a fiery red as they fill with her blood.

"Now, Amber, focus on her blood. Refresh the proteins, like we would someone's skin or hair."

"I've never done this before."

"Me either."

She looks at the queen.

"You have to try," she cries.

Amber nods, a bead of sweat swooping down her nose.

The door starts to crack. The wood is being chipped away. The queen hollers. Lady Zurie beats back against it.

"I'm afraid," Amber whispers. "And I'm so tired. I can't feel the arcana anymore."

"I'm tired, too." I turn her wrist over and trace the veins. "It's still there. It has to be."

Her eyes are heavy with exhaustion. I lean over Charlotte and hug Amber. I fall neatly into the crook of Amber's neck. The scent of orange blossom is still faint in her hair, even underneath the stench of the dungeons. "We can do this." I hope my words burrow down inside her. "We're strong together."

Arabella's hand squeezes my shoulder. "I'll help, too."

A door panel breaks. Sophia demands to be let in to see her sister. Amber, Arabella, and I clamp our eyes shut.

The arcana hiss underneath my skin.

The rhythm of Charlotte's heart beats alongside mine. I see the pulsating organ—fleshy, red, thumping. Blood rushes through it and sluggishly moves through her veins. I push the arcana to reset the proteins, as I would her bones for beauty work. Amber and Arabella's arcana combine with mine; it all showers through me like a hot rainstorm in the warm season.

Charlotte's body jerks.

The queen screams.

Amber topples forward, crashing into me.

"Amber!" I shake her and hold her up.

Charlotte coughs and moans.

"Oh, my little girl." The queen rushes to her side. "Wake up, please open your eyes."

"You must go," Arabella says to me.

Rémy helps me lift Amber's body from the bed.

"Use the passages. I've left trunks for you that contain all you need."

"I'll lead them," Arabella says, lifting a wall tapestry and pushing out a hidden panel.

"Thank you." The queen kisses my cheek.

Rémy disappears with Amber into the dark passageway. I linger and hear Charlotte gasp for breath and mutter.

The bedroom doors shatter, wood flying in all directions.

"Go," the queen shouts.

Hands find my shoulders. Arabella yanks me through. The door shuts us into darkness.

## 51

We follow behind Arabella. Her long veil sweeps along the cobblestone passage. "There will be guards here in a moment's time. Sophia has her own tunnels beneath the palace. Hurry."

She ducks and turns, seemingly at random, down a series of dark corridors. Pockets of gloom and dead air lurk about. Night-lanterns are hooked to the walls, creating quivering, infrequent splotches of light along the walls and floor.

My body quivers. Shadowy corners lie ahead. Spiderwebs spin a network of time gone by, stretching from lantern to lantern. I have no sense of where we are in the palace. Arabella knows every stair and turn and pathway through the darkness. The clomping of Rémy's heavy boots matches the racing pattern of my heart.

Finally, Arabella slows down. The noise beyond the walls quiets. The scent of fresh bread creeps in, and the stone walls are warm to the touch.

Arabella drops to her knees and runs her fingers along the

ground. She pulls on a latch, lifts a door, and exposes a Belle-trunk. Rémy sets a sleeping Amber on the floor and hoists it out.

Arabella flips it open and gazes up at me. "You are no longer a Belle." She pulls a simple green dress from the trunk. "Out of those clothes."

Rémy turns around while I change. I shiver with cold and fear. Dread fills every part of my body.

"Your name is Corinne Sauveterre, and you're the daughter of a dragon merchant from the Gold Isles." She ties the House of Rare Reptilians emblem around my neck, and shoves a parcel into my hands. Transport documents. A miniature portrait of me stares back. My new name and the names of my parents. "No one will ask for it unless you draw attention to yourself." Arabella digs farther into the trunk.

"Why petit-dragons?"

"They're lucky. And they're worth a lot." She holds up a pouch and flashes its contents at me. Five tiny eggs. They're swaddled. "The queen gave them to me for safekeeping so that Sophia wouldn't get to them. The shells are shatterproof. Just carry them on you. Keep them warm." She laces the pouch around my waist, then covers it with a waist-sash embroidered with the house emblem. "Sell them when you have to. If you must. But they are also excellent and natural messengers."

We lock eyes through her dark veil. She removes it. Her face is as smooth as mine. Her coiled russet hair is studded with jewels in her Belle-bun, and a Belle-emblem circles her neck. Her mouth curves into a smile. She has the same dimple in her cheek that I do. We could be a matching set. Mother and daughter.

I gasp.

"You haven't figured it out yet," she says.

"Figured what out?" I ask.

"I told Du Barry to keep you home," she says, while packing a small toilette box.

"You did what?"

She glares at me. "I knew something terrible would happen if you came to court."

"I don't understand."

"You and I are the same. You're me. They tried to make another version of me in you. Your mother, Linnea, even gave you my mirror." She points at the place where I've hidden it under my undergarments.

"What do you mean?"

"You know that we aren't born. We're grown like flowers."

"I saw Sophia's pods." A thousand questions about who and what I am bubble up on my tongue, even though I know there isn't the time to answer them.

"Yes, that's why I'm kept at court. To watch over this process. They use my blood to ensure that enough Belles are born."

I step back, and crash into the wall behind me. "You allowed them to do this?"

"Allow? I do what I'm told. Just like you. Up until today."

"You could end it all."

"I could have killed myself, but then they would've just brought you here and bled you every day. As long as there are strong Belles to use, it will never stop."

"It has to," I say.

"I know."

Noise echoes on the other side of the wall. I suck in a huge breath and hold it until the sound drifts away.

"Help me change her clothes." Arabella undresses Amber, who is sitting, spent, on the floor. I rush to help her. "And when you get to a safe place, you should both dye your hair. Especially Ambrosia."

There's a clatter overhead. The sound of rushing footsteps.

"We need to be on our way," Rémy says.

"Yes. I will be in touch again. Send word when you're safe." Arabella lifts my chin and lets her fingers drift up the sides of my face, just like Maman did. "Open your eyes wide."

She inserts two films to change my eye color. I squeeze my eyes shut after and reopen them. My eyes blur and water.

"Keep blinking. They will settle into place. There's more of them in the toilette box, along with skin-color pastes," she says. "Your faces will be plastered all over the kingdom in a matter of hours. The few who don't already know you by sight, will."

Three knocks rattle the wall.

"Time to go." She shoves the toilette box in my hands and drapes a hooded cloak over my shoulders. "I will help you in any way I can." She kisses my cheek, then turns to the wall and gives it one giant push. The wall cracks open like a hinged door, leading into the palace kitchen.

"To the courtier dock," she orders Rémy.

He nods and leads the way forward. Amber's still a rag doll in his arms. We go through the servant entrance. The dark wood of the underground palace dock gleams under low-lit sea-lanterns. The whole thing seems carved out of the bottom of the palace, opening up onto the ocean like a great mouth. Glittering boats are loaded with well-dressed passengers.

"Dock closing," a man hollers. "Load your boats and go, if you're going. By order of the queen."

"She's got to stand." Rémy tries to hold Amber upright.

I shake her shoulders. She moans. "Amber, you've got to wake up." Her eyes flutter. "I need you to walk."

She tries, but her legs buckle under her. Rémy drapes one of her arms around his shoulder and the other around mine. We join a line of passengers boarding several boats. We drag her forward.

"Gold Isles—this boat," one shouts. "Docking at Céline."

"Glass Isles and one stop in Silk Bay," another says.

"Spice Isles," a man hollers through a voice-trumpet.

Men and women drop fat coins into his hands and shuffle aboard.

I pull the hood over my head. "This way, Rémy. Spice Isles."

Rémy places a hand on my waist. "Three seats for my wife and me, and her very drunk sister," he tells the man.

The man laughs at the sight of Amber but doesn't look twice at us as Rémy gives him money. Our tickets secure us seats in the steerage class on the boat. Porthole windows expose night views of the water.

"What's going to happen?" I ask. "Where are we going to—"

Rémy brings one finger to his lips. "Say nothing for a while."

The boat slides out from the dock and into La Mer du Roi.

# 52

My sisters and I threatened to run away from Du Barry once. Edel made us all pack a tiny satchel full of stolen bread and cheese from the kitchen. Three of us hooked night-lanterns to our Belle-buns. We climbed out our bedroom windows and into the dark. Our nightdresses picked up mud and sticks and leaves. Edel led the way. Amber cried the entire journey. Valerie whimpered and jumped at every sound. Hana held her breath. Padma and I held hands. We marched to the little dock at the south wing of the island, and prepared to get in a bayou boat. White cypress trees grew out of the shadowy water like bones, and fireflies skipped along the surface, their little bodies red sparks brightening the night. We argued about the bayou octopus rumored to be living in those waters, waiting to eat us if we ever tried to swim away.

None of us had the courage to get in the boat before Du Barry caught us. The same feeling creeps into me now as the vessel oscillates under me.

The sea seems endless, the space between us endless, the

questions that I have endless. Du Barry forced us to study the map of Orléans, and I remember the big wall-length tapestry in the main salon of the Belle apartments, but being out on the water— moving away from the imperial island and into the unknown— gives me the dizzying feeling that we are headed to the edge of the world.

"Are you hungry?" Rémy asks. It's the first thing he's said since the ship left the underground palace dock.

"Yes. Should I go?"

"No, it isn't safe. You could be recognized still."

I nuzzle the cloak Arabella gave me, pulling it more tightly under my neck, and I cradle my waist-pouch full of dragon eggs. Amber's head is in my lap, and she sleeps peacefully. I wish I could sleep, too, but worries and questions hum through me, keeping me awake.

Rémy leaves in search of food, and I watch his back disappear up the ship's stairs to the surface. The people on this deck hold bundles, and some have jackets embroidered with merchant house emblems like mine.

"Barley water?" a ship-vendor calls out. "Eases the stomach on the sea. Barley water, anyone?"

I hold my breath as he comes closer.

"Barley water, miss?" He taps my shoulder. I jump, and shake my head no.

I'm flinching at every sound. *Is this how your new life will always be?* says a voice inside me. I wonder if Charlotte is awake, and if the queen is stronger.

I shudder and gaze around. Has Sophia sent someone after us? Are all the soldiers in Orléans searching? What bounty did she place on our heads? What is she doing to my sisters? What will Du Barry say when she learns of what happened? What happened to Bree?

After a few more moments, I become certain that Rémy has been identified and taken into the ship's custody. I watch the staircase he ascended, and when I spot his familiar shape, I exhale with relief.

He slips back into the seat beside me like he's only been gone for a few seconds. He hands me a sausage roll. "All they had. Pick around the meat. Smelled a little rancid."

I unwrap the paper and sniff the oozing roll. "Where's yours?"

"We have to save for when we dock."

"We'll share it."

"No, you eat."

I break it in half.

"Why can't you just follow instructions?"

"I thought you knew me by now."

We chew in silence. It isn't the worst thing I've ever tasted, but it's pretty close.

Amber stretches.

"Wake up," I whisper.

Her eyes flutter and then pop open. "Camille..."

"Shh." I cup her face.

She sits up slowly. "Where are we?"

I lift her hood. "On a ship to the Spice Isles."

"What happened?" she says groggily.

"I'll tell you when we get off."

"Look." Rémy points out the window. The glowing towers of the Spice Islands' port city rise in the distance. Gilt-lanterns hang out of windows, casting an aurous glow over all the buildings. Blue-sailed ships are docked in the port.

"Port ahead! City of Metairie," a man shouts and rings a bell.

People gather their belongings and shuffle to the stairs.

Rémy stands. He shapes the hood around my face. "Eyes down, all right? Both of you. You're merchants now, not such an esteemed birth."

Amber and I nod.

The boat docks. We shuffle off with the crowd. The pier is a chaos of bodies and sounds and movement. Newsies hold up papers, and a storm of post-balloons whirls overhead.

"The queen is dead!" one shouts. "The queen is dead!"

"What?" I gasp, my eyes wide. "No!"

"Metairie's latest news!"

"Read all about it. Ten leas a pop for the *Spice Isles Sentinel.*"

"I've got the latest pictures in the *Orléansian Times.*"

"My tattler tells all. Reputable sources only. Firsthand accounts."

I try to glimpse the headlines. The newsies' hands wave in the air, scattering the ink across the pages. I catch pieces of it.

QUEEN'S HEART STOPPED

SLEEPING PRINCESS CHARLOTTE HAS DISAPPEARED

KING IN RETIREMENT

REGENT QUEEN SOPHIA TO BE CORONATED

PALACE IN MOURNING

THE PRINCESS TO MARRY MINISTER OF
SEAS' SON, AUGUSTE FABRY

QUEEN'S LONGTIME LOVER LADY PELLETIER FLEES PALACE

My heart shatters. I stop, doubling over. Shopkeepers are working to swap their pier-lanterns with mourning ones. A black glow settles over the small market.

"We must move," Rémy says.

"Where?" I ask dumbly. It is all too much.

"This way." Rémy navigates through the crowd, dodging bodies. The crowds thin out. Pockets of men are hunched over wooden crates. They're playing cards, slamming down chips and hollering out insults.

"It's here," Rémy says. We pause in front of a building with a tiny sign that reads PRUZAN'S SALOON AND BOARDINGHOUSE, FINE WHISKEY, BEDS, AND DECENT FOOD. The saloon has a pass-me-by appearance, with boarded-up windows and post-balloon slots that look wired shut. A wobbly porch wraps around its face like a crooked smile. Stretching five stories high, it swallows nearly half the street, and has three empty storefronts on the first floor with cobwebbed windows and faded signs.

We climb the stairs.

"Wait here with Amber," Rémy says.

The card-playing men look up.

"Why are we here?" Amber asks.

I don't hear her question at first. My head is buzzing with the headlines about the queen and Auguste.

Rémy returns with a dangling key. "A room with two beds for my wife and servant."

"Servant?" Amber scoffs.

"You weren't awake to have an opinion," he says.

Inside, the saloon feels like one of our old dollhouses in the playroom at home. Banisters hold constellations of cobwebs. Sitting rooms spill over with tipsy sofas and moth-eaten covers, and the furniture is piled high with old-fashioned post-balloons, buckets, house-lanterns, drapery, older télétropes, bolts of lace, half-burned candles, broken spyglasses, ear-trumpets, and more. "This way." A woman leads us up the front staircase. She slumps forward, limping like she's walking over hot coals. "I put you in the back, where it's quiet." She wears a long handmade dress that drags at the hem, and little heeled shoes that probably leave sores on her big toes. The halls creak with each step she takes. I keep my head lowered and don't make eye contact. She shows Rémy how to open the door, and points the way to the bathing room. The humble space has two beds, a desk, a tiny cookstove, and a large window overlooking the street.

"Dinner's at eight. Kitchen closes before the midnight star."

"Thank you," Rémy says.

She shuts the door behind her. I set Arabella's toilette box on a small table.

We all find places to sit. A silence stretches between us, and we're too tired and weary to talk about what we have to do next.

A knock pounds at the door.

Rémy steps carefully to it. "Who is it?"

"Fresh macarons," the voice says. "For you and your wife."

The hairs on my arms lift.

"We don't want any. Thank you."

The knocking persists.

Rémy puts a hand on his dagger.

"They're the best in Matairie. Best in all of the Spice Isles."

"Go out there, and shoo them away," I say. Amber and I pull up our hoods.

Rémy opens the door. A cloaked woman stands there, holding a tray of yellow macarons. She reveals her face and I gasp.

Edel smiles back at us. "It took you long enough."

Dear Reader,

This book contains my personal monster.

I started *The Belles* almost a decade ago, but it's a story that's been living inside me since I was twelve, long before I ever had dreams of being a writer, before I even thought that was possible.

When I was a pimply, puffy-haired preteen in the mid-1990s, I overheard a conversation at my local suburban mall among several men about their respective girlfriends' bodies. They were thumbing through a popular magazine as they discussed how much better their girlfriends might look if they had longer and leaner legs, bigger breasts, different hair textures, a more slender frame, softer skin, and on and on, comparing them to the celebrities voted the most beautiful women in the world that year.

This conversation broke something deep down inside of me, and in that fissure grew a monster.

I checked out magazines from the public library and spent hours poring over the pages, dissecting the images and studying the women photographed. I housed my obsession in a secret little space inside my childhood bedroom. If you go in my closet and push back the clothes, there's a tiny door made perfect for a hobbit, a reading nook built by my bookworm parents to foster my love of reading. But I used that little room to explore all the thoughts I was having about bodies and beauty. I cut out pictures of women I thought men would consider beautiful, and pasted them on the little walls: legs, breasts, arms, torsos, eyes, hair textures, skin tones, and hairstyles.

Over time, the walls held the wishes I had for my own body, and filled me with questions. What would I do if I could change myself completely? How far would I go? How ugly could it get, and why? Was there a way to be the most beautiful woman in the world?

The world of Orléans is built from the flesh and bones of that monster. It's ugly, painful, unsettling, and oftentimes disturbing.

As uncomfortable as it might be, I hope this book pushes us to talk about the commodification of women's body parts and the media messages we send young people about the value of their exterior selves, what is considered beautiful, and the forces causing those things to shift into disgusting shapes.

I haven't been inside that little room since I graduated high school. I'm afraid to look up close at the monster I left behind. But maybe this book will help many interrogate the monsters that live inside us all.

Thank you for reading.

# ACKNOWLEDGMENTS

This book has haunted me for almost twenty years, and so many people have helped me translate it to the page. It took a village and an army, and I'm eternally grateful.

I couldn't do this without the support of my parents. Thank you for dealing with teenage me. Thank you for always saying *yes* and helping me chase my dreams. None of this would be possible without you.

The biggest thanks to my agent, Victoria Marini. Thank you for always going over every cliff and down each rabbit hole with me. Your endless support and enthusiasm and nudges and pep talks are the reason I'm here. Thanks for always having my back.

Massive thanks to my editors, Emily Meehan and her niece Annabel. Thank you for embracing my world, understanding its complexities, and starting this journey with me.

The largest and most massive and gargantuan thanks to Kieran Viola, who is the streamliner-of-bulls@$t, the fixer-of-broken-things, the brilliant, the talented, the most *patient* editor in the whole wide world. Thank you for understanding my brain, my anxieties, my neuroses, and the things I want to dig into. This book wouldn't be *the book* without you. I feel so lucky. I am a better writer because of you.

Marci Senders, brilliant cover wizard, your design will change how little brown girls feel about themselves forever. You've changed the worldview of so many little ones who look like me. Thank you for this gift! You are profound. You are wonderful.

Thank you to the whole Freeform team: MaryAnn Zissimos (the magic maker who is the best champion ever!), Deeba Zargarpur, Anna Leuchtenberger (made me fall in love with copy editors), Seale Ballenger, Elke Villa, Holly Nagel, Dina Sherman, Andrew Sansone, Mary Mudd, and Shane Rebenschied. You are amazing and put so much love into everything you do. Thank you for taking such great care of this book and helping it find its readers.

Thank you to my We Need Diverse Books team. You are *my* people and I wouldn't be here without you. Ellen, oh you are a force and you always feed me the most delicious Korean food and make sure I am powered up to do this important work. I will never leave you. Lamar Giles, thanks for always sending me Idris Elba pictures and helping me push through these deadlines. I appreciate you. Olugbemisola Rhuday-Perkovich, you are the angel on my shoulder. Thank you for your wisdom, guidance, and friendship.

Thanks to all the folks who have had my back and given me so much love, support, and advice along the way: Zoraida Córdova, Marie Lu, Elsie Chapman, Nicola Yoon, Tracey Baptiste, Scott Westerfeld, Renée Watson, Adam Silvera, Karen Strong, Justina Ireland, Alex Gino, Preeti Chhibber, Laura Lam, Ann Marie Wong, Sabaa Tahir, Megan Shepard, Daniel José Older, Leigh Bardugo, Kami Garcia, Marie Rutkoski, Danielle Paige, Heidi Heilig, Elle